Dov Silverman was born in Brooklyn, N
Immediately after high sch
the Korean War. He work
auctioneer before moving t

A *cum laude* graduate o
Brook University, New
teacher, high school princip
time between writing and re_____ English
school with the help of his w___, Janet.

The Fall of the Shōgun marks Dov Silverman's distinguished
début as a novelist.

DOV SILVERMAN

The Fall of the Shōgun

GRAFTON BOOKS
A Division of the Collins Publishing Group

LONDON GLASGOW
TORONTO SYDNEY AUCKLAND

Grafton Books
A Division of the Collins Publishing Group
8 Grafton Street, London W1X 3LA

Published by Grafton Books 1987

First published in Great Britain by
Grafton Books 1986

Copyright © Dov Silverman 1986

ISBN 0-586-06761-2

Printed and bound in Great Britain by
Cox & Wyman Ltd, Reading

Set in Bembo

In memory of our son, Jeff.
He said, 'Life isn't fair.'
He lived his with courage,
to the fullest to the end.

So long as men can breathe or eyes can see,
So long lives this, and this gives life to thee.

William Shakespeare

... but there is neither east nor west,
   Border, nor breed, nor birth,
When two strong men stand face to face,
   'Tho they come from the ends of the earth.

RUDYARD KIPLING
1893

PROLOGUE

US State Department, Washington DC, April 1853
Director William Whittefield of the Japanese Section and
Secretary of the Navy, Jason Spaulding, listened intently to Harold
MacDonald. '... and men such as Moryiama Einosuke can change
the course of Japan's future. In that country there are a few
influential people seeking western education. They want to equal
and better the power they saw Admiral Biddel bring into Yedo
Bay in 1852.'

William Whittefield and Jason Spaulding exchanged cautious
glances. Then the Director said, 'Mr MacDonald, please continue.
Tell us what happened when you were shipwrecked.'

'Luck was with me when I landed. Instead of having my head
lopped off according to Japanese law, I was thrown into prison.
Later I was shipped south to the island of Dishima in the port of
Nagasaki, the only place in the Japanese empire open to foreigners,
exclusively the Dutch. I became an English instructor and assistant
to Moryiama Einosuke at the government's School of Interpreters.
Of the fourteen very bright men in the school, he was by far the
most brilliant. I was told he spoke Dutch like a native, he studied in
Latin and his English was fluent and grammatically correct with
what I took to be a peculiar New England twang. I asked him if he
had ever been out of Japan but his answer was negative. Moryiama
was a confident man, sure of himself even when working with
those of superior rank. Other interpreters told the Japanese lords
what they wanted to hear. Mangiro had about him a genuineness
you often find in clergymen ...'

William Whittefield's body stiffened. His pockmarked face
blanched. He jumped up and crossed the room, advancing on
MacDonald who flashed a surprised look at the Secretary of the

Navy. Jason Spaulding shifted forward in his chair, wondering what had disturbed the Director.

'Describe this Moryiama Einosuke, or Mangiro as you just called him!' William Whittefield said to MacDonald. 'Describe his build!'

'He was about five feet eight inches, taller than most Japanese. Light-skinned, with fine features, except for a broken nose which lent a rugged dignity to his face.'

Whittefield looked down into the pupils of MacDonald's eyes, holding them with his before asking the next question. 'Why did you first call him Moryiama Einosuke and then Mangiro?'

'Mr Whittefield. I came here at the request of the US State Department, and was directed to you because I spent two and a half years in Japan. I don't know what I've said to antagonize you ...'

William Whittefield held up his hand. 'Pardon my aggressive behaviour, Mr MacDonald. For several years now I've concerned myself with learning about Japan and its people. You are the first westerner to come out of a hermetically sealed kingdom in two and a half centuries. Your information and observations are extremely important to us.'

'What do you mean by hermetically sealed?'

'It's a new word scientists use to mean air-tight or completely shut off from.'

MacDonald thumbed his nose, staring thoughtfully into space for a moment, then said, 'I wouldn't use the word hermetically.'

'Why not?'

'It's true the Japanese are centuries behind us in scientific and technical knowledge. However there are, in that country, a handful of nobles who promote Dutch Learning, a term meaning modern education. That's why I've been using Moryiama as an example. He and a few select protégés in the Shōgunate are studying the western world. Officially the school does not exist, as trade with foreigners is forbidden. Yet the Japanese built the artificial island of Dishima to allow them to trade with the Dutch on a limited basis, and the school is a reality.'

8

'Are you saying that the Japanese are in the process of modernization?'

'No, but the word hermetically doesn't fit. It's true that for more than two hundred years foreign seamen and shipwrecked crews were usually killed on the beaches, and any Japanese landing on a foreign island or boarding a foreign ship were and still are beheaded when they return, but there are people in high places who want western knowledge. They have used the Dutch to sneak it into the country.'

'Why didn't they kill you?' Jason Spaulding asked.

'Maybe because there are *daimyos* in the north where I landed who are loyal to Lord Nariakira and the Emperor and who seek Dutch Learning.'

'Why do business only with the Dutch?' A long blue cloud of cigar smoke emphasized the Secretary of the Navy's question.

'About three hundred years ago the Jesuits, led by Francis Xavier, began to make Japanese converts. The missionaries mixed religion, politics, and business. A small Roman Catholic uprising gave the Shōgun an excuse for killing over three hundred thousand people and consolidating his political position. The Dutch, being more interested in trade than promoting Christianity, were allowed this small trading concession.'

'Mr MacDonald,' Spaulding said, 'your initial report tells of a Mr Levysohn, who heads the Dutch Trade Delegation on Dishima, who stated that trading with the Japanese has been done at a loss or breakeven point for a long time. Why have the Dutch continued?'

MacDonald turned his broad impassive face towards Jason Spaulding. 'There is an Indian proverb that says don't try to clean your ass with the money a trader tells you he lost on a business deal.'

The three men laughed and the tension was broken.

Then MacDonald said, 'More important, and this information was put in my ear in a polite but firm way by Mangiro. From the late seventeenth century until now, the Dutch pay unofficially in books, designs, or small mechanical devices which can be secreted in one's clothing en route from Dishima to the mainland in order to

9

obtain the results of the national census of Japan taken every five years. According to Moryiama, the population figure has remained stable at about thirty million on the four main islands for as long as the Shōgun has been in power. You will agree that thirty million is a potential market worth waiting for.'

Jason Spaulding's cigar remained suspended in mid-air, held between thumb and forefinger. Smoke drifted from his open mouth. Then he pulled a notebook from his breast pocket and wrote quickly.

William Whittefield walked to the window overlooking the Potomac River. Without turning, he asked, 'What is the disposition of their military?'

'I have no idea. Certain classes of people carried weapons, almost always swords. Some were guards; others wore them for ceremonial purposes or as a sign of rank. I could never distinguish between them. I did see a few antiquated muskets. I must add that in two and a half years I only left Dishima for a few restricted walks through the dockside market in Nagasaki, and no interpreter ever answered my questions about their military.'

'What is their attitude or feeling towards Christianity now?' Spaulding asked.

'At the beginning I was questioned for two months. They frequently asked about my religion. I am an Episcopalian. Once I began to recite the Apostle's Creed but when I said "and in Jesus Christ his only son born of the Virgin Mary", Moryiama quickly stopped me, probably saving my life. He interpreted what I had said as "there are no gods". He also told them I cultivate my mind and will, and revere Heaven in order to obtain enlightenment and happiness.'

'Mr MacDonald,' Director Whittefield said, 'I must ask you again. You used the name Moryiama Einosuke and then Mangiro for the same man. Why?'

'Because he was Mangiro before he was given the rank of junior samurai. With that honour came a more prestigious name given him by his lord and benefactor, the *daimyo* or feudal Lord Nariakira. The rank also enabled him to speak freely to aristocrats, which he had to do as an interpreter.'

'The census figure of thirty million, do you think it's true?' Spaulding asked.

'Yes. There were two things Moryiama wanted to impress on me before I was brought back on the USS *Preble* with the shipwrecked American sailors. First was the number of people inhabiting Japan. Second that the feudal Lord Shimatzu Nariakira of Satsuma in southern Kyushu, an adviser to the Emperor, is one of the leading exponents of Dutch Learning, and opposed to the Shōgun.'

'You have used the term Shōgun as a euphemism for political and military power in Japan,' Whittefield said. 'We know that the Emperor, who claims direct descent from the Sun God, has the loyalty of all the Japanese people. Therefore, President Fillmore's correspondence was addressed to His Highness, and Commodore Perry has specific instructions to deal with the Emperor in Tokyo.'

Harold MacDonald's expression became a puzzled frown. He cleared his throat and took his time before answering. 'Why did you send Commodore Perry to Yedo, or Tokyo as you call it?'

'Because it is the seat of the government.'

'You're correct. But the Emperor is in Kyoto with the Imperial Court. The Shōgun in Yedo is the real power, not the Emperor.'

A heavy silence filled the room. The Secretary of the Navy leaned forward. 'Are you certain, Mr MacDonald? This has great significance! Are you very sure?'

'Yes. To the best of my knowledge, the Emperor is only a revered figurehead. Decisions of state are made in Yedo by the Shōgun.'

Spaulding let the stub of his cigar plop into the shiny brass spittoon at the side of his chair. 'Why did the Japanese allow Admiral Biddel to think he was dealing with the Emperor when the fleet entered Yedo Harbour?'

MacDonald paused again. Secretary of the Navy Spaulding and Director of the Japanese Section Whittefield awaited the words of this man who had returned from Japan with information which would change the foreign policy of the United States of America.

'The Japanese are generally small in stature,' he began slowly. 'They have a method of fighting called jujitsu, which means the gentle art. The principle of this form of hand combat is to use the opponent's own strength to defeat him. A man leaping at you is not stopped, but his forward motion is used to throw him to the ground. In other words, they trick you into making mistakes.'

'Daniel Webster, fresh in his grave, must be turning over in it now,' Spaulding said. 'How his tongue would cut us to ribbons if he knew we were dealing with the wrong people.'

'Mr MacDonald,' William Whittefield said, 'do you mean to say that the Japanese knew Admiral Biddel was coming, and tricked him?'

'No, but they do know something of what the Europeans have been doing in China. Moryiama told me about an English war to pressure the Chinese into buying opium brought from India. He also spoke about unequal trade agreements forced on the Chinese by other European countries.'

William Whittefield stood up abruptly. 'Sir, we thank you very much for your time and patience. The information you have brought us is extremely valuable. We hope you won't think it an imposition if we call on you again.'

'I am glad to be of service.' MacDonald stood up and shook hands with both men. 'Good day, gentlemen.' He departed through the heavy oak-panelled door.

Director Whittefield, hands clasped behind his back, watched wind puffs ripple the slow-moving Potomac. Then he said, 'Reevaluation of our approach to the opening of Japan is necessary, if only because of one man. Mr MacDonald has given us insight into that oriental kingdom, the depth of which even he is unaware. He was right in his judgement about Moryiama Einosuke having the ability to change Japan's future. The story of Einosuke's original name Mangiro is true, but he also had a third name. I and my crew on the whaler *J. Howland* gave it to him. He is John Mung! My adopted son!'

'My God, William!' Spaulding gasped.

Whittefield reached into a lower desk drawer and withdrew a ship's log. 'Harold MacDonald did not overly praise the abilities of Mangiro or Moryiama or John Mung as we called him. He was an extraordinary boy when I met him, a brilliant man and seaman when we parted.'

Jason Spaulding watched Whittefield leaf through the logbook. Scrawled at the top of each page in large bold letters was written A JOURNAL OF THE VOYAGE OF THE *J. HOWLAND* FROM FAIRHAVEN, MASSACHUSETTS BY GOD'S PERMISSION AND RETURN BY HIS GRACE. The former sea captain's finger ran down a familiar page, stopping at 8 January 1841. He read aloud, 'Ten AM: Spout sighted. Lowered boats two and three. Deacon Gilhooley, in charge of boat three, struck his iron at one PM. After a long ride, the whale shook free. Returning to ship, boat three sighted castaways on volcanic atoll, longitude 132.3, latitude 33.25. Two castaways were taken aboard, unconscious and suffering severely from exposure. One other refused to leave the island. This is not unusual for Japanese. I requested the crew to make a bundle. It was agreed, and the men contributed generously. Boat crew number three requested the right to return to the atoll. They saw the two bundles pulled safely from the surf. We are all God's children, but especially sailormen.'

CHAPTER
1

Nakanohama, Japan, January 1841

Lying on a raised, matted platform over the hard earth floor, watching a thin line of smoke curl up through the opening in the thatched roof, Mangiro thought of his father's death three years before. He was only eleven then but shortly after the funeral had conceived a mature, detailed plan. Now, after all the weeks, months and years, his scheme was about to be implemented. His father's constant repetition of the Warrior Code echoed in his mind. Knowledge and Bushido will return our name and status to the rank of samurai. It was the father's pride in himself as a samurai which led to his death, but it was that same pride which planted seeds of a desire to learn in his younger son.

Mangiro's father had been reduced to the *ronin* class because his *daimyo* (lord) had the double misfortune to die while away from his estate at a time when he was at odds with the Shōgun. According to ancient law, when death came to a *daimyo* away from his feudal manor, the property reverted to the Emperor. The Shōgun, the real power in Japan, implemented this seldom-used law for political purposes. The *daimyo*'s samurai were retained by other *daimyo*s or reduced to the rank of *ronin*, meaning wave-man – one who floats masterless, virtually unemployable. Two hundred years of isolation and peace in Japan had created a vacuum for the samurai warriors. They were now primarily used in rituals and ceremonies or as district and area administrators. It was unthinkable for a former samurai to step down to the merchant or peasant class. Roaming the islands were many bands of unemployed *ronin* who had turned to piracy on the inland sea and banditry in the countryside.

Mangiro's father arranged a marriage of convenience which gave him a house and a woman to care for his needs in the small fishing village of Nakanohama. There he fathered two sons, Jakato and Mangiro. The former samurai worked at writing official correspondence for the community and personal letters for the illiterate villagers. He taught several students and his younger son. Jakato, his elder son, preferred to work, play, or build fighting kites, content when he was physically active.

Mangiro, who was able to study for hours on end without becoming weary, especially enjoyed his lessons in the martial art of jujitsu. At the age of four, he began practising tumbling an hour a day for a whole year. The next year he was taught by his father how to fall when thrown without being hurt. At six he began to learn the art of using an opponent's own strength to defeat him. These lessons, combined with literature, dance, mathematics, Bushido, poetry and painting, were taught with the sole purpose of preparing Mangiro to serve his Emperor.

The young boy showed an amazing ability to comprehend and concentrate. His capacity to memorize written passages was astonishing. He was six years old when a tax administrator from the government office in Kochi came to Nakanohama.

The official opened one scroll of names and another of tax regulations on a low table. He had known Mangiro's father as a samurai but now spoke to him as to any peasant. 'Do the computations for the village!' he ordered.

Mangiro's father beckoned his son to the table. The boy approached the two men respectfully and bowed. His father motioned him forward. The six-year-old looked at the scrolls of rice-paper. His eyes ran up and down the lists of names and figures. At first he did not hear the tax assessor's curt dismissal. With a shout that could be heard by those waiting outside the hut, and a wave of his hand, the administrator used the lowest form of the Japanese language to send the boy away. Mangiro bowed politely, stepped back, and returned quickly to his place in the corner. His father sat rock still, his face hard as flint.

The Kochi official commanded, 'Begin the calculations!'

The former samurai responded by ordering his son, 'Do the accounting for every family in the village, and write this year's

15

rules as they appear on this scroll.'

Mangiro bowed his little shaven head. His right hand began flicking the horsehair brush over the rice-paper on his small writing table, the fingers of his left hand causing the beaded abacus to snap and pop.

He was too intent to hear the official say aloud to the village headman, 'Why must every *ronin* in every little village try to impress me with his ability, or that of his students. They waste my time. The child can barely walk, much less understand this.' He turned to Mangiro's father who sat with legs folded under his body, hands resting on his knees, staring straight ahead. 'Begin!' he ordered.

Mangiro looked up at his father who, without turning, beckoned him to come to the front of the table, a place usually accorded to adults. He nodded, and the little boy handed over the rice-paper. He had written the name and amount of each villager's taxes in the exact order as on the tax official's scroll.

Mangiro whispered to his father, 'Two names are out of place.'

The Kochi official raised his eyebrows and shouted, 'Impossible! Impossible trick! You,' pointing at Mangiro's father, 'had him memorize last year's list. Trickster!' he screeched.

The government official had already lost face by showing his anger, but Mangiro's father was not about to let the opportunity pass to further degrade this pompous, overbearing man with whom he had once shared equal rank. He calmly pointed to the bottom of the rice-paper where his son had penned in this year's guidelines for assessment, line for line, character for character, correct in every aspect.

The official, mumbling threats, stormed out of the hut and left the village. Some time later an acknowledgement from the office at Kochi accepted Mangiro's accounting and the twenty *kurus* of rice (thirty-two bushels) paid by the village.

The many instances in which Mangiro showed himself to be

16

different did not bring him honour but only the disapproval of his neighbours and friends. Although his father had taught him that art was meant to rejoice the heart and feed the mind, he learned, at the age of ten, that it was the community's heart and mind which was to be pleased, not his own. The village elders seized his paints and brushes because his paintings of the human form frightened people. Mangiro had violated the concept of classical Japanese art by capturing his subjects in the perspective of light and shadows which made them lifelike. Those villagers who were his models feared their souls had been imprisoned on silk by his brush. When the Shinto priest came to the house and confiscated the paintings, Mangiro accepted the decision and satisfied himself by drawing, with charcoal, the animals, flowers, fish and insects which were a part of his daily life.

Before their father fulfilled his death wish, he called his sons to him. 'Jakato,' he said, 'you are strong and enjoy being physically active. For you life will be straightforward – simple and orderly. The gods have decreed there will be few complicated decisions for you to make. Your brother is not so blessed. You are the elder and must look after Mangiro.' The former samurai then addressed his younger son. 'You are a special boy, not only by virtue of your memory and intellect. You are one who enjoys all facets of life. Thus far you have been blessed by not being able to see evil. I am glad I will not be there when your eyes open to reality. Your exceptional abilities already bring you into conflict with those around you and I don't know how to advise you. Trying to stifle your natural talents will be like corking a volcano. People are impressed with genius only when it comes from an officially recognized source. Superior ability usually makes one's peers jealous and fearful.'

Now, as Mangiro watched the smoke curl out of the hole in the roof, he thought how right his father had been. Mangiro's latest idea of using pebbles in the mortar to quicken the polishing of rice had been met with anger and contempt. He could not understand why his idea was not accepted. He had proved it worked but still he was reprimanded before the entire village for

17

having tampered with the foundation on which all Japanese life was based.

Even his brother told him, 'It is queer to attempt change. There is an order to the way things must be done. It has always been that way.'

Jakato shook Mangiro by the shoulder. 'Come on. It's your plan, and a great one too. We've got to be there before Fudenojo.'

The two brothers dressed quickly. They wrapped their food in the tightly-woven bamboo sleeping-mats and made their way down the beach to the twenty-four-foot fishing boat which leaned on its side just above the high-water mark. They placed their straw rain capes, conical hats, and bundles of food forward under the transom. Fudenojo, master fisherman and owner of the boat, waved as he came up the beach with Shin-ho who carried two baskets, one on top of the other. Each basket contained one hundred and fifty yards of carefully braided line especially rigged for sea bass, belonging to Shin-ho's family. Mangiro had coached Shin-ho on what to say to get permission from his family elder to use the line. It was Fudenojo's fine reputation and a bad fishing season which convinced the elder to allow them to use it.

The date was 5 January 1841 – lucky year of the Ox. In another two days the New Year celebrations would begin. Sea bass was a sought-after delicacy at this time of the year. Mangiro's plan was based on Fudenojo's ability as a master fisherman and their luck in reaching the market at the district capital in Kochi just before the New Year with a fresh load of fish. If their catch was good and their timing right, the profits would be high and the year of the Ox would begin with a great happy swish of its tail. In order to convince Fudenojo to at least listen to his plan, Mangiro had had to teach him the basic use of an abacus. To get Fudenojo's consent to use his name to Shin-ho's family, Mangiro had agreed to teach two of his children the use of the abacus in the coming year. Mangiro and his brother would be the baiters and unhookers for the two senior fishermen.

'Mangiro,' shouted Fudenojo, 'I have a good feeling about this

18

plan of yours. Hai!' He slapped the boy's shoulders.

Shin-ho's round polished face beamed at Jakato. 'Are you ready to sing the triumphal song of the fisherman?' he asked.

The shorter, more muscular brother laughed. 'Yes, of course.'

'Then you will have to bait and unhook like a fiend.'

'Like two fiends I will bait and unhook, all the way to the geisha houses in Kochi.'

The two laughed, their breath whisked away in the cold morning air.

'Excuse me, Fudenojo,' Mangiro said, 'the wind is on my left as I look to the sea and the sun is not fully risen.'

The two older men and Jakato laughed.

Mangiro continued, 'Isn't it said that an early south wind shows its hind parts to the north wind for cleaning before the eye of heaven closes for the night?'

Shin-ho giggled and bumped Jakato with his shoulder, mimicking Mangiro, 'Isn't it said that a fisherman without fish is no better than a farmer without rice? Both will see the eye of heaven reflected in an empty bowl.'

Their laughter was cut short by Fudenojo's curt command, 'Prepare the boat!'

They would be out for a minimum of one day, possibly two. As Mangiro helped load the bait, firewood, fishing lines, and secure the two casks of water, he bit his lip, reprimanding himself for once again breaking the rules of good manners by questioning the master fisherman. More experienced men than he had been left on the beach for less. His question had been infantile, even his brother had laughed. Every child knew the proverb and any fool could tell which way the wind was blowing. The reality he knew was that they needed a catch. Times in the village were hard. Many days' fishing had been lost this year because of the weather. That in itself would make their catch all the more valuable. If they were lucky and the Kochi men did not go out, they could earn a year's wages by setting up a stall and selling the fresh fish directly to the holiday crowds.

'Put your shoulders to the boat. The tide is beginning to run,'

19

Fudenojo said.

The three joined the master fisherman and slid the boat into the water, then clambered aboard. Jakato hoisted the lateen sail, Shin-ho took the tiller, and the boat came alive with wind and tide taking her out to the open sea.

Fudenojo took his place in the bow. Once outside the harbour he shouted, 'Hai!' and his arm pointed to the north.

'Heads away,' responded Shin-ho, and let the sail swing out.

There was a fair wind with a following sea and the craft was well made. With her high stern, she easily ran ahead of the low rollers.

Jakato looked at his brother and said, 'We're sailing to the outer fishing grounds.'

Mangiro knew that as a master fisherman Fudenojo belonged to a guild which maintained fish spotters along the coast. Through codes and signals, they relayed the information about schools of fish to each other.

The boys pulled two baskets of clams they had dug the night before to the centre of the boat. They sat down and began smashing the clams together, letting the juice run into a sealskin bucket between their legs, scraping out the soft cream-coloured flesh into one bucket, throwing the broken shells into another. Mangiro looked to the north for a sign of bad weather, but the sky was clear, the sea fair, and the wind steady although from the south.

The boys worked and talked of what they would do with their share of the money. They recounted stories their father had told them of New Year celebrations in the big city of Kochi.

Jakato picked up the well-worn tale. 'Most people have already stopped work and started making the rounds of the parties.'

Mangiro continued, 'Even the beggars bow twice to each other and have a feasting.'

'Whole families and clans parade from house to house, from party to party, then to the fairs.'

The boys finished separating the clams and began cutting and twining the meat on to the hooks of the fishing line.

'There will be dragon dancers, kite fighting, musicians, and puppeteers,' Mangiro said.

'Jakato,' called Shin-ho from his position at the tiller, 'tell your brother about the Kappa fluid.'

Jakato fell silent and concentrated on baiting his hooks.

'Mangiro, do you know about the Kappa?' Shin-ho laughed and winked at him.

Mangiro looked over at Jakato and wagged his head.

'Oh ho!' Shin-ho said, 'and I thought you were the one with the education. It is important to know what to do when you meet a Kappa, for it has the strength to kill a man or beasts as large as a horse. It is only three or four inches tall and therefore very deceptive.'

Mangiro tried to catch his brother's eye, but Jakato avoided his gaze. Mangiro joined in the fun. 'Oh worthy sir,' he used the highest and most respectful form of the language, 'who guides our destiny with thy powerful right hand and keen eye. Condescend to enlighten an unworthy such as I about the secrets of a Kappa.'

Jakato stiff-armed his brother in the shoulder, knocking him backward against the bulkhead. Both boys giggled, but were cut short by Fudenojo's command, 'Stop wasting time and pay attention to baiting the hooks!'

They glanced at each other, up at the sea and sky and shrugged, surprised at the tenseness in Fudenojo's voice. They looked at Shin-ho resting easily on the big tiller, his bare right foot up on the side of the boat.

'The Kappa,' he smiled, 'is really a dreadful little beast that lives near rivers and streams. It looks like a cross between a frog and a turtle. The most amazing thing about it is its head. There is a cavity in the top which contains a strength-giving fluid. The Kappa can drag men and farm animals into its watery home and they are never seen again. The only weakness in its character is being extremely well-mannered. If you meet a Kappa there's only one way to escape. You must bow low to the ground. The

Kappa, being so polite, will return your bow, spilling the strength-giving fluid from its head, thus becoming weak and harmless. I will help Jakato to find this fluid at the creditor's market in Kochi on New Year's Eve.'

Shin-ho winked and they all laughed.

Mangiro thought of the silver charm he would sell at the market. His father, unable to cope with life, had given the charm to his younger son without a word on the morning of the day he committed *seppuku* (ritual suicide).

'An honourable death for a worthy man,' the villagers said.

For Mangiro, the loss was doubly felt. He no longer had a father or a teacher. His plan to catch the Kochi market with the sea bass and sell the silver charm would allow him to supplement the loss of income to the household. It would support them and provide him with a teacher for a year in the nearby town of Uwajima.

The boat dipped and rose, moving steadily forward over the ocean rollers to the offshore fishing grounds. The brothers finished baiting the line and secured a stone weight to the end, saying the proper incantations to the gods of sea and fish.

Fudenojo called Mangiro forward. 'Light the *habachi*, make tea, and heat the rice.'

This meant they would soon be at the fishing grounds.

At about 9.00 AM, Fudenojo hopped up on the transom, holding on to the short bow rope with one hand for balance. He directed Shin-ho to the right, then later to the left. To Mangiro's untrained eye one part of the sea looked as another, but he knew Fudenojo could read the waves and the waters.

'Hai!' the master fisherman shouted.

Shin-ho pointed the bow into the wind and the two boys brought down the sail. Fudenojo began singing the old sea bass song and the others joined in. Walking back to the bucket of broken clam shells, he threw a handful over the side, watching them drift slowly downward through the water. He motioned Shin-ho to come forward with him. Each man took one of the fishing lines and heaved the stone sinkers, allowing the curled

22

line and baited hooks to run out. Then they sat around the *habachi* to eat. The boys began sloshing the chum over the side and throwing handfuls of clam shells to raise the fish. The chum floated out and around the two lines on either side of the boat, each line about one hundred and fifty yards long with three hooks to the yard. Every hook made of fish bone was set and tied carefully into a small piece of wood which allowed it to float free below the water. The men came aft and exchanged places with the boys who washed their hands in the swells of the cold green ocean water and went forward to eat.

Mangiro gulped the hot tea. He noticed that no seagulls came diving and crying for the floating chum but would not insult Fudenojo again by calling it to his attention. The boys finished eating and went back to their buckets. The men went forward and held the lines to feel if the fish were biting.

'Chum faster, youngsters,' the older man shouted. He moved closer to Shin-ho. 'I had hoped for better weather. The wind is going to change.' He looked at the sun overhead and then to the north. The skies were clear and the sea calm. He called, 'I want you two to use all the chum in the next half hour. We'll make our pull soon after that and head for home.'

Fudenojo and Shin-ho sat down. It was the custom of fishermen to remain as quiet as possible while the lines were out, and for each to pray to his personal deity to influence a good catch.

The small boat bobbed on the sea.

Fudenojo motioned the two boys forward. He and Shin-ho stood up and placed their right hands on the line. Custom dictated the first pull be made with the right hand for a good catch. They began the line-pulling song, each taking a turn to sing a new verse. The boys, who stood close behind, ready to unhook, joined in the chorus.

The line is so heavy the fish pull the boat forward,
Awaii maru, awaii maru.
Because the big fat fish don't want to be taken,

23

Awaii maru, awaii maru.
Tell them they will spend the New Year in Kochi,
Awaii maru, awaii maru.
Ai! Here comes the first to celebrate the festival,
Awaii maru, awaii maru.

Pulling the line was slow hard work. The two men were actually dragging the boat through the water. Jakato stood behind Shin-ho on one side, Mangiro behind Fudenojo on the other. They removed the fish or bait from the hooks and curled the line back into the baskets. The high hooks were relatively empty, some small sharks and mackerel, but the weight of the line indicated to the fishermen that the lower hooks were well occupied. The boys sang louder as the first sea bass came over the side. Then there was little time to think as the fish came into the boat on almost every hook, ranging in weight from two to three pounds, perfect for the New Year's market. The holidaymakers would eat raw fish which was still alive, or gutted fish stuffed with sweetmeats, almonds rubbed into the scales and baked in such a way that set on a platter it would look as if it were about to swim off the table.

The heavily-laden line was coming in more slowly when the boat settled back on a big wave. The two fishermen braced their knees against the side of the boat and held tightly to the straining lines. The boat remained motionless at the bottom of the trough, then was picked up and pushed forward by the next wave. Both men quickly pulled in line as the bow raced through the heaving sea, the bottom of the boat a tangle of line and flopping fish. The wind had shifted one hundred and eighty degrees, blowing from the north. All four turned and saw, far behind them, one massive cloud line from sea to sky, from horizon to horizon. In the distance, in front of the oncoming storm, Fudenojo could make out the tops of the white caps being blown off by the strong wind.

'Jakato,' he yelled, 'go to the tiller and scull the boat forward so we may save as much line as possible.' He looked over to Shin-ho who pleaded with his eyes. The line was a family treasure.

24

'Mangiro, forget the hooks and the fish. Stand by the sail and prepare to hoist it.'

The men pulled furiously on their lines. Jakato sculled but the luck they had prayed for was now becoming a nightmare. The line, heavy with fish, held like an anchor. Another wave from behind picked them up, then dropped them backwards. Jakato shouted a warning before the next wave broke over the stern, pouring water into the boat. The wind was beginning to whisper around the mast. Mangiro heard the order, 'Make sail!' and pulled the sail up the mast. The boat leapt forward. The two fishermen hauled on the line hand over hand until it trailed behind, its weight combined with the fish dragging the boat back into another trough.

Fudenojo looked over at Shin-ho as a wave broke over the stern, almost swamping the boat. They pulled out their knives at the same moment and together hacked away the line. Freed from the dragging weight the boat leapt forward, climbing the back of the wave in front of them.

In one bound, Fudenojo leapt over the hooks and fish in the bottom. He ran aft and took the tiller from Jakato. The boys and Shin-ho began bailing. Fudenojo played each wave with an artist's touch, using the wind and following sea to drive the ship southward towards a safe harbour. He let the great rollers pick the small boat up, then actually sculled the craft sideways with the long steering oar. Catching the forward motion of each wave and riding it, he used the lateen sail to catch the wind. From the crest of each wave he looked behind, judging the distance to the might of the oncoming storm. It was a race.

'Shin-ho!' he shouted, 'pass out the food. Everyone eat as much as you can!'

They put on their straw rain capes and conical hats, eating with one hand and bailing with the other. The wind became stronger, the waves higher, and the troughs deeper. The boat slipped back into a giant trough and the lateen sail went slack, losing the wind from behind. The boat wallowed as Fudenojo sculled furiously with the tiller, trying to climb the wave, but the top blew off the following wave on to the boat. The weight of the water held the boat as the wave broke fully over the stern. The boys were washed forward, face down among the lines, hooks, and flopping fish. Shin-ho pulled them to a sitting position. The race was lost.

Fudenojo shouted over the roaring wind, 'Heads away, we're coming about.'

Shin-ho jumped forward, ready to trim the sail as they turned to face the storm. The boat turned sluggishly because of the weight of the water. Sailing into the storm the boat slowly climbed the oncoming wave. As it reached the crest the full force of the wind hit the sail, snapping the mast off, carrying the rigging away. A flash of lightning froze giant grey waves with white curling heads in the midday darkness. The boat balanced on top of the wave, then raced down its back, burying her bow in the smooth green water of the trough. Tons of water broke over them.

The four men held their breath under the water and clung to the boat, but Jakato had not caught his breath in time. He held on as long as he could, then fought his way to the surface for air. He was swept away with most of the ship's gear and the sea bass which returned from whence they had come.

The swamped boat was in no danger of sinking as it was made of bamboo, each cane having its own natural flotation chambers, but it could easily be smashed to bits by the waves. Fudenojo, waist deep in cold ocean water at the tiller, sculled the boat to safety every time disaster threatened.

Mangiro and the two men rode out the storm for almost two days, with no chance to talk because of the high winds and treacherous seas. When finally the wind abated slightly, Shin-ho took the tiller from the semi-conscious Fudenojo. Mangiro held the exhausted master fisherman so he would not drown in the bottom of the swamped boat. After a while he tied the sleeping Fudenojo to the bulkhead and waded through the pitching boat, feeling under water with his hands and feet for food of some kind. He found two sea bass held firmly by their spiny dorsal fins in the bamboo, and the mats he and his brother had stored under the transom. The three wearily ate soggy rice and raw fish. No one mentioned Jakato. As master of the boat it would be Fudenojo's task to bring the news into the house and the village.

The second night a cross-current pulled them further out to sea. They took turns at the tiller and tried to bail with their sealskin boots, but the fury of the storm had beaten the boat into a bundle of loosely held bamboo sticks – a floating sieve. Towards evening of the third day Fudenojo crouched in the bow out of the wind, then stood up and cocked his head to the left, then to the right. After a few minutes, he pointed left and Shin-ho, at the tiller, sculled slowly to bring the boat around.

Soon they could hear the booming surf in the distance. Fudenojo came aft, motioning Mangiro closer. The three stood in the rear of the boat, sometimes waist deep, sometimes ankle deep in the swirling water.

'We're near land of some kind and cannot go on much longer like this,' Fudenojo shouted. 'Mangiro, you help Shin-ho scull towards the sound of the surf. I'll take the tiller and beach her.'

The booming grew louder and louder. Soon plumes of spray could be seen ahead. The waves came from behind now, pushing the boat forward at a faster pace, sometimes breaking over the stern. Fudenojo took hold of the bow rope and climbed up on the transom for a better view of their landing place. The small boat pitched and rocked fiercely. He held on, swaying back and forth, then made his way to the stern.

The three huddled together as Fudenojo gave his instructions, 'You two continue to scull according to my directions. We're heading towards rocks, not a beach. I'll take the tiller just before we're driven on to them. Take your boots and rain capes off. When we hit – jump! Shin-ho first, Mangiro, then me. Don't fear the waves. Grab a rock, wait, then let the next wave push you forward. Like the Kappa that Jakato wanted, you must be half turtle and half frog. Squat and jump, squat and jump. Good luck!'

White columns of spray and the roar of tons of water breaking onto the rocks came closer. The master fisherman directed the

27

boat towards the thundering sound of pounding waves which sent geysers of foam into the air. He waited – judging the distance, timing the waves. They were coming in sets of five with a slight break, then the largest wave first in the next set of five. The boat rose in the heaving water and, for the first time, they all caught sight of the shore, glistening black volcanic rock surrounded by white foam being whipped inshore by the wind.

Fudenojo made his way to the bow. He stood on the transom for a final look, then jumped down, removed his sealskin boots and rain cape and waded to the stern. He relieved the two at the tiller with his final shouted instructions above the roar, 'Jump when the boat strikes!'

They went forward, took off their heavy clothing and waited in the bow.

Fudenojo knew he would have only one chance to catch the biggest wave of the set which could drive them as far inshore as possible. He gauged the distance to the rocks and the waves in the set. The boat pitched, wallowed and rolled. It climbed the fifth wave and was in position for the big one which came bearing down on them. Using his tiller, he sculled furiously, at the last second turning the boat sideways to the wave. He sculled again, putting the stern to it. Like a surfer the boat rode the wave, racing towards the black rocks ahead. It flew over small, sharp outcroppings.

Shin-ho, holding onto the bow rope, perched on the transom, Mangiro crouched behind him. The boat struck. Shin-ho catapulted forward like a stone from a slingshot, hitting the side of a large, smooth boulder. Stunned, he spread his arms and tried to hang on.

Mangiro and Fudenojo leapt onto smaller rocks and clung as the backwash of the wave tore at them. They leapfrogged forward towards Shin-ho, clutching the rocks as the next wave crashed over them.

Shin-ho lost his grip and they watched him slide between the boulders, his fingernails scraping down the face of the rock. The next wave covered the crevice he'd fallen into. The two scrambled to the top of the large boulder from which he had fallen. As they lay on their stomachs waiting until a big wave washed over them, their unconscious friend floated up from the abyss. Both reached out but Shin-ho's shirt was gone, his hands were at his sides, and his short cropped hair allowed no grip. Mangiro managed to grab an ear. Fudenojo jammed his hand into his friend's mouth. The wave raced out and they held Shin-ho suspended from the side of the boulder until the next wave lifted him up and they could drag him onto the rock. They lay over their companion, gasping for breath, holding him so he would not be washed off.

Shin-ho was breathing but his body oozed blood from hundreds of tiny cuts. He had been raked back and forth over the razor-sharp shells of black mussels clinging to the side of the boulder. Fudenojo and Mangiro dragged his unconscious, bleeding body away from the breakers.

Stopping to rest, they realized it was raining. They cupped their hands and drank, then washed the crusted salt from their eyelashes. They washed Shin-ho, but could not stop the blood. Fudenojo went searching amongst the rocks and returned with an armful of seaweed in which they wrapped Shin-ho's naked, wounded body. In a place between the boulders, out of the wind and rain, Fudenojo and Mangiro lay on each side, covering him with their bodies for warmth. They covered themselves with seaweed and shivered to sleep.

Mangiro woke but could not tell the time of day. The pounding surf sent white spray towards the grey sky only to fall on to the rocks and run back into the dark sea. Shin-ho's body was hot with fever, Fudenojo was gone. Mangiro climbed on to a large boulder and caught sight of the older man coming towards him.

Fudenojo, stark naked, made his way among the rocks carrying a dead penguin. He swung the large bird up on the rock at Mangiro's feet and said, 'There are fresh eggs in the stomach. I tried to cut her head off but my knife is too dull, so I gutted her. It was then I saw the eggs she was sitting on. You know the strangest thing, I thought she was dead but when I bent down to get the eggs she jumped up and pecked at my legs.'

The man and boy sat down to a meal of raw penguin meat. They saved the eggs for Shin-ho.

'Didn't you have more clothes on when we landed?' Mangiro asked.

'Not too much more. Come, I'll show you.' Fudenojo led Mangiro to the other side of the volcanic atoll, no more than one hundred and fifty yards across at its widest point. 'There!' He pointed at a rock, its top white with the droppings of seabirds. 'I tore my clothes, what was left of them, into strips and made some nooses to spread on the rock. When the birds land, if they step into a noose it will close around a foot and they won't be able to fly. Your job will be to find a place out of the wind to watch from. When a bird gets caught, grab him before he flaps into the sea. Keep an eye out for any wreckage from our boat in the surf. I'll return to Shin-ho and see what else is around that we can use.'

Mangiro found a place between the boulders, out of the cold wind. Birds landed, walking in, on and over the cloth traps without getting caught. Every once in a while a bird snagged its foot on the cloth and Mangiro held his breath, but the noose did not close. He began pulling thread from his roughly woven trousers and braiding it into a cord. He knotted a loose-fitting noose, then tied the end to wet seaweed and laid his traps on the rock. Taking in the nooses Fudenojo had made, he braided that material into a smoother cord.

Concentrating on pulling the fibres apart, Mangiro suddenly heard a screeching on the rock. He jumped up and leapt quickly from rock to rock. Landing on all fours, he tried to grab the end of the line which had closed around a seabird's leg. Other birds took flight, screaming in anger. The captured seabird flapped its large wings, screeching into the wind as Mangiro caught it just at the end of the rock. He tucked the wings and body under his right arm, unconscious of the wind and cold salty spray. He held the large beak with his left hand, taking off the loop with the fingers of his right.

Out of the corner of his eye, Mangiro caught sight of a moving boulder just below him. Suddenly he was looking into the face of one of the monsters of the sea. The bird struggled free of his arms and flew away. The boy sat motionless, staring at the horrible creature only five feet away. It was seventeen feet long with rough hairless skin over rolls and rolls of fatty blubber. The body came to a point at the small ugly head with beady eyes and long whiskers above the long mouth. It is the kind of sea monster who eats men, he thought. Held by the eyes of the beast, he could not make his body move. The monster lowered its head into the water, raised up to within three feet of the kneeling boy, stared him in the eye and spat water in his face.

The shock of the cold water freed Mangiro from his spell. He jumped up, running and leaping from boulder to boulder, rock to rock, until he fell panting at Fudenojo's feet and breathlessly told his story.

The two returned cautiously to the rock. The master seaman slid on his belly over the boulder, peered carefully over the edge, then began to laugh. He motioned for Mangiro to join him. The boy hesitated, but then crept closer. The monster sat in the same place, looking up at them.

Fudenojo laughed again. 'This is a sea elephant, one of the ugliest and most harmless beasts of the ocean.'

The huge creature put his head into the sea, then spat sea water over Fudenojo's head. Mangiro tried to suppress his laughter but when Fudenojo giggled, the two of them, naked on the rock, began to howl with laughter. The sea elephant added to their hilarity by spitting more water at them.

In the afternoon Shin-ho was still feverish. The cuts on his body were beginning to fester. With great effort, Mangiro tried to control the cold fits of shivering that periodically racked his own body. He wondered how Fudenojo, his long muscular torso and sinewy arms set over short bowed legs, was seemingly immune to the cold, rain, and wind. The older man knew it was only a matter of time before the boy would succumb to exposure. He ordered Mangiro to lie on top of Shin-ho for body warmth.

Towards evening, Fudenojo returned with the bird traps and one empty water cask from their boat. He had Mangiro and Shin-ho put their heads and shoulders into the cask, then crawled in on

31

top of them, forming a pyramid. The cask gave some protection from the wind and rain that night.

The next morning Mangiro and Fudenojo ate more of the raw penguin meat. Shin-ho would only swallow some rain water scooped from depressions in the rocks. He shivered continually and his body burned with fever.

Fudenojo roamed the atoll's surf line looking for usable flotsam or wreckage of any kind that would give them some protection. He saw, here and there, pieces of bamboo tossing in the foaming surf, but little else.

Mangiro set out the loop traps on the bird rock and took his watching place. He dozed from time to time while birds stepped in and out of the traps. But his shivering body soon brought him back to the reality of the wind and cold. One trap did not even close when a bird dragged it to the rock's edge. It seemed the bird was laughing as it kicked the loop over the side and into the surf.

Mangiro crawled out on to the rock. The birds flew over the sea, screeching their annoyance, then swooped back and hovered over his head, using the wind and their wide-spread wings to hold position in the air and berate the intruder with their high-pitched cries. He gathered the traps and, with stiff fingers and total concentration, untied and retied knots, making one loop with a long line which he could hold from his position. He lay the single trap and trailed the cord to his place between the rocks.

The birds returned to their perch, arrogantly stalking the top of the white dung-crusted boulder. Now two big seagulls had their feet in the trap. Mangiro slowly pulled the loop closed. One of the birds stepped out of the noose just in time. The boy jerked the line hard and the second screeching gull, caught by one leg, beat the air furiously with its wings. The wind picked the bird up in the air like a kite, but Mangiro began hauling it down.

'Ahoy! Ahoy on the island!'

One hundred yards beyond the surf line, a sleek, white boat rode easily on the swells. Men were seated at long oars, unlike the Japanese who stand when rowing. Mangiro waved one arm, holding the trap line with the other. He and the rowers hailed each other back and forth until the oarsmen began pulling for the other side of the island. Fudenojo was waving the boat on. Pulling the limp bird from the surf, Mangiro ran towards where Shin-ho lay.

Fudenojo was already kneeling by his friend, pulling the stiff seaweed from his body. He looked up at Mangiro. 'You will go with Shin-ho on to the foreigner's boat.'

'What of you?'

'I will stay.'

'You will die!'

'Perhaps. But I am responsible to tell your mother about you and Jakato, and Shin-ho.'

'You will never survive! I absolve you of the obligation to tell my mother!'

'You absolve me?' Fudenojo was shocked.

Mangiro's head bowed at his breach of etiquette.

Fudenojo pounded his chest with his fist. 'It's my duty to stay! It's your duty to go!'

'We will never see Japan again. It's forbidden once we go with them.'

'As master fisherman I order it! Now take hold!'

They bent low and caught Shin-ho under the arms and legs. With great difficulty, they managed to carry him to a large outcropping of volcanic rock overhanging the surf. Fudenojo waved the longboat closer. A rope thrown expertly from the boat uncoiled in the air and on to the rock. The master fisherman worked quickly, taking two turns around the chest of his unconscious friend and again around Mangiro. He looked into the boy's eyes, then pushed Shin-ho and Mangiro off the ledge and into the cold heaving water. The men on the boat hauled them quickly through the water. Mangiro's head and shoulder hit the side of the bobbing boat. He looked up to see the legendary great red, hairy-faced, green-eyed monster, and from its shiny skin two large hairy hands reached out, gripped the ropes, and lifted Mangiro and Shin-ho clear of the water, into the boat in one motion.

'Oh Lord of the sea and sky, to whom have you delivered me?'

CHAPTER

2

On board the *J. Howland*, the two unconscious fishermen were immediately taken to the galley, the warmest place on a whaler which had not killed a fish in two months. Cooky ordered the castaways wrapped in blankets and placed near the stove. He tried giving them hot tea thick with sugar. Only the younger one was able to drink, and was then bundled down to the crew's quarters. Acting as the ship's doctor, Cooky kept the older man next to the stove, tending as best he could to the festering sores covering the man's body.

Mangiro slept for two days. He was awakened by the second mate, Deacon Gilhooley, shaking his shoulder. He rubbed the crust from his eyelids and saw red hair bristling on the pale face which hovered over him again. Distorted round green eyes stared at him. The monster reached down with one large hand and lifted him to a sitting position on the edge of the bunk. Mangiro searched his mind. Which god should he pray to for mercy? But no prayer surfaced. He couldn't think clearly.

The monster placed a hot mug of tea into his hands and pushed the cup to his lips. Despite his fear, Mangiro swallowed the sweet brew, never taking his eyes from the ugly face before him. Then the warmth of the tea in his stomach and the sugar coursing through his blood caused Mangiro to suppose that perhaps this monster was like the sea elephant, just a repulsive, smelly but friendly giant.

The red hair on the face parted and words came out of pink lips lined with large, shiny white teeth. All Mangiro could think of was Shin-ho's story of what to do when you meet a Kappa. He jumped up, letting the blanket fall. Stark naked, he bowed low to the floor. The monster shouted, then picked him up and pulled a sweater

34

over his head, pointing to the other things on the floor. Mangiro understood he should get dressed but did not know how. He was gently helped into the unfamiliar clothing and shown how to tie the Wellington boots.

'Deacon,' the monster repeated several times, pointing to himself.

The boy immediately understood. He tapped his chest, saying his own name. The bearded one nodded, then beckoned him to follow.

When Mangiro's head poked through the hatch, the sea breeze and spray struck the side of his face. He looked down the slanted deck, over the rail, and saw great waves racing by. Overhead, as high as he could see, were tangles of rope, sails, and the trunks of giant trees. Two men reached down, grabbed him under the armpits and lifted him onto the deck. From there the waves looked smaller because the ship was so big. He was led to a large group of men standing amidships near the rail. They parted to let him through. The wind and spray whipped his face. Hockmeyer, the big first mate and master of flensing operations, took off his woollen hat, put it on Mangiro's head, and pulled it down over his ears. On the deck, feet towards the railing, lay Shin-ho, his body sewn into a canvas bag with rocks tied to his feet. His eyes were closed and the wax look of his face was a familiar sight to a boy from a poor fishing village. Mangiro touched Shin-ho's face, letting his fingers linger on the cheek. Then he stepped back.

Captain Whittefield nodded to Deacon Gilhooley and said, 'You were once intended for the church. It would be better done by you.'

Cooky finished sewing the sack closed.

The Deacon turned to the boy. 'You don't understand a word, and being a heathen your ceremony would be different, but this is a Christian ship and we believe the Creator made all men.'

He pulled a worn Bible from inside his jacket and read the words so familiar to those who follow the sea. Then, taking Mangiro by the arm, he stepped back. Four men came forward and lifted the board on which Shin-ho lay. At a nod from the captain, they tilted

35

it and the body slid neatly into a passing wave. The men milled around the deck and the captain started for the bridge.

'Town-hooooo! Town-hooooo!' came the ancient whaler's cry from the crow's nest high above the deck. Everyone looked up. Old Peter, perched a hundred feet above their heads in his position as lookout, shouted, 'Four humps. Two points off the port bow about three miles.' Captain Whittefield was already on the bridge with the telescope to his eye when Old Peter sang out again, 'She blows! She blows! Goddammit she blows! Three more, Captain. A pod of seven sperm.'

Deacon Gilhooley looked aloft shaking his fist. 'Watch your language, Peter ...'

The rest of his words were drowned out in the joyous shouts of the crew.

Pistchiani, commander of boat number one, who dwarfed all men aboard but the two mates, grabbed Mangiro by the waist and hoisted him in the air, dancing with the boy as if he was a child's doll. 'You're our luck, Mungi, Mungo.'

Mangiro feared he was going to die. The devils had buried Shin-ho and now it was his turn.

The crew took up the chant, 'Mungi, Mungo ...'

The white satans danced with him like a band of round-eyed maniacs.

'Prepare to lower away all boats!' came the order from the bridge.

Mangiro was dropped unceremoniously to the deck. The crew scattered as the whaler turned to port, everything vibrating as the big-bellied whaling ship slapped through the waves. He staggered to his feet as men ran to their boat stations, some climbing the rigging to get a better look at their quarry.

It now seemed to Mangiro that the foreigners were really honouring Shin-ho – the shouting, dancing and singing all a part of their strange customs of burial. Then he realized they were excited by something in sight ahead of the boat.

'Captain,' Cooky called out, 'may I bring the lad to the bridge? He probably never saw a great whale.'

'Bring him up, Cooky.'

On the bridge, Mangiro viewed the ocean from horizon to horizon. A mile ahead he saw what looked like steam from small volcanoes booming out of the water, then big black humps rising and falling as the behemoths wallowed in the sea. He had seen porpoises and narwhals from the shore. Once Jakato had taken him half a day's walk to see a beached right whale claimed by another village. But this scene, from a whaler on the high seas, filled him with awe.

'There go flukes!' came the cry from above.

Mangiro saw the tails rise out of the water, one of them twenty feet across. Half of the sixty-foot body rose into the air before it came down again in a thunderclap and gigantic spray.

'They've sounded,' shouted Old Peter.

The captain closed his telescope and picked up the bullhorn. 'All hands stand down! Get some food! Boat captains to the bridge!'

Cooky pulled Mangiro down the ladder and into the galley with him. From a big steaming pot on the stove, he ladled thick stew into tin bowls. Dropping a biscuit and large spoon into each, he handed them to Mangiro and pointed to the men lined up at the door.

On the bridge Captain Whittefield spoke to the three boat captains. 'The pod knows we're chasing. That's why they've sounded. Swimming underwater will give them no more than an hour before they'll have to surface for air. In thirty minutes lower all boats. Sail an inverted fan ahead of us, keeping a half-mile distance between boats, first mate Hockmeyer's boat in the centre. Any suggestions?'

Pistchiani, a second generation Sag Harbor whaler, said, 'Sir, if that's a pod of bulls a fan is best, but if it's a harem then a point would be better. We'd be looking to wound one of the cows so they'll bunch up around her and the bull will drop back to protect. Then two boats can cut him out and the third go after the cows.'

The captain pointed his bullhorn upward. 'Peter, are they bulls or cows?'

'A harem, sir. A bloody blue harem!'

The navy way is always best, Captain Whittefield thought.

Consult with one's junior officers before attacking, then make a decision. 'A point it is,' he said. 'Fill your stomachs! Keep the half-mile distance between boats! And bring back some oil!'

At 11.00 A.M. Mangiro watched in wonder as the giant mainsail was lowered in preparation for launching.

'Boats away!' came the order from the bridge.

On the port and starboard sides of the whaler, three 28-foot round-bottomed boats smacked the water, the half-inch cedar planking and six-foot beams providing a buoyancy which let them skip over the waves like greyhounds through the rolling hills of a newly-scythed field. The oars were shipped and the sails run up. Mangiro watched the three boats dart away from the slower mother ship in a spanking breeze.

It was the custom of whalers that the bow oarsman was also the harpooner. When the whale breached within striking distance, the boat captain, at the twenty-two foot steering oar, would call to the harpooner who might have been rowing for an hour or more. The harpooner would ship his oar, stand, turn, grab the weapon from its place in the bow, and throw. Very often, because his muscles were strained from rowing, he did not reach his mark. Or if he did the barb would not enter deep enough and was shaken loose by the behemoth. If the iron struck fairly, the harpooner and the boat captain immediately changed places from bow to stern, this acrobatic stunt usually taking place as the boat leapt through the water, being pulled by the wounded, enraged whale.

Captain Whittefield, in only four years' whaling after his retirement from the navy, had seen too many fish lost because of the weak arm of a tired harpooner, or a man lost overboard in the exchange of places. He began using an unorthodox seven-man crew in his whale boats. At first, the men were sulky about the navy man's innovation, but soon realized the practicality of the change. An extra man at the tiller, in a long chase, relieved the other oarsmen. The boat captain also became the harpooner. He used the lance for that fatal thrust into a whale's lungs, sending blood showering up and blowing out of the spout.

Now Mangiro saw the three boats sailing in a V ahead of the

38

mother ship, the boat captains watching the big ship's topgallant for signal flags. When Old Peter in the crow's nest spotted dark shadows rising just ahead of the lead boat, he ran up a flag signalling fish ahead.

First mate Hockmeyer, in his boat at the point of the flying V formation, moved close to the mast and pointed to an oarsman. 'Up you go, man!'

Black Ben put his foot in the mate's cupped hands and stepped up on his large shoulders. Holding onto the mast, he looked ahead. The sun, almost directly above, illuminated the depths of the light blue water. His eyes searched port and starboard for the telltale shadows.

'Holy cow shit!' he shouted. He lowered his voice, trying to whisper, 'They're under us! We're over them!'

Ben jumped off the mate's shoulders and into his seat. Everyone looked over the side at a mass of black rising rapidly from below.

Hockmeyer released the sail line, dumping the air. In a hoarse whisper he said, 'Quietly boys, they can hear us. Back oar. Ready! Together! Back oar!'

The men dropped their oars into the water, the strain of the braking motion lifting them off their seats. They peered over the side at the ominous shadows coming up towards them.

Through clenched teeth, Black Ben said, 'I'll shove Old Peter's beard so far down his throat he'll have to shave his ass!' His feet set, arms straining at the oar, he grunted, 'Give me a razor. I'll shave his ass and cut off his balls!'

Their boat began to rise out of the water.

The captain put the telescope to his eye. Cooky and Mangiro watched with him as the head of the giant bull whale rose out of the water like a great black mountain just under the point whale boat. The long, sleek, white craft slid backwards off the whale's huge head. At the same time a smaller cow breached, spouting just to their left. The boat was sliding into the saddle between the sixty-foot bull's head and its dangerous flukes. Hockmeyer grabbed the harpoon.

'B'Jesus,' shouted Brannigan, 'don't stick him now or we're all dead!'

The boat rolled in the backwash of the bull's head. The big mate drew back his arm and threw with all his strength at the cow. The iron shaft buried itself in her body up to the wooden handle and she shot forward. Hockmeyer caught a full turn of the harpoon line around the bow block and the boat leapt after the cow, out of reach of the deadly flukes of the bull.

Captain Whittefield's telescope followed as the mate's boat streaked through the water. 'A special breed, Yankee whalers,' he said.

Mangiro licked his lips, eyes shining with the thrill of the hunt. He saw the spray and heard the explosion of the big bull's flukes pounding the ocean, warning the boats closing in on him to beware. The five remaining cows swam slower, the bull dropping back to protect his females.

Deacon and Pistchiani lowered sail, using their oars to close in on the bull. Chanting, they encouraged their men to row harder. The two boats shot over the water, the long oars bending in unison as they bit into the sea, then snapped the sleek craft forward.

The Deacon's green eyes sparkled; his red beard rustled against his oilskin jacket as he sang out his favourite hymn, 'Oh it's blessed to die a Christian. So pull men, pull.'

The rowers responded with a slap of the oars and a bent back, singing out, 'Heave-ho, heave-ho. Oh, don't be afraid of the big whale. So pull men, pull. Heave-ho, heave-ho. Oh, God created the big whale. So pull men, pull. Heave-ho, heave-ho. Oh, God created man to kill the big whale. So pull men, pull. Heave-ho, heave-ho. Oh, twenty thousand families live off the big whale. So pull men, pull. Heave-ho, heave-ho. Oh, a million light the dark night with the big whale. So pull men, pull.'

Pistchiani's boat came straight in from the starboard side. He sent his harpoon flying into the black body just behind the head. Deacon's boat was crossing the bull's flukes to attack from the port side. When the enormous flukes came out of the water in a twist of pain, the backwash almost swamped the boats. The whale turned

40

to port in an effort to throw the barb stuck deep in its flesh. This gave the Deacon his chance. He stood up and pointed to his target on the side of the enraged whale with his left hand. He raised the harpoon in his right and threw, hitting his mark. In quivering agony the whale's flukes came higher out of the water.

Pistchiani looked up at the giant tail rising above his boat. 'Jump! Jump!' he cried.

Every seaman dived overboard before the big black flukes came crashing down in a thunderous explosion, splintering the cedar planking. The whale tore off through the water, the Deacon's boat and wreckage of Pistchiani's flicking over the waves, held fast to the large body by the harpoons. The wreckage made a rooster tail shooting through the water in the wake of the big bull.

'Three points to starboard!' Captain Whittefield ordered. The muscles under his clean-shaven pockmarked skin jumped back and forth over his jawbones. 'Cooky, prepare to lower the lifeboat.'

The big ship, with its mainsail lowered, lumbered towards the foam and wreckage where boat one had been.

'Two heads up!' Old Peter sang out from above. 'Three! Five! They're all up but some are in trouble!'

Through his glass the captain saw three men swimming for pieces of wreckage. Two appeared to be struggling to stay afloat, the others trying to push broken fragments of wood to them.

'Ready to lower away!' the captain ordered as the whaler bore down on the wreckage. 'Hard to port!'

The *J. Howland* answered the helm. Dumping the wind from her sails, she wallowed as Cooky's boat hit the water. Mangiro ran to the rail and saw one man trying to hold another above water, both of them going down. The big ship was sliding by them. Cooky was hauling another seaman into his boat. Mangiro untied his Wellington boots, pulled them off and ran to the stern.

The captain saw the boy streak down the deck and, without breaking stride, leap over the rail into the sea, landing near the struggling men just as one of them went down.

Mangiro reached under the water and the seaman's thick

41

woollen cap came off in his hand. He ducked his head and groped blindly. Grasping the man's hair, he pulled the seaman up but could not lift his own face clear of the water to breathe without letting go. Then suddenly it was he who was being tugged by hands which gripped his collar. He kept his hold, and both were hauled into the bottom of a boat.

The number one boat crew stood with Cooky and Mangiro in the galley. Crowded together, they drank hot bowls of porridge from one hand and steaming cups of sweet tea from the other.

'Mungi or Mungo,' toasted Pistchiani with his tea, 'you may be a heathen Japanee but you've got the heart of a Christian and the luck of a baby born in whale shit.'

'Hear! Hear!'

'What do we call you? Mungi or Mungo?' the big man asked the boy.

Cooky slapped Mangiro's shoulder. 'I've been calling him Mung after an old Cape Town recipe known as Mung Juice.'

'Then Mung it'll be.' Pistchiani raised his tea again. 'But he needs a Christian name.'

'John,' Old Peter shouted from the doorway. 'John, after the captain's dead son!'

CHAPTER

3

Fairhaven, Massachusetts, 10 September 1840, 4.30 A.M.
The double note of a cornet carried through the town. Over and over the high and low notes were repeated. Fourteen-year-old John Whittefield threw off the quilt, pulled on his heavy woollen socks and trousers, then dropped his nightshirt on the bed. Within three minutes, his pockets stuffed with bread, cheese, and apples, he was heading for his boat, joining the procession to the beach.

A large blue flag hung from the top of the mast on the main dock, the flag and cornet signalling that a school of menhaden was in the bay. John knew that four large nets, owned by the community for such an occasion, would be used to drive the menhaden into one of the small coves opposite the port, and drawn closed. The fish could then be scooped up and brought back to the dock, from there to be hauled to the cornfields. The founders of Fairhaven had learned from the Indians to till the fish into the earth in the autumn, plough them under in the spring, and reap a better harvest in the summer.

When John reached his surf-boat he saw four longboats, with six rowers each, pulling away from the main dock carrying the community nets. Smaller boats followed. He placed a smooth tree limb under his keel, ran around to the bow and pushed, rolling the boat backwards over the tree limb into the water. His wasn't a swift craft, but it was sturdy. Long Islanders had built it out of stout oak, of lapstrake construction sweeping up high at bow and stern for breasting the surf.

At high tide, the water in the harbour was still, full, and glassy. Seagulls dived into the school of fish across the bay. Even at this distance their familiar cries carried across the water, greeting the sun and ending the quiet of the dawn.

John splashed through the shallows, his heavy wool trousers, tucked into the high oilskin boots, sending ripples over the placid water. He heaved himself into the boat, and pushed off with one of the oars. Warm with exertion from rowing, he took off his oilskin, folded it under the seat, and continued at a steady pace across the harbour. The four longboats were already in position and dropping their nets. The smaller boats coming across the bay were directed to tie on at various places, to combine the four nets and seal the trap pushing the school of fish into a marshy inlet.

John pulled off his woollen hat and rolled his eyes upwards to watch the steam rise from his sweat-soaked head. He flexed the muscles in his forearms, enjoying the feeling. He was taller than most of his friends, and already broader in the chest and shoulders than he was at the stomach and hips. He liked using his strength, especially when combined with planning and detail. Clearing a field of stone and building a fence from the rocks, placing them so each interlocked with the other, was good work. Better was to fell trees with one of his uncles, rip them into boards at the mill, measure them out, and help build furniture. Best was using the ingrained sense of generations, the knowledge his father had taught him, of how to use the wind to drive a boat through the water. He already had plans to make a sail for his surf-boat.

A hail from the last longboat in line brought his mind back to the work at hand. The sun was full up, its warmth raising a light mist off the cold water of the harbour. The tide was beginning to turn, and John sculled to hold his place. He was directed to a point near the end of the last net. In front of him were Mr Knox and his grandson, Timothy. The old man was tying on about fifty yards away. Past the Knox boat was the last longboat, ready at the end of the net to pull the trap closed at a sandbar one hundred yards beyond.

John gave two quick jerks on both oars, backwatered with the left, reached over the side and made fast to the net. The outgoing tide turned the surf-boat around. He looked over his shoulder and saw a long line of bobbing corks and boats. The pressure of the outgoing tide and the weight of the boats along the combined nets began to swing the trap closed on the menhaden. He pulled on his oars, setting them in the water, then using the strength of his back, shoulders, and legs to drive the boat. He watched the water boil in several places inside the net, and fish flip in the air.

He was impressed by the use of tide and current to set the nets and drift them into place. Because his father was in New Bedford buying supplies for the coming voyage, this was the first time John had come out alone to help trap the fish. He more fully appreciated his father's words on the cooperation of man and nature, and man and God.

It did not seem as if he and the net were moving, but the jumping of the fish intensified. A glance over his shoulder confirmed the closing of the trap. He could hear Timothy Knox talking to his grandfather, and the slap of oars. He noticed the seagulls had stopped diving and screeching into the school of fish. They circled above. He became aware of the sounds of their flapping white wings etched against an eerie grey-blue sky.

A hail from the longboat was repeated by Mr Knox.

John dropped his oars, cupped his hands around his mouth, and passed on the cry. 'Stand by.'

The call went from boat to boat along the mile-long net. John saw Mr Knox and others pointing towards Fairhaven. He pointed also, then noticed that the large blue flag on the town dock, caught by a sudden strong wind, was bending the long staff. The water near the dock was being whipped into whitecaps. Suddenly a barge broke loose. Driven by a fierce wind, it crashed into the pilings of a wharf which collapsed on top of it. The peaked roof of an equipment shack on the main dock sailed up and out over the water.

'Cut line!' Mr Knox shouted.

Before John could repeat the call, his feet flew out from under him. He was thrown to the bottom of the boat. His shoulder hit an oar, flipping it out of its socket and over the side. The boat bounced and bucked as the wind howled. John got to his knees, peering over the high sides of the surf-boat. Waves erupted at him from all directions. He jerked at the remaining oar to get it inside the boat.

45

He saw Mr Knox hacking at his line attached to the net, then everything was blotted out by a wall of rain. He could not see the shore in the fury of the sudden storm.

Holding on to the side of the boat, squinting through the water running down his face, he drew his knife from his hip holster and hacked once. The Toledo steel cut cleanly through the rope. The boat whipped away, rolling from side to side, rocking from stem to stern. He tried to make his way forward to the bailing-tin. Now that the boat was free of the net, it was no longer taking waves over the side, but was filling quickly with rain water. He was spun about in the darkness of the deluge, losing all sense of direction. Holding on to the centre seat for stability, kneeling in the bottom with the floating oar clamped between his legs, he held on as best he could.

As quickly as the rain had come, it ceased. The wind blew hard from the north-east in the same direction as the outgoing tide. Many boats were overturned. Others, demasted and rudderless, were being pulled and blown as he was, out past New Bedford. Not twenty feet away, Mr Knox was holding his boat steady with an oar he had jammed fast into the sandbar, now two feet under water.

As John drifted parallel to the old man, he jumped forward and threw out his anchor. It held. He grabbed the bailing-tin and worked furiously, throwing water over the side. He heard the old man calmly reassuring his six-year-old grandson. John felt relieved that the wind had stopped and he could hear the conversation. He looked up at the sun, circled by a strange halo. The shouts and cries of people in trouble carried across the water.

'Mr Knox,' John shouted, 'are you all right?'

The old man continued to coax his frightened grandson towards him in their boat.

John went forward and pulled in on his anchor line, drawing closer. 'Mr Knox, can I help you?'

The grandfather, not more than ten feet away, both hands holding fast to the grounded oar, opened his mouth to speak, but his voice was lost in the roar of the storm. The force of the wind and renewed downpour blew the boat out from under his feet. It left him hanging on to the oar on the sandbar, watching Timothy being whipped away in the untethered boat. The water was around the old man's knees, the next moment chest high. He saw his grandson fall to the bottom of the boat. Casting a quick glance at John, he struck out after the boy.

John's one hand was stretched out to the old man, the other holding the anchor rope, his chest forced against the bow. A wave hit him full in the face. He dropped the rope and it ran out quickly. Once again he drew his knife, and cut the anchor line before he was swamped. The pouring rain filled the boat. He grabbed the tin, sat in the bottom, his back braced against the seat, and bailed furiously. Water sloshed back and forth around him.

Bailing water blindly over the side for more than an hour, at times he had to hold his breath to keep the rain from choking him. He closed his eyes. There was nothing to see in the darkness of the downpour. Suddenly the rain stopped again and the sky began to clear. He continued bailing until he could feel the bobbing motion and familiar roll of his high-sided surf-boat. The wind and tide were flushing him and the storm debris through New Bedford Harbor out into Buzzard's Bay.

John ate an apple, then bailed the boat dry. He pulled his wet clothing as tight as possible to retain his body heat. He could see boats putting out from the far shore of New Bedford. Volunteer search and rescue teams would soon be combing the area. He braided together what little rope he had, and lashed the remaining oar to the high stern. Because of the boat's upward sweep, it was difficult for him to scull. He could only direct it somewhat.

At about 9.00 A.M., a cloud bank closed in the Massachusetts coastline. Several times during the day, he heard fog horns searching out survivors. He shouted into the mist, wishing for the old brass trumpet on the family sloop. Eating the cheese and last apple made him feel a little better. He saw the mast of a fishing schooner and dropped the steering oar. He shouted and waved, but to no avail.

A light drizzle settled on the water. He tried sculling once more, judging himself to be close to Mishaven Point, but the oar wasn't long enough to give speed or direction against the fast-running tide.

A fog horn sounded nearby.

'Ahoy!' he shouted. 'Ahoy! Ahoy!'

There was an answering hail and his spirits rose, but suddenly he was lost again in the white darkness of the cloud bank.

John felt the heave of the waves and change in the sea. He was out of the bay and into the Atlantic Ocean.

He dozed on and off and when he brushed the salt from his eyelids, it was already dark. The fog had lifted and the sky was clear with a fair north-west wind, taking him further from the American coastline. He drew the soggy bread from his slicker pocket, squeezed out the water and forced himself to chew it.

Kneeling in the bottom of the rocking boat, he prayed, 'God, give me strength to face the trials You have seen fit to put before me.' The boy wiped his nose on his sleeve. '... and if I survive, open Thy secrets to me that I may serve Thee in truth.'

John Whittefield kept watch through the night. Twice he saw the running lights of inbound ships, and once an outbounder, all too distant to be hailed. He knew he was close to the largest commercial shipping lane in North America and there was a good chance he would be sighted.

The sun came up over the ocean rollers, giving every indication of a fair, warm, autumn day. In the first three hours of morning light, he saw five packet-boats making the run to England and France. He untied the oar and shoved it through the sleeves of his oilskin, waving it high over his head, but drew no attention; no boat turned towards him. Most of the day passed without sighting another ship. It was more than thirty-six hours since he had heard the bugle calling the townsmen to net the menhaden.

There was little wind and the sun was beginning to settle towards the water. John caught sight of a smoke trail coming over the horizon, the red ball of sun behind it. He looked away to the three points of the compass, then again to the west. The steamer appeared closer. He forced himself to scan the darkening sky and sing three hymns, twice each, before looking again.

A large steamship was indeed coming fast in his direction. His heart quickened. The distance between the steamer, his boat, the sun and water, made it difficult to calculate if they would see him before dark. John realized that hailing a noisy steamship at night would be impossible. He put the oar in the oilskin and waved it over his head. He tried standing on the seat, but almost fell overboard. As the steamer drew closer, outlined by the setting sun, the shadows of the waves grew longer. His arms trembled from the exertion, and perspiration chilled him in the evening air. Darkness closed out the ship while it was still more than two miles away.

He took his oilskin off the oar and pulled it tight around him, shivering as he knelt in the bottom of the boat and prayed, 'The Lord is my shepherd. I shall not want. He maketh me to lie down in green pastures.' John had a vision of the hills and valleys around Fairhaven – the green of the trees and white sand at West Beach. '… my cup runneth over.' He pictured his mother at the Sunday dinner table, her head bowed in a prayer of thanksgiving as his father blessed their table. He was to have accompanied his father, who secretly still held the rank of Commander in the US Navy, on his second mission. The first had been a two-year whaling voyage to the Far East. This time John was to have gone along. He'd listened to Secretary of the Navy Spaulding tell his father of the importance of coaling stations for the new steam-boats preparing to cross the Pacific, and of the need to know more about the isolated island kingdom of Japan. 'Yea though I walk through the valley of the shadow of death, I shall fear no evil. For Thou art with me. Thy rod and Thy staff comfort me.' November was to be the beginning of his great adventure, chasing whales to Hawaii and up the coast of Japan with his father. He shivered in the bottom of the boat and raised his voice, 'Oh Lord, please help me or I'm going to die!'

Eeeeeyoow-weeeeee!

The screeching noise frightened him so badly, his body jerked and his muscles twitched. Still kneeling, he peered over the side of his boat. The whistle of a steamer ripped through the night.

Eeeeeyoow-weeeeee!

It sat like a bandstand lit up by oil lamps, reflecting in the heaving sea.

Pssh paww, pssh paww!

The sound of pistons turning and steam escaping filled the night. The steady beat of the engine slowed, then sighed to a stop.

'Ahoy! Ahoy!' came the cry from the steamer. 'Where away?' John forced himself to cough, cleared his throat, and swallowed. His voice cracked, 'Four points to port!'

He heard an order given, 'Lower the boat!' and saw silhouettes of men on deck. There was the splash of a boat hitting the water, and then the slap of oars.

As the boat approached, a figure in the bow raised up and shouted, 'From where do you hail?'

He called back the answer his family had given for generations, 'From Fairhaven and, with God's help, return.'

The bow lantern of the oncoming boat threw its light on the boy in the surf-boat. 'Aye, and so it should be, laddie,' the voice called back.

John was lifted aboard the rescue craft, his boat put in tow, and the rowers pulled smartly for their ship. They were New Englanders from the steamer *Barbara Chase*. Two knew someone in his family, and almost all had heard of the Whittefields of Fairhaven.

'Will we make port tonight?' John asked.

The first mate in the bow turned away, cupped hands and hailed the steamer, 'Prepare to raise two boats. We have a shipwrecked sailorman out of Fairhaven.'

The captain's wife usually entered the galley only on holidays and birthdays. Otherwise she was served as one of the ship's officers. She took advantage of this rare opportunity to start an apple pie while John ate the second bowl of pork and vegetable stew, washed down with hot tea.

'Mrs Link, how long before landfall?' he asked.

The small, thin woman pushed a wisp of hair back into place. 'Have you had enough to eat?'

'Yes, thank you. It was fine.'

Mrs Link poured more hot tea into his mug, adding large dripping spoons of honey, and passed the cup to the boy. 'My husband's instructions are for you to be sent to bed immediately.' She turned back to her pie, dusting the batter board with flour. 'The captain will speak to you in the morning, so finish your tea.'

John gulped the last of the sweet brew and followed her out of the galley onto the deck, passing the twin smoke-stacks amidships on the way to a cabin.

He only remembered Mrs Link helping him off with his boots, but awoke in a nightshirt between a thick homespun cover and a hard bunk mattress. He seemed for a moment to be inside a blacksmith's anvil. Clanging bells, pumping pistons and hissing steam from below deck filled the small cabin.

A bearded man sat on the opposite bunk. His forearms rested on his knees as he whittled on a piece of wood without looking, the shavings piled neatly between his sea boots.

'Sleep well, did you, lad?' he shouted over the noise.

'Yes, sir. You the ship's carpenter?'

'Nope. MacDougal's the name. Chief engineer.'

'How can you stand the noise?' John asked.

'It goes away when you get used to it.' He nodded his head. 'Mrs Link herself gave your gear a proper wash in fresh water.'

John sat up, leaning forward to take the clothes from the foot of the bunk. The wool sweater was bone dry. 'How long have I slept?'

'Close to eighteen hours.'

'Shouldn't we have made port?'

'The captain wants to speak to you. Quick now, on with your clothes.'

MacDougal bent forward, sweeping the shavings with one hand into the other. John dressed, and followed the engineer down a short passageway, then up the steps to the deck. The boat ploughed ahead into the wind at about eight knots, sails furled, and two lines of black smoke trailed out of the stacks.

MacDougal pointed to the bridge. 'Up you go, lad, and mind your manners. The captain's an old navy man.' With his big hand on the boy's back, he directed him to the steps leading to the quarterdeck.

As John's head cleared the top of the steps, he saw Mrs Link sitting back out of the wind, reading. 'Permission to come on deck?' he called to the back of the man standing near the rail, scanning the sea ahead with a telescope.

'Permission granted,' the Captain said without taking his eyes from the ocean.

After a minute or two he closed the telescope, and placed it in the leather case hanging from the rail. Without turning, he motioned the boy forward with a wave of his right hand. John looked up into the smooth wind-burnt face of Captain Link. The corners of his thin lips ended in red cheeks and sandy sideburns. The black bowler hat, clamped down over thinning blond hair, caused the Captain's ears to curl forward. Although the black suit was sober, it was offset by his broad smile.

The ship's master clasped his hands behind his back and examined the boy, trying to gauge the metal of this youth who had survived the freak hurricane. 'Son, I call you that for in every way you will be treated as such on the *Barbara Chase*.' He nodded at his wife and the helmsman who was making minor adjustments with the large steering wheel. 'Your father and I served together in the United States Navy.' He paused, then continued, 'John, we are not heading for port, but are making the China run around Africa to Canton.'

The boy took a step backward as if slapped. 'They'll think I'm dead.' He reached for the rail. 'My parents ...'

The captain stared at the hand holding the rail until John dropped it and stood straight.

'Aye, son, I fear they already believe it. You have been gone almost three days now.'

'Can mail be sent?'

'It's not likely we'll meet another ship for there aren't many sea-going steamers. And we're not travelling the normal shipping lanes. Cape Town is where we'll load coal and supplies, and look for a returning ship for you.'

'Sir!' The boy stood at attention. 'I can do the work of an able-bodied seaman although I have never been on a stinkpot ... a – a – a steamer before.'

The captain harumphed into his hand. 'You have a lot to learn about steamers, young man.' He bent so close that John could see the veins in his pink ears. 'That will be a part of your education on board. School subjects will be taught you by my wife who has the experience of many years teaching our three children at sea. They are all grown now. The lessons will be at regular hours, six days a week because rough weather may sometimes cause interruptions. I will direct you in knowledge related to instruments of navigation, and introduce you to Matthew Fontaine Maury's masterpiece *Wind and Current Charts*.'

The captain drew a small blue-covered book with gold lettering from his pocket, the same book John had seen the Secretary of the Navy present to his father. He was sure Captain Link must also be on a mission for the American government.

John stood as straight and tall as he could. 'Aye aye, sir!'

Eleanor Link believed lessons should be as practical as possible. She was able to talk of the world's capes, straits, islands, seas and oceans from personal experience because, like many New Englanders, the Links had gone to sea as a family. Her lessons to John were stories of the geography of the world.

With the captain, John calculated the daily run based on coordinates he entered in the ship's log. Of all his subjects, he gave this the most time. He enjoyed the exacting work. His calculations on paper were based on computations done with sextant and compass under the stern eye of Captain Link, who would later examine the entries.

The *Barbara Chase* was a tight, disciplined, happy ship. John hardly noticed the noise of the steam engine after a while, but always thrilled to hear the watch called on deck and sent aloft to the voice of the bosun singing, 'Unfurl the mainsail.'

The chanted response of the men filled the void of the vast and empty sea as the steam engine hissed and clumped to a stop. They sang and hauled the lines.

> The ship went sailing out over the bar. Oh Rio! Oh Rio!
> Turn away, love, away. Away down Rio!

John was accepted as an honorary member of all watches. He sprang into the rigging with the seamen – up the ropes, out on the spars like spiders in the web of lines, swaying over the sea and back over the deck. He sang with them as they untied the billowing white canvas that snapped tight in the breeze.

> We're outward bound this very day.
> Goodbye, fare you well. Goodbye, fare you well.

At first the boy did not realize the honour being bestowed on him by the chief engineer whose engines were off-limits to all. MacDougal, that dour Scot who spoke in sentences of not more than three words, and only on the subject of steam engines, allowed John to enter the inner sanctum. The weather, distance, or height of the running sea had importance for MacDougal only in reference to boiler pressure and pistons. Within a month after his rescue, John fell into the habit of carrying a wiper hanging out of his hip pocket, unconsciously imitating the chief engineer. He dabbed at the throbbing power plant here and there, to clean a real or imagined smudge on the gleaming engine.

By systematic computations and expert seamanship, Captain Link guided the *Barbara Chase* into Cape Town Harbour. 'John, look there,' he said. 'That's Table Mountain.' He pointed towards the South African coastline. 'It has its linen on today.'

Behind the red tiled roofs of Cape Town's white stuccoed houses arose a gigantic wall of stone. Over the flat top of the mountain flowed fleecy white clouds, etched against the crystal blue of the African summer sky. It's a mural by the hand of God, John thought.

'Look well to starboard.' The Captain pointed to a naturally sculpted peak. 'That's Lion's Head. Entering this harbour you must keep your bow pointed between the two mountains to stay off the reefs. Drop off two points to starboard or port and it's tickey beer and dop. These Dutchmen will have to pull you out of the bay.'

The search for a ship bound for the United States being fruitless, Captain and Mrs Link decided John should continue with them to Canton, to return via Hawaii, San Francisco, and New York on the *Barbara Chase*. The boy tried to hide his joy, and to keep it from showing in the letters he left at the Seaman's Mission. He'd be part of the first attempt by an American steamer to complete the passage around the world.

The three went to church, then toured the town for two days. They saw Hottentots, small African Bushmen, Bantus, and watched a tribal dance of the fierce Zulus. On the outskirts of town, baboons roamed like packs of wild dogs. They watched a race in which men sat on ostriches, they ate ostrich steaks, and took a supply of biltong – dried ostrich beef – back on board ship. John, with the help of Captain Link, sold his surf-boat at a good price to a ship's chandler. Choosing very carefully, he bought presents for home – a shield, spear, and Zulu head-dress with which he did a dance for the crew, imitating the Zulus. He collected beautiful shells along the beach, and looked anxiously seaward for fear an American-bound ship might enter port.

On a clear day they steamed out of Cape Town, took on coal at Port Elizabeth, then headed for the Mozambique Channel. Out of sight of land and other sails, the engine was stopped, sails lowered, and according to the Captain's instructions, a block-and-tackle were made fast to the mainmast. John watched two canvas-covered crates winched from the hold, then set into prepared positions on the bow and stern. When the canvas was removed and the crates opened, two 20-pound naval cannons with rifled barrels sat on the holystoned deck under the burning African sun.

Captain Link explained to John, 'We are heading into pirate

territory. The Madagascar Strait and most of the Indian Ocean are policed by Arab Corsairs. Java, Malaya, and other islands in the South China Sea provide enough cut-throats to man all the slave-raiding, buccaneering privateers on the seas of the world.'

John watched the longboat pull away, trailing four empty casks with flags on top. The casks were left bobbing at seven hundred yards, and the crew of the *Barbara Chase* ranged their guns in target practice. It was immediately clear they were experienced hands. They manned the guns with minimum instructions from the mates. Probably all navy men, John thought.

Under sail and steam, the ship travelled on. For two days, hour after hour, the crew ran dry gun and repel boarder drills as Captain Link and the mates checked their time and discipline. On the third day, sails were furled and the longboat, trailing casks, lowered again. Under a full head of steam, the gun crews and expert riflemen fired at the moving casks until the Captain was satisfied. The crates were then placed over the big guns, and tied down with rope and canvas.

Water rushing by its hull, the *Barbara Chase* beat to starboard, sail augmenting the steam engine to conserve fuel.

Captain Link pointed out to John the difference between the Arab dhows they began to see as they entered the Mozambique Channel. 'The season has just begun. We'll see hundreds of those lateen sails because November begins the monsoon. These Arab traders and merchantmen ride the Kaskazi, the following wind from the north-east.' He handed John the telescope. 'Look well at that one to port. All dhows are built on the principle of using the following winds; in November from the north-east, in April the Kusi or southerly monsoon. The giant lateen sail is used to catch the wind from behind, the high stern to prevent being swamped by a following sea. The long pointed prow extends upward to prevent the dhow from burying its nose in a trough. Some of those craft come from the Red and Arabian seas, as far away as Persia and India.'

John spent many hours after his studies in the shade of the bow

56

gun, away from the throb of the engine and beat of the paddle wheels. His chest bare and shoes off, trousers rolled up, he watched the dhows swoop down, daydreaming of the distant and exotic places from which they had come. It was his secret place to be alone and catch the breeze on those sweltering January summer days.

The lookouts were doubled when they entered the narrowest part of the channel. The coast of Madagascar was sighted, and they were now opposite Zomba to the east.

'Sail, three points to starboard,' came the call from aloft.

John peeked out from his hiding place in time to see the captain, on the quarterdeck, raise the telescope and slowly sweep the horizon. Every man on the *Barbara Chase* watched the ship's master, and marked to himself how many times the telescope stopped in the course of the scan from port to starboard.

The captain nodded and the first mate grabbed the steam whistle, giving signal to man guns and prepare to repel boarders. The gun crew came running forward, chasing John aft as they uncovered the cannons. The first mate ordered him to the quarterdeck. He climbed the steps with his shoes in one hand, shirt in the other, and a book tucked under his arm, looking up as sharpshooters climbed into the rigging with their new Henry breech-loading rifles. Gun crews fore and aft were laying out their powder and shells. Seamen were taking up positions on deck with their muzzle-loaders and rapiers.

'John.'

He spun around and saw Mrs Link sitting in her usual place, holding her knitting needles.

'You really should be fully dressed before coming on to the quarterdeck.'

The book dropped from under his arm. He bent to pick it up, and a shoe fell from his hand. 'Yes, ma'am.' He gathered everything to his chest, went quickly behind the helmsman at the wheel and dressed, all the while trying to peek ahead to see the sail causing all the excitement.

57

'Come and stand with me, John.' The Captain motioned him forward to the rail, and put his hand on the boy's shoulder. Then he pointed far ahead to the horizon, his finger moving from left to right. 'Those are pirates, lad.' Coming towards them over the skyline were five sails spread out in a semi-circle. Handing John the glass, he said, 'Look how high they ride in the water. Those are no honest traders or merchantmen. Focus on the one in the centre. They're all dhows, but that is one of the largest you will ever see.'

John trained the telescope on the centre ship, its huge prow far ahead of the bow wave, the stern so high and ornate it reminded him of an old-time Portuguese galleon.

'That big one is at least 130 feet long, and weighs over 225 tons,' Captain Link said. 'It's called a baggala. The other four, two on each side of her, they are booms, each about 100 feet and 170 tons.'

John looked at the lateen sails. Hauled tight, they resembled Saracen scimitars coming down with the wind behind to envelop the *Barbara Chase*. 'Why aren't they using all their sail?' he asked.

'They will. They'll try to use those long prows to ram us, then as bridges to send their cut-throats aboard. These dhows usually don't carry cannon. They'll use the sail for a last burst of speed to ram or drive us towards the shore.'

John looked at the Madagascar coastline. It was much closer than before as they continued their starboard tack under steam and sail.

'I hope these bloody buggers don't know what a steamer can do,' the captain said as he raised the bullhorn. 'Deckhands aloft! Prepare to furl sail!'

Captain Link and his crew would have been more concerned had they known that from the time they left Port Elizabeth they had been tracked. A combination of coast watchers and passing dhows sent signals up the African coast and across to the island of Madagascar, a pirate communications system built up over generations.

Ibrahim Kahysin, captain of the baggala and commander of
the five-ship pirate fleet, trained his telescope on the *Barbara
Chase*. He had heard of ships using fire instead of sails to move
through the water but had never seen one before. He watched
smoke curling out of the twin stacks but the big wheels were
stationary and the vessel was under full sail. He looked to the
right and left. His ships, in perfect position, were closing the
trap.

'At least two of the booms will ram the infidel before we do,'
he growled to his helmsman, then shook his fist. 'Don't hit too
hard! We could break her in half and lose everything!'

The helmsman, muscles knotted under dark skin as he tightened
his grip on the forty-foot rudder, nodded his understanding.
Although he had served eight years with Ibrahim Kahysin, he
knew a mistake might mean his life. He had seen others killed for
less.

A slow smile, revealing large evenly-spaced yellow teeth,
spread on the pirate captain's face as he watched the *Barbara
Chase* tack across his path. He slammed his fist into the palm of
his hand. 'We've got him! He's trapped!' Ibrahim shouted to a
seaman by the mainmast, 'Up the green signal!' Then to his first
mate on the lower deck, 'Are you ready?'

The mate pointed to the hundred and fifty cut-throats from
the dregs of the ports along the African coast, armed with knives,
swords and flintlock pistols. 'Aye captain, we're ready!'

'Watch the sails on the smaller booms, John. They'll be first to
close the trap on us. They're making eight knots now, but in this
wind they can do twelve to fourteen.'

Something on the giant baggala in the centre caught Captain
Link's eye. He trained the telescope on the big ship's mast. A long
green pennant fluttered as it was hauled up. He swung the glass
over the oncoming semi-circle of pirate ships.

'There it is!' Captain Link pointed to the two booms on the
port side. 'They've let out all sail.' He pulled the speaker's tube to

his lips and shouted to the chief engineer, 'MacDougal, I'll be needing all the speed you can give. Stoke her up!'

'Aye Captain. You'll get all we've got and then some!'

Captain Link brought the telescope down. The dhows were clearly seen now. Their teak hulls, rubbed red with shark oil, glistened in the burning sun. He continued on course, seemingly oblivious to the five corsairs bearing down on him. He put his hand on John's shoulder.

John stared ahead, eyes wide, fear in his heart. Was this how his life would end after surviving a freak storm?

'Up the blue signal!' Ibrahim Kahysin shouted.

A blue pennant went up the baggala's mast, under the green one. The other two booms jumped forward as they let out their sail to close the trap.

The pirate captain shouted to the men on the lower deck, 'I will kill anyone or all of you if there's fighting over the women or young boys we take captive! After it's over, you'll draw lots for the prisoners!' He raised his clenched fist over his head and roared, 'Now we ram that unbeliever's scum bucket! *Allah il Allah*! Death to the infidels!'

'*Allah il Allah*!' The cry was taken up by the pirate crew.

'Steady as she goes,' Captain Link repeated over and over, his eyes fixed on the baggala. 'Eleanor dear, please come and stand with me,' he called without taking his eyes off the big dhow.

His wife put down her knitting and went to her husband's side. The captain leaned forward, slowly bringing the bullhorn to his lips, then straightened and shouted, 'Furl sails!'

At the same time, John saw the giant dhow in the centre let out sail with the wind behind, now committed to a course, angry white water burst from under its bow.

This is what Captain Link had been waiting for. 'Full steam!' he shouted in the speaking tube. Then to the helmsman, 'Hard aport!'

Engines pumping, paddle wheels coming to life, the *Barbara*

Chase heeled over as the seamen aloft gathered in the sails. The tempo of the pistons and the slap-swish of water increased as the side-wheeler received full power from the throbbing engine below deck.

'Can they be so stupid?' Ibrahim asked himself out loud. Snatching the telescope from its holder for a closer look, he saw the big wooden wheels begin to move. He brought down the scope and saw thick black smoke belch from the twin stacks. He felt the hair raise on the back of his neck. A cold chill made him shiver and his testicles shrink into his body. For a moment he was paralysed. He was witness to a violation of the laws of nature. Without sail, the infidel ship headed into the wind. Ibrahim ran the back of his hand over his dry lips and muttered, 'If it be the will of Allah to test me with the devil's tricks, then I beseech thee O Mohammed, messenger of God, allow me to be equal to the task.'

It was clear to the pirate captain that the steamer's manoeuvre would take it between his baggala and the booms on his right. There would be no chance to ram. He shouted to his helmsman, 'Hard right!' To the man at the sail he gave an order forbidden to any craft with a lateen sail while running before the wind, 'Come about! Come about!'

The helmsman, responding immediately to the order, threw his weight against the big steering oar. But the second mate, in charge of the sail, shouted back, 'We'll tear the mast from the deck!'

Ibrahim snatched a musket from the nearby rack.

BAM!

The second mate fell dead with a hole in his forehead and a hundred men jumped to the lines. The baggala moved to answer her helm. The sail lost wind and, from the pressure on the ropes, swung inboard. The seamen dropped the lines and dived to the deck, struggling desperately for any hand-hold. The mast, creaking and groaning in its socket in the belly of the ship, screamed its protest as the wind caught the giant sail, spun it

61

around, and bellied out on the opposite side. The half-million-pound baggala was jerked halfway out of the water. Men clawed the planks for a hold. Equipment slid down the sloping deck as the port side rail dipped into the Indian Ocean.

On the high stern, Ibrahim clutched the rail with one hand and steadied his helmsman with the other. They listened for the expected deafening crash of the cracking mainmast, but it didn't come. Inconceivably, the big ship fought her way up from under tons of sea water. Looking at each other, the men began to laugh.

On the quarterdeck of the *Barbara Chase*, John realized the manoeuvrability of the steamer allowing her to make the ninety-degree turn meant they would escape the trap of the pirate ships. The four booms were out of position, unable to change course. But John's feeling of relief changed. His stomach dropped when he saw the baggala's giant sail swing across its deck. Captain Link had said it was an impossible manoeuvre for a dhow but the pirate captain was attempting it. The baggala was changing course before the wind.

John could control himself no longer. 'Look! Look!' He pointed at the big dhow heeling over on its side, revealing the barnacles on her bottom.

Captain Link took his wife's hand and said, 'If that pirate doesn't lose his mast and can right himself, he'll have an angle on us to ram.' He slipped a double-barrelled pocket pistol into Eleanor Link's grasp.

She leaned towards him and whispered, 'God is with you, Theodore. I am not afraid.'

All eyes aboard the *Barbara Chase* were on the big Arab ship. Slowly she righted herself and caught the wind, gathering speed, bearing directly down on them.

Captain Link raised his bullhorn to the crow's nest. 'Show our colours!' he ordered.

The American flag fluttered up the mainmast, snapping in the wind as the side-wheeler ploughed across the path of the oncoming pirate vessel. Captain Link ordered his bow gun to fire at the pirate ship's helmsman, his stern gun to aim for the mast.

Ibrahim Kahysin danced about the stern, aglow with the conviction that Allah had bestowed his blessings by not destroying the baggala. It was meant for the infidels to be slaughtered!

'Uncover the cannon and fire at the motherless bastards!' he roared.

Three carefully concealed old Portuguese twelve-pounders were quickly uncovered, and torches put to their touch holes.

BARROOOMM! BARROOMM!

Both ships fired simultaneously.

John ducked when he heard the two shells whizz over his head.

'It's too late to duck when you hear it,' Mrs Link said.

But John noticed that even she flinched when the third enemy shell ripped away fifteen feet of the port side railing.

The steamer's stern gun had missed completely, the shell falling harmlessly into the sea, but its bow gun scored a direct hit on the baggala's stern, killing the helmsman. John saw the pirate captain with his white turban, catch the big tiller and hold his ship on the ramming course. Chest bare, pantaloons whipping about his legs, the big man seemed oblivious to bullets splintering the deck around him, fired by snipers high above John's head.

'Prepare to repel boarders!' Captain Link bellowed through his megaphone.

John saw half-clad brown- and black-skinned men running out on the long, pointed ramming prow coming directly at him. He heard their shouts, saw flashing swords. The whap of a musket ball hitting the railing near his hand made him realize there were snipers in the baggala's rigging too. For a moment his feelings were hurt. Could someone be angry enough to shoot at him?

Captain Link watched his gunners, fore and aft, taking careful aim. Although they had reloaded their cannon before the pirates, they waited for the precise moment. They were experienced men, not to be rushed.

63

The Arab guns opened fire and twenty feet of decking was ripped up near the bow of the *Barbara Chase*. Five men lay mortally wounded.

BARROOMM! The stern gun on the steamer fired. John saw the base of the baggala's mast explode. The billowing sail pulled the entire mast up in the air. It hovered in front of the prow, then crashed into the sea.

The pirate ship ran onto its own rigging, stopping dead in the water. The men crouching on the ramming prow were thrown into the ocean. The snipers in the rigging swung and fell to the deck below, smashed like ripe fruit in a hurricane.

Both crews, braced for the shock of combat, now stood dumb-founded. The side-wheeler ploughed by the wallowing dhow with barely ten feet separating them, the only sound the steady sweep, swish of the paddle wheels.

John stared at the smooth startled face of the big Arab captain, his bare feet braced, still clutching the useless rudder.

Ibrahim Kahysin watched the steamer passing by. He looked to heaven, seeing only the burning African sun. He spat over the side and shouted to his first mate, 'Haul in on the rigging and bring our guns to bear!'

Men jumped to the lines, by sheer brute force turning the ship around. Ibrahim, in his frustration, gave the order to fire too soon. The shells fell harmlessly in the steamer's wake and the big baggala drifted downwind, her guns no longer able to reach the steamer, her crew trying to haul the sail from the water.

Captain Link called down the speaking tube, 'Half speed, MacDougal. A job well done!'

'Aye aye, sir. Do you agree to a tot for the black gang?'

'Agreed, but not just yet. We still have work to do.' The captain turned to his wife. 'Dear, would you please go below. This will be a gory business.'

Eleanor Link's years of experience at sea had bred unquestioning compliance. She left the quarterdeck.

Captain Link manoeuvred his ship behind the big pirate

baggala, out of danger from their cannon. He gave the order and his twenty-pounders opened fire, shooting until the big dhow began to settle, stern first.

Two longboats, each carrying thirty men, put out from the sinking ship, as did many makeshift rafts.

Crew and mates on the *Barbara Chase* looked to their quarterdeck. Captain Link's raised arm came down swiftly, his finger pointed at the rafts. His gunners sighted and fired. The water was soon dotted with wreckage and floundering men.

In the first longboat, Ibrahim held the tiller under his arm. He cast backward glances at the steamer, mouthing curses at the infidel captain, his own crew, and Allah himself for the fate which had befallen him. He saw his beautiful baggala sink, her green and blue battle pennants still attached to the floating mast.

'Row you bastards!' he shouted at his men. 'There's sharks all around! They smell blood!'

Fins knifed through the water from every direction. John saw the first shark tear a man in half. He shuddered as blood spread in the water. The shark rolled over with the upper half of the man's body clamped in its jagged teeth. Other sharks found their own prey and tore them apart. The waters turned red as the thrashing beasts gorged themselves.

John was thankful for the noise of the paddle wheels and engine which muffled the screams. He braced himself and turned to the captain. He had to choke back the bile welling up in his throat. 'Sir.' Pointing at the blood red water, he asked, 'Is this a Christian act?'

'John,' Captain Link said, 'I'm glad to have you scrutinize the moral aspects of my actions. Give me a few moments, please.'

Lining the bow of the steamer with the fleeing longboat of Ibrahim Kahysin, the captain ordered his helmsman, 'Two points to starboard!' Satisfied they were on course, he gave his full attention to the boy. 'Pirates are mad dogs. They rape, burn, pillage and murder, always choosing the weakest members of society to prey upon. Muslim, Christian, Chinese or Hindu – it makes no difference. Human kindness is unknown to them.' He pointed to the longboat. 'That captain with the turban is a daring fellow. Far too adventurous to be allowed to roam these waters any longer.'

Ibrahim Kahysin, seeing the steamer aimed at his boat, dropped the steering oar and grabbed up an old camel rifle. He cocked it and aimed at the bow of the oncoming ship. Cursing and firing his last futile shot into the hull, the pirate captain went to his death under the churning paddle wheels of the *Barbara Chase*.

Into the megaphone, Captain Link ordered, 'Stand down from battle stations!' To the mate he said, 'Send two men to help Mrs Link with the wounded, and give a double ration of rum to the crew and the black gang below.'

'Sir,' John said, pointing at the men in the remaining pirate craft who slumped over their oars waiting the same fate as their captain, 'why leave that last longboat after all?'

'To tell others,' Theodore Link said. He pointed at the American flag above. 'They have seen our colours. They'll spread word among the pirates of the Mozambique Channel to stay clear of the Yankees.' He patted John's shoulder. 'Now it's time for us to have that rum. We're on our way to China.'

CHAPTER
4

The *Barbara Chase* beat into the monsoon winds to the northern tip of Madagascar. Putting in at Comoro Island, the crew piled the deck high with firewood for the long journey across the Indian Ocean and through the Java Strait. They sweated a month in Sumatra while Scotty and his black gang tore down the engine, set up their own forge, and made repairs on the drive shaft and bearings. The ship sailed from Sumatra to Singapore, staying only long enough to have the decks piled high with more firewood, then went into the South China Sea. For almost two months, they ran up the coast of the Chinese mainland. Then, one warm March evening, under a full moon casting shadows on the rolling sea, the crew was sent aloft to furl sail. The *Barbara Chase* heeled to port and steamed up the Pearl River, passing the Tiger Gate, a fort at the entrance of Canton Harbour, at sunrise.

Thousands of boats were moored at the southern end of the harbour, which spread in a straight shore line to the right, then curved back again sharply to the entrance of the river. Masts poked through a white morning mist, swaying gently in the wake of the steamer. Giant war-junks, large floating hotels, restaurants, and spacious houseboats towered over sampans that housed two hundred thousand sleeping people. Lacquered red and black, the damp, slick hulls shimmered in the rays of the new sun.

The pastel blue of the morning sky blended with the soft greens of the rice paddies and the mountains beyond Canton. The colourful flags of thirteen western nations flew over the trading factories dominating the waterfront. Canton was the only port in China officially open to foreigners.

The captain pointed out a fifteen-man fastboat putting out from the American trading area. 'We've been sighted, John. That will be an agent to act for us. Bribery is an accepted way of doing business here. Europeans call it squeeze. It's listed as a legitimate expense in the course of trading in China.'

John watched the narrow boat heading straight for them, surprised to see the Chinese oarsmen standing up and facing the direction in which they rowed.

The captain's voice was tinged with excitement as he pointed at the only other steamer in the harbour. 'And that's the East India Company's *Nemesis*. She's an English paddle-wheeler. Centred in the hull just ahead of her 120-horsepower engine. One hundred and eighty feet long with two 32-pound cannon. She draws only six feet of water. She can go up almost any river and close to shore for trading.'

Canton's port was beginning to awaken as the sun burnt off the mist. Sampans glided down hundreds of canals. Work junks moved across the harbour. The 6.00 A.M. signal gun boomed from the Peak, a mountain behind the city. In addition to the boat people Canton proper had a population of over two million, more than three hundred souls per acre in three-storeyed narrow buildings. Artificial lakes, sustained by an intricate system of feeder canals, supplied the city's fresh water. Every day, almost three hundred tons of rice and foodstuff came down the canal network from the interior, hauled on six thousand government barges, worked by seventy thousand men.

Municipal services existed, but over the last half-century had deteriorated because of corrupt officials and an opium-drugged population. After centuries of having to pay silver and gold for Chinese silks, spices and tea, the British hit on an ingenious method of prying open the Mandarin's treasure chests. Opium, purchased in the Calcutta auctions and shipped to China, became an intense and highly profitable business.

The fastboat came alongside the bow of the *Barbara Chase*. A large, square-set American climbed nimbly up the ladder and strode quickly towards the quaterdeck, a white Panama hat and unbuttoned three-quarter-length jacket flopping and flapping as he came. He was followed by an elderly Chinese in what looked to

John like beautiful black silk pyjamas.

Jake Tillim extended a large, hairy hand. He spoke around the cigar tucked in the corner of his mouth. 'How are you, Captain Link?' Without waiting for a reply, he continued, 'Theodore, you had better arm your crew.' He pointed in the direction of the boat people. 'Scrambling dragons.'

Captain Link grabbed the whistle cord and blew the signal to repel boarders. John saw several large boats coming fast towards the steamer. They were similar in style to the fastboat but five times longer, each with eighty standing oarsmen. He caught the sound of a deep-throated rowing chant as the crew of the *Barbara Chase* took up their positions.

'There's an opium war between the Tongs in the city and among the boat people,' Jake said. The cigar shifted in his mouth from one corner to the other. 'Captain Link, are you carrying opium?'

The captain's eyes flashed. His top lip flattened against his teeth. 'Mr Tillim, I am an upright man and master of this ship! Everything on this vessel is legal!'

Jake was unperturbed by the captain's anger. He turned and spoke to his interpreter in Chinese. Then he asked the captain, 'May I have your bullhorn?'

The interpreter accepted the loudspeaker from Jake and was on the bow just as the first scrambling dragon closed in. He shouted to the longboats.

'He's telling the Tong leaders you will shoot the first son-of-a-bitch over the rail,' Jake said. 'Last week they overran the decks of the *Nemesis*. They wouldn't believe a British ship from India wasn't carrying Calcutta opium. Two navies were injured, ten Chinese dead.'

The captain nodded in a friendlier way. 'I'm indebted to you, Jake, but you should know me better.'

For more than fifteen minutes, shouting continued back and forth between the interpreter and the opium traders nudging the American steamer. Some of the rowers made a feint at climbing the rail but, in the face of the disciplined crew, none really tried.

Jake pointed to a beautifully decorated sampan approaching. 'A new bribeable harbour official name of Hwiang-si. Do I have your permission to negotiate the squeeze?'

'Yes, I am already in your debt,' Captain Link said.

The opium traders aboard the scrambling dragons disregarded the oncoming government sampan. One helmsman spat in that direction.

Jake shifted the cigar in his mouth and looked at the captain. 'Would you mind blowing your steam whistle and firing your bow gun over their heads? I want to maintain Hwiang-si's honour. It may lower the squeeze a bit, and it will wake up some of your old friends ashore who are tucked in with a hangover. Ha ha.'

The captain gave the order. The whistle shrilled and the cannon boomed harmlessly. The men on the scrambling dragons did not appear intimidated, although they did backwater to make way for the government sampan.

The interpreter went through the motions of official greetings, then escorted the harbour official to the quarterdeck. Hwiang-si conducted his transactions in Chinese with Jake. Without knowing the language, John could understand it was all business. The captain produced the ship's manifest and, after an hour of negotiations, Jake handed the captain two slips of paper – the amounts of the port duty and the squeeze.

When Hwiang-si left, Captain Link turned to the American trading agent. 'Jake, I would like you to handle the cargo both ways – buying and selling. Insure, pay, and collect debts at your usual commission. Mrs Link and I are going to do a bit of socializing. Are the parties as good as I remember?'

'Even better. More organized now. Each factory has its own day of the month, and except for the sabbath, there's always something happening.'

'Jake, I'm also interested and ready to pay for whatever reliable information is available about Japan from your private sources.' The captain motioned John forward. 'And this is young John Whittefield from Fairhaven, Massachusetts. Mrs Link will not be holding regular lessons while we're in port. I hope you won't mind teaching him about Canton and China?'

70

Jake Tillim took John by the shoulder and led him to the ladder. 'Be glad to. Come on, boy.' He started down the steps, then turned back and said, 'Theodore, if you did have opium, the scrambling dragons were offering 1000 Spanish silver for a 130-pound chest. Hwiang-si offered 1200. Ha ha.' He laughed around his cigar.

John Whittefield would become familiar with that laugh as he was introduced to China. He followed the agent off the ship and moved to his side on the dock. Barefooted, barechested, pantalooned workmen melted away in front of them as they walked around the growing stacks and heaps of goods being unloaded from the steamer.

Jake took the unlit cigar from his mouth, looked at the wet end, and heaved it away. 'Here we go, boy. It's time you learned just how inferior a soul you are. Ha ha. The Chinese believe themselves to be the most advanced culture on earth. You are about to meet the honourable Mr Wu. He's an honest man and a trader as sharp as any Yankee. He also performs one more function which no westerner is prepared to do – kow-tow. We hairy strangers from the west pay tribute for the right to trade – only in the port of Canton – and have to kneel before a representative of the Emperor. China doesn't need to export. It has a vast population as a permanent market, a people with no real interest in the crude offerings of us foreigners. We use men like Mr Wu, head of the family firm of Wu Hao-Kuan, to pay tribute and kow-tow for us. This fiction allows us to maintain our dignity and still buy and sell in China.'

Mr Wu's office was located in his home, a spacious building of many rooms, sliding doors, and a veranda around the entire second storey. The building enclosed a garden of delicate ferns and meticulously placed exotic flowers, surrounded by smooth river stones. The eldest son of the Chinese merchant never left his father's side, nor did he say a word, yet John was impressed by the young man. Only his intelligent dark eyes moved in that inscrutable face. In contrast, Mr Wu laughed and waved his arms, leaning back and forth in his chair as he and Jake bargained in Chinese.

71

When they left the office, the negotiating completed, they were led to the garden. Tea and delicate cakes surrounded by small pieces of dried, sugared watermelon were set on a low table.

Mr Wu's son served. John was intrigued by the intricate carvings decorating the posts, cornices and sliding doors. He looked across the courtyard. Watching them from the second storey veranda were Mr Wu's nine children, wife, concubines, and servants. There were almost twenty people, including toddlers, and he had not heard a sound. As if on signal, Mr Wu's family bowed. John found himself bending the upper half of his body in return to the greeting.

Jake took John to his home, an apartment over a warehouse at the dockside, and introduced him to the house staff. There were eight in all, three of whom were young and beautiful Chinese women. The agent slept, worked, and ate in one large room which had an unrestricted view of the harbour. A low bed with silk quilted covers stood in the far corner. Four large soft leather lounge chairs were positioned in a semi-circle facing the view. The chair nearest the desk was most worn, and had a telescope case sewn to its side. Next to the desk was a large teak cabinet half filled with books, the other half with bottles of whisky and gin. From this big room a hallway led to the toilet, tub-room, and servants' quarters.

Jake settled into his lounge chair with a water glass half full of whisky, which he raised. 'Here's to your captain, son. He's a good man, and it's been a good day.' He tossed off the whisky, put down the glass, and pulled the telescope from the case to scan the Pearl River and entrance to the harbour. 'It was just this way I spotted you early this morning. I'm a free agent and have to race others to the private ships making port. Company ships from the factories use their own agents.'

'How long did it take you to learn Chinese?'

'About fifteen years, and I'm still learning.'

'Is that why you use an interpreter?'

'Ha ha. No. There are two different kinds of Chinese. One is official. That's Mandarin, which I've learned. The other is for ordinary people, and that I'm trying to learn. Some day we'll open other ports in this country and do business with the common people. There are at least two hundred million of them. Ha ha. Can you imagine what a market that will be, and except for a few missionaries I'll be one of the only Christians able to speak with them. Why right now I doubt if there are five Americans who can do business in Chinese.'

John looked at the square-jawed agent with the unlit cigar, then around the room at the sandalwood walls covered by maps and delicate Chinese paintings. 'Do you think I could learn Chinese?'

Jake moved the cigar to the other corner of his mouth. 'Let me think about that. Right now, get yourself into the tub. Mr Wu's nose twitched a few times. You do smell a little strong. Ha ha.'

John went down the hall to a room where a huge tub was filled with hot perfumed water. Soft towels were draped over a chair and a silk dressing gown hung from a clothes tree. While he was in the tub one of the young Chinese ladies came in, her eyes lowered, to take his dirty clothes. John ducked in the water up to his nose. Without moving his head, his admiring eyes followed her to the chair and back out the sliding door. He felt a familiar ache in his loins.

After the bath, John put on the light silk robe and returned to Jake's room. While the agent bathed, John rested on one of the lounge chairs and looked out of the window. He watched a two-man racing shell pulling for the French factory, passing sampans and trading junks. It went out of sight behind a large war-junk with cannons sticking out of the gunports, the ancient muzzles capped like corked wine bottles. Far down the placid Pearl River, against the orange of the setting sun, he thought he saw a smudge near the skyline. He padded over the polished teak floor on bare feet and pulled the telescope from its case.

'Mr Tillim!' he shouted. 'Mr Tillim!' There was no answer. He ran down the hallway to the closed tub-room. 'Mr Tillim, a ship – a steamer coming up river!'

'Jesus Christ!' the agent shouted.

John heard splashing and the sound of wet feet on the floor.

'Get over here!' Jake ordered.

John, thinking the call was for him, slid open the door. Jake stood naked in the centre of the big tub, steam rising around his body, his arms reaching to take the dressing gown from the same beautiful young woman. She was nude, she was exquisite, her ivory body shining wet in the soft light of a paper lantern. Her outstretched arm held Jake's gown. It was John Whittefield's first glimpse of a woman's breasts. They were small and pointed. Her smooth, flat stomach flowed down to a small crop of black hair. Jake snatched the robe and the girl turned away. John held on to the door jamb at the sight of her rounded buttocks, sleek thighs and ebony hair glistening against the sheen of her skin. A voice called his name and he looked up.

Jake was robed and towelling his hair. 'Close the door!'

John reached for the latticework but his hand went through the paper wall, tearing it further when he jerked his hand out. Finally, sliding the door shut with a bang, he ran to the veranda. There, he grasped the railing and kept his eyes on the thin line of smoke barely visible against the last light of the sun.

He heard Jake shouting in Chinese and English. The only words he could make out were, 'Jesus Christ, Lulee!' Then, 'Get the fastboat!' Behind him, he heard the clink of bottles.

'Good job, lad,' the agent said.

John turned and saw Jake holding two bottles of whisky in one hand, taking another two of gin from the shelf. He held them up and smiled. 'If it's a Yankee – whisky, a Limey – gin. Be a good lad and give me a cheroot from that humidor.'

John jumped to the desk.

Jake bent his head forward, opening his mouth. 'Stick it in the corner and I'll be gone.' Then, with the cigar clamped in place, he said, 'You've done me a good turn, lad. Sleep well tonight. Ha ha.' He was out the door with the clinking of bottles and a shout, 'Lulee!'

A servant brought dinner for John – boiled potatoes, broiled fish, vegetables, tea and almond cookies. It was quite tasty but he was disappointed, having expected some exotic dishes from the

Chinese cook. He ate his lonely meal gazing at the panorama of the moonlit bay where thousands of bobbing lanterns of the boat people reminded him of fireflies on a warm Massachusetts night. Another servant came in to let down the bamboo curtains. John pulled the robe closer around him and curled up on the soft leather lounge chair. He was quickly asleep.

He became aware of a caressing pressure on his back, then a faint scent of perfume. He felt her soft belly slide up to his buttocks and the warmth of her thighs as her legs curled into the contours of his. In the faint light of the paper lantern, he watched a delicate hand, with long silver nails, untie the belt of his robe. He turned towards her, the robe opened, and the hard muscles of his young body felt her warm softness. He looked into the smooth face and dark eyes of the beautiful girl from the tub-room. She smiled and gently but firmly placed his hands around her waist.

Fingers spread wide, his hands explored her rounded buttocks. He shook with dread and desire but could not stop caressing her body, at the same time fearing she would cease the slow exotic movements of her hips. Her fingertips touched his nipples and he gasped, embracing her so tightly that his erection rammed into her stomach. Slowly, gently, she closed her fingers around his hardness and guided it into her. He felt himself following his penis inside as the trembling of his body became an undulating, never-ending series of waves which drove his hips back and forth, time and again, over and over. He heard himself laughing. Throwing back his head, he cried out, holding onto her for fear she'd break away. But her body was alive with pleasure – pushing towards him, pulling back only to gyrate beneath him, above him, causing him to explode inside her again, and again. She seemed to know exactly where and when to touch him. The interval between climaxes became longer and more pleasurable. John duplicated her caresses, and finally they fell asleep exhausted in each other's arms.

Sometime during the night she slid away from him. He felt her go, but remained quiet. Then he arose and raised the bamboo curtain. He stood for a long time watching the swaying lanterns of the boat people, not knowing if the tears in his eyes were for the evil he had committed or the joy he had experienced.

'Tomorrow,' he whispered, 'I'll go to church.'

'Come on, lad.' Jake was shaking him by the shoulder. 'You have lots to see. Mr Wu is sponsoring a special tour for us. Catch!' Jake threw a set of clothes at him. 'Put those on, get washed, and we'll eat and go.'

The clothes were new, of fine material, and perfect fit. John's Toledo knife was in the exact position on a new leather belt, and everything from the pockets of his old clothes was in the correct place.

Over fresh eggs and crisp fried beef, he asked, 'Where did my new clothes come from?'

'They were made last night. There's one thing you must understand about China,' Jake said. 'It's got labour surplus. The sewing machines you brought from America will do the job faster, but will also put many unfortunates out of work. Technology of the west is not a blessing here. You might even call it a curse.'

'As bad as opium?'

'No.' Jake wagged his head slowly. 'Nothing is as bad as the heavenly dust. That steamer you sighted yesterday was the *Lord Amhurst*, an East India Company ship just back from a trade survey mission to the north. The captain told me that wherever they went along the China coast, there was a demand for the drug. Boats put out from every town and village, becoming hostile when they found out his ship carried no opium. The drug is against Chinese law, but opium trading is unrestricted. According to the captain of the *Lord Amhurst*, there are at least nine million Chinese addicts.'

They finished their breakfast and looked out from the veranda. The *Nemesis* was now moored in the centre of the harbour, and the *Lord Amhurst* stood docked in its place.

Jake pointed downriver to what John thought were large houseboats. 'Those are loading stations for opium, floating warehouses, and they are heavily armed. When a deal is made, the scrambling dragons come out to pay and take possession of the opium, always under the guns of the factory. Then they race for shore for fear of being waylaid. There's not much the Chinese government can do considering the corruption, the squeeze, and the pitiful army they have.'

Jake Tillim was unaware of the increase of war junks in Canton Harbour and the reinforcements at Hu-men, the Tiger Gate fort. The giant fighting-junks had slipped into the bay over the past two months, mooring amongst the boat people. The Tao-kuang Emperor, from his Imperial Court in Peiping (Peking), had given orders to stop the illegal opium traffic once and for all, choosing Lin Tse-hsu to implement his orders.

Lin, an outstanding government administrator for almost forty years, began by strengthening the government's forces. He realized there were two enemies, the western traders and the Chinese Tongs. His agents scouted the empire to buy all the cannon they could without raising suspicions. They armed the Imperial war-junks and brought them one by one to Canton. The fact that neither Lin Tse-hsu nor his officers were acquainted with modern weapons or tactics made little difference. They planned to overpower the enemy with their numbers. They collected and mounted Spanish and Portuguese guns made in the 1700s. Dutch finbankers and Venetian twelve-pounders from the 1600s were bolted to makeshift carriages. Wheel-lock and flint-lock muskets, more than a hundred years old, were distributed to the crews. Of the twenty-two war-junks in the harbour, only six had captains with fighting experience against westerners. These were Malay pirates hired by the government.

The way to Mr Wu's house took Jake Tillim and his young charge by the Seamen's Chapel. John looked at the cross atop the small peaked roof and felt a sense of guilt, knowing he should go in to beg God's forgiveness, but just the thought of the Chinese girl caused him to have an erection.

'Are you well, John?'

'Oh yes, Mr Tillim.'

'Then keep up with me. Anyone who walks behind another man in China is either a coolie or a woman. Neither count for much here.'

John moved quickly to the trader's side, hoping the bulge in his trousers was not visible, and wondering how anyone could look down on the Chinese girl from the tub-room. He wondered if he should ask her to marry him. But he was too young and they would have to wait a few years.

At the merchant's house, they were received with tea and cakes dipped in honey. Mr Wu's eldest son led them to a room where they changed into Chinese garb – long black silk gowns buttoned to the neck, with sleeves, longer than their arms, embroidered at the cuffs. White silk stockings and black silk slippers completed the outfits.

Jake led the boy to a small courtyard off the garden. They entered an enclosed palanquin and were immediately hoisted by six bearers who placed the carrying poles on their shoulders. Another team of six relief bearers followed after them, and a man ran in front to clear the way. Sitting on cushions, they could see out through the bamboo curtains, but could not be seen.

Very soon they were in the centre of the city's crowded streets, passing cramped houses, stalls, and alleys far too narrow for the palanquin. John saw different styles of dress which, Jake explained, indicated social rank. The smell of peat used for cooking fires, mixed with soya, pimento, garlic, ginger, vinegar, and other unnamed things, filled the air. They stopped to eat boiled pork and wheat cakes with rice wine at 'Wei The Big Knife Restaurant' near the Bird Bridge, and watched the barges pulled and poled down the canal.

Resuming the tour, Jake and John saw factories where hundreds of people worked, and men who carried their business on their backs. A few animals pulled carts, but it was mostly people, people, people with bundles, or baskets swinging from shoulder poles, who filled the streets. Wheelbarrows were everywhere, some even mounting sails to help them along the road. To John, the Chinese of Canton appeared an industrious people, always on the move, very clean and, most of all, multitudinous.

The two ate their evening meal at 'Wah-Ling's Purple Dragon'.

It began with egg soup, thin strips of beef laid carefully around the edge of the bowl. In the centre were fried noodles, like a nest, supporting a pickled egg. Filleted fish, white rice, many strange vegetables, sauces both sweet and sour, sharp and bland, surrounded the food. These dishes were consumed with teas of various blends.

The sun was setting, and already paper lanterns cast their coloured lights from the houses and shops. The palanquin moved through the crowds. Then it was set down before what appeared to be a long wooden factory building. John could see no doors and only a few windows indicating three floors. Mr Wu's eldest son came from behind their palanquin. Flanked by two of the stronger looking bearers, he walked towards the building. Jake and John followed. Inside, several men stood about, obviously guards from the assortment of knives and pistols hanging at their belts. The group was expected, and greeted by a young man in a long embroidered silk gown. He bowed low, exchanged a few words with Mr Wu's son, then led them down a hall and through two doorways covered by beaded curtains. John was almost overpowered by a thick, heavy, sweet smell. He felt it in the back of his throat, and almost choked.

'This place reeks of opium,' Jake explained.

Mr Wu's son drew open a curtained doorway on the right. In the small cubicle, a middle-aged man lay on a thick quilt. Propped up by pillows, he leaned on his elbow, his cheeks sucking in to draw smoke from a short straight-stemmed pipe. By his side, a young girl squatted. Barefooted, in dirty torn clothing, she was packing the combination of tobacco and opium into another pipe. The merchant's son walked down the hall, pulling back curtain after curtain on both sides. Reaching the last cubicle near a staircase, he literally threw the curtains back, almost tearing them off the bamboo rods. The pathetic addicts inside paid little heed. Their unblinking glassy eyes could not focus; their heads lolled on pillows.

Mr Wu's son spoke in Chinese to Jake Tillim. John, watching the young Chinese face very closely, saw no sign of emotion. Jake

79

nodded his head affirmatively.

They started up the stairs and Jake turned to John, 'There are seventeen rows of sixty-five cubicles on this ground floor. Two more floors above are for the not so wealthy clientele.'

John followed them up worn wooden steps which showed the grain of lumber through the lacquer. A strange whispering noise grew louder as he went up. Smoke curled like thick fog against the low ceiling. Paper lanterns, hanging from supporting poles, gave out an eerie luminescence which hovered over row upon row of wooden pallets stretching the length and breadth of the building. On these opium beds lay sallow-skinned, emaciated men with blackened teeth, faces caved in on skulls from which their unblinking eyes caught the strange light. No one spoke. The unfamiliar whispering sound was made by the hundreds and hundreds of men sucking on pipes. In the narrow area between rows, small dirty children filled and lit opium pipes. Several two-man teams moved on signals from the children, carrying bodies to the far side of the room where they disappeared in the glowing fog.

John choked from the sweet heavy smoke. The young Mr Wu turned and John saw tears streaking his smooth impassive face. Without a word the young Chinese took John's arm and led him downstairs, followed by the others. They exited on the opposite side of the building. John coughed, trying to empty his lungs of smoke and breathe fresh air at the same time. Jake pounded him on the back. Mr Wu's son spoke in Chinese, pointing at a second-storey window with split bamboo curtains. A wooden chute led from the window down to a donkey cart. The curtains parted. A man's body was heaved on to the chute and slid down into the cart with a whooshing sound. The curtains flapped closed. At the other end of the building, John could make out a crowd of people on either side of a doorway.

Jake put his hand on John's shoulder. 'Those coming out the window have left this world; those waiting outside are hoping to buy a better one, if only for a short time.'

They walked to the palanquin. On the return trip the Chinese lanterns did not appear as gay, and the people seemed less happy.

'That's why Captain Link became angry with me when I asked if he had opium aboard,' Jake said. 'He has seen places like this. It's one of the largest but there are small dens in every nook and cranny of this city.' He shook his head. 'More than nine million addicts. That's equal to the population of the entire United States of America.'

'It has to be stopped!' John spat out the words with such vehemence that it caught Jake Tillim by surprise.

'I guess,' Jake said, 'as much as I'm against the opium trade, I've become used to it.' He sighed. 'There have been some Chinese and westerners who have tried to stop it. They were discouraged or done away with by their own people. You see, a good part of the English and European economies is based on opium.'

'But why don't the Chinese people do something. It's their country. They are being destroyed!'

'Someday someone like Mr Wu's son may find a way. In the meantime there are highly-placed Chinese officials making a great deal of money from opium. And most of the Chinese people don't even know about it.'

'With nine million addicts in the country, everyone must know.'

'John boy, there are over two hundred and fifty million Chinese, spread over four million square miles. Although they speak the same language, the dialects are so different that they can't even understand each other very well. Only the rich merchants and public officials learn Mandarin.'

John flopped back against the rear of the palanquin. He heard one of the bearers underneath the carrying poles grunt with the shift of his weight. He became angry with himself for causing the man pain, for being carried by other men, for wanting the Chinese girl, and most of all for not being able to do anything. 'If the Chinese ever do find a leader and form an army ...'

Jake's dry chuckle cut him off in mid-sentence. The agent pointed a finger at John. 'You're mature for a youngster. You've just pinpointed the nightmare haunting every white trader in the colony. The surest way to become unpopular in the port of Canton is to raise this subject. Everyone knows it would take just one spark to turn hordes of Chinese loose on us. There's so many of them they could throw us in the bay like a pot of slop – if they had leadership. Every trading factory has a contingency plan for just such an event.'

Back at his apartment, Jake dressed for a party at the Swedish factory. He said goodnight to John and recommended a few books from his collection. John immediately headed for the tub-room as soon as Jake was gone. The same girl entered while he was in the bath. Her head lowered, she took the clothes from the chair. John did not duck down in the water this time. He stared straight at her. Before sliding the door closed, she raised her eyes to meet his, holding him with her gaze, then was gone. He stepped out of the tub dripping wet, rubbed himself dry with a towel and slipped into a light silk robe. Instead of returning to the big room, he stopped and looked back the length of the dim corridor. Light from an open door spread over the floor of the hall and onto the opposite wall. His silk slippers whispering over the teak floorboards, he approached the light and stood in the doorway. She lay on quilts, covered by a pale blue silk sheet which revealed the contours of her body. Her shoulders were bare, cheeks slightly rouged, and her dark eyes invited him. John slid the door closed, dropped his robe and went to the bed.

The active social life of Canton took Jake away each evening and John was happy to remain in the apartment. But, a few nights later the girl was not in her room. Since they had never spoken, he did not even know her name. Wandering up and down the corridor he coughed softly, hoping for a sign. Hearing an answering cough, he opened a door and his face coloured scarlet as he bowed quickly to the startled cook. He heard the cough again, bowed a second time, slid the door closed and opened the next one. It was another beautiful girl. He stood in the doorway wishing he could speak Chinese. When she beckoned to him, he entered.

The next evening, Jake was home for dinner. John was glad for the conversation. 'Lulee has some queer ideas about westerners,' he said.

'Well,' the agent said, 'from the Chinese point of view, we are slightly out of the ordinary.' He raised his porcelain tea cup. 'We take their tea, put so much sugar in that the flavour is smothered, then squeeze in lemon to make sure there is no trace or scent of tea.' Jake leaned back and stretched his arm forward, pointing at John. 'They think you and I are barbarians. Inferior. But look at it from their side. We do pay tribute for the privilege of doing business with them. They think of the western countries as they have thought of other tributary nations for over five thousand years. The only imports that interest them are cotton and opium. They can do very well without both.' He threw his arms forward, got up from the chair and took a Chinese book from the shelf. 'This,' he tapped the book, 'is required reading for all officials dealing with foreigners. It is called *A record of things seen and heard about overseas countries*, written in 1730.' Jake went to a wall map. 'See anything strange? I drew this myself from the descriptions given in this book.'

John looked closely at the map. England was in Holland; Spain and Portugal were in Turkey; Sweden, Denmark and Norway were lumped together in Austro-Hungary and Germany.

Jake tapped the map with the book. 'They think the French were originally Buddhists and the source from which Christianity evolved.' He put the book on the shelf. 'There's an updated version almost as bad as this.' He sat down and leaned back in the lounge chair, looking out over the harbour. 'They describe England as a land with competent administrators who have built three bridges, brought fresh water to the capital city in pipes, and allow their ships to help seamen of all nations, in distress. America is an island. In the first book, America didn't exist. Now it's an island belonging to England. Americans specialize in fast boats and ships with fire in the belly which turns the oars. Men in America insist the women tie themselves around the waist so they won't eat so much. Ha ha.'

John enjoyed talking with Jake Tillim but it was beginning to get dark and Jake hadn't said anything about his plans for the evening. 'No party tonight, Mr Tillim?'

'Oh yes, yes. In fact I thought to take you along.'

John's head came forward, mouth open.

'You're catching flies, son.'

John snapped his jaw shut. 'I thought the parties were only for adults.'

'Well that is true, but you've become a big, active fellow. Would you rather stay here?'

'Yes, I think that might be best. I would rather read and rest up.'

'Whatever you think best,' Jake smiled.

He left the table and dressed to go out. As soon as he was gone, John bathed and hurried down the corridor, wondering which girl was waiting.

5 April, 1842: Jake Tillim sent word to Captain and Mrs Link to make quickly for the ship. John was told not to leave the apartment. Drunken navies had inadvertently killed a Chinese girl in the centre of Canton, a place legally out of bounds to the seamen.

The death set in motion a series of incidents which came to be known as the Opium Wars. It was to end the squeeze – the tribute system – open new ports north and south of Canton, and put the legal administration of these new ports and their populations into the hands of the western nations. In addition, the Chinese would be forced to pay the cost of implementing all these new services.

After a friendly brawl between the crews of the *Lord Amhurst* and its sister ship, *Nemesis*, each crew went its own way, embellishing stories about the free-for-all as they walked, talked and continued drinking. Big Bill Hooker, a first-class seaman from the south of London, reached over the counter of a food stall in the street and took himself a handful of smoked eels. When the owner protested and grabbed his arm, the big seaman punched the merchant in the face. The little man went down like a rock and his young daughter ran to his side.

Hooker jumped onto the stall counter. Waving the eels, he began to sing a sea shanty. Before he finished the first verse, the counter collapsed, throwing him on top of the girl and snapping her spine. It took her ten screaming minutes to die. Neighbours, family, and passersby, drawn by the screams, cornered the seamen. If not for the Chinese guards, they would have been killed by the angry mob.

Lin Tse-hsu, the Emperor's representative, was notified of the incident. He immediately ordered the foreigners imprisoned, to be tried collectively under Chinese law for murder.

One of the Chinese jailers, interested in seeing how his torture methods would work on an Englishman, obtained the information that the original stories about the *Lord Amhurst* were true. 'She's loaded to the gunwales with opium,' the sailor cried. The confession was untrue, but the seaman would have said anything to stop the pain.

The sailors from the *Nemesis*, hearing news of the imprisonment, invaded the jail. Forcing their way in, they injured several guards, then freed the seamen and everyone else in the bamboo cages. Still in a drunken rage, they set fire to the jail. Chinese military reinforcements, joined by people in the streets, chased the seamen to the English factory area.

From Jake's veranda, John looked for the source of the frightening noise – like the roar of some giant prehistoric animal. Thousands of howling people massed around the British factory, three hundred yards away. The *Lord Amhurst*, churning the water white, pulled away from the dock loaded with seamen and British nationals. Jake, from the street, motioned John to follow him to the fastboat. Almost before they were in, the boat shot out into the bay, heading for the *Barbara Chase*.

Meanwhile, the information about opium on the *Lord Amhurst* had been sold by the jailer to the most powerful Tong leader in Canton. Eight hundred cut-throats, on ten scrambling dragons, set out to stop the ship from leaving the harbour – to bargain or board her, whichever was necessary. Word of a large opium cargo spread among the boat people, reaching other Tong leaders who organized their men to pursue the steamer. The captains of the war-junks put their crews at the ready, believing the time had finally come for action.

John scrambled over the rail of the *Barbara Chase*, across the deck and up the ladder, taking his place to the right of Captain Link on the quarterdeck.

Mrs Link, on the other side of her husband, peered at him. 'John, don't become overexcited. These things usually amount to nothing.'

But the boy could see that Captain Link was taking no chances. His men were at their fighting stations and two new twenty-pound swivel-guns had been mounted amidships. The captain pulled the black bowler down on his head until his ears bent, watching intently as twenty-five more scrambling dragons shot out from among the vessels of the boat people, angling to cut the *Lord Amhurst* off before she could reach the Pearl River. Over the noise of the steam engines, John heard the chant of the two thousand rowers from a mile away. A roaring cheer from the mass of people carpeting the British dock encouraged the scrambling dragons.

Jake Tillim took Captain Link by the arm and led him away from the others. 'I must get back, Theodore.'

'Will you be safe?'

'I couldn't live anyplace else.'

The captain nodded and shook Jake's hand.

'I didn't forget your request,' Jake said. 'The information from my sources is that China imports some copper from Japan, government regulated of course. A little smuggling goes on from both sides, but recently they've caught Japanese with maps and paintings of western boats and people.' Jake shifted the cigar in his mouth. He called to Mrs Link, 'I bid you goodbye.'

She nodded.

Slapping John on the shoulder, Jake said, 'It's been good to watch you mature in China. Now that you are back aboard, you can get a little sleep. Ha ha.'

He was down the steps and going over the railing before John caught his full meaning. Just before Jake stepped onto the fastboat he looked up, winked and was gone.

How stupid to think Jake didn't know what was happening, John thought. When he turned around, no one noticed his crimson face. They were all watching the dragon ships gaining on the *Lord Amhurst.*

The captain of the *Nemesis* had steam up and anchors hauled in. He ordered a signal gun fired and flags run up asking the *Lord Amhurst* if she required assistance. The firing of the signal gun unnerved the commander of the Tiger Gate fort. Seeing the oncoming steamer being chased by dragon boats, he ordered his gunners to fire on the *Lord Amhurst.* Some of the ancient cannons exploded on their carriages, killing the gun crews and setting off powder-kegs nearby.

To the captains of the Chinese government war-junks, it appeared the fort was under fire from the British ships. The commander of the Chinese fleet gave the order and three red rockets whooshed off the stern of his boat, trailing smoke, bursting high over the bay. Thirty Chinese warships cut their anchor lines, raised sail and slowly ploughed through and over the sampans of the boat people to engage the British in battle.

The first salvo from the fort splashed harmlessly around the bow of the *Lord Amhurst.* But the British captain could see that if his ship held course, it would be in point blank range for at least two barrages from the fort.

Through his bullhorn, he gave orders, 'Ladies below! Gentlemen, you will be issued small arms. Please assist the crew if it is necessary to repel boarders.' He barked into the speaking tube, 'Stop engines!'

The pistons slowed and the paddle-wheels stopped. There were sounds of hissing steam and the chant from the approaching dragon ships.

'And you,' he roared through the bullhorn at the crew, 'you bunch of drunken bastards! You let one Chinaman dirty my deck and I'll flay the skin off the lot of you!' Into the speaking tube he ordered, 'Reverse engines!' To the signalman, 'Notify the *Nemesis,* yes we need assistance!' To the cannoneers on the stern and two small swivel-gunners on the quarterdeck, 'Aim well and fire true!'

The giant paddle-wheels of the *Lord Amhurst* slowly slapped the water. There was a whooshing sound as the forward drift stopped and she picked up speed in reverse. The paddles began pounding the bay like a locomotive. The big ship moved stern first, backwards through the water. Another barrage from the fort roared out, every gun ranged for the forward motion of the steamer. The shells and old cannonballs exploded and splashed harmlessly, well in front of the retreating ship.

The steersmen on the closest dragon boats were taken completely by surprise when the steamer reversed and came towards them, quickly closing the gap. One was rammed, another overturned. Both were chewed up in the paddle-wheels, men and boats spat back out into the bay. Two other boats trying to close in were overturned by the wash of the paddle-wheels. The two swivel-guns and stern cannon of the steamer fired, splintering and smashing the slim dragon ships. Another disintegrated, hit by the thirty-two pounder from the bow of the *Nemesis*.

Three dragon boats, their men straining at the oars, shot in over the backwash of the paddles to ram the *Lord Amhurst*. The rowers dropped their oars and jumped for the railing on the low deck. Two hundred and forty of them came pouring on to the ship, armed with rapiers, pistols, and sabres.

The captain, watching from the quarterdeck, pulled the whistle cord. His seamen, hiding behind hatch covers and deck housings, armed with large-bore, short-barrelled muskets loaded with scatter shot, jumped up. The murderous fire swept the deck clear of all boarders. Bodies of dead and wounded were dumped over the rail. The wake of the *Lord Amhurst* ran pink with blood. Gunners on both English ships continued firing at the scrambling dragons as they turned and fled. The *Lord Amhurst* and the *Nemesis* moved into position and shelled the Tiger Gate fort.

John was looking to see if Jake's fastboat had reached shore when a movement caught his eye. They were coming out through the sampans like large lumbering animals, their red and black lacquered hulls and dull white sails dwarfing the other boats. Thirty war-junks, sails up, cannon run out of the gunports, were breaking out into the open water, the closest less than a mile away.

'Captain Link, sir!' John pointed to starboard.

Until the government warships joined in, Captain Link considered the battle a private British–Chinese Tong feud over opium.

But now he raised the bullhorn. 'Make signal to the British ships that we are coming to their assistance! Notify the European sailing ships at the shore that we need their support!' His orders were sharp and clear. 'Show our colours from the mainmast! Gunners fire the closest targets!' He turned to John. 'Pull that whistle until the Britishers have seen the danger!'

John, thrilled to be a part of the battle, grabbed the cord and pulled down hard. The *Barbara Chase*'s guns opened fire on the Chinese fighting ships but the shells caused small damage. A fire in the rigging of the leading junk only slowed it down. Then the big guns from the two British ships, heeding the whistle, opened up on the war-junks. The bow of the first one disappeared in smoke. She went down immediately. Before the water covered her stern, two more junks were seriously hit. But other junks were closing fast.

Captain Link, seeing the British steamers reversing engines and seemingly retreating, read the signal flags between the two English captains. He shouted into his speaking tube, 'Reverse engine!' The three steamers moved backwards in the face of the attacking Chinese warships.

Once again, from the wharf, the crowd cheered.

It seemed to John that the largest war-junk was a monster ship whose sail blocked the horizon. Two rockets blazed from its deck streaming smoke, and burst in a green cloud over the bay. The Chinese fighting-ships began a turn to starboard, attempting to form a battle-line to drive the three steamers towards the Tiger Gate fort and catch them in a deadly crossfire.

Captain Link handed John the telescope pointed at the two British steamers. 'Focus on their maindeck amidships.'

To John's surprise, English sailors were gathered around a series of tubes pointing up in the air. Then they scattered, taking cover. There was a flash. Another and another. He put the glass down and watched the fire trails in the sky.

'Congreve rockets,' the captain said.

They exploded in, on, and around the battle line of war-junks. Two were set on fire, one burning so brightly it hurt John's eyes to look in that direction. The powder magazine blew, and the junk disintegrated. Shock waves swept Canton Harbour. Flaming pieces of the hull rained down, setting fires on other war-junks and on the shore.

The heavy British cannon were still firing when the bay shook again. A Swedish sailing ship at the wharf had fired a broadside into the Chinese fighting ships. Again the harbour shivered as a German sailing ship cut loose a broadside, catching the Chinese in a crossfire. The Dutch ship joined in, there was another barrage of rockets from the English, and most of the war-junks dropped their sails as a sign of surrender. Seeing this, the crowd on the dock howled like a wounded animal.

The Malay pirate captains had held back in the attack, and now attempted to catch the wind for a fast run down the Pearl River. The commander of the Tiger Gate fort, realizing they were deserting, fired on them. Two of the Malay's ships were damaged, but managed to continue downriver. The others were sunk. The crowd on the dock turned its anger on the British factory, tearing doors off warehouses, trying to set fires, invading villas and ransacking them, until the British steamers turned to fire on their own buildings. The crowd scattered. Seamen were sent ashore to rout looters with sabres and pistols.

Several hours later, Captain Link returned from a meeting with the British captains. He gave orders to weigh anchor. The *Barbara Chase* had been loaded for two days. Her bunkers crammed with coal, sacks of it piled on the deck, the American steamer began the long nonstop journey north, up the Chinese coastline into the Sasebo Sea, into the Sea of Japan, through the Strait of Shimoneski and the Pacific Ocean. Captain Link spent most of the daylight hours on the quarterdeck at a chart table, mapping the Chinese coastline. When weather permitted, they sometimes went close to shore to take soundings. Coming out of the Shimoneski Strait, the bow was pointed for Hawaii. They met several whaling ships, three from America, from which they took mail for home.

The *Charles W. Morgan*, out of New Bedford on her maiden voyage, was trying out a whale when the lookout on the *Barbara Chase* sighted her. The newly-commissioned whaler had greasy luck. A year and a half off the ways and she had already caught forty-two whales yielding 1800 barrels of oil and 7000 pounds of whalebone. The *Morgan* had gammed with the *J. Howland* off the coast of Japan in January. They had heard of the death of Captain Whittefield's son. Upon seeing John alive, the Captain of the *Charles W. Morgan* led a thanksgiving prayer service under the hot August sun. The hardened seamen sang hymns, their voices joining in harmony over the water between the ships.

Captain Link said, 'Only those who make the sea their home, recognize the whitecaps above the troughs as markers of departed family and friends. Young John will return to his family. Each seaman standing here in the middle of the Pacific Ocean, maintaining his balance with the roll of these waves, shares in that joyous reunion, living it in his mind's eye and in his heart, as if it were he who has been resurrected from the deep.'

'Amen!'

CHAPTER

5

The try pots had been fired up ever since Mung awakened aboard the *J. Howland*. The ship's flensing master had shown him how blubber was stripped from a whale's carcass, then block-and-tackle used to haul the fatty slabs aboard and drop them neatly into the red-hot pots. Some of the crew believed the increased catch was their reward for having saved Mung's life. The less religious felt he had brought his own luck with him and every boat crew on the whaler wanted him to pull an oar. They rubbed his head for luck before they went after any whale. But it was the giant Pistchiani who taught him how to row backwards, to work the sail, and steer the longboat. A special bond slowly developed between the two. In a chase, Mung began to pull his own weight.

As much as the men liked him, they couldn't get used to seeing Mung tear into a piece of raw whalemeat, or eat dripping seaweed fresh from the ocean. For his part, Mung had difficulty keeping down bully beef. The dry biscuits and coffee tasted like sandstone and varnish to him. It also seemed that no one but he bathed, even though he had to resign himself to daily dousings with cold sea water instead of a hot tub. The sickening smells of bodies, whale oil and rubbing liniment drove him out of the crew's quarters. He slept on deck wrapped in his blanket until a storm blew up and Pistchiani allowed Mung to sleep in his cabin. The next morning the big boat captain woke to find the cabin spotless. Every corner had been cleaned, the shelves polished, the floor scrubbed. Theirs became a permanent arrangement.

In his free time Mung helped the master carpenter, or could be found in some corner of the ship drawing sketches.

Two months after Mung had come aboard, Pistchiani went to the captain. 'Sir,' he said, 'it's a shame to let a bright lad like Mung learn our language from the crew in the forecastle.'

'What's the problem?'

'He comes into my cabin saying things they taught him like, "How are you, you big balls son-of-a-bitch."'

William Whittefield made a useless attempt to stop from laughing.

'The humour's not lost on me either,' Pistchiani said. 'I know the young one means nothing by it. And that's just the point. Look at these.' He handed over several sketches done on old sail canvas.

The captain immediately recognized pictures of the burial of Shin-ho and the chase of the bull whale and his harem. He looked up puzzled from the third. 'It appears to be a long insect with many legs lying dead on its back.'

'That's what it is all right – the first in a series of four. They show how the boy's mind is working. In the next picture the body of the insect is thinner and the legs straight. The third shows the legs pulled to the side and bowed, and the body thinner still. Now look at the fourth.' Pistchiani tapped the canvas. 'You have a perfect reproduction of the interior hull of the *J. Howland*.'

The captain shuffled the pictures again, then looked up at Pistchiani. 'What does it mean to you?'

'It means, sir, that this young lad who comes from a country where they build boats from bamboo lashed together, has grasped the concept of modern boat construction using the keel and ribs to form the frame and support the outer shell. I'm also certain he understands the idea of centring the mast and the use of the keel to sail into the wind.'

'How long do you think it took him to do these drawings?'

'Less than a week. I've counted every rib and brace in that last drawing and he's got them all there in the right place. The sail too. Every rope is just where it should be for a starboard tack.'

Captain Whittefield handed the pictures back. 'I've noticed him in the rigging or on deck watching whenever I order a change of sail. What do you have in mind, Mr Pistchiani?'

'The lad should learn good English.'

'Then teach him.'

'Captain sir, I can do my sums and write lists of things connected with whaling, but not much more.'

'You think Mung should be taught to write?'

'Yes sir. Anyone who can draw as good as this won't have any trouble with penmanship.'

'I'll think on it. Thank you for bringing this to my attention.'

How could I be so blind, William Whittefield thought. I've been trying to gain information about Japan and here I have a direct source on my own ship. He summoned Hockmeyer to his quarters.

When the big first mate entered, the captain said, 'For reasons important to me, I want you to teach the Japanese boy English. I remember you taught Sunday School in Fairhaven.'

'Yes sir, I did. I'd like to teach the lad. May I borrow quills, paper and ink?'

'Yes. And any books in my personal library you may need.'

'Aye aye, sir.'

In two months Mung was conversant enough in English for Deacon Gilhooley to approach the captain with his request. 'Sir, may I teach the Japanese lad about Christianity?'

'Is it your desire to convert him?'

'It is, sir. If I could save his soul and teach him about our Lord and Saviour Jesus Christ, it would atone for some of the sins I've been guilty of during my life.'

'It would certainly be an accomplishment, Mr Gilhooley. Bringing a heathen soul into the house of God is no mean task.'

'I would appreciate the opportunity, sir.'

'Go to it.'

The captain followed the boy's progress closely, growing to like him more and more. He was impressed with Mung's ability to learn but disappointed to find that Mung knew little about Japan outside his own village. When Mung spoke about history, it sounded much like Homeric legends.

On several occasions the boy's intellectual ability and total recall astounded the captain and other seamen who were teaching him. However, some seemingly simple things, such as sitting in a chair comfortably, were difficult for the boy to master. 'I'm used to squatting,' he explained. 'Everyone in Japan is. I never saw a man sit on a chair before. We don't even have a word for it in Japanese.'

On the other hand, Mung had no problem accepting Jesus Christ as God. He was used to praying to any one of a number of gods and the idea of a choice between the Father, the Son, and the Holy Spirit, all male ancestors who seemed worthy of veneration, pleased him. Initially he had confused Jesus, the Son of God, with the Sun God from whom he believed the Japanese Emperor to be descended. Deacon Gilhooley tended to overlook these small misunderstandings in his zeal to have Mung more enthusiastic about his teachings. When Mung did sort it out for himself, the difference made little impact. Since he was with another people, travelling to another country, it seemed natural to worship their gods.

One attitude which disturbed him though was the lack of respect for elders. Old Peter was often last in line at meals, and rarely deferred to when decisions were made. The Americans seemed to follow the best man, regardless of age.

First mate Hockmeyer brought another problem to the captain's attention. 'Sir, the boy is brilliant. On paper he can do arithmetic. He even uses Arabic numerals as we do. But ...'

'What's the trouble?'

'I'm not exactly sure.' Hockmeyer looked at Mung standing near the door and motioned him to a seat. 'Sir, the difficulty is that the boy cannot do even the simplest mathematical problem in his head, even though he can memorize anything he sees. If I ask him to do the sum of eight and four in his head, he's baffled. Watch this.'

The mate crossed the cabin to Mung and lifted a wood-framed instrument from the boy's lap. It had beads which slid back and forth on wires and was tied by a cord to the boy's belt.

'He made this thing, Captain. Mung,' he asked, 'what is the square root of sixty-four and the cube root of twenty-seven?'

The boy positioned the instrument on his knees and bent his head. The fingers of both hands flew, popping the beads back and forth. Then he looked up. 'The square root of sixty-four is eight.' He turned back to the instrument and soon looked up again. 'The cube root of twenty-seven is three.'

'He's always correct when he writes or uses that instrument,' Hockmeyer said.

The captain moved closer to the boy. 'Son ...' He coughed and cleared his throat. 'Mung, count how many fingers I'm holding up on my left hand.'

He took Mung's left hand with his right. As he touched each of his own fingers with the boy's hand, Mung counted out loud, 'One, two, three, four.'

Then the captain held his right hand up. Mung touched and counted, 'One, two, three.'

Holding both hands aloft in front of the boy, he asked, 'How much is four and three?'

Mung's hand automatically went to the abacus.

'No!' Captain Whittefield ordered. 'Don't use that!'

Mung looked up, confused.

Still holding both hands up, fingers outstretched, Captain Whittefield said, 'Count again.'

Mung started on the left hand. When he reached four, the captain brought his right hand up next to his left and said, 'Go on.'

Mung hesitated, then continued counting, 'Five, six, seven.' His dark eyes scanned the two hands back and forth. He separated them, counting each by itself, then brought them together. His almond-shaped eyelids opened wide. Looking into the captain's eyes, he sucked in his breath, the air whistling through his teeth. 'Hai!' he shouted. 'Hai! Seven! Seven!'

The captain slapped Mung on the shoulder and turned to Hockmeyer. 'This boy can learn anything! This inability of his to add and subtract in his head may be related to something I learned from him about the Japanese and the way they relate to time. They generalize it. Children born before a certain date are considered a year older. The time of the day is blocked into early morning, late

96

morning, early afternoon, and so on. It may be a custom to use the abacus or write numbers. It could be possible they have forgotten how to cipher.'

'That may be true, sir, in Mung's village, but would it apply to the entire country?'

'You have a point there. Maybe we can have Mung speak with the Japanese in the oriental compound in Hawaii.'

'Sir, what about his memory? Do you think all Japanese can remember so well?'

The captain rubbed his jaw. 'I doubt that. I doubt it very much.'

From that day Captain Whittefield began teaching Mung the use of the compass, map, and sextant, thinking often of his son John and making mental comparisons between the two boys. On the quarterdeck just at the end of one of these lessons, Mung revealed another aspect of his character. It was a warm day with a light breeze and calm sea. Mung snapped the clasp closed on the wooden box containing the sextant. Captain Whittefield turned from checking Mung's computations which were accurate as usual. He saw the boy's head jerk around as he looked at something in the sea. Then Mung whipped out the knife Pistchiani had given him after his first chase and kill. With the weapon in hand, Mung ran across the quarterdeck and dived head first over the rail into the sea.

The whaler was making a moderate four knots. Captain Whittefield and the helmsman stood dumbfounded. The crew, lolling in the warm sun on deck, were unaware of what had happened.

'Man overboard!' The lookout's cry from above galvanized everyone into action.

'Hard aport!' the captain ordered. As the helmsman spun the wheel to put the ship into the wind, the captain snatched the megaphone and shouted, 'Lower away a boat on the starboard side!'

From their boat stations, the men could see Mung swimming underwater with the knife in his hand.

'He's after the turtle!' Pistchiani pointed to the creature swimming slowly by them.

Mung had spotted the giant sea-turtle from the quarterdeck and acted instinctively. In Nakanohama the meat of a 700-pound turtle would support a family of three for a year. The shell would bring twice as much.

His dive took Mung close to the swimming creature. He thought to come up from underneath and cut the reptile's throat while the neck was extended but as he neared he saw the powerful flippers with their sharp extended claws, and knew they would cut him to ribbons if he tried. He broke the surface behind the front flipper and grasped the top of the shell. His hand slid off. He jabbed the knife into the shell hoping to pull himself up but the point would not penetrate. The turtle withdrew into its shell as Mung tried to board from every angle and slipped off at each attempt.

Pistchiani's longboat was already in the water; the rest of the crew stood at the rail.

'Mung! What on earth are you doing?' Captain Whittefield asked through the megaphone.

Treading water and pointing with his knife, Mung shouted, 'Sir, turtle steaks!' He went under and bobbed up again. 'Turtle soup!' Under he went once more and popped back up. 'Best damned eating in the world!'

The crew, eight months without fresh food, cheered loudly and looked hopefully at the captain.

William Whittefield put the megaphone to his lips. 'Mr Pistchiani, bring the supper aboard but perhaps we should leave that impulsive boy in the drink.'

The big whaler plucked Mung from the water. 'You're the craziest Japanee I ever knew!'

Mung giggled. 'I'm the only Japanee you ever knew.'

On board the whaler Cooky raced to the galley, shouting for firewood and deciding how to cook the unexpected delicacy. The crew, their mouths watering, threw a line to Pistchiani and hurried the block-and-tackle in place to haul the giant turtle aboard.

That evening everyone ate on deck in honour of Mung who could not stand to eat in the smelly quarters below.

The closer the *J. Howland* approached to Hawaii, the warmer and silkier became the air, and the more excited the crew. The wind blew fair and steady, the Pacific living up to its name of peaceful ocean. They approached the seventy-mile channel between the islands of Kauai and Oahu on their way to the big island of Hawaii for rest and refitting.

'Sail-ho!' came the call from aloft. 'Two points to port!'

Some of the crew sauntered to the rail.

Then again from above, 'Sail-ho three points to starboard!'

More of the crew came to the rail.

Then the entire ship was electrified by the lookout's shout, 'Town-hooo to starboard and she blows! Town-ho to port! She blows! She blows!'

The men on deck watched the lookout in the crow's nest jabbing his arm. 'Town-ho! She blows all over the ocean!' he cried.

Gilhooley shouted up, 'What do you see, man? What do you see?'

From above came the reply, 'The whole damned channel is full of spouting whales. There are ships all over chasing them.'

'First mate to the quarterdeck,' Captain Whittefield ordered.

Hockmeyer took the ladder in two leaps. He accepted the telescope from the Captain and scanned the horizon.

Finally the mate spoke, 'Captain, I was into something like this off the coast of South America about twelve years ago. It's one large herd or many, grouped up. Whales do that sometimes, though I never heard the reason why.'

The Captain took the scope. 'There must be twenty ships out there.'

'At least that many; they are whalers heading for the autumn rendezvous and refitting in Honolulu.'

'Hockmeyer, take Gilhooley and Pistchiani and my telescope aloft. Meet me in my cabin with a proposal on how to attack that herd of whales.'

The three big men went up the rigging and into the sheets, side by side, feet swaying on the ropes, stomachs pressed against the cross-trees. Seventy-five feet above the deck, the ship's pennant snapping thirty feet over their heads, they watched the oncoming scene of whales and whalers. They remained up there for two hours as the *J. Howland* ploughed forward.

The three boat captains filed into their chief's cabin, standing silently until Mung finished pouring coffee and left.

Hockmeyer began, 'They are still there, sir; whales blowing all over the ocean. Your estimate of twenty ships is correct, some foreigners, but mostly American whalers. It's something like a circus. Some of the skippers and many in the whaleboats have no experience at all.'

Gilhooley said, 'There must be over one hundred harpooners out on the water, and ten times that many whales. The whales seem to be using the Kauai channel to play in. Raising their flukes, catching the wind, and sailing along. Sounding, coming up, and jumping out of the water. They're having a frolic.'

Pistchiani lowered his coffee mug. 'The problem is that they're too easy to harpoon but the greenhorns don't know how to finish them off. We saw lines crossed, longboats ramming, mother ships drifting into each other. Right now, there's a Russian ship almost turned over, trying to cut loose a dead whale that's sinking on them.'

'Sir,' Hockmeyer said, 'that's a free-for-all out there. It's got to be every man for himself. There can be no planned attack on the herd.'

The Captain thought for a moment, then said, 'Two things are necessary. First, protect the *J. Howland*. I'll take you in as far as I can, drop the boats, and stand off. Second, a sharp watch in the rigging for directing the longboats. Have your men keep a lookout for our signals. We'll be on the whaling ground in an hour. Hockmeyer, see to it every man is fed a double portion. Gilhooley, put extra rations and water into the longboats. Pistchiani, see that the longboats are fully equipped and shipshape.' He snapped open his pocketwatch. 'We'll have five hours of daylight. I'll meet you gentlemen on the quarterdeck at two bells.'

The helmsman rang the hour as the boat captains stood behind their chief on the quarterdeck. Ahead of them, they could see

100

whaleboats, mother ships, and spouts crisscrossing the Kauai channel.

Captain Whittefield looked at them, then below to the crew on the maindeck. He said, 'We came out to get the whale. It's one of the bounties God put on this earth for man to use. Be sure you all arrive in Fairhaven safely to divide the rewards.' He raised his voice. 'Remember, a whale fast is a whale made. A free whale is anyone's for the taking.' He pointed his arms upwards, towards the mainmast. 'Watch the signals from above.' His arms came down slightly, the hands open, fingers spread wide over the heads of the men. 'And may God be with you.'

He nodded to Hockmeyer who turned and bellowed, 'Man your boats! Prepare to lower!'

Pistchiani pulled a sparkling gold Spanish coin from his pocket and grabbed Hockmeyer's arm. Holding the doubloon between thumb and forefinger, he waved it under Hockmeyer's and Gilhooley's noses. 'Wager a doubly on the first whale back to the ship.'

Hockmeyer took a doubloon out of a pouch tied around his neck. Gilhooley took out one he had secreted in the back of his large pocketwatch.

Gilhooley said, 'To be spent in the House of the Sun?'

The other two men smiled and together said, 'Done!' They each dropped their doubloon into Cooky's hand and went to their boats.

Mung, handling the tiller in Pistchiani's boat, was directed into the mêlée of drifting mother ships, running whales and pursuing longboats.

A Swedish boat captain, whose crew had been after a big cow for several minutes, saw Pistchiani's boat drawing parallel and after the same whale. He waved the Americans off.

Pistchiani jammed his left fist into the crook of his right arm. 'A whale free is for the taking,' he roared.

The big blond oarsmen from the northern country chanted after their captain, 'Ho ya! Hoo har!' They picked up their pace and pulled ahead of the men of the *J. Howland*.

Pistchiani sang out, 'Yankee doodle went to London just to buy a pony. Stuck a feather in his cap and called it macaroni.'

His crew picked up the stroke and chorus, 'Yankee doodle keep it up. Yankee doodle dandy. Mind the music and the step, and with the girls be handy.'

The Swedes chanted faster, matching the Americans stroke for stroke as they raced across the water.

The big cow, with no time to draw breath enough to dive, was tiring fast. Closing on her, the two boats rocked in the wake of her flukes, the Swedish boat on the inside. Mung steered the longboat as close to them as possible, watching the blond oarsmen, their fair cheeks blood red, sweat pouring off their brows, eyes glazed, arms working like pistons. They began to pull further ahead, riding over the whale's wake.

The Swedish captain shouted an order to his lead man who shipped his oar and stood. He snatched the harpoon and made ready to throw. Mung saw the muscles in the seaman's arm jumping from the exertion of rowing. The tip of the harpoon wavered. With one oarsman less, the Swedish boat dropped back slightly. Mung held his tiller steady, passing just as their harpooner threw his weapon. It arched through the air and the razor-sharp point pierced the side of the leviathan. The flukes went up and smashed down again with a thunder clap on the water. The wounded cow shot forward, pulling the Swedes' boat after her, but the harpoon's barb tore itself out of the blubber. The boat slid backwards off a wave, then wallowed in the wake.

'She's ours!' Pistchiani cried. 'She's ours! Pull! Pull men! Pull and we'll each buy our own whorehouse in Honolulu!'

The wounded beast charged a hundred yards forward, then circled to port, taking her directly in front of Pistchiani standing in the bow. He hefted his harpoon as the whale came closer. 'Pull! Pull!' he whispered. Mung held the tiller steady, watching him point the harpoon and plant his right foot behind. They heard the bow wave of the whale as she ploughed through the water, crossing in front of them. Pistchiani looked into the small eye of the beast.

'Yaaagghhh!' He heaved the harpoon and its steel point went into the great body up to the wooden haft. The whale spun towards

102

them. Pistchiani let out the line and ordered, 'Backwater starboard oars!' Mung threw the tiller over hard and the boat spun away from the whale.

Catching sight of the rocking Swedish boat, its crew slumped over their oars, the great beast charged, pulling the Americans over the waves behind her. Dipping her big broad forehead, she bashed into the Swedes, then lifted her head, rolling men and boat down the flat snout into her gaping mouth. She continued her upward motion, the powerful flukes driving her body high out of the water. Then she crashed back down, on men and wreckage. The line to the American's longboat went slack for a second, then whistled and whipped out of the water as the wounded whale shot forward again. The boat flew through the water and into the wreckage, the thin cedar planks of the American boat splitting apart amidships on the submerged hull of the Swedish boat. Pistchiani's crew was thrown into the water. He sledded alone behind the dying whale on the wreckage of his bow.

Old Peter in the crow's nest and the captain on the quarterdeck tried to keep track of the *J. Howland's* boats. At the captain's instructions, Old Peter ran out the signals directing the two remaining longboats to pick up survivors.

Captain Whittefield watched the bleeding whale running with Pistchiani skiing behind. Finally the cow tired and Pistchiani quickly pulled in his line until he bumped her side. Grabbing his lance from its place in the bow, he dropped the line, took hold of the wooden haft sticking out of the whale's side and jumped up on her back to drive the lance home. He held on as the cow used her last burst of strength to rush another fifty yards, then wallowed in the turbulent water, sucking in deep draughts of air and blowing them out the hole in the top of her head. Pistchiani braced himself on the harpoon, leaned against the side of the whale to draw the lance out, then plunged it in again. The great body quivered. The eye on the side of its head rolled back and watched the whaler manipulating the lance handle, searching with the point for the large vein leading to the lungs.

Mung saw a pink cloud of blood and steam billow up out of the

103

cow's blow-hole and shower down on Pistchiani. The behemoth gasped and died.

Meanwhile the men from Pistchiani's boat had been pulled to safety, one suffering a broken elbow, another with torn chest muscles. Three of the Swedes were missing. The rest had been picked up and brought aboard the *J. Howland*. Captain Whittefield sent Deacon Gilhooley's and Hockmeyer's boats for Pistchiani and his whale, allowing Mung and Black Ben to go along.

'Ahoy on the Good Ship Blubber Belly,' Gilhooley shouted to Pistchiani on the back of the whale.

'It took you long enough to get here, Gilhooley. How is my crew?'

'All safe and sound. They send congratulations on your new command.'

'Stop all the gabbing and come alongside.'

'Do you consider you've won the bet?' Gilhooley asked.

'Of course. Mine is the first whale, isn't it?'

Hockmeyer waved his arm and slapped his chest. 'But you want us to tow you and that mound of blubber so you can take our money. The first whale that reaches the mother ship wins the bet.'

'Aha!' Pistchiani shook his fist. 'I've got your drift. That ain't sporting!'

Gilhooley gave his red beard a tug. 'We're whalers, not sportsmen. It's getting dark. So if you'll agree to sharing the doubloons with us in the House of the Sun, you won't have to stay the night out here with your big girlfriend.'

'I want to go to the Sun House too,' Mung shouted.

No one paid him any attention. He nudged Ben. 'What is the House of the Sun?'

Ben shrugged. 'I don't know either but I'll see if I can fix it for both of us to go.'

Pistchiani waved the boats in towards him. 'You two may be first and second mates on a whaler but getting out of a losing bet like this means you're no gentlemen. Get me off of here!'

Captain Whittefield saw the longboats take Pistchiani aboard, then hook into the dead whale and begin towing her back. By the time they arrived, the Swedes had been taken back to their mother ship. The whale was secured alongside and the process of cutting in began. They rolled the cow over and over, peeling her blubber like an orange. Block-and-tackle were attached to the head which was separated from the body and hoisted on deck. The men began slicing away the baleen, that flexible bone used for umbrellas, corsets and girdles.

Mung, the last one on the body of the whale, signalled for a line and swung aboard ship. About to give the sign to cut the white carcass loose, he glimpsed a movement inside the headless remains and shouted for the winchman to lower him into the maw. The crew, alerted by his call, stopped their work and watched as Mung took a couple of turns of rope around a long sausage-like membrane and gave a thumbs up sign to have it and himself hoisted aboard.

On deck, one of the flensers neatly ran his five-foot razor-sharp knife down the length of the membrane. By the flickering light of the try pot fires Mung and his shipmates saw the body of a man lying face down in the muck. They stared at the still form in silence.

From the quarterdeck came Captain Whittefield's command, 'Examine the body!'

Cautiously the flenser touched the sweater and trousers. They were wet with the slime of the whale's digestive juices. He turned the seaman over on his back.

'Captain sir, it's one of the Swedes. His clothes are partially eaten away, his skin and hair are turned a satiny white. Arghhh...'

The flenser felt something grab him. He jumped away but the hand clutched his trouser leg. The Swedish seaman sat up, his eyelids fluttered open, and two dark blue eyes shone from that ghostly white face. The flenser tore himself loose from the grip and leapt into the sea.

'Man overboard!' the captain shouted.

Deacon Gilhooley ran to the Swede's side, kneeled next to him and cried, 'You have been in the belly of a whale! Like Jonah you have been to the bottom of the sea! Bless Jesus Christ our saviour,' he intoned. 'You must believe!' He looked around at the crewmen, then straight at Mung. 'You all must believe!'

The seaman gazed up at the Deacon and made sounds like the soft mewing of a crying kitten. The mewing became pinging noises through his fluttering lips, high-pitched sounds of uneven lengths. He then began to jabber in Swedish.

'Leave him be!' Pistchiani pulled the Deacon away. 'He doesn't understand a word of English and,' tapping his head, 'has probably gone bonkers.'

The Swedish crew took their shipmate off the *J. Howland* next morning. Until they did, no one slept. The flenser was pulled from the sea but would only consent to sit in a lifeboat until the Jonah was gone. Deacon Gilhooley, eyes burning with the fervour of a missionary, related the story of Jonah and the whale to Mung.

CHAPTER

6

Ten days and five whales later, Captain Whittefield navigated his ship into Honolulu Harbour. It was crowded with whalers from all over the world. He noted the unusual number of warships and entered each one in his ship's log and personal diary, '30 August 1842: British ships of war – *Sulphur*, *Action*, and *Ambuscade*; French – *La Place, La Bonite, Vénus*, and *Armetise*; USS *Potomac* and *Constellation*.'

The Hawaiian harbour-master came out to the whaler in a canoe and guided them to safe anchorage amongst the eighty ships in port. Sails furled, moored fore and aft, the mast and crossarms of the *J. Howland* became another bare tree in the rocking forest of the harbour.

Mung looked over the rail into the crystal-clear water. It was as if the ship floated on air. He saw exotic fish swimming lazily around the coloured coral, fathoms below. He looked into the depths of the water and remembered a dream from the previous night. He was back on Fudenojo's fishing boat, his hand caught in the fishing line. He could not let go. The tug-tug of the line dragged him over the side. He was being pulled down through the water, deeper and deeper. His lungs were beginning to hurt. Then he saw the distorted faces of his brother Jakato and Shin-ho below him. Their images became clearer as they pulled him towards them. They were smiling. They stopped pulling on the fishing line, smiled at one another, and looked up at him. He hovered above them, returned their bow, and accepted a bowl of fluid from the concave head of the mystical Kappa.

Jakato said, 'Mung, my little brother, always remember how to catch a Kappa.'

Shin-ho cut the line and Mung shot up towards the surface,

holding his breath with his last bit of consciousness, wondering why his brother had used the name Mung.

A big hand grabbed his shoulder and spun him away from the rail. Pistchiani said, 'Come on, my little Mung. It's time for you to go out in the world and learn the facts of life.'

Deacon Gilhooley came from behind, lifted Mung off his feet by the back of the belt, then carried him like a sack of potatoes towards the ladder.

The Deacon called over his shoulder, 'Pistchiani, lend me a hand with this sack of Japanese rice. He's grown in the nine months he's been with us.'

Pistchiani grabbed the other side of Mung's belt. The two men strode down the deck, swinging him back and forth between them. They reached the ladder going over the side and suspended him out over the rail and the canoe below.

'What do you say, Deacon? Shall we drop him?'

Mung looked up at both men, then down at the outrigger canoe. The Hawaiians dipped their paddles and backwatered.

'Don't call me Deacon. You know that when I go ashore on these heathen islands, I leave my Bible aboard ship.'

The two men let go of Mung. He dropped like a stone into the water.

When he surfaced and knuckled his eyes clear, Pistchiani shouted down, 'That will teach you to bathe more often.'

For a moment, Mung was dumbfounded. Then he shouted back, 'I'm the only one on the ship who washes every day. You and the others haven't taken a bath in a month.'

Gilhooley motioned the paddlers to pick Mung up. He shouted down, 'It's because you're a heathen. You need more washing.'

The Hawaiians were dragging Mung into the canoe when he shouted, 'But you taught me that cleanliness of the soul has nothing to do with the shape or colour of the body.'

Pistchiani looked at Gilhooley and said, 'What the hell have you been teaching the boy? Everyone knows that an American Christian is better than any other kind.'

'Ah,' Gilhooley sighed, 'you're finally beginning to understand.

108

Bringing a heathen into the fold is a complicated affair, not to be taken lightly.'

'Well,' Pistchiani said, 'if we're going to make him into a proper Christian American seaman, he'll have to go with us to the House of the Sun.'

Gilhooley nodded, swung over the side, and climbed down the ladder.

Mung sat in the centre of the canoe, Gilhooley and Pistchiani ahead and behind him. The two Hawaiians, big, powerful, handsome men, sat one in the bow and one in the stern. Other boats pushed off from the *J. Howland* and they followed, moving easily through the calm clear water. Mung stuck his hand over the side to measure the freeboard. It was only the length of his forefinger from the top of the canoe to the water. Other canoes raced ahead to the beach. Some manoeuvred their craft to catch a wave. There were Hawaiians laying belly down on boards ten feet long by two feet wide, paddling with their hands until they caught a wave to ride. Mung saw canoes and boards overturn in the surf, but the Hawaiians seemed to enjoy that as much as riding the waves.

The pace of their canoe picked up. The two paddlers pointed the craft directly at the beach. Mung felt the stern lift and the canoe race forward. From the corner of his eye, he caught sight of the frothy head of a wave hanging over them. He started to turn but Pistchiani held him from behind.

'Mung, don't move now or we'll all go in the water.'

Mung sat up straight. He looked down at his wet clothing. A second later he dropped his left arm over the side and dragged it through the water, slowing and turning the canoe.

'You crazy Japanee,' Pistchiani cried.

Gilhooley turned in time to see the big wave come crashing down on them. They rolled and tumbled through the surf, and staggered to the beach, laughing, pushing, and wrestling. Others from the crew joined the fun in a big pile of arms and legs on the sands of Waikiki. They frolicked like children – singing, mimicking, making fun of each other's gait on dry land after more than a year at sea.

Hockmeyer, Gilhooley and Pistchiani led the men off the beach to a long two-storey white adobe building with a red clay tiled roof.

'Where are all the women?' one of the crew shouted.

Pistchiani walked backwards, facing the crew. 'Can't you farts remember anything? I told you Hawaiians on the big island have got religion.'

'What the hell, we need women.'

Pistchiani stood and held up his hands. They all stopped to listen.

'Religion, I tell you,' Pistchiani shouted. 'Religion,' his voice lowered slightly, 'until 6.00 P.M. Then you hear the Fucking-Gun go off and the whorehouses are open.'

He jumped into the air and they all began running, shouting, laughing, cursing, and shoving each other. In front of the steps of Mama's Seaman's House, they stopped. The big double wood slat doors swung open. Gilhooley and Pistchiani grabbed Mung and bounced him up on to the porch. He sprawled at the feet of a short stocky woman. She wore a blue seaman's long-sleeved sweater over a flowered print dress ending at the tops of her bare feet. Greying black hair framed a moon face, a bulbous nose, and dark twinkling eyes.

'What are you bringing me here?' she pointed at Mung. 'A Chinese blubber boiler?'

'He ain't no Chinee, Mama,' Hockmeyer said. 'He is pure bred Japanee and can speak English as good as you.'

She bent down and helped Mung to his feet.

'Then he should have no trouble understanding the rules. Pistchiani,' she said, 'your father brought you here and he taught you the rules. No exceptions.'

The six-foot-three boat captain spread his arms. 'Mama! Mama, don't I know the rules?'

'Knowing and doing are two different things. I better get it clear with all of you.' She motioned them to come into the big lounge.

Hockmeyer and Pistchiani pushed Mung ahead of them. Gilhooley picked Mama up and whirled her inside, swinging her round and round as the sailors swarmed in, then stood her on a rough wooden table.

'A year without a woman and the first one I see is ugly, but I mean ug-lyy!' Black Ben shouted. 'And with her own rules!'

'Ben, you think this sweater Mama is wearing is because she's cold? Oh no.' Gilhooley's red hairy face wagged from side to side. He pulled up the sweater to reveal a moneybelt around her waist on the outside of the long dress. Tucked into the belt was a pistol. The big redheaded mate pointed at the weapon and said, 'Now, don't she look beautiful to you? Well, don't she?'

Ben scratched his bald head. 'Yes sir, beautiful, beautiful, beautiiiifullll.'

'OK you blubber boilers,' Mama shouted, 'in this house you're safe. No Shanghai, no rolling you for your money, and no fights. No women in the house, fifty cents a day with meals and bath, and I'm not going to feed you until you wash. You all stink!'

The men let out a whoop and crowded towards the back door, following Hockmeyer to the showers, shouting out orders for whisky, gin, and rum, peeling their clothes off as they went.

Pistchiani grabbed Mama about the waist and swung her off the table. Holding her in the air, he said, 'Mama, there are five of us want to go to the House of the Sun tonight. Can you arrange it?'

'OK, but don't pay the paddlers. Pay Lord and Lady Boomer when you get there.'

'Good. Now, can you give me the same meal my father eats?'

'Only after you're clean. Now put me down. I've got work to do.'

They drank and showered; they drank in the showers. Mung hardly recognized them filing into the lounge, scrubbed, shining faces with glazed eyes. They had each been given a long white muslin robe with short sleeves. Black Ben's bullet head gleamed as he kept looking down, trying not to trip on the robe dragging along the sandalwood floor.

Most of the men ordered steaks, chops, or boiled pork. Pistchiani sat at a small round table meant for at least three people, but would not allow anyone to sit with him. When Mama brought his food, they understood why. The tray covered the entire table. It held a large platter of six whole herring laid out side by side, a dark black bread warm from the oven with whole red tomatoes and raw white onions around it. A quart of whisky and a large cigar were placed by Pistchiani's right hand.

Hockmeyer and Gilhooley sat across from each other, eating raw chopped beef and onion mixed with raw eggs. Mung had ordered two large bowls of rice and boiled vegetables prepared by the Chinese cook. As he ate and savoured the food, he remembered the diarrhoea which had plagued him until he got used to eating aboard ship.

Pistchiani leaned back in his chair, puffed on the big cigar and grinned around the room at anyone and everyone. Except for fish-heads and bones, the platter was clean and the bottle empty. He raised his arms up to shoulder height, flexed his biceps and shouted, 'Work whaleship all year, get muscles big like ox, come to Hawaii to eat, drink, and now is time for women.'

Mama came to take the tray. 'You eat any more fish, you're going to look like one,' she said.

'Haw, haw.' A smile lit Pistchiani's face. 'Mama, you're wonderful. The food was wonderful ...'

BOOM! The long rolling echo of a cannon shot reverberated through the house.

Everyone froze, the room was silent, then someone shouted, 'The Fucking-Gun!'

'Whorehouses are open!' another yelled.

Mung watched the faces of the men. Their mouths gaping, eyes bulging, they bolted for the front door. Someone fell in the entrance. Pandemonium broke loose as those in the rear piled on the ones in front. They stacked up in the doorway until the roar of two shots brought silence.

Mama stood in the middle of the lounge with the smoking pistol pointed towards the ceiling. 'When you go to the whorehouses from Mama's, you go like gentlemen. If you want to go in those robes, go ahead, but you'd better put your boots on and get your money. You have to pay to lay in Hawaii.' She waved at

Hockmeyer, Gilhooley and Pistchiani. 'Untangle those damn fools!'

Deacon Gilhooley, Hockmeyer, Mung and Black Ben, led by Pistchiani, waded out to board a thirty-foot twin-masted Hawaiian canoe. They climbed on to the platform between the two hulls. The six-man Hawaiian crew sat in the carved-out hulls on either side, working the sails and tiller. The easy rocking motion and warm air soon lulled the whalers to sleep.

They awoke about midnight to the deep-throated rowing chant of the Hawaiians. The canoe had entered a small bay, heading for the white sandy beach. Beyond the beach, stately palms more than fifty feet high stood behind grass shacks. Rows of palms led to a valley between two volcanic mountains, peaks shimmering silvery in the moonlight.

Pistchiani pointed to that unseen valley beyond the palms. 'The House of the Sun. The Hawaiians have a legend. Since Creation the sun comes here to rest every night before its journey across the heavens.'

One of the paddlers handed up a thick bamboo joint. Hockmeyer pulled the stopper and took a swig of rum. He handed it to Mung who drank deeply, then passed it to Ben. Mung wanted to ask if the Hawaiians really believed in the legend. Everyone knew that if the sun was going to rest anywhere, it would be with the Japanese people and the Emperor who is directly descended from the Sun God. He opened his mouth to speak just as the rum exploded in his chest. The flames scorched his throat, causing his face to glow and his eyes to start from his head.

Hockmeyer slapped him on the back and said, 'Mung, I can see you're a man who appreciates good liquor.'

The seamen roared with laughter and the Hawaiians joined in. They handed up two more bamboo bottles. The back of Mung's neck felt numb. A warm comfortable glow radiated through his body. Gilhooley quietly nursed a bottle of rum by himself.

Pistchiani said, 'Come on Mung. You must have another drink

113

or the Hawaiians will be insulted.'

This time Mung held it in his mouth and let it down his throat slowly. There was less of a shock and more of a glow.

Pistchiani said, 'Gentlemen, I am going to introduce you to Lord and Lady Boomer. From them you can learn to be true sinners.'

'Amen,' Deacon Gilhooley said, and looked away.

They splashed ashore, following one of the paddlers up the beach to a semi-circle of grass huts. A lone drum beat a slow rhythmic tattoo. By the flickering light of kuku-nut torches, Mung saw naked bodies of men and women strewn over the ground, mostly Hawaiians. Here and there the pale body of a westerner contrasted against a woman's brown body. Some were still making love to the slow beat of the drum. A bearded sailor, wearing only a cap, slumped over the back of a beautiful girl. Her smiling face cradled in her arms on the ground, she rocked back and forth to the motions of the sailor's hips behind her.

In the centre of the clearing, the drummer thumped on a hollow log with a sharkskin cover. Slumped in a high-back wicker chair was a big Hawaiian man with greying hair. Sprawled in a large cart, on woven coloured mats with a bamboo rum bottle in her hand, was the naked three-hundred-pound, six-foot-two Queen Kekaualohi. Her pillows were two naked young men.

Pistchiani made a grand sweeping gesture with his arm. 'Gentlemen, I present Lord and Lady Boomer.'

The big woman shifted her weight to allow the gas to escape. Phhhtttttttttt!

Lord Boomer, disturbed by the noise, sat up. His stomach convulsed and he opened his mouth. Brraaarrffffff!

Startled by this noise, he opened his eyes to see the men staring at him. He spoke in Hawaiian to Lady Boomer who sat up, wiping the perspiration from under her large breasts.

She said, 'Who the hell comes here in the middle of the night?'

'Pistchiani and his friends,' he shouted.

'Pistchiani? The father or the son?' She leaned forward to get a better look in the torchlight.

'The son,' he shouted.

She leaned back. 'Your father was a good fucker but I had to get him pisseyed drunk before he would consider coming into the cart with me.'

'Lady Boomer,' Pistchiani bowed, 'I'm glad to see you haven't become a Christian like those Bible-spouters on the big island. They ruin all the fun.'

'The old gods are the best.' She breathed deep and passed gas. 'Reverend Damon comes over to preach now and then but I tell him to go up on the volcano and jump in. If your god saves you, I say, I'll become a Christian.'

She motioned to one of the young men behind her and he put another bamboo bottle in her hand. She took a swig of rum. Her loud burp was answered by a burp from Lord Boomer in the cane chair. He stood up, towering over the six-foot-three Pistchiani.

His speech thick with rum, he said, 'We learn from the Christians. When you come to pray, you have to pay.'

Pistchiani walked over to Lady Boomer, raised his hand above her head, and let the three shiny doubloons fall between her big breasts. Her whole body quaked with laughter. She waved at Lord Boomer. 'Arrange for girls and huts.'

The big man leaned forward slightly. Phhhttttttttt! He passed gas and left. The Queen woke the two young men in the cart to wheel her over to a large grass hut.

'Is she really a queen?' Ben asked.

'Sure,' Hockmeyer answered, 'and he's a prince.'

'Isn't that her husband?'

'No, he's the king's brother by another mother. Pistchiani knows more about it than I do.'

Gilhooley was holding his hands to his ears. 'This is blasphemy! Did we come here to talk or get laid?' He walked off, following the path Lord Boomer had taken.

'Lady Boomer is a queen, a younger sister of the king she married,' Pistchiani said. 'When the king converted to Protestantism, they were divorced. They say he thought it was an easy way to get rid of her. She used to fart and carry on with her young lovers right in front of foreign dignitaries.'

A lovely Hawaiian girl approached, her arms full of bamboo rum bottles. She wore only a grass skirt. Mung, at the end of the line, watched carefully as she handed a bottle to each man, exposing more and more of her beautiful breasts. When at last she stood in front of him, he took the remaining bottle. His eyes roamed her soft, curving body as he raised it to drink. The warmth and glow spread through his loins. The girl made a graceful flowing motion with her hands, touching the hollow between her breasts, then touching Mung's chest. He trembled as the men laughed and walked away.

'Aloha,' she said, and with both hands led him to a nearby hut, drawing him down next to her on the grass mat.

They lay face to face. 'Aloha,' he said. 'What a beautiful name.' He remembered having read a pillow book written by an eighteenth-century courtesan, but for the first time in his life his photographic memory failed him. The girl began unbuttoning his shirt. She snuggled closer and massaged her breasts against his bare chest. Mung quickly unbuckled his belt and wriggled out of his clothing as she unfastened her skirt. He reached over and slowly ran his rough hand over her thigh. They moved towards each other and her mouth sought his. The touch of her lips in the first kiss of his life sent a thrill coursing through his body. Her tongue darted in and touched his, sending an electric shock down into his stomach. The sensations all began to concentrate between his legs. She pushed him onto his back and mounted him, taking his erection between her thighs. Her smooth golden body moved over him, up and down, back and forth. With both hands he caressed the erect nipples of her small breasts. She threw back her head, tossing her long dark hair over her shoulders, smiling, the motion of her body keeping time to the solitary drum beat outside. Suddenly Mung had an irrepressible urge to bury himself deeper inside her. He thrust his hips up, arching his back from shoulder to heels. Her mouth opened and a moan escaped her lips. Desperate to plunge deeper, he held her tight with both hands and rolled on top of her, driving his hips between her thighs. With each thrust she yelped, then grabbed him behind the neck, pulling his mouth to hers. He sucked at her tongue and each stroke of his body built up the pressure, until the energy was released in a burst which left them both limp. Mung lay back, out of breath but very pleased with himself. Suddenly he could remember all the details from the pillow book, and the girl was more than willing to try everything.

Mung's head bounced along the ground. He felt himself being dragged over the dirt on his naked back, pulled by both legs. He shaded his eyes from the bright, morning sun, trying to figure out what was happening. He could barely see Pistchiani's moustached face hovering above him, and heard the big whaler's voice echo in his head. 'Look at the little fellow, Hockmeyer. He can't even focus those slanty eyes of his but he won't let go of the rum bottle.'

As in a dream, Mung felt his legs fall. His heels hit the ground. Pistchiani said, 'The bottle is empty. Let it go.'

Mung wanted to answer but his tongue was too big and dry in his parched mouth. He released his grip on the bamboo bottle and it rolled off his chest on to the grass. Pistchiani helped him sit up, and Hockmeyer offered him a rough and hairy brown bowl, white inside and filled with sweet thin milk. They called it coconut. He drank it all, and they showed him how to scrape out the tasty white meat inside the shell. After a while Mung felt well enough to taste other fruits he had never seen before.

Lady Boomer came out of her villa and lumbered down the beach to bathe and swim. When she came out of the water, her attendants held her cart ready and she climbed in. Two young men with small hand-drums took their places on either side. They moved up the trail leading to the Valley of the Sun, with many followers around the cart. Leaving Gilhooley behind, the crewmen of the *J. Howland* joined the royal procession. It was an easy path, winding between green slopes of the extinct volcanoes, shaded by tall palms and ancient tamarind trees.

The sound of drums grew louder and the wail of the calabash echoed from the mountains as others joined the party along the trail. The procession stopped near waiting carts and the Queen donned a silk scarlet loin cloth, called a *malo*. Then an enormous

cape and helmet of yellow and scarlet bird feathers. Others of
the royal family also dressed in *malos*, cloaks, and helmets. One of
the young attendants opened a purple Chinese umbrella to shade the
Queen from the sun. The tempo of the music picked up and the
people began to sing. More and more participants came down
the slopes. Bamboo rum bottles were passed up and down the
procession. Bowls of a bluish paste called *poi* appeared, as did palm-
leaf platters of dried fish and baked dog.

Entering the valley, Mung heard a chanting sound ahead. He
saw at least a thousand people waiting to greet the royal party.
Arms folded over his chest, dressed in a magnificent cape of
feathers, was the Prince, Lord Boomer. He stood in front of a
newly built, 150-foot pavilion made of saplings, with a palm leaf
roof. To the left of the pavilion stood a man and a woman clothed
only in *malos*. Both were nearly seven feet tall, their young bodies
rubbed shiny with coconut oil. They stood in front of a ten-foot
pile of oil-soaked wood, holding blazing torches over their heads
with both hands. Lord Boomer strode out alone to greet the
Queen, then took his place by the side of the cart. The procession
came to a stop in front of the torch bearers.

Lady Boomer spoke to the hushed crowd in Hawaiian. She gave
a signal and the two giants threw their torches into the woodpile.
The flames rose high into the air, the crowd cheered, then became
silent again. Lady Boomer took off the beautiful feathered cape,
used for generations as a sign of rank, and threw it into the fire. The
drums beat louder; the people started to hum and sway. Lord
Boomer stepped forward to throw his cape into the flames. The
crowd began to sing a song of thanksgiving. This *luau* was the
Queen's way of thanking the old gods for giving her and the Prince
good health. The sacrifice of the ceremonial capes and helmets was
to ensure the favour of the old gods in the face of the young Christ
god. Others of the royal family followed the Queen's example.
The smoke from the treasured garments whipped away on the heat
waves of the fire.

Lady Boomer took the Prince's hand and led him to the centre of
the pavilion. He helped her on to the royal platform where they lay

118

down together and began to make love. The calabashes stopped wailing. Only the drums kept the beat.

People formed lines in front of the royal platform and the beat of the drums changed. They began a *hula*. Mung watched the movements of hands, torsos, and legs. The dance was easily interpreted. He had only to look at the royal couple. The dancers were pantomiming the love-making on the platform.

Someone put a bamboo container of rum in Mung's hand. He became separated from his shipmates and wandered in front of the dancers, passing between mounds of bananas, coconuts, melons, and other fruits. Men were digging cooking pits and lining the bottoms with hot coals from the big fire. Mung saw the girl he had been with in the hut. He stood in front of her, watching the perspiration form a sheen on her golden skin as she undulated to the primitive drum beat. Her head was thrown back, eyes turned upward. Her feet stamped the ground, bare breasts trembling, her outstretched arms flowing in time to the music.

Suddenly, delicate hands slipped under Mung's arms from behind. He turned, feeling the soft nakedness of a woman's body. He looked into an unfamiliar but beautiful face, body rocking back and forth in time to the drums. She took the rum from him and drank, then handed the bamboo bottle back. He drank. Her fingers undid his shirt and unbuckled his belt. The rum was in his blood; his body swayed with hers. She kept the motion of the *hula* as he stepped out of his trousers. Between the lines of dancers and the pavilion she fell in front of him on her knees and took his erection into her mouth. He buried his fingers in her shiny hair to push her away but the movement of her tongue and lips weakened his arms. She locked her hands behind his knees and continued, until he raised both hands, his eyes gazing heavenward, straight into the sun. The muscles of his flat belly convulsed, his juices gushed forth, and they sank to the soft earth together.

Mung became aware of the warm sun relaxing him. The vibrations of the drum beat and the pounding of the dancers' feet flowed through his body. He reached out for the woman but she was gone. Suddenly his clothes, bundled around his sea boots, landed on his stomach. He sat up.

'You crazy Japanee!' Pistchiani grabbed both Mung's hands from behind and dragged him closer to the pavilion. 'You want to get killed?' He pointed to the Hawaiians riding bareback on galloping horses which pounded towards them. 'Get your clothes on or they'll think you're a native,' he laughed.

The riders whooped as they reined up their horses before the pavilion in a cloud of dust. Laughter and screams came from the dancers, some of whom were bowled over by the drunken horsemen. Finally Lord Boomer ordered the riders off their mounts, lined up and holding the reins.

Queen Kekaualohi stood up, holding a bamboo rum bottle in one hand and a spear in the other. The crowd quietened and she raised her voice, thanking the old gods for giving rain and sun in correct proportion for the trees to bear fruit and the fish to multiply. She pointed to the white conch shells marking one side of the race course and the half mile trench on the other, to the turning marker at the far end of the valley, then bent forward slightly.

Phhhaaatttttt!

The crowd cheered.

The three-hundred-pound Queen reared back and threw the spear into the ground in front of the horsemen. Twenty riders leapt on to their mounts, three so drunk they fell off the other side. Two more fell off backwards at the start. Fifteen horses tore at the turf, throwing clods of dirt into the air to the roaring cheer of the crowd. They raced down the valley towards the turn marker. It was difficult to see who was leading as they moved away from the pavilion. Coming into the turn, they all bunched up. One horse stumbled and two others collided, throwing three riders to the ground. Another rider at the back of the pack on the inside of the turn, realizing his mount was not strong enough to continue, tried to jump on the back of another horse. Both riders crashed to the ground. Ten horses came round the marker, riders kicking their mounts. The crowd screamed, calabashes wailed, and drums boomed, as the racers flew down the last stretch, riders beating their horses with plaited grass whips.

The Queen and her entourage began to move away from the centre of the pavilion as the horses came closer. Pistchiani pulled Mung back with him. A chestnut, a big black stallion in the centre, and a dappled mare were in the lead, pounding neck-and-neck towards the spear. The rider on the stallion leaned over, preparing to grab the spear, but the rider on the chestnut kicked his horse with his right knee, driving the chestnut's left shoulder into the stallion's rider. The man fell off, tumbling between the horses. The chestnut slowed a fraction because of its shoulder block on the other rider. The dappled mare was knocked out of position when the stallion was bumped. The mare's rider put his bare feet on his horse's back, his hands on her shoulders. He crouched, then leapt on to the riderless black stallion, leaning over and swooping up the spear. The momentum carried the three horses and two riders crashing into the pavilion. The riders were thrown, then pulled to safety from the bucking horses and collapsing roof.

For two more days and nights the *luau* went on. Whole pigs, wrapped in taro leaves and stuffed with delicacies, were steamed in the ground. Bowl after bowl of cool blue *poi*, chickens basted with coconut milk, baked mullet on ti leaves, arrowroot puddings, steaming mounds of snowy white rice mixed with shrimp and sprinkled with macadamia nuts, were consumed. Empty kegs of Jamaican rum littered the area.

Late in the morning of the third day, Hockmeyer gathered his crew. They staggered back down the trail to the beach with hundreds of sick Hawaiians, to an empty hut where they could sleep.

Twenty-four hours later, they woke to the sounds of Hawaiian voices and sweeping brooms.

Hockmeyer poked his head outside. 'They're cleaning up,' he announced. He looked around the hut. 'Where the hell is Mung?'

Ben wiped his mouth with the back of his hand. 'The last thing I remember, he lay down next to me.'

'I'll go look for him,' Hockmeyer said.

Mung was cleaning Gilhooley's hut. The floor was covered with chicken and dog bones, rinds, fruit peels, and bamboo rum bottles.

Three naked women were still asleep amidst the debris. The big red-bearded second mate sat in front of the hut crosslegged, his bowed head nearly touching his knees. He was trying to sing, emitting sounds like a wounded water buffalo.

Hockmeyer slapped Mung on the back. 'You're a good lad to clean up here but the Hawaiians always put things in order after we leave.'

'It's all right,' Mung said. 'I'll clean here like I do on the ship.'

The first mate put his thumb and forefinger on his chin and considered the problem. Then he said, 'Well you're not really a white man so it won't upset things with the natives. But you don't have to. They always do it. I'm going to look for some Hawaiians to take us back.'

Gilhooley lay outstretched on the sand, unconscious. The Hawaiian crewmen refused to take him in their canoe because he was filthy and smelled so bad.

'Everyone lend a hand,' Hockmeyer said. 'Mung, you get his boots and socks off. Ben, get his trousers. Pistchiani, you and I will take the top half.'

Mung almost choked on the smell of puke, rum and urine as he bent over the second mate to undo his boots. When Gilhooley was stripped, the men picked him up by the hands and feet.

'All right lads. Carry him to the water's edge,' Hockmeyer said. 'At the count of three, let him go.'

The big redhaired body was swung back and forth, then arched out over the water. Gilhooley turned in the air and landed face down, smack into a wave. He tried to stand but the outgoing wave pulled him backwards. Then he was slammed forward when an incoming wave hit him from behind. He struggled to his hands and knees, afraid to get up, letting the waves break over him. He saw his shipmates on the shore laughing at him. Shaking his fist, he struggled to stand and was knocked down by another wave.

'You're trying to kill me,' he roared. 'You're trying to kill a good Christian!'

He attempted to get up again but fell in a sitting position, his back to the waves, legs out in front. He began to cry, tears running down his cheeks into his fiery beard as he shouted at his shipmates.

'What is he saying?' Mung asked Pistchiani.

'He says he is too far from a proper place to receive a Christian burial.'

'I would like to be buried in Japan, but I don't know if they'll allow even a dead Japanese to return,' Mung said.

Pistchiani pointed at Deacon Gilhooley. 'He thinks we would let his bones bleach on this heathen soil.'

Mung felt a pang of anguish. More than anyone else, he understood Gilhooley's fear. He fought back the feeling of loneliness that swept over him. There would be no Buddhist priest to arrange his funeral in America. No one to light a lantern for him on the Feast of the Dead holiday, or send a small straw boat carrying fruit for him afloat on the waters of the nether world. He would have to rely on the mercy of Jesus. This concerned him too. Would Jesus really give him mercy? Even the Deacon wasn't sure Christ had powers in Hawaii.

Mung watched Hockmeyer and Pistchiani wade into the surf and drag Gilhooley out. Everyone lent a hand lifting him onto the canoe. They shoved off for the big island.

CHAPTER
7

Honolulu, September 1842

On his return to Honolulu, Captain Whittefield was impressed by the progress and influence of the Protestant missionaries whose endeavours he supported. The entire royal family and courtiers on the big island had followed King Kamehamea's lead and were also converted. Sunday was observed more fastidiously than in Fairhaven. All shops, bars, businesses, and whorehouses were closed for the sabbath. Schools were staffed by competent, dedicated teachers from seminaries in New England. Students from wealthy families in California studied in Hawaii rather than the California Catholic schools or taking the six-month voyage around the Horn to east coast Protestant schools. Two hospitals had been built, staffed, and were maintained by the missionaries.

On the third day, after lunch at Reverend Damon's house, the two men adjourned to the den and lit up cigars.

'William,' the minister said, 'the natives here need our moral guidance and political experience. The schools we've built are laying a strong foundation for the future. We've erected churches and hospitals, brought in a printing press to establish a weekly newspaper, organized a library, Town Forum, Temperance and Christian Reading Societies.'

'You sound as if you're on the verge of creating a state.'

'A modern state. Exactly! Hawaii has a larger land mass, population, and is more strategically important to America than, for example, Rhode Island.'

BOOM! The harbour-master's gun interrupted the conversation, a signal that a ship of some importance had entered the harbour.

The reverend went to the veranda, then called excitedly, 'William, come quickly!' He pointed to the harbour. 'Look! By God look at it! The first American steamer in Honolulu!'

The two men watched the side-wheeler plough through the water, trailing smoke from her twin stacks, the American flag whipping from her mainmast.

BOOM! BOOM! BOOM!

'They're saluting her,' the reverend cried. 'Our warships are saluting her.'

BOOM! BOOM! Smaller cannon and muskets were fired from the decks of the Yankee whaling fleet in the harbour.

Reverend Damon shook the captain's hand. 'We did it, William! I feel as if I made that voyage myself!'

'I never thought I'd feel so excited about a stinkpot! Some things do change!'

'Yes, they do. And it's important that we give moral significance to these changes. You may retire from the sea but I trust not from the service of your country.' The reverend looked into the captain's eyes. 'Yes William, Secretary of the Navy Spaulding wrote me that you may be offered a position in Washington.' He pointed to the steamer. 'The *Barbara Chase* is not entirely a surprise either.' He led the Captain from the veranda. 'Come. Let's go and greet her.'

An hour later the two men joined the crowd on Hawaii's only pier. The steamer rested quietly, hawsers and lines secured. A gangway was being put into place. Captain Whittefield looked to the quarterdeck. The ship's master seemed familiar, but the bowler hat, pulled far down on his head, obscured his face. A small slim woman, attired in New England fashion, stood at the Captain's left. To his right, a tall blond broad-shouldered boy brushed the hair from his eyes. Captain Whittefield felt his stomach cave in, a sour taste rose in his mouth, and his legs buckled. He fell to his knees.

The Reverend shouted, 'William, what's wrong?' He reached down to put his hands under his friend's arms. 'Let me help you.'

The Captain was sobbing. His cap fell off his bowed head.

125

Hands clasped between his legs, tears running down his cheeks, he cried, 'My son! My son! Martha! Oh my God, he's alive!'

Honolulu, 7 September 1842.

My dearest Martha,

Our son John is alive and well with me in Hawaii. He was rescued by Captain Theodore Link aboard the steamer *Barbara Chase*. I have asked the Captain and his good wife, Eleanor, to write an account of John's rescue and his time on board their ship. They have graciously consented to do so and it will be enclosed in this packet. John has also written his account of what took place since the freak storm in which he was lost.

The Captain and Mrs Link are special people. They took our son to themselves as if he were their own. Mrs Link, having raised three children at sea, attended to John's academic education. The Captain taught him seamanship with an added advantage. John was able to learn both sail and steam on the high seas. They sent letters from Cape Town, South Africa and I do hope you have already received this wonderful news. I am giving this packet of letters to Captain Link tonight at dinner. He sails tomorrow morning and will send them by the new portage service over the Isthmus of Panama.

The light has returned to my heart. I am not ashamed to tell you that at the shock of seeing John standing on the quarterdeck, I collapsed. After we were reunited (I will tell you about that in person for I cannot find words to put it on paper) John, I, Captain Link, Eleanor Link, and the Reverend Damon all locked arms and we walked together from the pier to the Bethal Seaman's Chapel, singing hymns. Hundreds, who had come to see the steamer, joined us in a thanksgiving service. In the name of our family I pledged one thousand dollars to Reverend Damon's Seaman's Welfare Fund. After careful consideration and in consultation with our son John and the Reverend, I have adopted a shipwrecked Japanese boy as our foster son. The crew of the *J. Howland* gave this Japanese boy our son's first name when we took him aboard. They could not pronounce his last name which is spelled something like Mangiro so they call him Mung. He is an unusually alert and intelligent young man, the same age as John, and will be a good companion for him. The Reverend Damon has found Mung well qualified for baptism. The second mate, Deacon Gilhooley, instructed him in religion during the nine months since his rescue. Mung, for his part, is delighted to be taken in as part of our family and told me he feels no conflict in religious conversion as it was explained by the Reverend.

We will sail in two weeks for the whaling grounds off the Pacific side of South America, then around the Horn to chase whales up the Atlantic side and finally home to you and Fairhaven. Please pass on the letter addressed to the owners of the *J. Howland*. Our voyage has been successful and they will be happy to know I have sold off three hundred barrels of prime oil at top price to the European packet service. This sale will enable us to store an equal amount, if our luck holds, on the return voyage. We hope to be home in the summer of 1843.

Martha, I love you. Life is too short to spend the rest of it at sea, away from you and John. This will be my last voyage. I hope you understand that I had to adopt Mung. It was as if God meant it to be. The boy's father is dead, his mother alive, but because of the savage laws of his country it is forbidden for him to return to Japan. As Captain and Eleanor Link took our son from the sea, so I feel we must care for Mung until he can be reunited with his mother, if ever. We have been blessed, Martha, and I doubly so by having you as my wife.

The third packet of letters from Captain Link, the Reverend, and me, addressed to Secretary of the Navy Spaulding, must be sent to Washington by special messenger and not regular post.

A bit of news to keep the sewing circle abuzz. Captain Robert Cathcart sailed the whaling ship *Otter* from Nantucket last autumn. He had a suspicion that his wife was having an affair with the owner of the *Otter* so he pulled his ship into port not fifty miles away, took a carriage back to Nantucket and confirmed her adultery. He returned to his ship and continued the voyage, catching whales until the ship reached Santa Catarina in South America. There he sold the oil and the ship, and has disappeared with the money.

Remember all the jokes made about that fellow Tudor who had crews collecting ice from the frozen ponds of New England for shipment to warm climates? He found that sawdust is the best insulation to retain the cold temperature and is now called the Ice King, numbering Maharajahs, sheiks, and other royalty among his clients.

Martha, with God's grace you will see your son John, your foster son Mung, and your loving, devoted husband this summer.

> *Signed with all good wishes and love,*
> *William*

The Links and Whittefields were dinner guests of Reverend Damon the evening prior to the departure of the *Barbara Chase*. They ate New England bread warm from the oven, bean soup, roast meat, potato pudding, boiled vegetables, sweet cakes, and tea. A cannon fired the six o'clock signal just as the Hawaiian houseboy was clearing the tea service.

The Reverend pulled out his pocket watch and said, 'Correct to the minute!'

Mung had not spoken during the meal and felt that further silence would be considered rude. He cleared his throat and said, 'That's the Fucking-Gun. The crew at Mama's are prob … a … bly …' He looked at the three men who appeared to have ceased breathing.

128

Mrs Link smiled at Mung and said, 'I believe your brother John would like to walk in the garden with you.' She turned to John. 'And when you're there you might explain to Mung that there are English lessons I'm not qualified to teach.'

John grabbed Mung's elbow. 'Come on, we'll take a walk.'

Mung almost fell backwards off the chair from the tug on his arm.

As they left the dining room John was heard to say, 'There is something about the language I really must explain to you.'

Captain Whittefield said, 'Thank you Mrs Link. Once again you have come to the rescue.' He turned to the head of the table. 'And to you Reverend, for bringing us together once again before we part.' He looked at Captain Link. 'To you and your wife for saving our son, my wife and I will be eternally grateful.'

Eleanor Link said, 'Since our children are grown and have their own families, time aboard ship often weighs heavy on Theodore and I. Your son brightened our days. Now that we look back, for us they passed all too quickly.'

Captain Link said, 'Your son was a joy to us and to the ship's crew. Ask him to show you the steps to the Zulu dance he learned in South Africa, and his thoughts about stinkpot sailors.'

Mrs Link said, 'I've packed a trunk of books for both boys to read on the voyage home. John tells me that he and Mung visit the oriental compound where Mung is teaching him Japanese.'

Captain Whittefield said, 'Yes, and part of the day John tries to improve Mung's English.'

They all laughed.

Captain Link tapped the table with his fingertips. 'Hear, hear. That is a fine idea. I've never met a white man who could speak Japanese.'

'When Japan does open its doors to the world, your son will be in an advantageous position to help America with his knowledge of their language,' Reverend Damon said.

'The boys will have almost a year on board to study together,' Captain Whittefield said. 'If John can master the language, it may mean special consideration when he goes before the reviewing board at Annapolis in a few years.'

Captain Link pushed back his chair and stood up. 'Gentlemen, you must excuse me. There's cargo to check on and engines to be inspected, but most of all I must make sure my crew is still alive. It will take a month of Sundays to sweat the liquor out of them.'

Captain Whittefield rose and came around the table with an outstretched hand. 'Words cannot express my gratitude. You saved my son's life and influenced me to adopt a widow's son from a foreign land. Thank you.' He leaned forward and kissed Mrs Link on the forehead. 'May God bless you both.'

The racial differences between John Whittefield and Mung, apparent to others, were forgotten by them in their desire to know one another. John, with blond hair, blue eyes, and a wide full mouth set over a square jaw, was taller by three inches than the leaner, darker-skinned Japanese boy. They were seen studying and fishing together, and spent many happy hours learning to surf on long boards and swim Hawaiian-style from the islanders.

On their visits to the oriental compound, Mung found the simple food delicious and the hot baths delightful. However, little could be learned from the people. They were illiterate and unknowledgeable about politics, commerce, or the geography of Japan beyond their own villages. John forced himself to eat raw fish, partially cooked vegetables, and tasteless rice. He controlled his desire to leap out of the boiling cauldron known as a Japanese bath, remembering Mung's admonition about losing face in the eyes of any Japanese.

Captain Whittefield instructed the boys to set regular hours for teaching each other their respective languages. Mung and John looked for a quiet, cool place where they could study and not be lulled to sleep by the heat of the day. On a small moss-covered beach, near a tree-shaded pool fed by a stream which splashed down the side of a mountain, they discovered two Hawaiian girls washing vegetables. The girls, wearing only the short *malo* skirt, stood up as the boys approached, their young, firm, pointed breasts exposed. They whispered to each other, giggling. Then, forming a circle with thumb and forefinger of the left hand, they both pushed the pointed forefingers of their right hands back and forth through the circled fingers.

John looked at Mung. 'I believe they wish to fornicate.'

The girls came closer.

'You mean fuck?' Mung said.

The two girls were touching the boys' shirts.

'I told you to use the word fornicate,' John said.

The girl in front of Mung was the same height. Her nails touched his chest as her fingers played with the buttons of his shirt. Mung's arms flapped at his side. He stretched his neck, turning his head from side to side.

'Did you ever do it, John?' he asked.

The girl in front of John put his hands on her breasts. 'Yes,' he said. 'In China I did. Did you?'

Mung's almond-shaped eyes widened. The girl was running her hands over his chest. His head bobbed. 'I did it on the beach and at the *luau*.'

The boys looked at each other's erections poking through their sailcloth trousers, and down at themselves. They grabbed the girls and fell on the blanket of cool, green moss.

There were other sessions at the pool with the girls. The boys made up for lost study time at night. Sitting opposite each other, Buddha fashion on the floor, they whispered memorized phrases and dialogues to perfect pronunciation, intonation, and increase their vocabulary.

'Mung, how do you feel about becoming a Christian tomorrow?'

He shrugged his shoulders. 'The way Reverend Damon explained it, I may continue to celebrate the anniversary of my father's death.'

'Is that all that's important to you?'

'No, but there isn't a great difference between the dos and don'ts of both religions. Besides, I'm no longer in my country.'

'Don't you have holidays and rituals?'

Mung considered the question, then answered, 'My father taught me there are two religions. Unless one is going to become a Buddhist monk or a Shinto priest, he doesn't have to learn anything about either one. When a child is born in Japan, a Shinto priest blesses it. When it dies, a Buddhist monk buries it. Most of Japanese religious life is divided between the priest and the monk. Now that I'm no longer in Japan, it's logical to observe the one God.'

'I'd rather die than be anything but a Christian,' John said.

'How could you serve God if you're dead?'

'I would serve him in heaven.'

'But if the other religion is not opposed to yours and there is only one God, why not?'

'I couldn't. I just couldn't.'

Mung said, 'Did I ever tell you the legend about the strange animal called a Kappa?'

John got up, pulled the light blanket back from the bed, and sat down on the edge. 'Why don't you tell me tomorrow. We have to get up early for your baptism.'

'John?'

'Yes?'

'Is fornicating with Chinese girls different from Hawaiian girls?'

'You know, Mung, after your baptism tomorrow you should stop fornicating.'

'Why? You're baptized. The Deacon and the others are too and you all do it.'

'That's because ... that's because it's always been that way on this side of Cape Horn for American sailors.'

'Well, tomorrow when I get baptized I'll also become an American, right?'

'Yes, I think so.'

'Then I can fornicate like an American sailor.'

'That's not exactly what I meant, Mung.'

'We'll talk about it tomorrow, John. Goodnight, brother.'

'Goodnight, brother.'

Six days a week, during summer rendezvous, the noise and stink from the bars and whorehouses lining Honolulu Harbour permeated the curving, sandy beach of Waikiki. But Sunday was kept as the Lord's day. By order of King Kamehamea, all businesses were closed. The whalers, merchant seamen and navies, on their first shore leave in months or even years, did not take kindly to this. They often threatened or bribed shop owners and then tangled with the ten-man Hawaiian police force led by six-foot-eight, 300-pound Iron Mike. The confrontations, known as Sunday Storms, usually quietened down at the sight of Iron Mike and his men. Each of them was over six feet three inches tall, wore only a scarlet *malo* and was armed with a war club.

On Sunday, 26 September 1842, Mung awoke at 6.00 A.M. to dress for his baptism. He put on a white cotton, button-up shirt with long cuffed sleeves, a black wool suit and stiff, new leather shoes. Captain and John Whittefield took their leave of him outside the house. They were going to church by carriage.

Two Hawaiians waited next to an outrigger on the beach. Reverend Damon and Mung stepped into the canoe, the Hawaiians slid the craft off the sand and hopped in. Dipping the paddles into the water, they propelled the canoe smoothly through the calm sea, heading away from the beach and around the point into Honolulu Harbour. Ahead, the crystal blue waters lapped at the pure white sand of the beach framed by tall, stately palms, tops bent slightly, waiting for the morning breeze to awaken them.

On the beach Mung saw a double file of Hawaiians, men and women, extending from the Bethel Church to the water. The paddlers picked up the soft rhythm of the song of welcome from the shore. As the outrigger approached, men rushed splashing into the water. Surrounding the canoe, they lifted it on to their shoulders and carried Mung and Reverend Damon between the two rows of people. They set the craft down before the church, singing with the others,

> Oh yes, we will gather at the river,
> The beautiful, beautiful river,
> Oh yes, we will gather at the river

To do the work of the Lord.

Reverend Damon and Mung stepped out of the canoe and were joined by John and Captain Whittefield.

A member of the Hawaiian royal court approached the reverend. 'King Kamehamea requests forgiveness that he cannot be here, but he has sent a *luau* in honour of the occasion.' He motioned to mats piled with roasted pigs, pigeons and baked fish, mounds of pumpkins, pineapples, bananas, papaya, mangos, and coconuts, and large bowls of rice, puddings and *poi*.

Reverend Damon said, 'Please tell the king we are overjoyed with his gifts. His presence is sorely missed and we shall make a time to visit him when he returns.'

They entered the church whose sides and front walls, made of reeds and pandanus leaves, had been removed to accommodate the large number of people. Navies, whalers, and merchantmen, drawn by the singing and the crowd, milled around. A few helped themselves to the food set out for the *luau*.

Daniel Opunui and Berita Kaikaula, converts themselves, assisted Reverend Damon in the baptism of John Mung. The Reverend, his long white robe buttoned at the collar, stretched out his arms, placing his hands on Mung's bowed head.

He spoke in a deep resonant voice that carried beyond the confines of the church to all those who stood outside. 'Bringing forth fruit worthy of redemption is our task here today. We are all trees in the garden of the Lord and our roots stretch forth in His fertile soil, seeking to absorb the nourishment. To direct our roots which stretch out blindly in the darkness of this earth, God has given us the Bible to act as a rule and guide. In the darkness it brings light, from confusion it brings direction.' His voice boomed. 'How shall man produce fruit worthy of His Grace? If thy roots be weak how can the essence of thy labour be meritorious in His Eyes?' He looked around the church and lowered his voice. 'Only if those roots seek out the nutrients, faith, love and charity, that God has put here on this earth. By diligent service to the Lord, like the process of osmosis, a transition begins at the roots, travelling up through the trunk into the limbs, to the leaves, opening the buds that ripen into fruit which in itself is an offering to God. Is the fruit perfect? In the Eyes of the Lord it will be, for He is an understanding God. Yes, He is perfection, for He is a loving God, and we are His children. Let us praise the Lord on this day. Let us thank the Lord on this day that John Mung has become one of us!'

Mung raised his head. The humming of the congregation swelled into the deep-throated, soft, swaying Hawaiian version of a New England hymn,

There is a happy land far, far away,
Where saints in glory stand, bright, bright as day.
Oh how they sweetly sing, worthy is our Saviour King,
Lord, let his praises ring, praise, praise for aye.
Come to this happy land, come, come away,
Why will you doubting stand, why still delay.
Oh we shall live with thee, blest, blest for aye,
Bright in that happy land beams every eye,
Kept by a Father's hand, love cannot die.
Oh then to Glory run, be a crown and kingdom won,
And bright above the sun, we'll reign for aye.

Reverend Damon put his arms on Mung's shoulders and looked into his face. 'You are now a Christian. Praise the Lord that He has brought you to us. Bless you, my son.'

Captain Whittefield and John walked on either side of Mung, following the reverend and the two Hawaiian converts out into the sunlight. The crowd parted before them. An old woman, standing in front of the *luau*, held a four-foot braided bread cradled in her arms. The reverend made a blessing on the loaf, on the woman, and the congregation.

He looked beyond the woman to the sailors standing at the edge of the crowd. 'Won't you brothers join us in celebrating the Lord's day?'

The congregants stood in a double line to break a bit of bread from both ends of the loaf held by the old woman. Then they rushed to help themselves from the piles of food. The sailors sauntered in, took what food they wanted, and walked to the line of shacks that served as the red light district during the week.

Captain Whittefield, his arm around Mung's shoulders, led him away from the crowd. 'Mung, if there ever comes a time that you can return home to your family, know full well that I will help you to do so. Until that time comes, consider yourself one of our family.' He looked down at the boy. 'John was saved from the sea and cared for by Captain and Mrs Link as their own until we were reunited. I can do no less for you. It is God's will.'

Mung's eyes held the Captain's as he said, 'Sir, my father taught me the code of Bushido when I was young. It is for honourable men. From Deacon Gilhooley I have learned the teachings of Christ. Your actions, sir, fulfil the first and imitate the second.' He bowed from the waist. In a tone a hair above a whisper, he continued, 'In the days that remain of my life I will remember you as I do my father. I will remember both the code and the teachings.'

Captain Whittefield slapped Mung on both shoulders. 'May the days of your life be long and happy!'

He turned Mung around and motioned to John who joined them. John reached into his pocket and took out a cross carved from a whale's tooth, on a leather thong.

He slipped it over Mung's head. 'Wear it well, brother.'

'Did you make this yourself?' Mung asked.

'Yes.'

'When did you find the time?'

'I usually had to wait until you fell asleep.'

'Hey you two Christian lads. Come over here so we can congratulate you.' It was Deacon Gilhooley standing in front of the crew of the *J. Howland*.

The men slapped Mung's back, shook his hand, then pulled him into the centre of the group. Someone opened a blanket and Mung was shoved on to it. The whalers grabbed the edges and began bouncing him high in the air. They pushed John in next to Mung and threw the two boys up, again and again. Then, wrapping both in the blanket, they carried them down to the beach and heaved them into the water. The crewmen took off their clothes and ran, rollicking and wrestling, into the waves.

The crowd around the *luau* swelled to over one thousand people, more than two thirds non-Hawaiians. Most of the Hawaiian men had gone to play in the surf with their boards. The sailors wandered among the women trying to persuade them to go behind the shacks.

Daniel Opunui and Berita Kaikaula came up to Reverend Damon, pointing to a long line of Hawaiian men approaching with food and kegs of brandy on their shoulders.

'It's Chief Kaneka,' Daniel said. 'He's bringing liquor in front of the church on the Sabbath.'

The chief, at the head of a hundred and fifty men, walked out from between the shacks. His tawny young body gleamed with coconut oil in the morning sun. Intricate black tattooed designs on his broad chest spread up over his muscular shoulders and down his arms, stopping at the shell bracelets around his neck and biceps. He strode through the crowd of sailors and Hawaiians, a path opening before him. Captain Whittefield moved to Reverend Damon's side as the sailors crowded in. Kaneka halted just in front of the reverend, feet planted wide apart, hands on hips, white teeth flashing and big nose wrinkled up between his eyes.

He shouted into the reverend's face, 'I've come to join the celebration.' He looked around and laughed, waving both hands to involve the crowd.

The reverend purposely lowered his voice. 'You are not welcome here, Kaneka. Not today.'

Although almost toe to toe with the reverend, the Chief shouted again. 'That's a first-class insult! You dare to tell a Hawaiian that he's not welcome to a *luau* on his own island?'

'You are breaking the Sabbath law and the law of King Kamehamea by bringing liquor here on the Lord's day.'

Kaneka turned to the crowd of seamen. 'That's a first-rate insult! They taught me in the missionary school that Jesus Christ drank wine at the Last Supper. That was just like a *luau*.'

The sailors shouted their approval.

Kaneka held up both hands for silence. 'I only came here to help make this a first-rate feast when I heard the king didn't send enough food.' He pushed his face closer to the reverend's, a scowl

137

replacing the smile. His voice cracked as he screamed, 'You Christians don't tell a Hawaiian Chief on his own island that he can't drink what he wants when he wants!'

Someone in the crowd of seamen shouted, 'Cut off the reverend's bloody ears and I'll eat them raw.'

The crowd cheered.

Reverend Damon turned to Daniel Opunui. 'Bring Iron Mike and his men. Hurry!'

Chief Kaneka shouted, 'These church people want Hawaiian to fight Hawaiian.'

The crowd responded with a roar, 'Yeah!'

Kaneka continued, 'The church wants to tell sailors what to do on shore leave.'

'Yeah!' the crowd roared.

'Take away your women!'

'Yeah!'

'Take away your whisky!'

'Yeah!'

Kaneka looked up at the sky and bellowed, 'The sun tires of all this!' He pounded his tattooed chest with clenched fists. 'I tire of all this. It's time to sit, drink and eat. To take women to our sides and to talk of the gods of olden days.'

The last phrase was a prearranged signal. His followers opened up the kegs of French brandy and pandemonium broke loose. More than six hundred seamen rushed at the liquor, crowding around the barrels, drinking from cupped hands when they could not get coconut bowls. Some crews succeeded in running off with a keg to the shade of the nearby shacks.

Daniel Opunui returned to the reverend's side. The small band of policemen, with Iron Mike at the head, bulled their way through the crowd, trying to get to Kaneka. Passing an open keg, one of them swung his knarled war club. As the sailors backed away, he smashed the barrel, showering them with splinters and brandy. The sailors reeled back, then like a many-limbed creature, howled and pounced on the policemen. The struggle was furious but brief as the Hawaiians were buried under a mob of seamen. Reverend

Damon, Captain Whittefield and members of the congregation pulled, shoved and pushed for some time before they were able to extricate the policemen.

To restore some order and show his authority, Chief Kaneka had his men set up boxing matches. Four posts, with ropes tied between them, were pounded into the ground near the line of shacks. When brawls broke out in the crowd, Kaneka's warriors were quick to intervene and throw the men into the ring. Many Hawaiians were drawn to the gambling at ringside.

The crew of the *J. Howland* lay on the sloping beach, out of sight and unaware of what was taking place at the *luau*.

'Either of you got any money?' Gilhooley asked Pistchiani and Black Ben.

The two men lay at the water line letting the waves wash up around their bodies.

'What are you going to do with money on Sunday?' Pistchiani asked.

Gilhooley squatted down behind them. 'I think I can get some liquor, if I'm lucky.'

Pistchiani pointed to a pile of clothing. 'There's a purse in the back pocket.'

Ben raised himself on one elbow. 'Get some for me too.'

Gilhooley picked up the trousers. He noticed three sailors staggering towards them. 'Hey there, mates,' he hailed, 'where did you get the booze?'

The three started laughing and slapping each other on the back.

'Come on now,' Gilhooley shouted. 'Tell us where we can buy some.'

'Buy? Why buy it, Yank? There's bloody barrels of the stuff at the *luau*, just for the drinking.'

Pistchiani and Ben turned on their stomachs to see who Gilhooley was talking to. Mung and John came out of the water in time to see a naked Gilhooley running up the beach, Pistchiani and Ben chasing him. The boys dressed hurriedly. They gathered all the clothes and followed. Ben and Pistchiani, standing naked by a

139

keg of brandy, were drinking with two hands from coconut shells. They accepted their clothes and cautioned the boys to stay close by.

Amidst the singing, shouting, swearing and laughter, Mung and John settled down on their haunches. Gnawing on chunks of roast pig and pineapple, they watched a pulling game. Two men, their right feet toe to toe, locked middle fingers together and tried to pull each other over. Betting was heavy and the cheering crowd added to the excitement.

Mung's view was suddenly blocked by someone standing directly in front of him. Tight-fitting stockings and trousers that buckled at the knees accentuated the large calf and thigh muscles. He looked up into the unshaven, pinched face of a sailor from one of the French fighting ships. Mung started to get up and the seaman struck him a blow on the right ear that stunned him and made his head ring. The sailor grabbed him by the shirt front and raised him to a standing position. He was not much taller than Mung, but broader in the shoulders.

He shook the boy and snarled in French, 'How does a yellow heathen bastard come to wear a cross?' He lifted the cross on Mung's neck and hefted it in his palm.

John tried to push the man's arm away and was pinned from behind by a burly French navie. The small Frenchman ripped the cross from Mung's neck and stepped back.

Mung was shocked but still realized the man in front of him was dangerous. Instinctively he bowed from the waist. Suddenly the front of his face exploded and his feet came off the ground. He was in the air, then crashing to the ground on his back. Pain shot through his head. Yellow, green and red thunderbolts flashed in his eyes. Darkness kept trying to crowd the thunderbolts out but he fought it back.

His eyes began to focus but there was an obstruction between them. He touched his broken nose and the pain returned the thunderbolts. He spat blood to clear his mouth in order to breathe.

Pistchiani looked over just as the Frenchman pulled back his right hand and hit Mung full in the face. Roaring like a bull, the six-foot-three-inch whaler charged through the crowd. Kaneka's guards had also seen the fight. Two of them tackled Pistchiani about the legs and waist and another two grabbed his arms. One big guard grabbed the Frenchman from behind.

Black Ben heard Pistchiani's roar and came running from the other direction. He did not notice Mung on the ground, but seeing the big Frenchman holding John, jumped him from behind. The Frenchman let go of John and flung Ben from his back like a dog shaking off water. Quick for his size, the big man pounced on Ben, pounding him with both hands before more of Kaneka's men separated them.

John bent down to Mung. 'What happened? Why did you bow?'

Mung tried to answer but his upper lip was swollen into his mouth and he needed air to breath. With John helping, he wobbled after Pistchiani and the small Frenchman. They were being pulled towards the fight ring by four guards with raised clubs.

'You want to fight?' one of the guards asked the big whaler.

Pistchiani looked down at the Frenchman. 'If I hit that little shit of a frog, I'd be sued for scattering garbage. If I piss on him, he'll drown.'

The guard nodded and Pistchiani was released. He turned to Mung and John. But as soon as the guard let go of the Frenchman, he darted after Pistchiani. Coming up from behind, he spat at the back of the whaler's head. Pistchiani put his hand to the back of his neck, looked at the spittle on his fingers and spun to face the Frenchman. The little man stood next to the ring with his hand on the top rope. He leapt over the rope, pulled his shirt off and threw it to the ground. Strutting to the centre, he put his foot on the line and struck the classic pose of a fighter – arms curled in front of him. Pistchiani stalked to the ring, ripping his shirt off as he went. The crowd followed, everyone rushing to get a better place from which to see the fight.

As the big whaler ducked under the top rope, the Frenchman pulled a purse from his waistband and held it aloft, swinging it back and forth. Mung saw his friend reach for his purse and throw it to Ben.

'Match all the little bastard can put up,' Pistchiani shouted.

Bets were made with shouts and curses, the crew of the *J. Howland* for their shipmate, the French navies matching their money as fast as it was offered.

The Frenchman turned his back on Pistchiani. He walked to the side of the ring and took a coconut bowl of brandy, which he drained. Then he strode to the centre of the ring where Pistchiani stood ready to fight.

'Have you ever seen a fist fight?' John asked Mung.

Mung wet his lips and managed to say, 'No.'

'The only rules are that after a certain amount of time the fighters must be able to come to the line in the centre of the ring. And no weapons allowed.'

Mung watched the muscles in Pistchiani's arms flit back and forth as the little Frenchman advanced towards the line. Pistchiani began to crouch so he would not have to punch down to the smaller man. The Frenchman dropped both arms to his sides. His head lolled over on his left shoulder and his tongue hung out between slack lips. Pistchiani dropped his guard and straightened up, looking puzzled. In a flash the Frenchman's leg came up and kicked him in the groin. The agony of the first swift kick was followed by a second dug into the pit of Pistchiani's stomach.

The French seamen cheered and began chanting, 'Sa-vat! Sa-vat! Sa-vat!'

Black Ben, standing behind the two boys, moaned and said, 'Damn! The Frenchie is feet-fighting. Look at the legs on that little shit. He's got muscles in his toes!'

Pistchiani bent double with pain. He kept his hands in front of his face, arms and elbows protecting his stomach and groin. The Frenchman planted several quick kicks to the kidneys and ribs, using either foot equally. As each blow landed, Pistchiani grunted but refused to go down.

The little man motioned for another bowl of brandy. He stood near the ropes drinking and joking, then threw the empty bowl into the crowd. Strutting to the centre of the ring, he placed two hard kicks into Pistchiani's side, then strode to the back of the whaler and kicked him behind the knees. The big man crashed to the ground as if in prayer, arms in front of his face. The crowd was silent. Pistchiani's heavy breathing was heard around the ring. From behind, the Frenchman kicked the fallen man in the back, then jump-kicked with both feet between the shoulder blades.

'Aaaaaaggggggghhhhh!' Pistchiani screamed and sprawled on his face in the dirt.

The Frenchman strutted to ringside and beckoned for another bowl of brandy. He drained it, then went to Ben and the boys, holding his hand out. 'Geeve mee theee moneee!'

Ben disgustedly began pulling the pouch out of his shirt, but his hand was stayed by a roar from the crowd. The Frenchman turned to see Pistchiani standing with his foot on the line in the middle of the ring like a hulking bear, hands held up in front of him. The little man's face was flushed with liquor. He approached the moustached giant, spread both arms wide, smiled and sent two more kicks to the whaler's stomach. The first one doubled Pistchiani up, the second hit his elbow and brought his hand down. The smaller man leapt high in the air, opened both legs wide and scissor-kicked Pistchiani in the head, opening a cut under one eye and swelling the other closed. The whaler staggered around, trying to keep the Frenchman in view of his good eye. The little man waited until Pistchiani came close, then pirouetted, back-kicking him in the left side, then in the right. He spat into Pistchiani's face and, turning his back, strutted to ringside for another bowl of brandy.

Pistchiani put both hands to his face and brought them away covered with spittle and blood. He howled and charged the Frenchman as he drank. Just as Pistchiani's big hands reached out, the little man bent double and stood on both hands. Kicking his feet up and back like a savage horse, he caught the whaler in the midsection, driving the air out of his lungs and a cry of pain from his throat. Pistchiani reeled to the centre of the ring. The Frenchman followed and aimed a kick at the unprotected head, but missed and fell. Pistchiani tried to fall on top of him but the little man rolled away too quickly and sprang to his feet. Pistchiani crawled on his hands and knees.

The French crewmen were shouting for their man to stop drinking and fight. He cursed back at them and motioned for another bowl, drinking it as he watched Pistchiani struggle to his feet.

With a bow, the Frenchman announced, 'And now, ze scissor!'

Dropping the bowl, he ran towards Pistchiani and leapt high in the air, opening his legs to execute the head kick. Pistchiani took one step forward and brought his big right fist up into the little man's groin. The Frenchman convulsed in midair. He hit the ground and the whaler's big sea boot caught him in the ribs, lifting him up again.

For several seconds there was only the sound of Pistchiani's sea boots thudding into the body of the unconscious Frenchman. Then the Americans cheered. The burly French navie jumped into the ring and Ben ducked under the ropes. With his head down, he ran across the ring and butted the big Frenchman in the stomach. The man doubled over. Ben locked both hands together in front of him and brought them up into the Frenchman's face, straightening him up. He grabbed the big man by the belt, pulled himself in close and jumped up and down, ramming his head under the big man's jaw until he toppled like a felled tree. Ben leaned down and took the purse.

Pistchiani, draped on the top rope, was trying to reach outside the ring to kick the unconscious Frenchman once more. Ben took Mung's cross from the pocket of the senseless, bloody body and held it high over his head. The Americans cheered again and the French navies sulked off.

Reverend Damon and Captain Whittefield had joined Dr Judd at the hospital. Most of the arrivals from the *luau* were not seriously injured. After patching up Pistchiani's wounds, the doctor worked on Mung's shattered nose. He inserted smooth sticks into each nostril to ensure the air passage would remain clear. Captain Whittefield held Mung's head steady as the doctor manipulated the broken bits of bone under the skin back into place.

Dr Judd stepped away. 'Young man, I'm afraid that long,

straight nose of yours is going to look like a short crooked trail from now on.' He patted Mung's shoulder. 'You're a very brave young fellow.' The doctor looked at Captain Whittefield. 'A brave boy, your son. He didn't cry out once. Can you stand up by yourself, Mung?' The doctor motioned to John. 'I think the idea of you and Mung staying with Pistchiani and the others at Mama's tonight is better than his remaining here. The hospital will be too crowded and noisy.'

Reverend Damon came in and said, 'Iron Mike just sent a message from the beach. He has to open the bars or the mob threatens to wreck all of Honolulu. More and more seamen are pouring into the harbour area. Over two thousand men, including five hundred Hawaiians, carousing around in search of whisky, women and excitement.'

Iron Mike used six of his men to open the first bar. A roar spread through the mob. The excitement of power possessed them and they set out on a mad rampage, ripping the doors off shacks, warehouses, and homes; kicking in the thin board walls or hacking their way through thatched roofs to reach the gin, rum, or any loot they could find. Fights broke out with no one to stop them. The number of knife wounds brought to the hospital increased rapidly. Iron Mike put his men into position around the hospital to protect it from the roving bands of drunks.

In front of the line of dismembered shacks and buildings, the crazed mob set up the Royal Court of Seamen of the Seven Seas. Their first decision was to send town criers through Honolulu's streets, warning the townsfolk that if the women were not sent to the beach, the buildings around the harbour would be burnt to the ground. If that warning was not heeded, the Seamen of the Seven Seas would level Honolulu. Whalers, merchantmen, and navies cheered as ten drunken Hawaiians staggered off to shout the message in the streets.

In the light of a roaring bonfire the Royal Court awaited the answer to their ultimatum. Half-naked dancers were silhouetted in the firelight, howling like animals. Men ran back and forth around the bonfire. Chief Kaneka staggered to the centre of the cursing, screaming crowd.

He brandished a gin bottle high over his head. 'I am chief in Honolulu! Tomorrow I will be king!'

The seamen cheered, jeered and shouted, 'Where are the women?'

The chief signalled for quiet, throwing the half-empty bottle at the head of a Hawaiian who continued to dance. 'You want women? If you want women, the only thing stopping us is the missionary laws.'

The crowd cheered.

'Before the king changed the laws there was never a problem of women in Hawaii.'

The crowd cheered again.

Kaneka's body perspired with the warmth of the liquor in his stomach and the heat of the bonfire. He raised both hands, outstretched to the sky. 'Before you can get women on Hawaii, we got to bury the new laws and the young god.'

The crowd chanted, 'Bury the laws! Bury the god!'

Kaneka, pointing at the seamen, screamed at the top of his voice, 'Build a coffin for the burial!'

'Build a coffin! Build a coffin!'

Several men ran up the beach to look for wood.

'Aaooaaaaaaooooooouuuuuu!' Kaneka yowled into the night sky. He turned to the Bethel Church, raised his arm and cried, 'A Bible to bury! Bring a Bible!'

More than one hundred men ran staggering across the open ground to the church. They ripped off the doors, pulled down the walls, and swarmed inside. A torch was thrown onto the roof and the dry pandanus leaves burst into flames. Fanned by the evening breeze, the entire building erupted. The sailors fled the blazing structure, then returned to feed the fire, throwing in anything that would burn. Kaneka led the mob up the beach towards Honolulu, looting and burning as they went.

At Mama's house, the little woman stood on her front porch, arms folded, jaw set. Pistchiani, Ben, Mung, and John stood in a row behind her. Kaneka halted at the bottom step, looking up at her with wild eyes. Mama shouted at him in Hawaiian. Kaneka held up his hand and the crowd behind him fell silent. He glared at the small, grey-haired woman. Her eyes blazed back at him and the purple veins in her bulbous nose pulsated.

A group of seamen broke through the crowd with a crude open coffin carried shoulder high. A dead baboon, arms folded on its stomach, a Bible tucked under its hands, lay inside. The chief's face relaxed into a broad smile. He turned his back on Mama and motioned to the men holding up the coffin.

Pointing at the dead baboon, he said, 'Look here! The young god of Christianity and his laws!'

The crowd roared its approval.

Kaneka ordered several of his followers to precede the column and proclaim at the top of their lungs, 'The ten commandments and all Christian laws are dead! By order of King Kaneka I!'

The crowd cheered again.

Kaneka pointed to the coffin. 'This is a first-rate way to bury a religion!'

He led the crowd into the city.

Mung, watching Kaneka and hearing the denunciations of Christianity, was frightened. What would the old Hawaiian gods ask of him? He had only just adjusted to Christianity. Now he knew he need not have worried, but when Deacon Gilhooley began teaching him he had felt faint upon hearing about receiving the body and blood of Jesus in the sacrament of the Eucharist. He was suddenly filled with yearning for the simplicity of seeing God in nature.

Mama stood on the porch, her arms still folded until the last of the mob was out of sight. They could mark the progress of the serpentine column as flames shot up along the road leading to Honolulu.

'Mama, what did you say to him?' Pistchiani asked through swollen lips.

The little woman smiled. 'I told him if he wants to be king and bury the new laws, that's his business. If he wants to burn my house, that's my business and I'll bury him with this.' She moved her left arm. The pistol, usually tucked in the moneybelt under her

147

sweater, lay cradled in the crook of her elbow.

Ben raised his hands, imitating Kaneka. 'Mama, that's a first-rate method of convincing a man to move on!'

The sun – big, round and orange – rose steadily over the sea. Smoke drifted lazily upward into the clear blue sky over the rubble of Honolulu. Men lay about the city as if thrown there by some irresponsible giant. They slept where they had fallen, in a drunken stupor. Vomiting, retching, unconscious moans of pain and the babblings of nightmares creased the quiet.

As planned, at 8.00 A.M. Dr Judd walked out of the hospital. He tied a yellow ensign to the lanyard and ran it up the flagpole. Down by the dock Iron Mike hoisted another yellow flag, then joined the men of his battered police force.

With grim determination on their faces and war clubs in their hands, they moved up the beach and into Honolulu, pointing to the yellow flags and shouting, 'Smallpox! Smallpox!'

Bleary-eyed, sodden seamen soon crowded the Waikiki beach to get back to their ships, afraid they would be quarantined on the infected island. Hawaiians, in their outriggers just beyond the surf, haggled over prices with men who waded out chest high in the water to be ferried off.

Captains on the whalers hoisted their recall signals and sounded fog trumpets to attract their crews to the longboats standing offshore. They feared a quarantine could mean the loss of an entire whaling season.

Captain Whittefield faced Reverend Damon and Dr Judd, both haggard and pale. 'I'll bid you farewell now. I still have to load a few supplies. I hope all the storehouses haven't been wrecked. You two have a difficult task ahead – rebuilding the church, the port, and the town. May the ashes serve as a foundation that will last till redemption day. God bless you both.'

Reverend Damon said, 'William, may God continue to bless you and your family. The return of your son gave many here the reassurance that God in heaven does not forsake his work on earth.'

The doctor took William's hand in both of his. 'On behalf of the king and the people of Hawaii, I wish you godspeed home and good hunting on the way.'

CHAPTER
8

The two brothers sat on the side of the hill below Reverend Damon's house. Waikiki Beach was deserted. The yellow flag waved in the breeze at the ships heading for the open sea. Only the *J. Howland* remained at anchor, its crew reassured by Captain Whittefield that the claim of a yellow-fever epidemic was a ruse to save Honolulu. The boys watched the surf pounding the white sand.

'Our father won't be here for another two hours at least,' John said. 'I guess your nose still hurts too much for a walk.'

'No. Just that it's a little hard breathing and it's throbbing like my pecker just before I'm going to fornicate.'

John pulled out a handful of grass and threw it into the wind. 'I told you to say penis. And besides, it's not nice to talk about fornicating.'

'The crewmen are always talking about it.'

'That's why our father arranged for us to bunk together in our own cabin. You have to get rid of some of the expressions you picked up from them. It wouldn't do to have you tell one of the seminary teachers at Harvard High School that your pecker is throbbing.'

They both laughed but Mung felt conflicting emotions. He was indebted to William and John Whittefield. They had truly accepted him as son and brother. But Mung was aware on shore and even aboard the whaler that he was Japanese and different – not as good as the white man. Now he would be leaving the Pacific and sailing to the world of white skin and round eyes.

'How long will it take us to reach Fairhaven?' he asked.

'Six months to a year. Depends on the weather and the whaling.'

Mung stood up. 'Let's take that walk.'

They ambled along until they reached the crossroads at a stand of palm trees. One path led down to the beach, the other to the pool where they had rendezvoused with the Hawaiian girls. Both boys stopped. They looked down the paths, up at the sun and at each other.

'Yeeehowww!' They shouted and ran up the path leading to the pool. When they broke out into the clearing the two girls were kneeling by the water washing their *malos*. They both stood up smiling, unashamed of their bodies. The soft sunlight filtering through the palm trees played on their golden skin. Their jutting breasts and curving hips seemed to undulate in the speckled light.

John pointed in the direction of the sea with one hand, then at Mung and himself with the other. The girls understood he meant they would be leaving soon. They approached and inspected Mung's swollen nose, then talked to each other in Hawaiian. Suddenly they snatched their *malos* and ran off.

Mung sighed. 'Six months to a year is a long time.'

'Yes,' John said. 'And there is no fornicating for us in Fairhaven.' He kicked at the emerald green moss. 'We might as well take our last fresh water bath.'

They stripped off their clothes and lolled in the crystal-clear shallows, listening to the call of exotic birds and the rustle of the palm fronds high above their heads. Mung tried to visualize what it would be like in Fairhaven. His mental picture was a confused conglomeration of Nakanohama superimposed on the town of Honolulu with tall pointed church steeples the Deacon described as scraping the bottom of the clouds.

John lay on his back, toes just touching the bottom and arms moving enough to remain afloat. His thoughts were of his mother, of the coming reunion with her. Aboard ship he would help prepare Mung for the entrance examinations to Harvard High School. His father had already explained that foreign students of oriental background were given special consideration, with the expectation that they would enter the Divinity College, then join a mission abroad.

Splash! Splash! The two nude girls dived into the pool, one

151

surfacing between John's legs. He felt a thrill of vulnerability and excitement as she slipped forward, his legs under her arms until her breasts moved back and forth over his genitals. He paddled with his hands to remain afloat, and watched his penis rise. He tightened his legs around her. Placing one hand on each of her breasts, she caught his erection between them and massaged it slowly up and down, back and forth.

Mung was standing chest deep in the water when the second girl's hands clasped his ankles and she slithered her entire body up against his. Her dark slick hair broke the surface and their lips met. They fondled each other and he probed her with his hardness. She put her hands on his shoulders and pulled herself up, embracing his thighs with her legs until he had penetrated her with a strong thrust. Gasping, she locked her legs behind him.

On the beach other Hawaiians were setting out *poi*, melon, bananas and coconut meat on grass mats. Then they withdrew behind a clump of trees with their musical instruments. Soon the haunting wail of the calabash and the beat of a drum gave rhythm to the lovemaking in the pool. The slow and flowing drum-beat gradually quickened, becoming fevered, blending with the wild melody played on the calabash.

Mung staggered forward, the panting girl speared on his erection. He fell on her, driving her down in the shallow water to the sandy bottom with furious thrusts. She battled back, turning him over and sitting on him, trying to take as much of him as possible inside of her.

John had climaxed between the girl's breasts. Seeing Mung and his girl thrashing in the shallows reminded him of the sharks attacking the pirates. He became hard again and began pushing the girl backwards through the water to the moss-covered beach. There they made love slowly, he with a control he had not had before. He heard his cries of pleasure join hers, blending with the whine of the calabash. His spurting climax reduced their movements to the slow beat of the drum. John revelled in the minor eruptions which overtook him, until he lay back exhausted, looking up to the sky.

A short while later the four young people sat in a circle. The girls fingered *poi* into their lovers' mouths, feeding them choice cuts of melon and bits of snowy white coconut. They each chewed and sucked on stalks of sugar cane.

'Is it better than this in Fairhaven?' Mung asked John.

It took several seconds before John responded. 'It's nicer there. In a different way.'

Suddenly John jumped to his feet. 'My father will be waiting!'

The boys snatched their clothes and ran up the path, hopping into their trousers and calling aloha to the girls. John dashed ahead. Hearing Mung call out in Japanese, he looked back to see his adopted brother dart off the path and go down on all fours in the grass, charging from tree to tree.

A cold sweat broke out on John's face. 'Oh God,' he moaned, 'Mung's gone crazy from too much sex!' He held onto the trunk of a palm tree for support, waiting for the madness to overtake him. 'God,' he prayed looking at the sky, 'I fornicated a lot today. Before I lose my mind know that I love you and I promise never to do it again.'

'Town-ho,' Mung shouted. 'Cut it off!'

Bounding ahead of Mung, its head just visible in the high grass, was a mottled yellow and brown kitten. John went limp with relief. He began to laugh. 'I thought we were both going to be demented for the rest of our lives.'

'Get it,' Mung cried.

John intercepted the frightened kitten, catching it by the nape of the neck. 'Why are you chasing her?'

Mung came up breathing hard. 'If it's a her then it makes no difference. Can we check?'

John held the kitten up for inspection.

'It's a him,' Mung shouted. 'It'll be good luck to take him aboard.'

'Only male cats are good luck?'

'Only male cats with the yellow and brown colours like a turtle. In any Japanese village, boat-owners would bid a lot of rice for this little guy.'

153

Mung took the kitten in his arms and it began to purr.

Aboard the whaler with Captain Whittefield's permission, the kitten was dubbed Lucky in a knighting ceremony performed by John. It was given the equivalent name in Japanese and raised to the rank of samurai according to the protocol of Bushido. Lucky lived up to his name. The wind remained constant, the weather fair, and a number of whales were taken on the way home. The cat followed the boys everywhere, responding to commands from either one in Japanese or English. Mung sewed a sling to carry Lucky under his arm or behind his back when he went up into the rigging.

By the time the *J. Howland* rounded the Horn, using the books Mrs Link had given him and with John's help, Mung improved his grasp of English grammar, composition and history. He taught John the same subjects from memory in Japanese. They learned games and sang songs in both languages. John taught Mung to box and he learned to fall, flip, and throw an opponent in the art of jujitsu.

One day Captain Whittefield called Mung into his cabin. 'Tomorrow is March fourth,' he said. 'It will be sixteen years ago to the day that John was born. It's a tradition within families to give presents on one's anniversary of birth.'

Mung nodded. 'Thank you for telling me. It is so in Japan. But there everyone celebrates becoming a year older on the first day of the new year. I too am sixteen.'

William Whittefield listened to his foster son and appraised him at the same time. He was not as tall nor broad in the shoulders as John, but he had a fluid grace like his pet cat and the muscles of his neck stood out like whipcords. Two calm, intelligent, dark eyes watched and absorbed everything from either side of his bent nose. How great the physical contrast between the boys and yet how similar their personalities and intellect, William Whittefield thought. I must read Genesis again and give more thought to the fact that we are all sprung from the same seed. He dismissed Mung and said a silent prayer, thanking God for allowing him to find his own son alive and adopt another.

The following morning the crew gathered before the quarterdeck. William Whittefield called John to his side. 'Today is my son John's birthday. I now have two sons.' The men all turned to Mung who stood among them, then back to the captain. 'Japanese people celebrate birthdays differently, everyone on the first day of each year. Since we have rounded the Horn and are on the Christian side of the world, I propose to celebrate both my sons' birthdays today, March fourth in the year of our Lord Jesus Christ. May they be blessed forever and ever. Amen.'

In unison the crew responded, 'Amen,' and then chanted, 'Hip, hip, hurray!'

They hustled Mung up to the quarterdeck next to the captain who presented both young men with identical polished brass pocket-compasses.

After recovering from the initial shock and beauty of the gift, Mung excused himself. He went behind the helmsman and brought forward a kite he had made, on which he'd painted a picture of the *J. Howland* chasing a whale. He handed it to John, anxiously watching for his reaction. When John's face lit up, Mung was delighted. Even more so when John presented him with a large wooden top he had carved.

After the crew sang 'For They Are Jolly Good Fellows,' the boys were asked to sing a song in Japanese. John was proud of himself for being able to do it. But the response to the song was only polite applause and blank looks because to everyone but the boys it sounded as if they were tone deaf and howling sick. The captain quickly ordered rum for all hands and gave John and Mung the remainder of the day off.

They immediately went to the fantail to fly the kite and practise tricks with the top. Later on, in the galley, they got under Cooky's feet in hunting cockroaches. In their cabin with the black-backed beetles, Mung stuck fine sewing thread to the shells of five roaches with bits of tar he had chewed to stickiness. He then attached the strings to a paper chariot. When John had the other five set up, they raced their teams on the floor, shouting and cheering their chariots on.

Once around the Horn the mood and atmosphere altered aboard the whaler. Mung first noticed it in the forecastle. There was less cursing and card playing, and more men in attendance at the Deacon's Sunday church services. Mung was frightened by the changes in behaviour. Although he tried to explain it to John, he hadn't the maturity to understand that he felt threatened. His first reaction was melancholy.

He often found a corner to be alone with Lucky and poured out his heart to the little cat. 'I miss Jakato and Mother. Fudenojo and Shin-ho are often on my mind lately. In my dreams I can smell the village, see the thatched huts, drying nets, and the people. I don't know what it will be like in Fairhaven.' The kitten looked up into Mung's eyes as if understanding every word. 'I might embarrass my new father and brother if I fail to pass the high school examination. Or worse that I will be accepted there and then put out for my stupidity.' He picked Lucky up under the belly, holding the cat high over his head. 'You may be a lucky cat but you're not very academic.' Mung repeated the word academic several times. He had learned it from John the previous day. 'I have to study!' He slipped Lucky into the sling under his arm.

Mung pored over his books but unconsciously began to push aside the westernization process. His first act was to make an abacus for John and teach him how to use it. He carved two little Buddhas for himself and his brother to carry as lucky charms on their belts. He gave up trying to make John take off his shoes in the cabin because they were in the Atlantic Ocean and it was colder. He did make a *tokonama* – a small shelf in the cabin on which he placed a picture he'd painted of a plum tree in bloom.

He explained to John, 'This is traditional in every Japanese home. It's in honour of the Emperor. If he were to visit he would know we were expecting and thinking of him. This is his place in our house.'

156

'How could he possibly ever visit us? We're off the coast of South America.'

'It's symbolic,' Mung answered.

There were other symbols he unconsciously used to save himself from complete divorce from his Japanese soul. He painted lotus flowers because they grew from beneath the surface of the water, similar to the way he had come to this ship. Their petals were wheel-shaped and gave him the pleasure of remembering the teachings of his father about the infinite cycles of life and death upon which man is bound to travel for eternity.

On the practical level, Mung often found himself spending time in the galley. He had persuaded Cooky to buy soya sauce and several bags of rice in Honolulu. Cooky insisted on serving boiled rice with toppings of onions, beets or cabbage, or sometimes all three. Mung showed him how to prepare puddings and porridge. The fried rice Mung made was welcomed in the mess. He ground rice to flour and made sweet cakes, bread, pancakes and noodles. The crew responded by encouraging Mung to spend more time at the stove. He always marvelled at the amounts the men consumed at one meal. It would have sufficed the whole of Nakanohama for a week.

Cooky quickly realized how versatile and cheap rice was. It also stored well. Before they reached Fairhaven, he knew it would be a large part of his supplies the next time he sailed. In less than five years, most American merchant vessels were stocking quantities of rice on long voyages.

Mung's problems were low on the list of priorities aboard the *J. Howland*. The ship was a whaler, chasing whales from March to August up the east coast of South and North America. The ship's hold once again filled with neatly stacked barrels of prime whale oil, and the deck was piled high with baleen.

On a clear August night they raised Montauk Light off the port bow. In nine hours they sailed past Martha's Vineyard, Gay Head, the Rhode Island Light, and into Buzzards Bay and the channel by New Bedford to the Fairhaven Wharf.

Church bells rang throughout Fairhaven long before the

mooring lines were heaved ashore. The townspeople came running, waving as they streamed towards the dock.

The town crier could be heard. 'The *J. Howland*! William Whittefield commanding! Three years out and returned by God's grace!'

John pointed. 'That's the Fairhaven dock. And opposite, by that sandbar, is where I was when the storm carried me out to sea.'

Mung was overwhelmed by the comparative wealth of the fishing villages they had passed coming upriver. Now he saw the sturdy docks, solid wood and brick houses, horses and carriages. On the dock itself people were gathering from every direction. Their dress gave him no indication of rank or importance. The men mostly wore dark trousers and white shirts with the sleeves rolled up in the summer heat. Some wore hats but as with the women, it did not seem to denote class status. The female clothes were a riot of colour but with no clan design. He remembered learning there was no class distinction in American society. It will take much getting used to, he thought.

The greetings shouted from ship and shore drowned out the orders of the mates but eager hands heaved the lines ashore where they were secured. The creaks and groans of the whaler's timbers ceased as she lay tethered to the land. Mung felt as if the life had gone out of the large vessel. Then he heard the hymn-like sound of women's voices singing.

Didn't the Lord deliver Daniel from the lion's den.

Didn't the Lord deliver Jonah from the belly of a whale.

Now the Lord has delivered our son

like Noah from the raging gale …

The crowd on shore and the men on board fell silent as the churchwomen of Fairhaven, arms linked, approached the ship.

'That's Mother!' John cried.

In the centre of the group, tears streaming down her cheeks, Martha Whittefield walked forward to meet her son. The gangplank was lowered and Captain Whittefield motioned John to precede him ashore. Five inches taller, sun-bronzed and well-muscled, John ran to his mother's loving arms. William

Whittefield embraced them both.

Mung watched from the ship, swallowing hard to hide his emotions. Where was his mother? Would he ever see her again?

A woman's solo voice rang out clear and sweet,

> Amazing grace, how sweet the sound
> that saved a wretch like me.
> I once was lost, but now am found.
> Was blind, but now I see ...

Voices joined in the song and Captain Whittefield waved for Mung to come to him. When he did, Martha hugged him with as much warmth as she had her own son. The family was too excited to realize that many people stopped singing at the sight of a white woman embracing an oriental boy.

Captain Whittefield shouted to his first mate, 'Mr Hockmeyer, the entire crew is invited to join my family in giving thanks to the Lord.'

'Aye aye, sir!'

The seamen and many townspeople followed the Whittefields up Main Street to the tall steepled Methodist church, singing hymns on the way.

As they entered the sanctuary, the captain told Mung, 'Martha's great-grandfather and mine helped build this church. They were British subjects then. Both our families have continued our affiliation and support. I hope you will come closer to the Lord here.'

Mung kneeled with the others and joined in the prayer of thanksgiving. He added a prayer to his mother's household Buddha, certain that Jesus had no domain in Nakanohama.

The first home-cooked meal at the Whittefield house began with cream of clam soup spiced with peppercorn, thyme, and sweet marjoram. Two four-pound shad were split, boned, laid skin side down on a well-oiled hickory board, flavoured with hyssop, and baked for thirty minutes. The fish were served with wedges of lemon and fresh butter brushed on. Martha put the second loaf of hard-crusted warm bread on the cutting board as sizzling steaks and baked potatoes were placed before her men. A pewter jug of milk, cool from the cellar, washed down the fruit pies for dessert, which had been sent by unseen relatives and friends.

The four sat most of the day talking in the country kitchen, sharing the happenings of their lives during the time they had been apart. In the evening they moved to the porch to catch the cool breeze. The hall clock struck eight and William Whittefield asked the boys to fetch a bundle from his cabin aboard ship. Mung scooped up Lucky who lay at his feet satiated with milk and left-over shad. He slipped the cat into the sling under his arm.

The boys walked down the street, John telling Mung about the town, its shops, and the different buildings they passed. Nearing the dock they heard the sounds of loud music and laughter coming from those bars closest to the *J. Howland*.

Mung stopped near the gangplank. 'John, we promised to have a farewell toast with the crew. What if you get the bundle and I look for them. I'll meet you back here.'

'Agreed,' John said. He bounded up to the ship.

Mung walked to the nearest bar. He entered and stood near the door, searching for a familiar face. Most of the people had drinks in their hands, including the women whom he recognized as prostitutes from his experiences in Hawaii. They wore frilly, bright clothing, breasts popping from the tops of their dresses. He had been nine months at sea. Even through the clouds of tobacco smoke and stench of stale liquor, he sniffed the scent of perfume and felt an erection coming on.

Silence spread from the people at the bar to those on the dance floor and at the tables.

'Hey!' someone shouted. 'No Chinamen allowed in here!'

Seeing neither Chinese nor any crew member of the *J. Howland*, Mung turned to leave. As he opened the door, two prostitutes coming in barged into him. The taller of the women grabbed Mung's head and pulled his face between her ample breasts.

'Leaving so soon, honey,' she laughed. 'Maybe we can take a turn in the stall before you go?'

The soft roundness and overwhelming female smell stunned

160

Mung. He vaguely heard her saying, 'Oh, you've got a pussy under your arm. Want to see my pussy?'

She stepped back, got a look at Mung, and screamed, 'A fucking Chink! God Almighty, my reputation's ruined!'

Mung, completely aroused, bowed slightly and said, 'Would you like to fornicate?'

'What!' The woman's painted face screwed up in surprise. Her high-pitched voice alerted the men in the bar.

'I would like to put my pecker ... Excuse me. I mean my penis into your ...' Mung pointed between her legs.

'You slant-eyed son of a bitch!' she screamed.

Instantly Mung was encircled by a group of hard-looking dock workers. They pushed him out the door and the biggest of the bunch demanded, 'What did you say to the lady?'

'I asked her if she wanted to fornicate.'

'What the hell is fornicate?' He shouted into the bar. 'Hey Millie, what did the Chink do?'

Brushing the tops of her breasts with painted fingertips, she said, 'The little yellow bastard wants to screw me!'

The large man turned back to Mung and stepped closer. He smiled and said, 'You want to diddle a white woman?'

'I have money. I can pay.'

'You'll pay all right. Look over there.'

Mung's head followed the man's finger. Before he realized it, Lucky was snatched from the sling. The big man threw the trusting kitten into the air, caught it by the tail, whirled it around, and smashed its head against the side of the building. He flung the little body into the gutter and rubbed his hands together.

Mung moved as in a dream. He pushed people aside and knelt beside the dead cat, tears in his eyes. He looked up in time to see the murderer aiming a kick at his head. In cold fury, Mung gauged the kick. Deflecting it with his left forearm and throwing a punch, as John had shown him, straight from the shoulder with all his might, he aimed at the man's groin.

'Eeeeaaaggghhh!' The tough screamed and fell over backwards. Someone jumped from behind and was flipped over Mung's shoulder, landing flat on his back. A third rushed from the side. Using a hip roll, Mung threw him to the ground. He saw a clear path to the big man writhing on the ground, clutching his groin. In one leap Mung was on him, driving a wedge punch into his Adam's apple. In the next instant Mung was buried under an avalanche of punching and stomping men. He felt his arms pinned. Blows rained down on him. His unconscious body was kicked across the street, off the edge of the dock and into the water.

John, coming down the gangplank with his arms full, saw the group of angry, cursing men heading back across the street. Three others lay on the ground near the bar, moaning.

'Oh my God! What's Mung gotten into?' John ran to intercept the group. 'What happened?'

One of the men thumbed his nose and pointed to the river. 'We took care of an uppity Chink.'

At that moment John saw Lucky's broken body sprawled grotesquely in the dirt. He dropped his bundle and ran to the edge. Mung lay face down in the river. John leapt in and grabbed him by the hair, lifting his face out of the water.

Holding on to his brother, he swam to the nearest rowboat, and thanked God to hear Mung cough and spit.

John rolled Mung into the boat, hearing him mumble through split and swollen lips, 'Why did they kill Lucky? Why don't they like orientals?'

John shook his head. 'I don't know.' There were tears in his eyes. 'It's not just orientals. People like that hate anyone who's different.'

Two weeks later Mung had recovered well enough to attend Sunday services but it wasn't in the church built and looked after by generations of Whittefields. The church fathers had made it known to the family that a non-white was not welcome. The Whittefields turned to another church in Fairhaven which accepted Mung as part of their congregation. Although he made no comment about the incidents of prejudice against him, Mung began to understand the bitter truth on the Christian side of Cape Horn.

Very soon after, Mung and John passed their entrance examinations at Harvard High School and were welcomed without reservation by all of the faculty and many of the students.

William Whittefield travelled to Washington DC where he quietly resigned his naval commission. With the sponsorship of Secretary of the Navy Spaulding, he took up his appointment in the Far Eastern Section of the State Department. His wife, Martha, remained in Fairhaven until the boys completed three years of study. Both did so with honours. John was accepted at Annapolis and Mung to Harvard's Divinity School, the only college ready to receive him. Shortly after their graduation in June of 1846, William Whittefield was appointed Chief of the State Department's new Japanese Section in the Foreign Office in a simple, private ceremony. Mung knew it was because of him but kept his thoughts to himself. There was nothing he could do if the American government didn't want a yellow man at the formal appointment.

As each prepared to set out on his new path in life, Mung made a different decision. 'I'm not cut out for the ministry,' he explained to the Whittefield family. 'Some of the happiest days of my life were on the whaler. I'd like to go out again.'

'It's a noble profession,' William Whittefield said. 'Martha's father and mine both chased the big fish.'

'You'll be keeping up our tradition,' John said. 'At least there'll be one whaler in the family.'

Mung was pleased they approved his decision. With William Whittefield's help, he signed on a trim-looking whaler in New Bedford.

John Whittefield had taken to his studies at Annapolis like a seal to water. His mind revelled in the problem-solving situations posed by his teachers. His six-foot, 180-pound body gloried in testing its physical limits. His experiences aboard the ocean-going steamer and the whaler marked him as exceptional in the eyes of his superiors. He was encouraged to expand his knowledge of Japanese with special language instructors.

John rarely took leave from the Academy, even though his

parents were only hours away in Washington DC. He was determined to perfect himself to serve God, man, and country to the best of his ability. But, in June of the second year, his parents had insisted he attend the ball at Secretary Spaulding's spacious home. He felt out of place among the guests who were accustomed to balancing tea cups and making insipid conversation. He made his way across the room to a place near the French doors, determined to slip out at the earliest possible moment. He checked the wall with his fingertips to make sure the powder-blue paint would not smudge his immaculate white uniform.

'John, this is Beth Spaulding.' His mother had found him. 'You two played together in this house eight years ago.'

He turned to the girl, resigned to putting up with her, unprepared for the golden hair and intense blue eyes before him. He watched her red lips part and expected her to speak. She only smiled and he became aware of his heart. Noting the full bodice and dainty waist swelling into rounded hips, his eyes jumped and his lids fluttered. He could hear his heart beat in his ears. She laughed and the musical sound drew the strength from his legs.

Accustomed to social life in the nation's capital, Beth recognized John's unsophisticated reaction and was delighted. She had watched him move stiffly across the floor trying to avoid contact. She sensed the rippling power of his muscles under the stiff dress uniform. When he flashed a brief smile, the whiteness of his teeth against the bronze of his skin was startling.

'Do you remember our first meeting?' she asked.

His sun-bleached blond hair still fell in front of his blue eyes, and he brushed it away in the same boyish manner she recalled.

'Yes,' he said. 'We rode horses. You insisted on a race and made me jump two fences. You won and scared me half to death.'

They both laughed and Beth saw that his smile was even more perfect close up. 'Do you remember your promise?' she asked. 'You said you would take me sailing and scare the wits out of me.'

'We were children then. I didn't mean it.'

'Does that mean you withdraw the invitation?' She looked up at him in feigned dismay.

'No. Oh no,' he said. 'Will Sunday be convenient?'

Her eyes flashed. 'Yes. Very convenient.'

It was the beginning of their relationship. From then on, whenever John had leave, they were together. They sailed and picnicked on his family's schooner, or rode horses. He became her escort to parties, balls, and official functions in the capital and at Annapolis. She was a mirror image of him – forthright, religious, intelligent and in love.

Mung was twenty-one years old when he returned to Martha and William Whittefield's new home in Washington DC. They welcomed him with open arms.

'Tell us about your voyage.'

Mung smiled. 'Most important was the way the crew accepted me. An officer jumped ship in South America and I was voted second mate. On the return voyage, the captain went out of his head and had to be forcibly restrained. I navigated the ship around the Horn and directed whaling on the way home.'

William Whittefield was gratified to hear Mung's account. 'We're very proud of you, son. I'm pleased to know that your exceptional intelligence and leadership qualities were recognized. What are your plans now?'

Mung shrugged. 'I really haven't decided.'

Martha Whittefield hugged him. 'This is your home.'

He looked into her eyes and thought again of his mother in Nakanohama. Martha looked at her adopted son and admired him. Not tall but well-muscled, he had a confident stance and look of assurance set off by that broken nose which some women found attractive. His conduct was beyond reproach yet families worried about his contact with their daughters. The old slights began again.

John came home for a visit from Annapolis. He introduced Mung to a lovely young blonde woman. From the adoring glances passing between John and Beth, it was clear they were in love. This shook Mung more than any single event since his beating the first night in Fairhaven. He said nothing of it to anyone but was reminded that in Nakanohama he would already have been

165

married. Here in America even the lowliest whore wouldn't let him touch her. He had considered taking a Chinese wife and encountered his own deepseated prejudices.

When word of a gold strike reached the nation's capital, Mung decided to go to California. He bid farewell to the Whittefields, presented a carved whale's tooth to Beth, and shipped as a mate on a steamer bound for Panama. Along with other Forty-niners he took the train across the Isthmus and booked passage on the Pacific side to San Francisco. From there he made his way north to the gold fields.

After some time the Whittefields received a letter in which Mung explained that he was driven, no matter the danger, to return to his homeland. He had to know if his mother still lived, seek a wife to continue his family name, and honour his father's grave. He expressed his regrets and was most appreciative of the kindness shown him by the Whittefields.

Then a letter came from Reverend Damon in Hawaii. Mung had visited and told the reverend about a shootout in the gold fields in which two former shipmates were killed, and of his determination to return to Japan.

Later there was another letter from the reverend. He had received word from the captain of the whaler *Brentwood* that on 9 January 1851 Mung was lowered off the coast of Ryuku Island (Okinawa) in a small boat. He was last seen pulling for shore in a calm sea.

CHAPTER
9

January 1851

The ship lay off Ryuku Island in a calm sea, the sun's glow beginning to colour the dark horizon. He looked over the rail of the whaling ship *Brentwood*, his face beaded with cold sweat in the warm, muggy air. Although he had eaten, he felt an emptiness behind his belt buckle, a weakness in his knees. There was a gauntness in the twenty-four-year-old's features and the friendly face with the indented nose was solemn.

'Have you changed your mind, Mung?' Captain Abrahams asked.

'I'm thinking about what's ahead,' he said.

The whaling master leaned on the rail next to Mung. 'I've told you before, don't feel obligated to leave the ship here. I'll return your money. When we put into Hawaii you can go ashore, or travel around the Horn with us and back to New England.'

'Thank you, Captain, but I must see this through.'

'Even if it costs your life?'

'Yes, even that.'

'Son, life, human life, is the most precious and unique thing God put on this earth. I'm asking you not to put yours in jeopardy.'

Mung looked at the older man. 'When my father took his life, it was with honour. He would not have done so had he been childless because of his obligation to honour his ancestors. My brother, Jakato, died in a storm, and I am forced to wander in foreign lands, from which I cannot pay homage to my father or our forebears. I have found no Japanese women in California or Hawaii, nor heard of any on other islands in the Pacific. If my life and my family's name is to end, let it be by the hand of a Japanese, in Japan.'

Captain Abrahams stepped back from the rail and extended his hand. 'I wish you good luck. The wind is coming up. I've seen that your provisions are on the skiff.'

'Thank you,' Mung said. 'I appreciate your help.'

Captain Abrahams pointed up to the crow's nest. 'As soon as our lookout can see the island, we'll lower your boat. When we make a one hundred and eighty degree turn, sail directly away from us until we are out of sight. That will give you your bearings and the island should be in view by then.'

The crew of the ship presented Mung with a whale's tooth and a cheer for good luck before they lowered the skiff. Once away from the *Brentwood*, he changed into the simple fisherman's garb purchased from a castaway in the oriental compound at Honolulu. He sailed steadily for two hours before the whaler disappeared over the horizon.

Mountains in the northern part of Ryuku were soon visible. From charts he had studied with Captain Whittefield, he knew that flat land lay below the horizon stretching southward. Four sails moved away from him to starboard. They were the same kind of boat he, his brother Jakato, Fudenojo and Shin-ho had sailed when they left Nakanohama ten years before. He and Jakato had not even taken leave of their mother for fear she would forbid them to go. That had also been part of his plan. He remembered a saying often quoted by his father, 'Men plan and the gods laugh.'

Mung lowered his sail, wanting to get as close to shore as possible unobserved. His greatest fear was that he would be decapitated by a samurai without a chance to speak. Over and over, he practised greetings for various situations. He had not spoken Japanese since he left Hawaii three months before.

It was ten in the morning when Mung ate the sourdough bread and hard cheese the cook had provided for him. The pistol, given him by Captain Whittefield, lay alongside navigating instruments in a wooden box in the bottom of the boat. He picked up the oars, took a deep breath and began rowing into the centre of Nakagusuku Bay, being purposely conspicuous. He did not want to give the impression he was sneaking ashore.

No one challenged him as he neared the beach. The harbour was empty; he had seen more fishing boats leave. Old men sat mending nets, smoke rose from cooking fires and women washed clothes at the water's edge. The sound of wooden mallets drifted across the quiet bay from a small boat-yard. The children sighted him first and came running to see the man who rowed backwards. The skiff slid neatly into the sand. He stood up on cramped, quivering legs, and stepped ashore, expecting to feel some special emotion, but did not. The children gathered around, watching him.

He called to them, 'Bring the village headman.'

Hearing him speak, they knew the language was Japanese, but did not understand. Although Ryukun islanders paid tribute and taxes to the Emperor, they were not taught the Japanese language. Frightened of anyone from Japan, the children ran away. Mung thought to look for someone in authority but decided it would be better for him to stay by the boat and wait.

Ryochi Okuda, the Japanese prefect in Nakagusuku, sat cross-legged in his open-sided hut, performing the only task that passed time pleasantly for him, thinking up possible schemes to be transferred back to Japan. Only three months ago he had finished his first six-month vacation at the manor of the Satsuma Lord Nariakira on the island of Kyushu, but it seemed much longer. Many *ronin*, those unemployed samurai, told him how fortunate he was. They willingly would have committed themselves to five years on Ryuku just to be in the service of some feudal lord. Two hundred years of isolation had meant a long period of peace for Japan, but peace brought unemployment for soldiers. For Ryochi, beginning his second five-year assignment on Ryuku, Japan was paradise. Here, the air was always hot and sticky, except when blown away by a passing typhoon. The Ryukuns built their houses of flimsy material, knowing they would be destroyed in the next storm.

Deep in his familiar thought pattern, Ryochi did not notice the three Ryukun elders waiting respectfully, heads bowed, in front of

169

his hut. Their hair was tied into topknots with a copper skewer passing through, to signify rank. Eventually, he recognized their existence.

In Ryukun, the leader said, 'There is a stranger on the beach.'

Ryochi snapped, 'From which village is he?'

'It is not clear. He is Japanese, but has a foreign-type boat.'

Ryochi heard this information as he would the daily catch of fish, until the full meaning exploded into his consciousness. He catapulted his short stocky frame from the low sitting platform, grabbed his two-handed sword, and ran past the elders. They watched his short bowed legs kick up dust as he hurried to the beach.

Villagers circled around the Japanese stranger and his foreign boat. Two of Ryochi's Japanese subordinates had pushed the crowd back. One, named Tsunajiro, prepared to draw his sword and kill the stranger.

Ryochi was just in time to shout, 'Stop!'

Tsunajiro, filled with the importance of the situation, said, 'He must die. Look at the foreign boat. We've already begun burning his books and that wooden box.' He pointed to the fire nearby.

When Ryochi thought back on the events, he realized it was probably Tsunajiro who had saved Mung from being executed. Ryochi was also determined to kill the man on the beach if he was a foreigner or returning Japanese, but when his subordinate used the words, 'must – he must die', Ryochi bridled at the breach of discipline and etiquette.

BAM! BAM! Two explosions shattered the wooden box in the fire.

Ryochi noticed that the young stranger was as frightened as everyone else by the explosions. He walked to the fire and, with his scabbard, pushed the books and smouldering box away from the flames.

He barked at Tsunajiro, 'Put out the fire! Clear the dirt off everything and bring all to me immediately! Have these Ryukuns put the boat next to my hut! If they steal one nail, I'll have your head!'

170

Ryochi grabbed Mung by the arm and shoved him forward. The villagers fell back to either side of the road. Ryochi hurried Mung along, jabbing him in the small of the back with his scabbard until they reached his hut. There, he questioned Mung long enough to be certain he was a fairly well-educated Japanese, more intelligent than the ordinary fisherman he was impersonating.

Ryochi examined the four-barrelled pistol. He had seen a large muzzle-loading hand-gun once, but nothing like this. He looked at the small pouch of gold nuggets, the navigation instruments, and the books. He paced back and forth in front of Mung, who kneeled with his head bent.

Mung felt a tug at the thong he wore. His head snapped back when Ryochi tore the cross from around his neck. The stocky Japanese stared at the cross in his hand, then closed his fist over it. He tucked it into his kimono and drew the two handed sword from its scabbard. Mung looked up to see Ryochi brandishing the blade high over his head.

'I'm sorry, Father,' Mung said aloud. Clapping his hands once in Buddhist fashion to speed the prayer on its way, he bowed his head and waited.

The blade whistled through the air, then stopped, the cold, razor-sharp steel resting on the back of his neck. Mung's body began to shake. He wanted to shout, 'Do it!' but could not. A hard kick in the side rolled him over on the mat.

Ryochi stood over him and shouted, 'You are not to speak to anyone!' He kicked Mung in the stomach. 'Don't open your mouth, or you are dead!'

Ryochi summoned Tsunajiro and ordered him to take Mung away. Tsunajiro, in turn, ordered two Ryukuns to drag Mung from the hut. For the first time since landing on the beach, Mung knew he had a chance to live. He wanted to tell the men dragging him that he had to move his bowels, but was afraid to speak. Tsunajiro ordered the Ryukuns to strip Mung of his clothes. On the dirt in the square in front of the crowd, they rolled him over, ripping away his shirt and trousers. The crowd enjoyed the spectacle of a Japanese being humiliated. They laughed and cheered. It was just as the two Ryukuns began to drag him across the square that his bowels moved of their own accord. The crowd roared with laughter. The two men jumped away from Mung as he dirtied his legs and the ground. The villagers imitated the children, holding their noses and pointing. Tsunajiro shouted. The Ryukuns became silent. Several men brought buckets of water to douse Mung. Tsunajiro aimed a kick at his head but missed and almost lost his balance. A twitter of laughter rippled through the crowd but quickly stopped as the Japanese sub-prefect glared at them, infuriated. He pointed to the four-sided open cell with its bamboo bars and Mung was thrown into the twenty-by-twenty-foot jail. He hunkered down in the corner, with his naked back against the bars. Eyes cast down, he avoided looking at the jeering crowd.

Ryochi paced back and forth in his hut. There was no doubt in his mind that Mung should have been executed. That cross around his neck made it doubly certain. But he was positive no one else had seen it. If he killed Mung now and forwarded his belongings to the capital city of Naha, Ryochi knew his superiors would suppress his name and take whatever credit they could for themselves. They wanted to get off this island as much as he did. If he sent Mung to Naha alive, they would claim credit and possibly accompany Mung back to the mainland to be examined and probably executed. Ryochi knew that if he bypassed his superiors, he could lose his own head. The least punishment would be dismissal from the Satusma Lord's service and exile on Ryuku. He looked around his open-sided hut, then outside at the stark village square and the Ryukuns who hated all Japanese.

He mumbled to himself, 'I'm already in exile and too stupid to realize it.' He shouted to his servant squatting outside. 'Bring my writing desk and have a runner prepare to go to Naha!'

Ryochi knelt at the low desk and addressed a letter to Sakuma Shozan, the senior scholar at the Satsuma Court.

Sir

I have not done my duty as the law is known and written, in the hope I may be of service to my master, Lord Nariakira. A young man named Mangiro of the fishing village of Nakanohama, from the island of Shikuku, was shipwrecked ten years ago on a fishing voyage at the age of fourteen. Three others of the crew were lost. He was rescued by westerners from a country called America, who named him Mung. He claims to read, write, and speak their language. He says he spent three years studying in their schools, almost six years on two different ships catching whales, and one year searching for gold. He returned to what he thought was Japan to live with his people again. This is his statement. He landed here in my district on the island of Ryuku in the village of Nakagusuku. He was dressed as a poor Japanese fisherman, but his speech is cultured. He arrived in a small well-made western-style sailing boat which is intact. His belongings, though few, are remarkable. They include a small pouch of gold nuggets, foreign books, instruments he claims are used for navigation, a hand-gun with rotating barrels, a whale's tooth, and pieces of clear glass which were broken when he landed. I am sending these items for your inspection. The burn and dirt marks are from the action taken by my subordinates in accordance with the law when Mung landed. I, not they, am responsible for not destroying these items and executing the man. I have interrogated him only briefly because the weekly ship to the mainland leaves on this evening's tide. There is no copy of this letter. If I have done wrong by not implementing the law, or not informing my superiors in Naha, I will do my duty to my most honourable Lord Nariakira.

The phrase 'do my duty' was formal Japanese. It meant Ryochi would commit *seppuku* after he executed Mung. Ryochi sealed the letter, placed it in the bundle of Mung's belongings, and sent the runner with specific instructions to place the package aboard the ship heading for the mainland. He was ordered not to talk to anyone, not to rest in Naha, to deliver the package and return.

Ryochi Okuda sat crosslegged on the platform in the middle of his hut so he could see Mung in the open jail cell across the square. He had taken an irreversible step that would change the course of his life. It was a bold move worthy of a samurai. If it failed there would be no one to write a poem, a play, or song about his desire to serve his Lord. For that matter, if nothing had changed and Mung had never landed here, there would have been nothing to sing about anyway. Ryochi did not want songs as much as getting back to the mainland with a proper position in the Lord's service. This plan of his had its roots in whispers he had heard while on leave at Lord Nariakira's manor. It was rumoured that the Lord was supporting the senior pedagogue Sakuma Shozan in his quest for western knowledge. It was further whispered in utmost secrecy, at low breath, that the Lord Nariakira was a supporter of returning real power to the Emperor and doing away with the title and authority of the Shōgun. Beads of perspiration broke out on Ryochi's forehead. He controlled his urge to wipe his brow for he knew the Ryukuns were always watching for signs of weakness. He had forgotten to write in the letter of his special relationship with the prisoner, which was to be his ticket home if it was decided not to kill Mung. He sat still, grinding his teeth and muttering, 'I should go out and kill that bastard!'

Later, Ryochi watched Tsunajiro put seven Ryukun prisoners returning from a work gang into the cell with Mung. They too were stripped before entering the cage. They made no attempt to speak among themselves until the guard was out of sight. They did not try to communicate with Mung. Two women brought a bowl of rice, a cucumber, and bowl of water for each prisoner. Mung sat alone, fingering the rice into his mouth. He took a drink from the bowl and choked, spitting the salt water out. He was tempted to throw the bowl at the woman and was about to pour it on the dirt floor when a prisoner approached him. The man took the bowl from Mung's hand and sipped the water. He pointed at the bowl, used the word for salt in Japanese, and handed it back. The prisoners ate nothing other than rice and cucumbers morning and evening, day after day. Their only salt intake came from this one cup of sea water after work. Mung drank it.

Ryochi thought several times of strangling the life out of Mung with his bare hands, wanting to feel the stupid bastard quiver before he died. He also realized that any chance he had depended on Mung staying alive. Ryochi stalked from his hut to the cage and ordered Mung outside. He threw a short work jacket and trousers to him and motioned to be followed, then waddled down the road to the beach.

The sun was still hanging over the horizon when they reached a dung heap at the end of the village near the water's edge. Ryochi threw the whalebone cross with its broken thong on to the dung heap. Flies buzzed up angrily.

He pointed to the cross and said, 'I don't ever want to know if you believe in that. If you tell anyone of its existence, we're both dead.' He raised his voice. 'Jump on that dung heap and stomp it to the bottom!'

Mung, frightened by the emotion in Ryochi's face and voice, leapt on to the pile and began stamping, first with his right foot, then with his left.

Ryochi's hysterical voice screamed, 'Faster! Faster! Faster!'

Mung was running in place, sinking down into the silt and slime. Filth was creeping up his legs and flies swarmed around his head. He was waist deep in the pile and completely exhausted when Ryochi ordered him to stop. Mung opened his mouth to take a breath and flies swarmed in. He spat and touched his mouth with unclean hands. Trying to climb out, he rolled down the pile.

Ryochi shouted, 'Stop wallowing like a Ryukun pig! Go and clean yourself!'

Mung staggered into the water far enough to duck his body under. He stripped, grabbed handfuls of sand and scrubbed himself clean. He drifted out to let the water take the weight off his trembling legs. His body shook violently in disgust at the filth that was on him. He swam a few quick strokes away from the beach, then back to try to control himself.

Ryochi shouted, 'Where did you learn to swim with your hands over your head and kicking the water with your feet?'

Mung answered, 'In Hawaii.'

'Do it again!'

Mung was made to swim out and back, then parallel to the beach, so Ryochi could observe the unusual stroke. He was ordered out of the water to squat on the beach.

Ryochi sat in front of him on a piece of driftwood and asked, 'What is the penalty for any Japanese who boards a foreign vessel or steps foot on foreign soil?'

Mung answered, 'Death according to the Exclusion Edict of 1638.'

'Do you want to die?'

'No.'

'Why have you returned?'

'To honour my father and our ancestors; to seek a wife; to return my father's name to the status it once held; to leave children to carry on our name. I am the only surviving son.'

Ryochi stared out over the water. Then he asked, 'Was life so desperate for you in a foreign country?'

'No, not in the physical sense, but it's the Japanese culture I yearn for.'

Ryochi said, 'It certainly wasn't in the physical. You returned with things worth more than a village fisherman earns in a lifetime. Explain about these cultural differences.'

'I was accepted into an American high school, but excluded from most churches.'

Ryochi slammed Mung on the side of the head with his scabbard, then kicked him as he rolled over in the sand. 'You will not mention the church!'

Mung sat up again, trying to disregard the pain. He obeyed Ryochi's command to continue. 'It was easy to earn money and the work was not too hard. The standard of living for most people is very high. It was not acceptable for a dark oriental to marry a white American girl, even if she is a whore.'

Ryochi shouted, 'What! A Japanese marry a white whore! I would die first!'

Mung did not answer. For the first time their eyes met. A sense

176

of understanding passed between them. Ryochi waved Mung to continue.

'It would probably have been acceptable for me to marry a Hawaiian, but I would have had to live with the other shipwrecked Japanese in the special compound.'

'These Americans and Hawaiians must hate Japanese,' Ryochi said.

'Not the Hawaiians. But most whites are against people who have different colour skin than theirs.'

Ryochi put his sword across his knees. 'What made you decide to leave there? What was the final grain of rice that tipped the scale?'

'I had done enough whaling, having been two years on a ship when I was rescued and another three after I finished high school. At the end of my last whaling voyage there was nothing for me to do on land. The people who adopted me, Mr Whittefield and his wife, were living in the capital city of Washington DC. The community there wasn't any more friendly to me than they were in Fairhaven. I felt I was an embarrassment to the Whittefields.' Mung paused, deciding not to mention that his foster father was in government service or that John was in the Naval Academy. 'My adopted brother was studying in the university. Word came of a gold strike in California and I heard of an opening for a second mate on a steamer bound for Panama. From there, with many others heading for the gold fields, I travelled to San Francisco. I also thought I might find a Japanese wife there. Instead I met Raphael DeSylva. He mistook me for Chinese because many of them are shipped from Canton as cheap labourers. He wanted me to work for him on a gold claim. Raphael had barely enough money to pay for the claim. He was looking for a partner to share the expenses of equipment and food. I had the money but was cautious about offering to be his partner before I knew what kind of man he was. We agreed I would watch his horse, cook the food he bought, and share his tent outside of town until he found a partner. The big Mexican was very friendly and good company.

177

Each day I went with him into San Francisco.

'On the fifth day, Raphael went into a casino and I was standing by the horse. Crowds of people moved up and down the street – teamsters shouting at their animals, Mexican caballeros sitting on prancing horses, Americans in buckskin, and immigrants wearing their native dress from countries all over the world. Two men, my former shipmates, stood out like a red dragon kite against a blue sky – the giant Pistchiani and the short bald-headed Black Ben. The two were walking down the opposite side of the street. "Town-ho!" I shouted, and ran to meet them. We were laughing and pounding each other on the back but I glanced over in time to see someone trying to untie Raphael's saddlebag from his horse. I leapt off the high pavement and ran over, demanding to know what he was doing, and another man jumped me from behind. All this in broad daylight. I used a jujitsu shoulder roll, bending forward and throwing him to the ground. The thief at the saddlebag sprang at me and I went over backwards. I pulled my knees up as I fell, put my feet in his stomach, and flipped him far behind me. I came to my feet in time to see him draw a knife from his belt, but in the next second he was running away, screaming in pain. Pistchiani had snapped his arm like a stick. I turned to see the first one also fleeing.

'Black Ben smiled at me and said, "If you had only known how to fight like that in Hawaii, your nose wouldn't be so bent."

'Raphael had come out of the casino with others to see the fight. I introduced him to my friends. He and Pistchiani were almost the same size. When they shook hands, a look passed between them of men who know they are going to be friends. Since Ben and I weren't allowed in most bars, we all sat on the pavement drinking whisky. Before we finished the first jug, we were playing with the idea of a four-way partnership. By the time we were halfway through the second, I remember agreeing to put up all my money to cover part of Ben and Pistchiani's shares. They had lost most of theirs playing poker. The last I remember was sitting with them on the high wooden pavement, swinging our legs. I was trying to teach them to sing the Peach Blossom song in Japanese and became annoyed when they could not pronounce the words. I awoke tied belly down over the saddle of a walking horse, feeling as if my life was ending. The horse smelled bad and jounced me up and down as he walked. I must have spoken because Raphael brought his horse around to ride next to me.

'He had a big, toothy smile. Slapping his chest, he said, 'Don't you say thank you to your new partner for sobering you up Mexican style?' I moaned and he said, 'You're an ungrateful Japanese who sings like a fart. Look at your two friends. They don't complain.'

'Behind my horse, and hanging over their saddles in the same position as me, were Pistchiani and Ben. Ben fitted over the horse as I did, but Pistchiani's head and legs almost touched the ground.

'"Mung," Raphael said, "you introduced me to two good people. They know how to enjoy themselves just like me. If we'd stayed in San Francisco any longer with your friends and your money, we would lose both."

'That day Raphael cooked breakfast and dinner for all of us. We grumbled and shaded our eyes from the sun as we moved north. It seemed to anyone who saw us that we were a most diverse and unsuited group to be partners, but they were mistaken. Our camp along the river became an evening meeting-place for other prospectors. If people didn't come to us, we walked to wherever we heard singing and were always welcomed. We found some gold, and the times around the campfires, swapping stories after panning and sluicing all day, were among the best I have known.

'At first there weren't many people along the river, but they soon came pouring into the gold area from all over the world. Fights and thefts increased. Walking between camps became dangerous after dark. Work time on the river was reduced because we had to stand guard. Sometimes, at night, shots could be heard echoing through the hills.

'It was about four in the morning when it happened. Pistchiani and I were on guard. He was sitting on a camp stool in front of his tent. Ben and Raphael were asleep. I sat on the ground, my back against Raphael's saddle. The first shot came from behind my tent.

I felt the impact as the bullet hit the saddle and I rolled over on the ground, frightened but unhurt. My rifle fell. I reached for it and another bullet tore up the ground near my head, throwing dirt in my face. I rolled over and pulled out the four-barrel pistol you found in the box.' Mung looked at Ryochi. 'It's one of the newest, a gift from Mr Whittefield when I went to California.'

Ryochi gestured for the story to continue.

'Pistchiani came around the tent firing both barrels of his shotgun in the direction of the muzzle flash. There was a loud scream and shooting erupted from all around us. I heard Pistchiani grunt twice, then turn to face the muzzle blasts. He took careful aim with an over-and-under pistol, and fired, walking stiff-legged straight into the blazing guns. I fired four shots at the muzzle blast. The shooting stopped from that side, but Pistchiani fell like a tall tree. Ben rushed out of the back of his tent with a short French muzzle-loader packed with shot, meant for repelling boarders on ship. He fired at the shadows amongst the trees and we heard more screams of pain. Ben turned to run around to our side of the tent when a double load of buckshot tore him in half. Raphael had emptied both his double-barrelled pistols. He picked up my rifle from in front of the tent and charged into the brush. We heard the raiders shouting and cursing as they withdrew. Raphael returned after he was sure the perimeter of the camp was safe. Ben and Pistchiani were dead.

'Raphael and I each loaded two pistols, Pistchiani's shotgun, and Ben's blunderbuss, and headed upstream after the raiders. Before long we heard moaning and cursing in the morning quiet.

'One of them cried out, "Don't leave me!"

'"Shut up or we will!" his friend shouted.

'I suggested to Raphael that we cross the river to get ahead of them. Moving quietly over the boulders, we forded the stream and went easily up an old trail paralleling the river for about a mile, then recrossed. Raphael said we must get them close, very close, and he chose the spot. We could hear them long before they were in sight. Raphael carefully explained his plan. We laid out the weapons on the rocks, out of sight but close at hand, and our ambush was ready. Raphael had judged correctly, four of them were heading right between us. The man helping his badly wounded companion seemed unhurt. The other two had minor wounds.

'One of them whined, "I told you it was bad luck to bushwack a Chink."

'Another shouted, "If you goddamn well had shot all the bastards, you wouldn't look like that!"

'Raphael fired first. The man wasn't ten feet from me when the buckshot hit him in the side. The blast picked him up and he sprawled at my feet. I fired Ben's musket and the other pistols until they were empty. When I stopped firing, the echoes continued down through the hills, the gunsmoke hanging in a little cloud around us. Only one of the raiders was alive, on his knees begging not to be shot.

'Raphael ran out and dragged him upright by his shirt front. He shouted in the man's face, over and over, 'Do you know me?

'Rattling and shaking the man like a chicken until he began to blubber and answered, "No, no, I don't know you."

'Raphael shouted, "Then why do you want to kill me? Why did you kill Pistchiani? I bet you didn't know him either." The big Mexican sobbed. He kept shaking that raider. "Did you know Ben? Did you know Ben? He was my partner, that little black bastard!" Tears streamed down Raphael's cheeks into his moustache. "I loved them," he shouted, and pulled the man towards him until their noses almost touched. Both were weeping. So was I. "How can you kill someone you don't know?" Raphael asked. "What's your name?" Shaking him. "Your name, what is your name?"

'"Holkee," the raider answered. "My name is Holkee."

'And Raphael stuck his knife into Holkee's belly, turning it up into his heart.

'He stood for a while over the dead man, then waved his arms at the trees and sky. "The fun's gone from here," he said.

'I felt the same. Before either of us could move, we were surrounded by armed men. Thrown to the ground, kicked and punched.

'"A fucking big Mex and a shit-faced Chinaman killing decent white people," the head of the Vigilantes shouted at us. "It's time for some gold-field justice. We'll hold court here and now, then decide which way to kill this Roman Catholic papist and heathen Chinee."

'They would have too, if not for older hands along the river who came by and identified us. Raphael told the Vigilantes we would take care of the dead men and they left us. We didn't talk much. I helped lay the four bodies side by side near a big rock. I painted the word "Raiders" on the stone with their blood. Returning to camp, we found three more dead men in the woods. We hung them from trees near the river so they could be seen, then buried Pistchiani and Ben almost where they fell, side by side.

'We sold the gold claim with the graves marked as a cemetery and got rid of everything else. Ben, we knew, didn't have a family. We sent a letter to Sag Harbor, New York to contact anyone from Pistchiani's family. Raphael decided he wanted to be with his people in Los Angeles. We divided the money into three parts, a third for each of us and a third in a bank for Pistchiani's family.

'It was just outside of San Francisco, the last night Raphael and I were together, that I decided to come home to Japan. There was nothing for me anywhere else. My adopted brother was married. My two closest friends were dead. I wasn't accepted in the societies of Washington DC, Fairhaven or even the gold fields. I knew my decision was right, no matter what. It was like a stone lifted from my heart.'

It was already dark but Mung's eyes met Ryochi's and held them. He saw agreement there. How could he know Ryochi was also risking his life to return to Japan. Mung and his captor were sailing the same craft of destiny in treacherous seas.

Ryochi got up and motioned Mung to follow him. When they had gone a short way, in a more dignified form of the language, Ryochi said, 'Your treatment of those who killed your friends was just. That Raphael must have the soul of a Japanese.'

It was thirty-four days before a messenger came from the Satsuma

Court to the village of Nakagusuku. He showed his credentials to Ryochi Okuda, handed over a packet and retreated to wait outside the hut. Ryochi knelt at his writing desk, the packet before him unopened. He stared at the heavy rice-paper envelope with the red seal and black insignia of the Satsuma Lord Nariakira. Then he reached out, hefted the package in his hand, breathed deeply, and ripped it open. There were two letters inside.

The first was brief and Ryochi sucked wind through his teeth as he read,

To Ryochi Okuda, Prefect at Nakagusuku, Ryuku Island.
You will perform your duty as it should have been done. The execution of Mung will take place out of sight of all peoples. You are allowed the honourable path only if it takes place immediately after Mung's execution, away from all eyes save this courier who will act as witness. You will follow his instructions implicitly.
Signed, Sakuma Shozan, Satsuma.

The second letter contained official notification transferring the authority of prefect to Tsunajiro.

Ryochi summoned the messenger. In a flat, emotionless voice, he said, 'What are the instructions from Satsuma?'

'Prepare yourself and the prisoner,' the messenger answered. He pointed to the skiff outside the hut. 'Have it put into the water. You will perform the deed at sea.'

As if in a trance, Ryochi nodded. He sent his houseboy to summon Tsunajiro and have Mung brought back from the work party in the fields. After informing Tsunajiro of his promotion, Ryochi officially transferred the duties of Prefect of Nakagusuku to him. Then he ordered the boat taken down to the beach and his hut cleaned in preparation for a last tea ceremony which Tsunajiro would serve. He went to bathe.

After the bath, dressed in his finest robe, Ryochi found Tsunajiro waiting, prepared to begin the ceremony. According to ritual, a simple vase stood on the low lacquered table in the centre of the

183

room. Its contents, three different sprigs of flowers, were cut to three lengths, the tallest representing heaven; the shortest earth; and the third, man who stands between both.

Ryochi sat at the table, nodded his head and Tsunajiro knelt. He shook a little bell, its tinkling sound signalling the start of the ceremony. He measured the tea into a cup, poured hot water, and leaned back on his heels to watch it brew.

Ryochi looked around the room. It had been dusted but not too meticulously. If I was returning, he thought, Tsunajiro would have had it cleaned properly. Maybe I'll just come back and haunt the stupid bastard. He looked at his beloved tea set, incense burner, hanging scroll of Mount Fuji, and sighed. I have to leave everything to him anyway.

He accepted the cup from the outstretched hands of his junior and, in the formal manner, each slow movement dictated by tradition, drank the thick hot tea.

Tsunajiro rang the bell again to end the ceremony, and accompanied Ryochi from the house. Outside he handed the former prefect his two swords. Ryochi placed them in his *obi*. 'Whatever is mine is now and forever yours,' Ryochi said.

'Hai, noble samurai,' Tsunajiro responded.

Ryochi Okuda threw back his shoulders, raised his head, and strode down to the beach on bowed legs. He laughed to himself. I wish I could will you my death sentence, Tsunajiro you stupid bastard!

At four in the afternoon the three men were pushed off from shore in the skiff. Mung, as yet unaware of the orders from Satsuma, rowed out to sea.

A while later, the courier addressed Ryochi. 'In your report you stated that this boat can sail. Have you seen it do so?'

Ryochi shook his head. 'No. I only repeated what the prisoner said.'

'Then tell him to sail it.'

Ryochi gave the order and Mung fixed the mast in place. He took the sail from its locker and raised it. Quickly the wind caught the canvas and the boat began to move. Mung drew the sail tighter and

184

the skiff heeled over slightly, picking up speed. Her graceful hull made a swishing sound through the water as droplets flew by.

The messenger sat near Mung at the tiller and asked, 'Are all western craft this fast?'

'No,' Mung answered. 'Some are slower. Others, because of the amount of sail and the hull design, are faster.'

'How close to the wind can this boat come?'

'Not quite directly into the wind, about two points off. That is the closest any boat can go into the wind except a steamboat which moves without sail.'

'Do you know about steamboats?'

'I know what their capabilities are, but I don't know about the workings of the engines.'

Ryochi listened in a disconnected way to the conversation between Mung and the courier. He had come to like Mung and his stories about America, Hawaii, and especially whaling. Ah, Ryochi thought, I would have liked to travel with him. Then he began to think about his duty. If I have him kneel with his head over the side, one stroke with the two-handed sword and it will all be over, painless. His head will fall into the sea. If I kneel on the bench near the transom, place my knife here, he touched a point just below his waist, and cut quickly, I can fall in the sea and this messenger will not report that I screamed like a woman. He laughed dryly to himself. I have no experience at committing suicide and if I am good at it, who can I tell?

Hearing the messenger interrogating Mung about whaling, Ryochi became interested in the answers. The questions were quite intelligent, yet the courier was foolish. The mountains in the north of Ryuku Island could no longer be seen. When he and Mung were dead, the messenger would have to sail the skiff back alone. He did not look like a seafarer or one who could handle this foreign craft. Ah, that's his problem. Mine are all over. Ryochi stood up and said, 'There's been too much talking! Mung, you knew the law when you returned to Japan! Now it is your time to die!'

Mung stared at the shining blade of the sword as it cleared Ryochi's scabbard, catching the last rays of the setting sun on its

185

polished surface. 'What happened? Why now?'

Ryochi shrugged. 'It's really not important why. It's the way things have to be.' He motioned to the bench by the tiller. 'Kneel there with your head over the side and don't move. I want to make this as painless as possible and the rocking of this boat won't help.'

Mung had let go of the tiller. The boat lay dead in the water, canvas sail flapping. The three men were silent. Mung climbed up on the bench. Kneeling, he looked over the side and saw his reflection in the dark green water.

'If it's any consolation, I'll be following you,' Ryochi said. 'This one,' he nodded at the messenger, 'will try to sail back alone.'

The courier stood up quickly, lost his balance and almost fell overboard. Then, using the imperative and a higher form of Japanese to the superior-ranking Ryochi, he ordered, 'Sheathe your sword and sit down!'

The former prefect of Nakagusuku drew himself up. 'Why do you speak to me like that? Where do you get the authority to cancel an order of Sakuma Shozan?'

'Listen to him!' Mung shouted at Ryochi. 'Don't argue!'

Ryochi snapped at Mung, 'Silence! He doesn't know his place! He is speaking to a Satsuma samurai!'

The messenger reached up and pulled off the rag turban he wore as a sign of his profession. He tilted his head, displaying the topknot of hair drawn forward over the shaved front portion of his scalp. This was a coiffure reserved only for aristocrats. 'The letter from Sakuma Shozan directs you to follow my instructions implicitly, and I tell you there will be no death here today! Sheathe your sword!'

Ryochi remained standing, his legs braced against the rocking motion of the boat. 'What are you saying?' he growled.

Mung screamed, 'We're saved! You don't have to kill me! You don't have to kill yourself!'

Ryochi looked down at Mung. 'Silence! You don't know your place either!'

The messenger shouted, 'Look at me! They say you spent time at the Satsuma Court not too long ago. Did you not see me with

Sakuma Shozan? I am his most senior student, Yoshida Torajiro.'

Ryochi leaned closer, staring at the younger man's face. The boat rocked and he lost his balance. Grabbing for the slack sail, he missed and plopped down in the bottom, the naked sword resting between his legs.

'It was left to my discretion to see if this hammernose Mung was less than you indicated in your report,' Yoshida said. 'If so I was to see him beheaded and you commit *seppuku*. And now,' he turned to Mung, 'we sail for a point fifteen miles off Naha to rendezvous with a larger vessel waiting to take us to Kagoshima.'

Ryochi leaned over the side and retched until his stomach emptied into the sea. He slumped back again to the bottom of the boat. Mung felt his own arms and legs twitching as he steered according to Yoshida's directions, and thanked all the gods under his breath.

Two weeks later they were towed into Kagoshima harbour under cover of darkness. During the fortnight of their journey, Yoshida questioned Mung thoroughly. Upon landing, Mung and Ryochi were sent to a shack on a lonely spit at the southern tip of the harbour. The skiff was buried in a sand dune.

A report was sent to Sakuma Shozan by Yoshida Torajiro. It read,

Sir
The haste with which I forward this report can be seen in its lack of organization. Mung spoke most freely when I wasn't writing down everything he said. I decided to let the conversations wander amongst the subjects which are most important to us. His knowledge about whaling is impressive, but it would take a master fisherman to correctly estimate its value. I've written down what he said about seamanship without understanding. I have tried to remember all those questions we discussed so many times. I humbly request you excuse the limitations of my knowledge.

The United States is a large country with few people in

relation to its land mass. The government encourages people who are not wanted in other countries to come to America and work the land. They are often given free land if they farm it. The immigrants come mostly from Europe.

The man who discovered America made a mistake and thought he was in India. Therefore, the natives are called Indians. They are primitive people, nomads who do not value the land. The Americans value land as much as money, sometimes more. Americans are very industrious and daring. Business is an honourable profession and men train their sons for it. Because most Americans came from other countries and the government was only formed about seventy years ago, it is difficult to describe a national character. The feeling of freedom is infectious and people who were serfs can aspire to be anything they desire. There are no class distinctions and all men stand equal before the law. People walk straight and are proud to call themselves Yankees which is another name for Americans.

Meat of pigs, cows, sheep, and fowl are considered delicacies. Horses and dogs are kept for work and pets. Horse is sometimes eaten, but dog is only eaten in time of famine. Gold and silver are used for money, not rice. Rice is imported from China. Bread is eaten as we eat rice.

Drinking whisky is restricted to men, considered manly except by religious people who detest drinking and those who drink. The religious people often stand outside the taverns and sing songs to charm the drinkers away from their cups. They are usually not successful and are sometimes beaten soundly about the head and shoulders for their efforts. Many have dyspepsia from drinking whisky which is also used for medicine and has opium in it. That is why it is called medicine. Religious people are allowed to drink medicine. Payment is made to a doctor for each medical treatment, not as in Japan where a semi-annual fee covers treatments for all illnesses.

People living in towns whose laws are strictly enforced are

law-abiding, polite, and keep their towns clean. If someone breaks the law, the people are gathered and a vote taken to determine his guilt. The majority rules and everyone abides by the vote. Where there are no laws, violence is common and sanitation disregarded. Goats, sheep, pigs, cows, and fowl are allowed to wander about and slops are thrown out of windows. Guns are common. The pistol found amongst Mung's belongings is called a Christian Sharps and the four revolving barrels are of the most advanced design. Christian is the name of the man who made the gun and has no connection to religion.

The people are clean but take cold showers or bathe in warm water which would not be satisfactory to a Japanese. A Japanese bath is too hot for white skin.

When a gentleman meets a lady, he takes off his hat and says, 'How do you do?' The lady always answers, 'Fine, thank you,' even when she is ill. When two men meet, they hold right hands. Smoking big cigars is a sign of wealth and prosperity. Women do not smoke. Most shops have glass windows to display their goods and glass in the door so people can see who is in the shop. All except the poor have glass windows in their homes. This is why Mung brought a piece of glass with him. He never heard of glass in Japan.

Americans build bigger and faster ships than anyone in the world, and they are better whalers too. Time and calendars are based on the sun. There are twenty-four periods in a day, each divided into sixty units. The opposite of our calendar, their months have names and their years have numbers. They have the same number of months in the year as we do. It is considered important to be on time. Many people carry time-pieces. Americans like to build machines which do the work while they watch. They build machines for pulling carriages, pushing boats, working wool, and cutting trees into boards. When a man desires to marry, he looks at a girl. If she pleases him and if he pleases her, they both speak with their parents. If all agree, they go to the church and bring friends from each side of the family as witnesses. The priest asks them questions aloud and they answer so all can hear. After the marriage, the woman must please the man. Most families are happy, loving, and industrious. Americans like to sing and they honour musicians highly. They do not like to be seen when they sleep and retire to a special sleeping room. Every house has sleeping rooms. They sleep on raised platforms and cover themselves even when fully clothed or in warm weather so if anyone comes in they won't be seen sleeping. Toilets are either beautiful ceramic-ware which are placed under the bed and emptied first thing in the morning, or a shack built over a hole in the ground enclosing a seat with a hole. It is considered a good place for contemplation and reading.

The major holiday celebrates the birth of a man who became a saint and started Christianity. They also celebrate the new year, spring planting, autumn harvesting, and, in the summer, the war which freed them from the British seventy years ago. On that day, men take weapons from the armoury and march around to music while the crowd cheers. Later there are contests of strength for the men, cooking for the women, and games for the children. Everybody eats too much on this day and the women are told they shouldn't have cooked so much and so well, but this pleases them. At the end of the day the guns are returned to the armoury and locked up for another year.

Horses and oxen pull the farmers around to spread seeds because the fields are so large. Businessmen form groups to pool their money for a large enterprise. It costs about three thousand five hundred pieces of gold to build a whaling ship. The instruments Mung brought with him are standard equipment for offshore sailing vessels. They are used to tell time, the ship's position, and its speed. One quart of whale oil is sold for one dollar. The western whaling ships only want the blubber covering the body of the whale, the oil in its head, and certain bones which they use for umbrellas and corsets.

The meat, which we consider a delicacy and represents the major weight of the carcass, is cut loose and allowed to sink.

Women are chaste, kind, and beautiful. Those who choose to be prostitutes are shunned by respectable men during the day. Gentlemen always arrange visits at night so they won't be seen. Prostitutes stay in certain areas and respectable women never speak to them.

Americans believe freedom is good and should be given to all people. They say all people are equal, but Americans are best. The government buys land to expand the United States as they did in Louisiana from the French, and in Panama from the Spanish. Sometimes they take land as they did from the English in Canada, and the Spanish in Texas and California. Many Americans live there since gold was found. The Mexican government lost a war to the United States recently and ceded five hundred thousand square miles of land. This gives the Americans access to the Pacific Ocean. The treaty was signed three years ago.

The Hawaiian Islands are ruled by a king. He is greatly influenced by missionaries and businessmen from America, England, and Europe. Whaling ships rest in Honolulu in great numbers. Most of them are American. The weather is moderate most of the year, the natives pleasant and peaceful. Western sailors use the islands as a playground and call it paradise because they are not bound by too many laws and think their god does not see sin on these islands. Syphilis was brought to Hawaii by the western seamen so the missionaries built two hospitals to care for the sick. The natives could not read so the missionaries built schools and brought fine teachers. The natives live in huts but are learning from the white man to build houses of wooden planks. The natives are the world's most accomplished swimmers on and under the water. They often harvest shellfish from the sea floor at great depths. There are many unusual and exotic fruits on the islands. Sugar cane is grown by contract labour brought from China, working on plantations owned by Europeans and

191

Americans. Natives who are not baptized are indifferent to their nakedness. Those who have been baptized are ashamed to be seen naked.

Japanese fishermen lost in storms, rescued, and brought to Hawaii are well fed and clothed, but must live in a special compound which is locked after evening roll call. As the foster son of Captain Whittefield, Mung had complete freedom of movement. Whalers believe Japanese are primitive people who kill all who land on their shores or cook and eat them. There are many tales of islands in the Pacific inhabited by cannibals.

Protestant and Catholic Christians don't like each other when they discuss religion, but otherwise work well together. Latin is taught in Protestant schools but is not used in their liturgy by the priests. Latin is not taught in the Catholic schools but is used in the liturgy. Mung denies ever being influenced by Christians and there are no signs to the contrary. According to the prefect, Ryochi Okuda, he ordered Mung to dance on a symbol of Christianity and bury it in a dung heap. He says Mung did this without a moment's hesitation. Along with this scroll are detailed charts of the harbours of Honolulu and Fairhaven, Massachusetts drawn by Mung. His memory and talent with a brush are exceptional. I have penned in some explanations to better orient the viewer, as Mung learned cartography from his adopted father. Mung knows about western incursions in China and about the Opium Wars.

He is an exceptional young man. His memory is only one facet of his intellectual ability. His only desire is to return to Japan, honour his father's name, marry, and live quietly among his own people. He was well schooled by his father until the age of nine. He was educated partially on board the whaling ship which rescued him and then for three years in a secondary school in the United States. He served as an officer and then captained a whaler for another three years. Whales have become scarcer and the demand for oil stronger, which is why we see more western ships off our coast searching for the giant fish. It is my belief that Mung could never return to his former life-style in a small fishing village, but he is most suited for your project.

Ryochi poses no problem and is a good companion for Mung. I await your instructions.

Your humble student, Yoshida Torajiro.

CHAPTER
10

Three weeks later, two master shipbuilders and twenty carpenters brought with them six leather-bound books and orders to Yoshida Torajiro from Sakuma Shozan. 'Build a whaling ship based on western designs.'

Sailmakers, iron workers, rope and barrel makers, arrived at Kagoshima daily, with apprentices and tools. Yoshida became so involved with the housing coordination and administration of men and materials, he appointed Ryochi to act as liaison between Mung and those of superior rank with whom the former fisherman had to work.

Mung knelt on the mat floor of the isolated hut and stared at the books on the low writing desk in front of him. One was an ancient Portuguese shipbuilding manual written in Latin, which he had learned in high school. Four others were detailed instructions for building a brig, a sloop, a bark and a whaler, all written in Dutch. The last was a shipbuilding manual in English with a brief description of constructing a whaler.

Ryochi sat across the room. He had been watching Mung closely. 'If you don't build that boat, we'll both lose our heads.'

Mung looked at him with a blank stare, his lower jaw hanging loose.

Ryochi jumped to his feet, stomped on the floor and shouted, 'Don't give me that dumb look! You have the books! Read them!'

Mung's mouth was dry, his tongue thick. 'But I don't know Dutch.' He waved at the books. 'I don't even know where to begin.'

'If they gave you Dutch books, then they'll get you a translator. We have two master shipbuilders who will tell you where to begin. It is the size of the ship, the purpose for which it's built, and the principles of how it's moved through the water by those special sails they don't understand.'

Mung stood and looked at Ryochi, the emptiness leaving his eyes. 'I can get a translator?'

Ryochi smiled and his head bobbed up and down. He really did not know if it were possible but he had to stop Mung from going into shock.

Mung began to pace the hut. 'I'll learn Dutch,' he said. 'It's the only way.'

Ideas came to him in a jumble. Impressions began to crowd his mind. He cleared his writing desk and sat crosslegged, back straight. He placed charcoal sticks and paper in front of him. Then, closing his eyes and using a form of meditation his father had taught him, Mung concentrated on the centre of his forehead. Unconsciously his fingers grasped the charcoal as memories of his five years aboard two whalers and summers spent working with John Whittefield in the Fairhaven shipyard rushed into his thoughts. He saw the dry dock clearly. And a keel with curved ribs supported by wooden beams. He could even picture different kinds of wood and buckets of varnish, oil and tar. His brow creased. Ryochi was right. These details were unimportant. The master shipbuilders would know.

Freed of the encumbrance of specifics, his mind raced ahead, focusing on the ship itself. He floated around it from stem to stern, topgallant to keel, inside and out. He could see it all.

At three in the morning, there was no more paper. Ryochi was asleep. Drawings lay scattered over the earthen floor. Mung looked at them for the first time with conscious eyes. They were strangely familiar and he knew he had drawn them. He stood stifflegged, then gathered the drawings and piled them on the desk. He would have to examine each one and put them in some kind of order.

With permission of the guard, he walked alone along the beach. He bent down and cupped his hands. Sifting sand through his fingers, he listened to the gentle lapping of the ocean waters.

I've come home and am still alive. If I can build this ship and captain her, I might be able to restore some honour to my family. He tried to keep thoughts of his mother out of his mind. She was not young. She might have died in the ten years since he left her. But there was no way of knowing without exposing himself as a returnee to the authorities of the Shōgun. He began to tremble, perspiration beaded his face and tears streamed down his cheeks.

He looked up at the pale moon and said aloud, 'God, if I finish this ship and then die, I will not complain for I have been allowed to return home. However many days I will have, my life is dedicated to the Emperor and Japan.'

Mung and Ryochi were moved into a house with Yoshida, next to the shipyard. Restricted to the town but no longer guarded, they worked outside by the light of the sun, and in their quarters by candlelight. During the hour immediately following their evening meal, Yoshida began teaching Mung the Dutch language. Mung soon realized that Yoshida lacked certain basic grammatical concepts which were familiar to him because of his background in Latin and English. In the following months, Yoshida taught him the spoken language and he became the teacher of written Dutch.

Mung began his construction project by describing to the master shipbuilders and carpenters the size of the craft they were setting out to erect. On the beach he marked off three lengths in the sand – sixty feet for the stern mast, eighty feet for the foremast and one hundred and twenty feet for the mainmast. The craftsmen were overwhelmed by the enormity of the enterprise. Mung used brush, paper and ink to draw a picture of the whaler. This caused more confusion as he sketched in the stern and the location of the three masts.

For some minutes they gazed at the picture and the marks in the sand. Then senior shipbuilder Yokumbora said, 'Since the Exclusion Edict it has been forbidden to build a ship with a closed stern, or with more than one mast. Although we haven't ever built a ship with multiple masts, the knowledge has been passed down in our families.' He pointed to Mung's sketch. 'This will never work. Not even with a single mast and the new type of sail. The craft will spin around on the water like a top.'

'That is because you are thinking of the traditional flat-bottomed junk. We are going to adopt a western invention called a keel. The sides of the craft will be rounded. Of lapstrake construction.'

There was the sound of whistling breath being sucked in through the teeth. The shipwrights bowed their heads and remained silent.

'Command us and we will carry out your instructions,' Yokumbora said.

'That's not enough,' Mung answered. 'I've never built a boat. You men are experts. I've seen this kind of ship built. I've spent years sailing them. I can read about it. But I need your experience and advice.'

There was a visible relaxation of tension as the craftsmen realized that the young man was earnest, respectful and willing to admit that he was out of his element.

Once again Yokumbora voiced the problem on everyone's mind. 'Even with this keel of yours, a boat with rounded sides and a one hundred and twenty foot mast will turn over on the first ripple.'

Mung snatched his brush and sketched furiously for several minutes, repeating the series of sketches he had done many years before of the unfolding beetle becoming the frame of a whaler. The shipwrights quickly grasped the concept of the frame supported by the keel and the sides attached to the frame but were still unconvinced that a hull with such tall masts, carrying so much sail, would not turn over.

'Follow me please,' Mung said. He led the way over the dunes to the sand spit where he, Yoshida and Ryochi had first landed. Once again the men thought he had taken leave of his senses. Mung went down on all fours and began shovelling sand with his hands, until the outline of a boat was visible. Then all joined in helping to dig up the skiff.

First to sail out with Mung was Yokumbora. To the amazement of everyone on the beach, the skiff didn't turn over. Following

Mung's directions, the senior shipbuilder brought the small boat almost directly into the wind. The craftsmen applauded, bowed in unison, then almost swamped the boat in trying to take a turn. These men, the product of generations of shipbuilders, talked excitedly to Mung with new respect. Later, they prepared endless diagrams of the concept of centring the sail and using the keel as the keystone of the vessel's construction.

The following week Mung and Yokumbora travelled to an ancient forest several miles inland. They spent five days selecting giant oak trees, some as old as Kagoshima itself, for the masts and keel. On their return Mung made cutaway sketches of the ship as it would be when completed, showing three decks, various cabins, holds, hatches and compartments to be built into the hull. These were copied by other artists and distributed to the shipbuilders.

The subject of much conversation and many jokes was the toilets. Mung overheard one of the shipwrights saying, 'What for? Just hang your ass over the side and let go.'

Someone else commented, 'Anyone stupid enough to piss into the wind should be locked in the little shit house for the rest of his life and fed only laxatives.'

Mung, well past his initial feelings of incompetence, was able to enjoy the joking. He continued his project in an efficient manner. He braided several thicknesses of rope, from a heavy hawser to the quarter-inch trailing line for the harpoon, as samples to be duplicated. The hammers of sword-makers and iron workers rang, making hundreds of iron and brass fittings, the razor-sharp flensing tools, and harpoons. Charcoal-makers soaked and sweated beams and planks trimmed by carpenters, until they were pliable enough to be bent and shaped into place.

The Japanese shipwrights digested the principle of western shipbuilding, working with speed, skill and imagination. They used bamboo for a dry dock without nails or spikes. They scaffolded with bamboo lashed together by braided rice stalks. The finished products were exactly to Mung's specifications, the scaffolding as sturdy as he had ever seen.

Since the average Japanese is smaller in stature than an

American, Mung revised the size of sleeping quarters aboard the whaler. He installed a tub-room for hot baths at sea. The keel was soon laid and the first ribs attached. Each day Mung saw an improvement in the organization, distribution and flow of work. Everyone in Kagoshima was involved in the building of the whaler. They were becoming an efficient team which began work at sunrise and finished at dark, seven days a week.

By Lord Nariakira's orders, the town of Kagoshima had been sealed off from the day Mung arrived. Incoming messages and equipment arrived at a station miles away, and were delivered to Kagoshima by special porters. No one else was allowed to enter or leave the town. Therefore, it was three months before word of mysterious doings at Kagoshima reached the Shōgun's palace; another month before two of the Shōgun's spies were caught by Satsuma samurai in the surrounding mountains. To Lord Nariakira, this was taken as another sign of weakness and indecisiveness by the Shōgunate. In times past the Shōgun would have sent a messenger displaying his royal banner to ride the post road with samurai ready to cut down anyone who did not grovel. Now he only sent spies.

The hull of the whaler neared completion. More spies were caught in the hills. If it were officially known that the Satsuma Lord was sponsoring the building of a foreign type of ship that might turn out a failure, he would have defied the Shōgun and lost face. For this he could be ordered to commit *seppuku*. He decided to pay a visit a Kagoshima. By his presence, he hoped to ensure the speedy completion and success of the project.

Mung lay sleeping, a book fallen open on the mat at his side, another held loosely in his hand. He felt himself being rocked and dreamed he was in a hammock on board ship. Someone was shaking him. He reached out with closed eyes for the books and put them on top of each other at the head of his sleeping mat, then struggled to his feet with a moan.

'Ryochi,' he said, 'it's getting more difficult to get up every morning. I feel like my body is standing and my ass is still on the floor.' He heard a short burst of laughter and said, 'Stop your laughing and give me the water.' He felt the lacquered bowl touch his arm, and used both hands to splash the water on his face. Rubbing the sleep from his eyes, he looked up to see Yoshida holding the bowl. Mung asked, 'Where's Ryochi?'

Yoshida reached out with his free hand, turned Mung around, and said, 'Bow to the Lord Nariakira of Satsuma and Sakuma Shozan, senior scholar.'

Mung fell on his knees, then prostrated himself full length on the floor.

'Rise!' Yoshida said.

Mung came to his knees with head bowed, eyes lowered.

The deep sonorous voice of Lord Nariakira ordered him, 'Raise your head!'

The Satsuma Lord wore a light brown robe of fine material with creases like a knife's edge. Two samurai swords were tucked into his *obi*. On each lapel were the symbols of the Satsuma family, a white circle intersected by a white cross on a black background. Under the brown robe was another garment of black, and one more showing just an inch of white which came to a V under a clean strong jaw. The Lord's hair was drawn back into a tight bun. His eyelids did not move as he examined Mung.

Beads of water clung to the young man's face, accentuating his jaw muscles and the deep lines on either side of his bent nose. He was tall for a Japanese, thin and wiry. Mung had lost twenty pounds since he landed in Ryuku.

Lord Nariakira asked, 'Will this ship float?'

Mung was so taken aback by the question that he answered, 'Of course.'

Yoshida sucked wind through his teeth.

Mung began to apologize but was cut short by the next question, 'When?'

'We shall float her in two months and she will be ready for trial runs in October – three months.'

In the same deep even voice, Lord Nariakira said, 'Work these men until the sweat runs out of their sleeves, but cut the time by one month. Yoshida will have the authority to requisition anything

200

or anyone in the realm of Satsuma. Can you do it?'

Mung said, 'The problem is not workers, for we have become a skilled team here. We need thousands of torches to extend the working day by three hours, and helpers to run errands and clean house. More prostitutes are needed. The men waste time waiting for the women when they could be sleeping. If the crew of the ship can be brought in, we can begin training them immediately.'

Lord Nariakira nodded to Yoshida who said, 'I will see to it.'

Sakuma Shozan stood next to his Lord, slightly to the rear. His clothes hung loose and looked heavy for his frail body. His skin crinkled like delicate rice-paper around soft brown eyes, his voice surprisingly powerful for such an old man. 'Mung, I've read the reports by Yoshida and the master shipbuilders that among other things you can do mathematics without an abacus. Is that because of your ability to remember so well?'

'No sir, it was taught to me by the ship's captain who saved my life.'

Sakuma Shozan wet his dry, thin lips and motioned Mung closer. 'Please explain it to me.'

When Mung had done so, just as William Whittefield had demonstrated the concept to him, a smile creased the old scholar's mouth.

'If you memorize by multiples of ten you can project enormous sums,' Mung said. 'The westerners are taught to memorize multiplication tables from the time they are children. Mathematics is used to teach children the discipline of learning. Higher forms of mathematics are learned in schools but never used except in a few specialized professions. On the lintel stone of the entrance to Harvard College is written that no one shall enter who does not know geometry, yet only a handful of the students will ever use it.'

Lord Nariakira spoke. 'It will be arranged for you to instruct a group of teachers from Kagoshima in this new method. They in turn will teach it to a select number of students as an experiment.' Then he turned abruptly and left the house, followed by Sakuma Shozan and Yoshida. There were noises outside the hut, tramping feet, then silence.

Yoshida returned with a big smile. 'Hammer-Nose, we passed inspection. You have pleased the Lord and the scholar of Satsuma all in one day. What more could you want out of life?' He took a porcelain sake bottle from a lacquered cabinet and sat down at the writing desk. 'Come join me, Mung.'

They drank together, then Yoshida said, 'We have to reorganize your schedule. You must begin training the crews and also have time for teaching mathematics.'

'I prefer to teach a group of students first. To experience any problems before I begin with the teachers.'

'Very well. It will be arranged.'

Another student of Sakuma Shozan, more proficient than Yoshida, came to tutor Mung in Dutch. Two full crews and captains were brought for training. Their exercises began after Mung's language lesson in the morning and again after his noon inspection of the shipyard.

A training station was constructed on shore. The crews learned to build and fire try pots, put together pre-cut longboats and barrels, and practised throwing harpoons. They climbed the rigging on stationary masts, set sail, gave signals, and learned the use of block-and-tackle according to orders from below. Mung had two ropes attached to the sides of each mast which were pulled from side to side, swaying the long poles. The crews would later say it was easier to handle sail at sea than ashore. In the longboats they rowed out into the bay, learning to sail, row and harpoon. When periodic storms made the longboats impossible to use, Mung kept the men in the stationary rigging for as long as it blew.

One morning during Mung's Dutch lesson, he was notified that a local fish-watcher had spotted a pod of five whales swimming one mile south of Kagoshima harbour. Three boats were training out on the bay, unaware of the whales. Mung and the captain of the crew on the stationary masts, climbed to the crow's nest. After pointing out to the captain the identifying characteristics of a right whale, Mung had him order his boat crews on alert. They scrambled down the rigging and jumped into longboats. Setting out on their first chase, the anxious seamen pushed off and raised their sails. The remainder of the crew and people on shore ran up the beach for a better view. Townsfolk heard the excitement and came to watch.

Mung, in the lead boat, ordered the conch blown to signal the three boats on the bay. The message received, they raised sail and joined the race out of the harbour.

As the boats passed the sand spit on starboard, one of the whales sent a spout of steam into the air. 'Town-hoooo! She blows, goddamnit, she blows!' Mung shouted, but no one understood him. He looked around, regretting that Pistchiani and Ben weren't there with him.

They closed fast on the pod, approaching, according to Mung's signals, in an inverted fan. As they moved in, the old bull upped flukes and the pod went under. Mung ordered the boats to scatter and attack independently. He and his crew sat in the rocking boat, waiting while the other crews spread out. Twenty minutes passed.

Suddenly the whales broke water behind the three boats closest to the harbour. The chase was on. The pod sounded again but the old bull breached in five minutes, with the three boats closing fast. The harpooner in the lead boat was anxious. He came too close to the flukes and his boat was swamped by the backwash of the tail. The other two closed on either side of the whale. The boat nearest Mung appeared about to ram just before the harpooner let his iron fly, sinking it up to the haft. The old whale shot forward. The harpooner had forgotten to take a turn of the line around the bow block and it zinged out of the first rope barrel. The boat captain at the helm leapt forward. Knocking the harpooner out of his way and overboard, he took a turn around the bow block from the second barrel just before the rope flew out. The boat jumped forward with no one at the tiller, zigzagging through the water after the whale. Suddenly it flipped, dumping the crew out.

The whale ran for five hundred yards, then slowed close to the third boat. Their harpooner buried his iron. The old bull shuddered, and wallowed. The harpooner pulled his boat alongside, drove the lance home and probed with the steel tip, as he had been taught. Deep under the blubber the samurai steel searched for the artery leading to the lungs and a blood red mushroom shot out of the spout hole.

There was a cheer from hundreds of people lining the beach. They had witnessed the first whale taken in what was to become a major industry for Japan. Because Mung had required every boat crew member to pass a swimming test, no one was lost. Spirits were high as the boats towed the whale into the harbour.

Everyone in Kagoshima came down to the beach to see the flensing operations and trying out of the whale. Mung had a good opportunity to learn how the meat was taken from the older fishermen. He sketched the types of block-and-tackle that would be used for the operation. That evening, all the townspeople and workers at the shipyard feasted around open fires on as much whale steak as they could eat. Later, one hundred and eighty casks of oil and two tons of whalebone were put into Lord Nariakira's warehouse for shipment to the Satsuma Court. The lesson was a valuable one for captains and crews and was taken as a good omen by all.

Mung had been teaching the students mathematics for a month and was now ready for the teachers. The supervisor of education arranged a meeting with seven male teachers at the school nearest Mung's quarters. As the teachers filed in, there was a disturbance at the door. Mung looked up and saw the men grouped near the inside wall. He glanced towards the doorway and saw a young woman enter, wearing a luminescent blue kimono and gold brocade *obi* with large pink bow at the back. She was taller than most of the men, and thin. Her head and hips tilted forward like an artist's swift S stroke on paper. When she turned towards him, he saw that her delicate face and lightly coloured cheeks were framed by raven black hair pulled to a tight bun in the back. He could not take his eyes from her. The male teachers drew in their breath, whistling through their teeth, as the young woman pitter-pattered across the mat floor on white stockinged feet to stand in front of Mung.

She bowed politely, raised her head and looked him in the eye. 'My name is Miss Saiyo Ishikawa, sir.'

To Mung, her voice was the sound of bubbling water in a rock garden. He stared at her.

She did not blush, nor did she lower her soft eyes. They opened wider and seemed to draw Mung in. 'I am also a teacher and have a school for girls.' She turned and nodded. 'These are my teachers.'

For the first time, Mung realized there were two other young women behind her.

She looked at him again and said, 'We too would like to learn this new method of teaching mathematics, and request to participate in your lessons.'

Yoshida, standing behind Mung, was shocked to see his friend's head bobbing up and down, saying, 'Yes. Yes. Yes.'

The men teachers began mumbling loud enough to be heard. 'What nerve of women wanting to study with men!'

'Mung,' Yoshida whispered. Then, raising his voice, 'Mung!' Then shouting, 'Mung!'

Finally Mung looked away from the girl.

'Didn't you tell me Lord Nariakira ordered you to teach mathematics as it is taught in America?' Yoshida asked.

'Yes,' Mung mumbled.

'And isn't it true that in America males and females study together, and the majority of teachers are women?' Without waiting for an answer, Yoshida's voice hardened, enunciating every syllable towards the men teachers. 'It is in accordance with Lord Nariakira's wishes that men and women shall study together!' he pronounced.

The men shuffled their feet, looked at each other, then took their places at the writing desks.

Try as he might, Mung was never able to recall that first lesson. Scheduled to meet the teachers twice a week, he became so impatient to see Miss Ishikawa that he rearranged an extra lesson each week. He took to walking through the town in the evenings, supposedly for his health. It neither improved his health nor his disposition for he never met her. He took less interest in food. He began strolling through the town during lunchtime, hoping for a glimpse of her. He literally jumped at the sound of children, thinking it might be her passing by with her students.

On his walks Mung often made comparisons between Japanese and American women. The former moved gracefully. They never shouted in the harsh tones so familiar in American bars, backyards and markets. Western women were hard, large and threatening compared to Saiyo's delicate, gentle manner. He thought often of caressing and making love to her, resulting in increased visits to the ladies of the Willow World at the building site. He emptied himself into their bodies with a vengeance. It served to relieve the pressure in his loins but not the ache in his heart.

He became a tyrant at work, driving the men and himself harder than before, becoming angrier each day as the time approached for the launching which would take him out to sea and away from Kagoshima.

At the end of the final lesson, Miss Ishikawa, who had proved herself a bright and capable student, was last to leave the room. Yoshida sat in his usual place at a desk slightly to the rear of Mung. He watched Mung's head follow the reed-like figure balanced delicately over tiny feet, as she glided heel and toe across the room. Mung noticed her lacquered writing box still on her desk and started to call out, but at the last moment held back the words.

She turned and said, 'Did you call me, sir?'

Mung shook his head, hoping she would not remember the box. To his relief, she went outside. He heard her put on her clogs and walk away. He counted to ten and let out his breath. Then went to the desk and gently picked up the writing box.

He chuckled to himself, 'You're one clever fellow, Mung. Now you can find out where she lives.'

He opened up the box, touched the brushes, and held it to his nose.

'What are you sniffing?' Yoshida asked.

Mung was startled. He held the box out. 'She forgot this. Miss Ishikawa forgot ...'

Yoshida interrupted, 'All right, I'll return it to her.'

Mung quickly withdrew the box. 'No, no. I'll take it back. Do you know where she lives?'

'I can find out.'

'Would you do that now? I wouldn't want her to walk all the way back here.'

'She really is quite intelligent, but she is also ugly,' Yoshida said. 'Too thin, and ugly.'

Mung stared at Yoshida. 'What! What! How can you say she is ugly?'

Yoshida began laughing and talking at the same time, tears streaming down his cheeks. He sank to the floor. 'Look at you. Half the girls in Kagoshima have pulled their kimonos so far back from their necks you can almost see their behinds, just to get your attention, and you fall for a tall, skinny intellectual whose kimono is so tight she will probably strangle.'

Mung pleaded with Yoshida. 'Stop rolling around like that. Get up and find out where she lives before she comes back.' He pulled Yoshida up and shoved him out the door.

In a few minutes, Yoshida returned with directions and a warning, 'Her father is one of those rare, intellectual, old-guard samurais.'

Mung set off down the street with a long sure stride that withered to a shuffle by the time he reached the Ishikawa house. He stood outside the gate, watching shadows moving back and forth inside. Someone came out of the house next door.

Mung quickly opened the gate, walked up to the front door, and called out, 'Mr Ishikawa.' He saw the shadows stop moving; then one approached the door.

It slid open and a tall, slightly bent, elderly man said, 'Yes? Why is it you call?'

'Your daughter forgot her brushes at school,' Mung said.

Mr Ishikawa examined Mung more closely. 'I don't know you. Which of my three daughters are you referring to?'

'Miss Saiyo.'

'Oh, you mean the eldest. Are you a fellow student?'

'No, I am her teacher in the evening.'

Mung did not see the smile in the old man's eyes nor pick up the inflection in his voice when he said, 'What are you teaching my daughter in the evening?'

'Mathematics. The western method of memorization.'

Saiyo's father said, 'Come in and have tea. Your hand must be tired from holding the box, and it must have been a long walk.'

Mung heard the patter of feet, hushed whispers, and giggling behind the *shoji* screen door to the next room. He sat with Mr Ishikawa and did not know what to say. He began examining a beautifully shaped bonsai about twelve inches tall. The dwarfed maple tree sat in a tray no larger than six inches in circumference and two inches deep. The gnarled trunk tapered up to exquisitely trimmed branches spreading delicate red leaves.

Mr Ishikawa said, 'It has been in my family for 120 years.'

'It is good to keep the family name by passing on things from generation to generation.'

'Yes, but I have only daughters. The family name will end with me.'

Mung remained silent. The door slid open and an older woman entered to serve tea. Mr Ishikawa introduced his house servant. Mung looked behind the servant, watching the door, then realized Mr Ishikawa was looking at the writing box and the servant was staring at him. He handed up the box with a mumbled explanation.

Mr Ishikawa said, 'My daughter has told me of this new method of mathematics. Do you think it is better?'

With his eyes darting towards the door, hoping Saiyo might enter, Mung answered, 'Both systems have their advantages. The Japanese student can learn to do more complicated formulas in less time with the abacus. The western student does his calculations on paper and can recheck his figures to find out where he went wrong.'

They talked for some time about American education before it dawned on Mung that he had stayed too long and was not going to see Saiyo. He regretfully bid Mr Ishikawa farewell.

Mung worked his men fifteen hours a day, seven days a week. He often slept on the whaler. No one could talk to Mung without him looking cross or snapping back an answer. He was most often found on the quarterdeck looking towards town, hoping to catch a glimpse of Miss Saiyo Ishikawa.

Finally, at the end of September 1851, the first commercial whaler in the history of Japan was prepared for launching. Shinto priests and Buddhist monks proffered blessings and incantations. The signal was given, chocks knocked out, and the *Shinto Maru* slid down the way to bury her stern deep into the water. The entire town and all the workers sent her off with a roaring cheer. The big ship heaved up and the crowd hushed as she rocked back and forth, men swinging from the rigging high up the hundred-foot mast.

Sakuma Shozan represented Lord Nariakira at the ceremony. He stood beside Mung on the platform with other local dignitaries, watching the ship rock violently from side to side. 'Will it capsize?' he asked.

'No. Our workers can be matched with the best in the world, and the ship will sail in much rougher seas than what you have just witnessed.'

'Then it's complete.'

The crowd roared louder than before as the whaler settled down and the Satsuma ensign, on twenty yards of silk, was run up the mainmast.

Mung said, 'We must have sea trials to learn how she handles. Each boat, even when made from the same design by the same men, is different. After the trial runs, we'll take her on a shakedown cruise.'

Mung was the only one in Kagoshima who was unhappy. The launching of the *Shinto Maru* meant he would have to stay aboard. He could not trust anyone else with the responsibility of the ship until their training was complete. His orders were to instruct both crews at the same time.

He turned to Sakuma Shozan. 'When I return, would it be possible for me to visit my village to see if my aged mother still lives, and to honour the grave of my father?'

The old scholar pursed his lips, and his eyes softened. 'I read Yoshida's report when you landed here in Kagoshima. I sent a confidential agent to your village of Nakanohama, but have received no word. It is possible a band of outlaw *ronin* have killed him. There are many unemployed samurai turned bandit roaming the empire. Know this, if you were to return now, it would mean your death. You have been out of our country. Only in Satsuma are you safe.'

Mung nodded listlessly. He bowed as the senior scholar of Satsuma left the platform.

On the whaler, initial exercises for the two crews were held in the harbour. They drilled well but Mung became melancholy. He took to his quarters except during the training, rarely spoke, and then only regarding the crew, ship, or drills. The crews' execution of orders were implemented so well that he grudgingly guided the *Shinto Maru* out of the harbour and into the ocean for open sea trials. It should have been a time of joy and triumph as the new whaler breasted the ocean rollers and beat her way out of Kagoshima harbour on to the high seas, but it increased the distance from Saiyo Ishikawa and the depth of his depression.

Once a shipboard routine was established, Mung took to his cabin and stayed there. The *Shinto Maru* sailed one hundred miles straight out from Kagoshima. The helmsman's orders were to steer away if any sail was sighted. Boat drills, rigging, and block-and-tackle exercises were continued. Two whales were sighted but the longboats never came close enough to throw a harpoon. Mung took to his bunk and refused to eat. When they returned to the coast, he ordered the drills continued outside the harbour.

The senior captain took it on himself to send a longboat ashore. It returned with Yoshida Torajiro. Upon boarding the ship, the young samurai went directly to the galley. He carried a bowl of steaming fish soup mixed with cracked wheat into Mung's cabin. Yoshida found his friend lying in the bunk, staring at the ceiling. Mung tried to ignore him, turning his face to the wall, but Yoshida reached out and touched Mung's shoulder. He felt Mung's body heaving in low sobs.

Yoshida said softly, 'Mung, Mung, you must know that I care about you. Sakuma Shozan is especially impressed by what you

210

have done. He is trying to find out about your family. Even Saiyo's father, a full-ranked samurai, did not drive you from his house. The social distance between you and Saiyo is far greater than from here to Kagoshima, yet I believe that even Lord Nariakira will help you bridge that gap.' He pulled Mung by the shoulder until they faced each other. In a stern voice, he said, 'Remember! Your father was a samurai! His rank may have been taken from him by law, but you, of all people, must believe that the blood of the father influences the son. Otherwise you would not have risked returning to Japan. If you are a samurai by blood, then act according to the rules of Bushido!' He pulled Mung by the shoulders until his feet swung off the bunk, then shouted, 'Up! Stand up!'

Mung rested his elbows on his knees, letting his head fall into his hands. 'All I wanted was to return to my mother, honour my father in his grave and live quietly in Nakanohama.'

Yoshida wagged his head. 'No, no, my friend. You can never return to that simple world of fishermen. You've seen and learned too much and your mind would not let you. The moment you opened your mouth, you would startle them with your knowledge. They would reject you. Remember the proverb, "The nail which sticks out is pounded down." This is one of the reasons we seek Dutch Learning. We want to understand democracy, so maybe, just maybe, a poor fisherboy as you can rise to be a leader in the new Japan.' Yoshida paced back and forth, then picked up the bowl of soup, shoved it into Mung's hands, and ordered, 'Eat this!' His face flushed and he growled at Mung, 'I said, eat it!'

Mung put the bowl to his lips and tasted the hot liquid on his tongue. Swallowing, he felt the warmth spread in his stomach. He sat up.

Yoshida pointed at him. 'Do you think we risked saving your life for wealth or prestige? Oh no!' He shook his head. 'We have those. In our society, all we must do is live according to the rules and we will be given more.' Yoshida made a slashing movement, like a sword blade through the air, with the flat of his hand. 'Power is what we seek! Knowledge is power! With power we can make change!' He jabbed his finger at Mung. 'You are alive only because of what you know!'

Mung held the empty bowl in his hand, looking up at a Yoshida he had never seen before. 'What changes do you want to make?'

Yoshida threw back his head, talking as he stalked the cabin. 'The first and most important change is to restore the Emperor to power!'

'But the Emperor is all powerful.'

'That is what you and the common people think. The people worship the Emperor but they obey the Shōgun, and have for two hundred and fifty years.'

'Doesn't the Shōgun heed the Emperor?'

'In theory yes, but the Emperors of Japan long ago delegated their powers to the Shōgun so they would not be bothered with the everyday workings of a country, so they could indulge their fantasies and whims. Now we have a situation which is just the opposite. An incompetent and uninterested Shōgun and the young vibrant Meiji Emperor who seeks the return of his rightful power over the feudal lords of Japan. This confrontation is not new. Your father was a victim of the power struggle between the Emperor and the Shōgun. Our historian researched it. Your father's feudal lord, a supporter of the Emperor, died while away from his domain. The Shōgun invoked an ancient law, took over the lands, reduced all his samurai to *ronin*, and gave the lands to another who would support him.'

'You mean my father was a victim of politics?'

'Of course politics. I believe politics to be the highest form of power.'

'What changes would you make if you got that power?'

'Internally, under the Emperor's leadership, unite the country into one nation, and do away with the select group of petty kings sitting in their feudal manors. From north to south, on all the islands, we will eliminate the stagnation and corruption which has resulted from over two centuries of isolation and complacency. While you have been building your ships, there have been rice riots. Something unheard of in the empire. We must open up our country. It's the only way to stabilize the economy. In times of

212

good harvest we can sell our surplus to other nations, and in times of famine we can purchase food from them. Introduction of modern industries such as whaling can raise the standard of living of the entire population!' Yoshida stopped in front of Mung and held his gaze as the muscles flicked back and forth over his cheekbones. 'We must gain western knowledge to stop the barbarians when they come!'

'Which barbarians?'

'The nations of the west.'

'How do you know they will come?'

Yoshida waved his arms. 'Haven't you told us about the English, French, Germans, Portuguese, and so on in China? The Dutch, Spanish, and French are in the South Pacific islands. The Americans, you told us, have gained access to the North Pacific after their war with Mexico, and are contesting England and France for Hawaii. We know also that most of India, Africa, Egypt, and smaller nations of the Middle East are being governed by a European oligarchy led by England, France, and Spain.' Yoshida squatted on the floor in front of Mung. 'When I say we know, I am talking about a small group of men dedicated to the Emperor and Dutch Learning. Even the majority of those who support us have no concept of western power and social reform. You tell us that in America it is an honour to be a businessman. In Japan that is the lowest class distinction. But, did you know that because of the inability of the government to export or tax Japanese businesses, the aristocrats of Japan have gone into debt to the merchants?' He pounded the bulkhead with his fist. 'An internal breakdown is taking place because titles of some of the most honoured families are being sold to eliminate these debts. The morality of our country is going rapidly downhill. The Gay Quarter in the Shōgun's capital at Yedo covers a larger area than the offices of the government. The Russians have been probing our northern shores from ports in Siberia. The English and French have actually tried to sail into Yedo harbour. They did force their way into Nagasaki harbour two years ago. And the Shōgun does nothing!' Yoshida pounded his chest with his fists. 'We seek power through Dutch Learning not

213

only to create internal change. But to be prepared to meet the foreigners when they come! Will you join us?'

Mung stood up, holding the bunk for support. He looked around the cabin and at his friend who stood beside him. 'I wanted to help Japan. That is one of the reasons I returned. I have seen the Americans. They are a good hard-working people. There is much to talk about, but first I must get something else to eat. That soup woke up my appetite.'

CHAPTER
11

17 October 1851

On the holiday for bringing the first fruits to the Shinto temples and shrines in Kagoshima, the streets were decorated with arbours of evergreen. In front of each home stood arches of pine boughs. Bamboo canes were staked at the corners of the houses, linked by short ropes of woven grass to keep away the evil spirits. So many dwarf trees and ferns were displayed in front of the houses that the streets resembled a miniature fairyland.

The elders, having decided that this year's offerings should be made at the mountain shrines rather than those near the seaside, led the procession of parents, teachers and children. The weather was warm and the leisurely walk up the winding mountain paths gave everyone a chance to enjoy the forests, the wild flowers, and the view.

Five hundred miles to the east of the town, in the Pacific Ocean just beyond the Bonin Islands, lay one of the world's largest sub-oceanic trenches. In this area, at ten-thirty the same morning, a violent earthquake shook the earth's crust at thirty-four thousand feet below the water's surface. The holiday-makers, climbing the slopes of Kagoshima, felt several tremors. Some, afraid of earth-slides, returned to their homes, but the festive air continued as most of the townspeople sang songs and picked flowers on their way.

The shock of the quake caused a titanic earth-slide in the subterranean trench, creating a new depression of major geographic significance in the earth's surface. The ocean rushed in to fill this depression and three two-foot tidal waves were born. The waves radiated out, heading for the Japanese coast at six hundred miles an hour. As they moved up the slopes of the trench, weight and mass caused them to lose speed because of bottom friction. At two thousand feet below sea level, they slowed to five hundred miles an hour but grew two feet. At a depth of one thousand feet, they reduced in speed to three hundred miles an hour and gained two more feet in height. The separation between the waves became greater as they surfaced. The southerly edge of the killer waves washed over low-lying atolls in their path towards Kagoshima.

Saiyo Ishikawa strode up the trail, disregarding the short mincing steps of a well-bred lady. She ignored the stares of adults she passed, continuing the long steps until she walked beside her father. 'Do you think it would be safer to return with the children to the town?' she asked. 'Others have for fear of earth-slides.'

'Earthquakes are a part of everyone's life in Japan,' her father said. 'Since their destructive force cannot be predicted, life must continue. We should also.'

Mung and Yoshida stood on the quarterdeck of the *Shinto Maru*, discussing the possibility of reforms in the social and economic structures of Japan. The two whaling captains stood by the rail, watching their crew members manoeuvre the longboats according to signals given from the crow's nest. The whaler, lying two miles off Kagoshima harbour, had proved seaworthy. The swelling of her planks in the salt water had sealed the hull, attesting to the expertise of Japanese shipwrights. The weather was moderate, visibility good, the sky a soft blue, and the sun warmed the surface of a calm sea. The ship was lying to an offshore breeze when she was gently but firmly lifted seven feet up and settled down again.

Mung said to Yoshida, 'That's a strange beam sea.'

He watched the longboats raise their oars and ride over the wave. The two captains rushed to the bow rail of the quarterdeck, looking wide-eyed at Kagoshima and the wave approaching the harbour.

The senior captain looked up to the crow's nest, cupped his hands around his mouth, and shouted, '*Tsunami*!!!! *Tsunami*!!!! Order all boats to return!'

The signal cannon boomed as the first killer wave drove in

towards the coast. It raced up the submarine slopes of the island of Kyushu, growing in density and height. At a speed of one hundred miles an hour it was eight feet high, at eighty miles per hour – eleven feet, at seventy miles – fifteen feet. It rolled over outlying reefs and islands, crashing on the shoreline to the right and left of Kagoshima harbour. The wave moved relentlessly up the V-shaped bottom of the harbour, slowing to fifty miles per hour, then forty. At thirty miles an hour, the wave was fifty feet high, causing a vacuum to form in the port. Parts of the harbour bottom no human had ever seen were exposed as all the water rushed out with a great hissing sound to join the massive wave. Those on their way back down the mountain were the first to see the wall of water come crashing down on their town.

Mung clutched the rail as he saw one of the basic laws of nature violated. The wave grew and grew. It seemed impossible. The town was lost from sight as millions of tons of water fell. Mung used all his mental strength to break his grasp on the rail. The sail was already set.

He shouted orders to the helmsman, 'Turn to starboard! We'll catch the offshore wind.'

He began giving orders to the two crew captains, then suddenly thought of Saiyo. He leapt into the rigging, was climbing higher for a better view, when the concussion of the wave crashing on land reached them. Mung saw houses, temples, horses, trees, and boulders washed inland. He looked down and saw his two captains standing where he had left them. They had not carried out his orders.

Mung swung from the rigging and jumped ten feet to the deck, the livid white line across his bent nose like a horizontal slash on his angry face. 'Why aren't you moving?' he shouted.

The senior captain stepped forward and bowed. Yoshida moved nearer. The captain said, '*Tsunami* is never just one. There are always others.'

Mung snatched the telescope from its case and scanned the open sea. He lowered the glass, grinding his teeth, and growled, 'I see nothing!'

Yoshida came between the two men, turned to Mung, and said, 'Don't sail into the harbour yet. The captain is right about *tsunami*. The killer waves never come alone. If this ship is destroyed, you will not be able to help Saiyo or anyone else.'

Mung's eyes burned into Yoshida's until his friend looked away. Pushing by him, Mung barked at the captains, 'Man the sails!'

Both men bowed, stepped back, and gave the orders to send their crews into the rigging. Like madmen the whalers flew up the lines, tearing at knots in anticipation of the next command to tack in to the harbour. They had become family to the people of Kagoshima.

Saiyo Ishikawa, with her teachers and students, was high on the mountainside when she heard the whaler's signal gun to summon the longboats. The boom caused her and others to turn seaward in time to watch the wave crush the town. The force and weight of the water shook the mountain. It washed through the town and towards the slopes. There was an eerie silence as the waters swirled below them, then receded, taking their homes and families out to sea. Children cried; women wailed and tore their hair. Some men ran back down the trail.

Saiyo's father, further down the hill at a small shrine, had also seen the wave. After the initial shock of watching Kagoshima being washed away, he hurried to a point where several trails met, trying to stop people from rushing down the hill. He was only successful after enlisting the help of several strong young men.

The *Shinto Maru* tacked slowly at first, then caught the wind. Her holds empty, she rode high in the water. Mung, his jaw set, stood at the forward rail of the quarterdeck, refusing to listen to Yoshida's pleas to remain offshore. He ordered signals made to the returning whaleboats to follow and help with survivors. His eyes wide and unblinking, he tried to judge the best place to make his port tack against the offshore wind to safely enter the harbour. The whaler began to pick up speed.

The wave still swirled around the ruins of Kagoshima when from the crow's nest came the long-drawn-out cry, '*Tsu ... naaa-aaa ... miiiii!*'

218

Mung looked up and saw an arm in the crow's nest pointing seaward. The second wave came on, slowing in speed, growing in height. They watched the longboats two miles further out ride over the ten-foot wave. Mung ordered the helmsman hard to starboard, heading the *Shinto Maru* into the wave. He ordered the signal cannon fired and the longboats further out to deep water.

'The gods of the sea have gone mad!' Yoshida shouted. He pointed at the wave coming towards them, now twenty feet high.

The *Shinto Maru* answered her helm, turning at eight knots with a following wind to face the growing tidal wave.

Mung, his face less taut, turned to the two captains, bowed and said, 'Everyone into the rigging but the helmsman and I!'

The crew of the whaler scrambled up amongst the billowing sails. Mung pushed Yoshida off the quarterdeck into the rigging. He grabbed a line, tying it around the waist of the helmsman, his own waist, and to the railing behind the wheel. Just as he finished the knot, the second wave came bearing down on them, a solid green wall forty feet high with flecks of white foam blowing off its top. The *Shinto Maru*, doing ten knots with a strong following wind, began her climb up the massive wall. The ship stood on her beam as she fought her way upward. Men in the rigging swung about like wind chimes. Mung and the helmsman interlocked their arms and held the wheel. The whaler hovered on the lip of the wave. She was carried backwards, then broke through the crest. Tons of water washed the deck and the whaler raced down the back side of the wave, burying her bow deep in the ocean. Again the decks were awash up to the lower sail, but the ship fought her way up from the weight of the sea and wallowed in the backwash of the tidal wave, allowing the water to pour off her decks until she could shake herself loose, catch the wind, and continue out to sea. The senior captain came out of the rigging and grabbed the wheel. Mung and the helmsman had been battered against the quarterdeck rail. Yoshida helped them up.

The backwash of the first wave, carrying the ruins of Kagoshima, joined the volume of the second, raising its height to eighty feet above sea level as it moved almost half a mile inland before it crashed down, washing part way up the mountainside. Mung turned away from the incredible scene on shore and looked seaward for the next wave, praying to Buddha, Christ, and the Shinto gods of nature to protect Saiyo.

'*Tsu ... naaaaa ... miiii!*' came the cry from the crow's nest.

The third and largest wave in the recorded history of Japan moved towards Kyushu Island. Mung measured the wave, using the technique applied to determining the height of mountains, and later entered it in the ship's log. Because the whaler was now further out to sea, she easily breasted the twenty-five-foot wave. The backwash of the first two waves were combined in the third which raced into the harbour, slowing to twenty-five miles an hour and attaining a height of 110 feet. It moved in three quarters of a mile before it broke, crashing against the mountainside to a height of 350 feet. Parts of the mountain were washed away. Hills were denuded of trees centuries old. Giant boulders rolled like pebbles into the bay.

The *Shinto Maru* and her longboats continued their course seaward on the calm ocean until the senior captain indicated it was safe to return. When Mung gave the order to come about, he had the whaler in position to make one long tack into the harbour. It was almost two in the afternoon when he commanded the signal guns fired. The longboats raced ahead of the whaler to search for survivors amongst the wreckage. Returning fishing boats also made up a small rescue fleet, but were left behind by the whaler as she sped into port under full sail. Twenty-seven thousand people died that day within twelve minutes on the island of Kyushu.

Mung anchored fore and aft in the harbour. He divided the men on board into crews, designating to each an area to search for survivors. There were few landmarks of any kind left in the town, and they found no survivors. Until the crews reached the slopes of the mountains, they saw no living thing, animal or human. Even the birds had deserted Kagoshima.

Running through the mud field that was once a town, Mung heard men ahead of him shouting and pointing. A line of people were making their way down the hillside. Spattered with mud, he ran with the others towards the oncoming column. The Satsuma men from the whaler grabbed Kagoshima children, hugging and caressing them, tears unashamedly rolling down their cheeks. Fishermen, returning to the village, ran up and down the column shouting names of loved ones. Sounds of crying and wailing filled the air.

Then Mung and others heard a rhythmic sound like the tinkle of bells. It became louder – the voices of children singing the song of the Weeping Willow, led by Saiyo Ishikawa. Her tall thin figure in mud-stained kimono appeared regal to Mung as she tried to keep her balance on the muddy trail, leading her students and teachers back to what was once their homes. Mung started forward to meet her but was restrained by a firm hand grasping his arm. It was Mr Ishikawa.

The old man pulled Mung around sharply and said, 'You and I have other duties that are more important.'

Mung looked at the older man and blurted out, 'I must see her.'

'You may see her when this is over. You are commander of the largest disciplined group of men in this area. You must take charge of feeding and housing the survivors. The town must be rebuilt. My daughter is the sixteenth generation born in Kagoshima. I take a vow here and now that Kagoshima will survive to see a seventeenth. Will you join me in this vow?'

Saiyo ran to her father and hugged him. She reached out to touch Mung, then withdrew her hand.

Mr Ishikawa said, 'Daughter, your children need you!'

Looking longingly at Mung, then at her father, and back to Mung, she stepped away, bowed to her father and went to her students. Mung's eyes followed. Could it be that his love was reflected in her eyes?

'Will you do your duty?' Mr Ishikawa demanded.

Mung looked at the distinguished samurai and fingered his bent nose. 'I will have the *Shinto Maru* towed in and made secure to shore. Have the elders, priests and leaders of the town guilds meet with me aboard the ship. It will act as town headquarters.'

Mung turned and began giving orders to round up the crews.

Realizing the men of Kagoshima would be of little value in their sorrow, he sent runners to bring others from the outposts guarding the trails to the town. Yoshida dispatched messengers to the Satsuma Court.

They divided their areas of responsibility. Yoshida and the two master shipbuilders were to supervise the rebuilding of the town. Mung and his captains were to arrange food supplies and repair the port.

The most pressing and tragic task, in which all participated the following day, was to bury the sixty-three bodies recovered from the mud or found floating in the bay. Buddhist priests, their shaven heads reflecting the sun, led the procession carrying the square wooden coffins to the mass grave dug on a hillock overlooking Kagoshima. A single rose, carved from stone by the town's master stonemason, was set on a pedestal at the site, in memory of those whose bodies were not recovered.

Mung had no need to prod his men. They worked until they collapsed. He alternated the crews between the work on shore and fishing to provide the town with food. They scavenged the bay and mouth of the harbour for all usable flotsam, piling it on shore near the *Shinto Maru* where Yoshida and his master shipbuilders established the reconstruction headquarters.

The elders tried to draw maps of the town as it had been, but without proper landmarks were hopelessly confused. Hearing of this, Mung set up an easel, rice-paper and charcoal on the quarterdeck. He requested Mr Ishikawa and others to advise him. They stood, overlooking the mud flats, the rivulets of water draining back into the sea. Here and there the stone base of a temple or shrine protruded through the muck. With these as identification points and strong clear strokes, Mung reproduced an accurate picture of Kagoshima as it had been before the *tsunami*. The elders were astonished and remained silent as, in awe, they watched their town with its winding streets and broad lanes, grow before their eyes on the rice-paper, exactly as they remembered it.

On 30 October a long procession from the Court of Satsuma made its way over the mountain and down the trail into the town.

Each porter carried a double load. The food and clothing were stacked at the reconstruction centre. At the head of the column, a samurai in full armour carried a single dwarf maple tree in an elegant pot. It was a bonsai of extreme beauty and had been in Lord Nariakira's family for three hundred years.

Sakuma Shozan, accompanying the column, ordered the townspeople assembled in what had been the main square. There, he made the presentation. 'Lord Nariakira wishes you to remember in your days of sorrow and grieving that in this world of tragedies there remains beauty and love. He commands you to rebuild your town and yourselves with this in mind. For that reason, he sends you this family treasure which he and his fathers before him have tended with their own hands. It is a sign of Lord Nariakira's will to have Kagoshima blossom once again.'

Sakuma Shozan, despite his age and the arduous journey by palanquin, ordered a meeting of the reconstruction committee aboard the *Shinto Maru*. He listened to the elders, to Yoshida and Mung, and then made suggestions for utilization of the porters he had brought and the distribution of food and clothing. He stressed that the dignity of every person receiving aid be maintained, then dismissed all but Yoshida and Mung.

'You two have done well,' he said. 'Now look at this.' He spread out a map of Kyushu, then with his finger circled an area around Kagoshima. He looked up at Yoshida. 'You are hereby appointed governor of Kagoshima and are responsible for rebuilding it and the surrounding hamlets.' The old scholar withdrew a scroll from his sleeve. Handing it to Yoshida, he smiled and said, 'This is a document raising you to the rank of full samurai with all rights, stipends, and privileges.' The old man's face beamed and Yoshida blushed, bowing as a son would to his beloved father. Yoshida started to speak but quietened when the old man held up his hand and said, 'It has been a joy being your teacher.' He turned his tired, deeply lined face to Mung. 'There are many things I would like to talk to you about, but there is no time. I have spoken to Lord Nariakira of your future. It is impossible at the present for you to return to your home in Nakanohama. Restoring your father's name to its original status is impossible for his feudal lord is dead. His family and lands no longer exist; they belong to the Shōgun. Therefore, we have created a legal fiction to raise your status. We have given you a new identity.' From the same large sleeve, the old scholar drew a second scroll. He handed it to Mung. 'You are hereby adopted into the family of Einosuke, and are bestowed the rank of junior samurai. All official correspondence will address you as Moryiama Einosuke.'

Mung accepted the scroll in his two outstretched hands and bowed. 'What does this mean?'

'It means you will be able to speak with those of various samurai rank in attendance at the Imperial School of Interpreters in Nagasaki where you are going. It is arranged for you to teach English, improve your Dutch, and translate certain books from Latin. This assignment is most immediate because of a foreigner who has arrived there for interrogation. He was born in America. His father, he claims, was English, and his mother he believes was originally Japanese. It is all very confusing. He speaks some Japanese words but there is no one to translate his English. His name is Harold MacDonald. Before going to Nagasaki, an old friend of yours will accompany you to the Court at Satsuma.'

Sakuma Shozan arose, indicating the conversation was at an end. He smiled at Yoshida and said, 'Samurai, show me to my room. I am exhausted.'

Yoshida bowed and escorted the old scholar to a nearby cabin. He returned to Mung who was still standing with the scroll held in both hands.

Yoshida jumped up and down, grabbing Mung by the shoulders and dancing him around. 'Don't you know what this means?' he shouted. Falling back against the cabin wall, he slid slowly to the floor, laughing. 'You can marry that stringbean, Miss Saiyo Ishikawa.'

Mung stared down at him, an incredulous expression on his face.

Yoshida pointed up at the scroll Mung held in his hands. 'You are now Moryiama Einosuke, samurai of Satsuma. I will always know you as Mung, but your new rank will allow you to marry the daughter of Samurai Ishikawa.'

Mung leapt high in the air, hit his head on the cabin ceiling, crashed to the floor next to Yoshida, and shouted in English, 'Town-ho! Goddamnit! Town-ho!'

Yoshida grabbed him and they began to wrestle. Mung tried to break free. 'I'm going to marry her!' he gasped. He tried to stand but Yoshida grabbed the back of his ankle with one hand and pushed hard on his knee with the other. Mung crashed to the floor. Sitting up, he looked wide-eyed at Yoshida. 'What the hell did you do that for?'

'Have you forgotten how it's arranged?' Yoshida shook his head. 'You've been out of the country too long. You need an intermediary and with my new rank of full samurai, I can act on your behalf.'

Mung jumped up and stalked the room, then turned to Yoshida. 'Go! Begin right now!'

Yoshida leaned back against the cabin wall. 'You must remember that these things take time. Besides that, her home has been destroyed.'

'And I want to help rebuild it with her.'

'You've been ordered to the Court at Satsuma and from there to the Interpreters School at Nagasaki.'

Mung looked around like a caged animal, muttering to himself.

Yoshida asked, 'What are you mumbling about?'

'I'm given the rank to marry her, then they take me away from her. Can't they leave me alone?'

Yoshida got to his feet. His voice hardened. 'Forget being left alone and remember what your father taught you about Bushido! You live to serve your Emperor and your Lord! Your actions have become childish! Pack your things! The escort will be waiting at the gangplank!' As he stalked out, Yoshida called back, 'I will speak to Saiyo's father for you.'

Alone in his cabin, Mung stuffed two small seabags with books and a change of clothing. On deck, he was greeted by the senior captain who bowed and escorted him to the gangplank. The few members of the crew who were aboard, bowed. Mung returned the courtesy.

The captain handed Mung a piece of intricately carved whalebone, depicting the *Shinto Maru* on one side and a whale being harpooned on the other. He said, 'This is from the jawbone of our first whale. It is carved for the sword you are now entitled to carry.'

Mung took the whalebone, bowed deeply, then looked around at the decks, masts, and rigging he had designed and helped build, and at the men he had trained. He stepped back and shouted, 'Greasy luck to all of you,' then turned and went down the gangplank.

Ryochi Okuda stood at the bottom, holding two horses. He laughed and shouted, 'Hey Samurai, can you ride?'

Mung let out a sigh. 'It seems they've given you the task of being my watchdog again. I hope it won't be too boring.'

Ryochi laughed and mounted his horse. 'Being around you is anything but boring.'

Mung said, 'I'm glad to see you.'

'And for me it was time to get out of the geisha houses. I was going into debt to those accursed merchants,' Ryochi said. He signalled to a runner who ran ahead of them, blowing a conch shell. 'I have to take you to a certain place before we leave. Yoshida ordered it.'

Mung kicked his horse until he trotted beside Ryochi. 'Was Yoshida very angry?'

'No. Why do you ask?'

Mung said nothing. He looked around as they rode. Several houses had been reconstructed. The main streets were clean of mud and debris. In the centre of the town square, on a carved pedestal, sat the beautiful dwarf maple tree. At the edge of the square, Mung saw Saiyo in the midst of a crowd of women, giving instructions. The women soon broke up into work groups and went off in different directions.

'Go to her,' Ryochi said. 'Yoshida ordered me to bring you here.'

Mung looked at Ryochi, then leapt from his horse just as Saiyo turned and saw him. He heard her draw in her breath. She bowed. Mung bowed. The two stood in the ruined city, gazing at each other.

One of the horses held by Ryochi whinnied. The noise brought Mung to attention. 'Miss Ishikawa,' he said. 'I have just been honoured with the rank of junior samurai. Yoshida Torajiro will speak to your father on my behalf about marriage. I hope this does not displease you.'

For lack of the customary fan, Saiyo brought her fingertips to her lips. 'I do hope Yoshida will be quick about it.'

Mung blurted out, 'What?'

Saiyo withdrew her hand, revealing a smile. 'It is only proper for a daughter to accept the decision of her parents,' she said.

A smile creased Mung's face from ear to ear as he stared at her. Saiyo's cheeks tinged pink. She lowered her head slightly.

He said, 'I am ordered to Satsuma and then to Nagasaki but ...'

Ryochi, from his place with the horses, shouted, 'Time to go.'

Mung and Saiyo bowed to each other. Mung walked backwards to his horse, bowed again and looked lovingly at his future bride. 'I'll be back,' he shouted. He leapt into the saddle and galloped up the trail, shouting at the top of his voice, 'Town-ho! Town-hoooo!'

CHAPTER
12

On the Imperial Road to Satsuma, Mung and Ryochi slept and ate at official stations, presenting their credentials and signing vouchers. Their horses were fed and the straw shoes changed as a matter of course. Mung saw more people along the road than he had ever seen in America – merchants, farmers, priests, samurai, mendicants, fortune-tellers, pilgrims, and parties of vacationers on their way to holiday resorts carrying banners which announced the names of their towns.

At the outpost of the Satsuma Court, the straw horseshoes were changed for the last time, and a runner assigned to precede them blowing a conch shell. Farmers had already finished their day's work in the fields, and the highway to the feudal court was deserted.

Alongside the road they came to a stone figure of the Buddhist patron saint Jizo, who protects pregnant women, children, and travellers. The two men dismounted and approached the statue with bowed heads. Placing their palms together in front of their faces, each said his own silent prayer. Ryochi prayed Mung would not get entangled in one of the intrigues at the Satsuma Court, for he had been assigned to protect him. Mung looked at the fat carved figure sitting in a stone lotus petal and thought, I hope to see you again soon, old Jizo, when I leave here to get married. Both men stepped back and clapped their hands once to send the prayers on their way.

They remounted and headed for the main gate in the long low wall surrounding the Satsuma castle. Ryochi presented his passes and orders to the samurai in charge of the guard. The horses were led away. Mung and Ryochi were assigned a guide whom they followed to their sleeping quarters. On the way they passed houses, shops, and government offices built into the fortress walls enclosing one and a half square miles. Crowds of people moved around the fish and vegetable markets.

In the last glow of daylight, gleams of white and gold quivered from the roof tiles of the seven-tiered pagoda castle of Lord Nariakira. It dominated all the buildings, temples, and shrines in the province of Satsuma. The guide led Ryochi and Mung to the right wall of the fortress, away from the crowds. He mounted the porch of a house built into the wall and slid back the *shoji* screens on two separate rooms. On the sleeping mats of each room were clothes appropriate for their rank of junior samurai, bearing the calligraphic insignia of Satsuma. They left their saddlebags and were directed to a bath.

Upon returning to their rooms, they were awaited by two beautiful young women attending *hibachis*, prepared to serve dinner. Ryochi instructed them to remove the screen between the two rooms so he and Mung could eat together. Mung noticed his bags had been moved and the knots tied differently, but said nothing. He sat down and ate ravenously with his friend. The women put everything away, replaced the screen, undressed, and got under the downy quilt covers.

Ryochi called from his side of the screen, 'I will never understand why Americans hold prostitutes in such low regard.'

Mung called back, 'It's one of their customs I don't understand either.'

'Well, anyone who uses the toilet for a reading room can be expected to have strange ideas,' Ryochi said.

Mung felt the girl's softness next to him. Reaching for her, he moved his hands over her warm, smooth body. He was quickly aroused and her training in the art of lovemaking caused him much pleasure. He imagined she was Saiyo but knew in his heart there could be none like her for him.

The warm body behind him rocked back and forth. He tried to open his eyes and turned to reach for her, but his hand was gently pushed away.

229

'It is time to rise,' she whispered.

Mung rubbed the sleep from his eyes and saw the faint glow of a light through the papered door in Ryochi's room. 'It's not dawn yet,' he said.

As she lit a tiny oil-lamp, the shadows played on the girl's hips and soft belly. He stood up and reached for her again but she said, 'It is time for you to go.'

Mung slipped into the robe she held for him and looked into her eyes. 'You are beautiful.'

She stepped back, slid open the outside door, bowed, and said, 'Thank you.'

Outside, he and Ryochi put on their shoes. A Buddhist priest with shaven head emerged from the shadows, beckoning them to follow. In the darkness, it was only the rustling of the priest's robe that guided them. They were led up a flight of stone steps and instructed to remove their shoes. Again they followed the whisper of the robe as their stockinged feet slid over smooth flagstones. Small oil-lamps in niches along a wall barely revealed that they had entered a temple. The guide separated the two, leading Mung to a room where he was told to meditate.

Sinking slowly to the floor, he stared ahead into the darkness and sat in the lotus position. Thinking back to his father's instructions, he allowed his body to relax, spine straight, head erect, arms forward, thumb and forefinger resting on his knees. He cleared his mind of every thought until there was a dark void. Slowly a light formed in his forehead, a third eye directed inward which watched his thoughts pass. The eye expanded until the luminescence became the opening of a dead volcano in which he floated up to the light. He flew out of the mouth of the volcano into a glorious blue sky, soaring over cliffs, down slopes and out over the plains surrounded by distant mountains. There were multitudes of people and ranks of samurai below. He swooped down to see them more clearly but they scattered at his approach. He searched for Saiyo but she was not there. He turned upward towards the sun but its brightness pained his eyes. He feared he had been blinded.

His eyelids fluttered open. The first rays of the morning sun pierced his retina. The tiled rooftop of the large, enclosed courtyard was outlined by the light. Mung could see that the alcove in which he sat was one of many in the castle. Each small room was occupied and looked out onto a sand garden of exceptional beauty. Seven large stones were ingeniously spaced on rippled sand to give the effect of the sea in motion. On the far side of the rectangle sat Lord Nariakira, flanked by his two sons.

The single chime of a bell sounded. Lord Nariakira stood and all bowed, touching their foreheads to the floor until he was gone. Mung felt a hand on his shoulder, and followed the priest from the temple towards the rear wall of the feudal manor. They passed farmers going out to their fields, women tending cooking fires, merchants and vendors cleaning in front of their stalls and shops, and children reciting their lessons for parents before going off to school. The ring of a hammer on metal grew louder as they neared a group of samurai crowded around a swordmaker's forge.

The priest whispered to Mung, 'Do not bow while the Lord works,' then directed him to the side of the group gathered around an open pit with a hearth of glowing coals. Lord Nariakira and his sons were in the pit, dressed in rough white work-clothes. The Satsuma Lord withdrew a sword from the fire, its blade half finished, a glob of molten steel glowing at the tip. He placed the burning steel on an anvil. Holding the hilt with damp rags, he brought down a short sledgehammer. His two sons, standing in front of him, brought down their long-handled sledges in perfect coordination, one after the other, showering sparks which peppered their white work-clothes. They worked at a rapid pace until the glow faded from the fiery lump at the end of the blade. Lord Nariakira thrust it back in the fire and his sons turned to work the heavy leather bellows.

His voice carried above the wheezing blow pipe. Using Mung's adopted name, he said, 'Moriyama Einosuke, will Kagoshima recover from the *tsunami*?'

Mung lowered his head and answered, 'Yes, my lord. The people grieve but they work at rebuilding the town. There is enough food; none go hungry. Your dwarf tree sits in the centre of

231

the town square and inspires all who look upon it.'

Lord Nariakira withdrew the blade from the fire. He looked at it, placed it back in, and said, 'The making of a sword is a fine art. After meditation, my sons and I work at the forge to blend our purified spirits and enlightened souls with the steel from the earth of Japan. The sword is a noble weapon. How would Americans appraise it in battle?'

Mung answered, 'Americans would respect its beauty and craftsmanship. They would wear it on the belt of their uniforms as a sign of rank, but they would use a gun. It is more efficient.'

The wheezing bellows stopped; silence lay heavy until broken by a baby's cry.

Lord Nariakira withdrew the glowing blade from the fire. He looked at it for a moment, then said, 'The cry of a child is the sound of new life. Rather than stifle it, I will capture its uniqueness in this blade.' He brought down his hammer.

Mung was jerked from his place and hurried away by the Buddhist priest. They went quickly down a small lane, then made several turns until they came to a wider street. The priest slid back a *shoji* screen, pushed Mung through, and slammed it closed. They removed their shoes inside and carried them. The house appeared empty. Mung followed the priest as he moved quickly through the rooms, across a courtyard, and into another house. Once again the guide moved through the rooms with familiarity until they stood by a bamboo screen. He motioned Mung to step forward and they peered through the bamboo slats on to a wide street. The priest indicated with a nod of his shaven head for Mung to look down to the far end of the street. People were running and ducking into doorways. Those who had not seen the three samurai in time, bowed low. The warriors swaggered shoulder to shoulder up the street, their grim faces set in hard lines, their hands on the hilts of their swords.

A merchant, wearing an expensive brocade robe, stepped out of his shop. He looked around at those running for cover, but stood his ground. As the samurais approached, he bowed. Not very deep, and the merchant stood erect too soon, Mung thought. The nearest

232

samurai whirled around, his long blade flashed, and Mung watched the merchant's head pop off. It rolled into the street. The body stepped forward as a stream of blood gushed from the severed neck, then quivered and collapsed.

Mung turned to the priest who clamped a hand over his mouth and whispered, 'They are looking for you.'

Watching until the three samurai were out of sight, Mung pulled the hand from his mouth and said, 'Why? Why are they looking for me?'

The priest shook his head. 'You certainly do have much to learn. The remark you made about Americans using guns instead of swords almost cost you your life. If Lord Nariakira hadn't told that tale about the child's cry and the sword, your head would have been rolling around like that merchant's.'

'Why did they kill him?'

Like an adult being patient with a backward child, the priest explained, 'First, he is of the lowest class and is of no real consequence. Second, his bow was less than perfect. Third, that samurai or one of his friends is probably in debt to that merchant. This method is the quickest way to cancel it. Have you forgotten that a samurai has the power of life and death over commoners?' The priest stepped back. 'You have that power now.'

'Is anyone safe?' Mung asked.

'Of course, if you know when and how and with whom to speak. That is why you have been brought to this house. We have been told you have an exceptional memory. You will need it. For the next three days you will be instructed in court etiquette and the way a samurai should conduct himself. You must never again make the kind of mistake you made this morning, not if you want to live to serve your Lord and Emperor.'

In a short while, Ryochi appeared at the house with five other samurai. He told Mung, 'These guards will be with you every moment during your stay here. They will sleep in their clothes with hands on the hilts of their swords. They are fighters, not papier mâché courtesans. You will be safe.'

'You mean I'm still being hunted?'

233

'No, that is mostly over, but there are always spies of the Shōgun around, even in the Satsuma castle. The Shōgun's generals already know that you built the whaler and that you have been raised from the rank of commoner to junior samurai. You wear the insignia of Satsuma on your clothing and the Lord Nariakira is a supporter of the Meiji Emperor. Therefore you are a target. The Shōgun's men know also that you are going to the Interpreters School.'

Ryochi led Mung to meet the first in what seemed a never-ending line of instructors. He was allowed to sleep only eight hours in three days. On the morning of the fourth day, Mung was ordered to bathe and don fresh clothing, then led outside by Ryochi. The five samurai surrounded him and they walked briskly through the streets to the seven-tiered pagoda castle. There, he alone followed a guide to a small room where he was seated facing a *shoji* screen. The guide left and shortly the screen slid back, pulled by unseen hands. Lord Nariakira sat straight, eyes unblinking, staring at Mung. Mung threw himself forward, face down, in homage.

'Be seated!' Lord Nariakira said. 'Your report to Yoshida about American expansion to the west coast of the continent, the war with Mexico, the land route over the Isthmus of Panama, events in Hawaii, and the Opium War in China, indicate a bright mind filtering this information.'

Mung was taken aback by the abruptness of the statement and the staccato beat of Lord Nariakira's speech. He sat quietly, head bowed, staring at the floor.

Lord Nariakira said, 'Most people tell me what they think I want to hear. You must always tell me the truth.'

Hidden in his large sleeves, Mung pinched the cuticle of his thumbnail to sharpen his senses.

'Will westerners come to Japan?' the Lord asked.

'Yes.'

'Why?'

'To protect their seamen who are sometimes shipwrecked while making passage to China, to reprovision whalers, to establish coaling stations for their new steamships, and to attempt to trade.'

234

'Will they come to invade us?'

'No.'

'How can you be sure? Your report says America took five hundred thousand square miles away from Mexico, that all major powers are in China and some of the islands of the south Pacific.'

'The western nations have not invaded China. They are controlling her ports for purposes of trade.'

Sharply Lord Nariakira asked, 'Are they all nations of traders?'

'It is considered a most honourable profession in western countries.'

The Satsuma Lord's eyes blinked and he said, 'Continue.'

'Americans saw California as part of their country. They consider Hawaii separate, but within their sphere of influence. A parallel in Japan would be Ryuku Island.'

The Lord waved his forefingers and Mung ceased talking. Lord Nariakira's eyelids slowly closed as he concentrated his thoughts.

Both men remained motionless until the Lord said, 'In your travels, have you heard anything about the Russians?'

'No.'

'They are probing our northern islands from Siberia. The British have been testing us here in the south. In the past ten years both have entered our ports, but were turned away without incident. There is a man being held at the official Imperial School of Interpreters. He speaks very little Japanese and we have arranged for you to interpret his English. You will also conduct an English class for the other thirteen interpreters. Do not teach the language too quickly, for it will be one of the reasons you stay alive. Most of the interpreters are the Shōgun's men. In their eyes you will always be suspect since you come from Satsuma and have been out of the country.'

Lord Nariakira crooked his forefinger and the *shoji* screen on his left slid open. The samurai waiting there bowed, then moved across the floor on his knees, the blade of a sword balanced on the back of his outstretched hands.

Lord Nariakira motioned to Mung, saying, 'You may prefer a pistol but a sword is a sign of your new rank. Take this and fit the whalebone handle to it.'

Mung shuffled forward, wondering how the Lord knew about the handle. He took the blade and bowed deeply, then moved backward and the screen door slid closed. Ryochi and the five samurai escorted him back to the house where he was allowed the first good sleep since entering Satsuma.

Some time later, Mung was awakened by a hand on his shoulder. Another closed over his mouth. In the darkness Ryochi whispered to him, 'Get dressed.' Clothing was put into Mung's hands.

The same Buddhist priest waited to lead them through the dark streets to the sword maker's shop. They passed around the pit of glowing coals, and through a beaded curtain into a room which was actually built into the rear wall of the fortress. Floor mats and boards were lifted and set aside. They followed the priest down a narrow stone staircase. Mung felt the cool dirt wall with his hand as he stooped over and they moved in darkness through the tunnel. After about twenty yards they stopped, his hand was put on the rung of a ladder, and he climbed up out of the ground. There were only the stars; then out of the night appeared a runner holding the reins of two horses.

Ryochi whispered to Mung, 'Mount up.'

'Good travels,' the priest said, and disappeared into the ground.

The runner pulled a woven bamboo grate over the opening. On to that he pushed dirt and placed tufts of grass, then turned without a word and set off at a fast trot over the field. Mung's horse followed Ryochi's. An hour passed before they stopped at a road. The runner whispered to Ryochi, pointed, then turned back to the castle. Ryochi kicked his horse to a fast trot. He and Mung rode for another hour, until at the first light of dawn, they entered a grove of trees. Ryochi pulled off his saddlebags and handed Mung a package of food wrapped in rice paper.

Mung began to speak, but Ryochi interrupted, 'Eat first. Then we can talk.'

They sat amidst the trees, munching their breakfast, watching the sky become lighter. Ryochi got up and went to Mung's saddlebags. He pulled out the sword and scabbard which were tied to the bag and brought them to Mung. While Mung was examining and admiring the sword and the whalebone handle, Ryochi returned once again from the saddlebag and handed him the pistol and contents of its original box.

Ryochi nodded his head in the direction from which they had come. 'They must think a gun has some merit. Personally,' he patted his sword, 'I prefer sharp steel.' He hunkered down. 'What I have to tell you now pains me very much. I've come to like you and ...' His voice drifted off.

Mung lay the sword across his knees and put the pistol, powder, and bullets in his lap. 'What is it?'

Ryochi reached out and touched Mung's shoulder. He looked him hard in the eye, trying to give his friend strength. 'Your mother died two years ago of consumption. Lord Nariakira orders you not to attempt to visit the graves of your parents. The feudal lord on whose land your village is located, serves the Shōgun. To return would mean certain death.'

Mung's chest heaved and a sigh escaped his lips.

Ryochi continued, 'The Lord Nariakira himself will send you to honour the graves of your parents as soon as it is possible.' He stood up. 'This is the way it is. Now we must go to Nagasaki.'

They hardly spoke to each other on the road – passing farmers, merchants, and craftsmen who bowed as they trotted by. They saw Shinto and Buddhist shrines, ate and slept at inns along the way, and climbed higher into the mountains. A tunnel of black pine almost obscured the sunlight. It was cool and quiet in the shade. Emerging, they found themselves on the crest of a mountain overlooking Nagasaki. Purple and pink hues edged the horizon where sea and sky met. The city spread back and away from the bay, hemmed on either side by trees of cedar and pine growing almost to the water's edge. Mung watched puffs of wind ripple the bay and seagulls riding thermal waves out over the water. He composed a poem for Saiyo:

> The wind and the sea are closer to you than
>   this longing soul.
> The radiance of the sun enters our eyes.

And the fragrance of the wild flowers we sense.

Only you enter my heart.

There is no room for anything else.

A high-pitched yell from behind brought Mung spinning around.

A burly man with dirty clothes and wild greasy hair burst out of the thickets. His eyes frenzied, a long sword raised over his head in both hands, he bore down on Ryochi who had been squatting, listening to Mung's poetry. With no time to draw his own weapon, Ryochi faced the crazed man who tried to hack at his head. The blade flashed downward and Ryochi side-stepped. Grunting, he threw a punch into the attacker's ribs, much like an American boxer. The force of the blow caused a cracking sound, followed immediately by the snap of the man's neck from a swift kick under the chin. The attacker was dead before he crumpled to the ground, the sword still clutched in his hands. Mung could hardly believe his eyes, it had happened so quickly.

Ryochi drew his sword, shouting to Mung, 'Bandits! Draw your blade!'

Five more sword-wielding men broke from the forest, rushing towards them. Ryochi backed quickly towards Mung until they stood side by side with the cliff behind them. Mung reached into his kimono and pulled out the pistol. He took deliberate aim and fired the four barrels, one after the other, placing a slug in the chest of each of the four attackers. The fifth, stunned by the devastation, froze with his sword upraised. Ryochi, recovering first from the shock of the explosions, brought his sword parallel to the ground in a flashing arc, cutting the bandit in half at the waist. Mung ran to the saddlebag to reload the pistol as Ryochi moved from bandit to bandit, lopping off their heads. He surveyed the scene with a self-satisfied smile, and replaced his sword into its scabbard.

Fists set firmly on his hips, Ryochi said, 'You certainly knew what you were talking about!' He waved his arms at the bodies. 'That pistol is really something!'

'Shouldn't we leave this place?' Mung said.

Ryochi shrugged his shoulders at the bloody scene. 'After this, there won't be a bandit in this area for a year.' He reached over and took the pistol from Mung's hand. 'Let me see that.' He turned it around and around.

'Be careful,' Mung said.

'Tell me how it works.'

'Only if you agree to go away from this bloody place.'

'I agree, after we make a sign on that big rock about *ronin* bandits as you did in California. We'll write it with their blood.'

Moving down the road to Nagasaki, Mung explained the workings of the pistol.

Then Ryochi explained how he had killed the first attacker with bare hands. 'Only one useful thing I learned from the Ryukuns, and that was karate. Since the islanders are subject to Japanese law, they are not allowed weapons on penalty of death. They developed this method of unarmed combat, using their hands and feet to kill. I had one of them teach me.'

At the outpost of Nagasaki, Mung and Ryochi registered and reported the attack of the *ronin* bandits. They followed their runner as he blew his conch shell, and entered the city of almost half a million people.

Houses spread in every direction. The hills were terraced out of the mountain to the edge of the forest on either side. The peaks of pagoda roofs, topping shrines and temples, dominated the city. Private homes with elaborate carvings of dragons and other mythical figures became more frequent as they approached the port. The runner led them to an enclosed compound on the waterfront where the gate was guarded by two fierce-looking samurai. They were admitted after showing their credentials to the scribe and taken to the prefect's office. The compound housed offices of the police, tax collectors, and served as the cultural and administrative centre for Nagasaki and surrounding districts.

Ryochi presented a scroll from the Satsuma Court to the prefect of Nagasaki. He was a stern-faced old samurai who read the scroll, then looked at Mung for some moments before he spoke. 'You are to translate what the American tells you in response to our questions. Look across the courtyard.' He pointed to a room

239

without a door. 'He is in there. You will never speak with him in this compound unless one of the other interpreters is with you.'

Mung bowed and remained silent.

The prefect glared at him. 'In my opinion you are as suspect as the American. Both of you should be dead.'

Ryochi said, 'Dead, can he serve the Emperor?'

'Alive, does he serve the Shōgun?'

Mung said, 'I serve both, for they are Japan.'

The prefect's head snapped around to face Mung. With a wave of his hand, he dismissed them both. 'Go!'

Following a guide across the square to their quarters built into the compound wall, Mung asked, 'Why is he so antagonistic?'

Ryochi answered, 'He is one of Lord Hayoshi's men, and a staunch supporter of the Shōgun.'

For the next two months Mung interrogated Harold Mac-Donald, the shipwrecked American seaman, always under the watchful eyes of other interpreters. It was only after MacDonald's transfer to the island of Dishima, at the mouth of the harbour opposite the compound, that they had the opportunity to speak freely and become friends.

The island of Dishima had been built at the order of the Shōgun two and a half centuries before. Stones and boulders, loaded onto boats and barges, were then rowed to the harbour entrance where a half mile square was marked off by wooden floats. The rocks were dumped there day and night, year after year, until they formed a mass which rose five feet above the water line. The Dutch traders, who had never tried to proselytize the Protestant religion as did the Catholics from Portugal and Spain before the Imperial Edict which closed Japan, were granted the concession to inhabit the artificial island.

The Dutch gathered seaweed for fertilizer, hauled dirt and manure to Dishima, and planted vegetable gardens. They kept pigs and sheep for meat, cows for milk, and netted plenty of fish. This was the only official contact Japan had with the western world.

Mung began teaching at the Imperial School of Interpreters

located on Dishima. He wrote his own English grammar book from memory, adapting it to the needs of the students and the idiosyncrasies of both languages. Using his high school Latin, he translated certain books according to instructions from Satsuma, writing summaries which were passed to the Court by Ryochi. Sakuma Shozan requested more detailed synopses of particular books, most dealing with western military strategy.

Mung had fallen into a routine. Early every morning he was taken to Dishima by ferry. He taught his English class for three hours, then joined the other interpreters in studying Dutch for four hours with Mr Levysohn. Afterwards he walked and talked with MacDonald for an hour, circling the half mile square island with its few houses lined in a neat row in the centre. Then Mung went to the room which contained books written in Latin and translated for three hours, until the ferry came to take him and the others back to Nagasaki. Ryochi always met him at the quay and they would go together to a restaurant or geisha house. Mung often cursed the work which kept him from Saiyo, but he did enjoy it and he had little time to brood. He received no letters from Yoshida nor word of Saiyo.

One morning the regular routine was broken when Mung prepared to leave his room. Two samurais, guarding the door, told him he was to remain inside. He slid open the screen between their rooms and woke Ryochi, speculating on what might have happened. On Ryochi's instructions, Mung began keeping his pistol in the sleeve of his kimono. For the three days they were captives, food was brought to them. They were escorted to bath and toilet rooms which were always deserted except for the silent samurai guards.

On the morning of the fourth day, Mung was notified to go to his usual classes on Dishima. The other interpreters greeted him on the ferry but thereafter remained silent. When he entered his classroom, prepared to give a lesson, he found twelve bedraggled, red-eyed American sailors with the prefect of Nagasaki who ordered Mung to interpret. He learned from the sailors they were from the merchant ship *Lila B.*, on a return voyage from China.

While trying to make passage through the straits of Shimoneski, they had foundered in a storm. Rescued by Japanese fishermen, they were bound hand and foot, almost starved to death, and finally brought to Dishima.

Mung slept on the island for a week, conducting the interrogation and interpreting the prefect's questions and the sailors' answers. The other interpreters were always present. When Mung finally returned to his room at the compound in Nagasaki, Ryochi was there.

He whispered to Mung, 'Be careful. I have been watched since you left to interrogate the Americans.'

'How did you know what I was doing?'

'Everyone has informers, but never mind. I want to hear the details.'

Mung told Ryochi how the merchant ship had set out from Canton and was wrecked, these sailors being the only survivors.

Ryochi shook his head. 'No, there were seven more sailors found by people from another village and beheaded, their bodies cast back into the sea.'

Mung said, 'You will have to send word to Satsuma. I have learned from these seamen of a group of American ships preparing to sail from Canton Harbour. They plan to travel through the Straits of Shimoneski, up the coast to Yedo, for the purpose of negotiating a treaty of trade and assistance with the Shōgun.'

Ryochi bent closer, eyes bright, voice tense. He whispered, 'Is this true?'

'Yes, but I did not translate that for the prefect. I am sure the other interpreters did not understand because I used sailor's slang when I realized what the Americans were saying. I warned them not to tell anyone else as it would endanger their lives.'

Ryochi sat back, thinking for several minutes. Leaning forward, he whispered, 'There is no other way. I must relay this message myself.' He pointed to the sleeping mat. 'Until I return, leave that where it is and sleep in another part of the room.'

'Do you think I will be attacked?'

'When I leave, the prefect and other friends of the Shōgun will know where I've gone. They will surmise you told me something I hadn't already learned from my spies.'

'But if they kill me, they will never find out what.'

Ryochi patted Mung on the arm like a patient mother. 'Their spies in Satsuma will learn of it shortly.'

Mung shrugged. 'Can you wait for me to write a short letter?'

'There is no time.'

'Then you must send a message for me to Yoshida asking about Miss Saiyo Ishikawa's health.'

Ryochi chuckled. He touched his swords, slid open the door of his room, and was gone into the night.

No one in the compound or at the Interpreters School mentioned Ryochi's disappearance. Soon after, his room was occupied by two stern looking samurai. Every evening for three weeks, Mung returned from Dishima and walked the streets of Nagasaki, dining out, going to a geisha house or to a theatre. He usually returned to his room to study, then placed bundles of clothing on his mat and curled up in a different place to sleep.

This night he was stretched out near Ryochi's screen door and just beginning to drift off. Hearing whispers from the adjoining room, he moved his head closer to the paper door, listening intently. There was the sound of running feet, then a scream, 'EEEeeyaaaahh!'

Two figures, side by side, burst through the thin, paper wall. One tripped over Mung's feet; the other leapt over him and hacked at the clothing on the sleeping mat. Mung threw off his blanket and the pistol dropped out of his sleeve. Rather than search for it in the dark and tangle of the blanket, he jumped up and ran through the hole made by the attackers. Their shouts followed him as he bent his head and rammed through the wall on the opposite side of Ryochi's room. An old man squatted over a chamber pot. Mung stopped, bowed, heard the noise behind him and ran through the next wall, the old man staring after him in astonishment. As the attackers ripped through the wall after him, the old man lost his balance and fell backwards into the pot. Mung broke through the next wall. By the light of an oil lamp, he saw a large mound in the

243

centre of the room. The mound rolled over to separate into two huge sumo wrestlers. Their erections seemed tiny, poking out of the folds of flesh. Anger creased the behemoths' faces. Mung jumped to the right when the two three-hundred-pound giants stood to their full height. As he fell through the screen door into the compound, the attackers ran full speed into the sumo wrestlers and were immediately seized. Mung heard them screaming but did not wait to see what happened. He raced barefoot to the prefect's office. Guards were already alerted and the prefect was coming out of his room. Two sentries grabbed Mung but were commanded to release him. The naked sumo wrestlers, followed by the old man, came to make their anger known.

After the prefect heard the story, he went to Mung's room. Ducking through the ripped walls, followed by Mung, the guards, the old man, and the wrestlers, from room to room through the holes, the prefect reentered the compound through the broken door. He began to giggle. Looking from one to the other, he laughed, trying to stop himself as tears ran down his cheeks. He pointed to the holes in the roof through which the two giants had thrown the attackers. The laughter was infectious. They all roared with laughter. Thereafter, the prefect assigned Mung to a guarded room next to his.

A few days later, Mung was summoned to the prefect's office where Yoshida and Ryochi were waiting. The old samurai looked at Mung who remained silent despite his surprise at seeing Yoshida. The prefect called for brush and ink. With a flourish, he signed the scroll and handed it to Yoshida.

He looked at Mung and said, 'Congratulations on your forthcoming wedding.'

Mung's jaw flopped open and his head bobbed. He barely muttered, 'Thank you,' then bowed and stepped back out of the office.

As Yoshida and Ryochi bowed, the prefect said, 'Tell his wife to be careful of him. He sometimes runs amok through the walls of houses. Thinks he's a billy goat.'

Yoshida and Ryochi bowed again, looked quizzically at each

other, and backed into the courtyard.

Outside the compound, away from the port area, Mung shouted to his friends, 'I refuse to go any further until you explain what happened.'

Yoshida stopped his horse, turned in the saddle, and said, 'You still want to marry skinny Miss Saiyo Ishikawa, don't you?' Before Mung could answer, Yoshida continued, 'Well, it's all arranged. I spoke, in your name, to Mr Ishikawa, and he agreed.'

Mung repeated, 'He agreed. He agreed. Just like that. You asked and he agreed. As simple as that?'

'Not exactly so simple. Lord Nariakira wants you in Yedo when the Americans arrive. Spies in China are sure to send the Shōgun word of the Americans' coming. Once they knew, you would never have been allowed to leave Nagasaki alive. The marriage into the Ishikawa family may also protect you in Yedo. It is one of the oldest and most respected families in the empire.'

Mung sat his horse a bit straighter. A grin spread on his face. 'What if the prefect would not have released me?'

'He couldn't refuse. Lord Nariakira is acting as your godfather. It was he who ordered your travel permit for the wedding.'

'Where is Saiyo?'

'She and her father are already in the Satsuma castle, and we've got a long way to go.'

Mung began to laugh. He threw back his head and shouted, 'Town-hooooo!' He slapped his horse hard on the rump, kicked her in the flanks and was off down the road with Yoshida and Ryochi hard after him.

They rode for eighteen hours, stopping only to change mounts and eat bean cakes and honey washed down with hot tea. They arrived in Satsuma at ten in the morning. Ryochi was taken to a bath and sleeping quarters. Mung and Yoshida were led to the pagoda castle, its golden cornices of seven tiers glittering in the morning sun. Ushered into a room where Lord Nariakira and Sakuma Shozan were sitting, the younger men prostrated themselves full length on the floor, then obeyed the order to arise and be seated.

Sakuma Shozan said, 'Tell us about this rumour of Americans sailing from Canton to Yedo.'

With hands folded and tucked into his sleeves, Mung tried to gather his thoughts before speaking. He pinched the cuticle of his right thumb and the pain brought his tired mind into focus. He forgot about his aching muscles and said, 'The men I spoke with were off the merchant ship, *Lila B*. They said there were five American navy ships anchored in Canton. Two are supply ships. The *Columbus*, *Vincennes*, and *Preble* are warships commanded by Commodore James Biddel. The Commodore has orders to negotiate a treaty for coaling stations, trade, and proper treatment of shipwrecked sailors.'

The old scholar asked, 'When will they arrive?'

'It is not clear, but they felt it would be soon.'

'How would the fortifications you saw at Nagasaki and Kagoshima stand up to these ships if they used force?'

Mung answered, 'Nothing was said of entering those ports.'

'Yes, but the design of those forts is similar to those in Yedo.'

'The fortifications you speak of are mostly dirt walls with ancient cannons, many of which have bird nests in their muzzles. The gun emplacements would be reduced to rubble in fifteen minutes.'

'How would our samurai fare in a pitched land battle?'

'I doubt they would have much of a chance,' Mung answered. 'The ships could enter the harbour and shell the city with fire bombs. Because of the paper and wood construction of our houses, the city could not be saved.'

'Do all these soldiers possess pistols such as the one you used to kill the four samurais?'

'No. Most carry muskets and rifles whose rate of fire is slower but more accurate at greater distances.'

The Satsuma Lord remained silent for several minutes, then said, to Mung, 'Go bathe, and prepare yourself for the *mi-ai*, the ritual meeting with your bride and her father.' He waved Mung out of the room.

Yoshida remained. Lord Nariakira addressed both the scholar

and his student. 'We want the Emperor's powers restored, but we do not want foreigners entering our country by force. We don't want to become another China, overrun by barbarians.'

The three sat silently, each taking stock of the possible alternatives.

Sakuma Shozan said, 'Unless we can convince the Shōgun not to use force, whatever we decide will make no difference. How much time before Mung leaves for Yedo?'

Lord Nariakira answered, 'The *mi-ai* is in three hours. He can be married later tonight and have a three day honeymoon before we send him off to Yedo with Yoshida and Ryochi.' The Satsuma Lord looked at Yoshida. 'In regard to the ritual of stealing the bride, you will act as my proxy.' Chuckling to himself, he said, 'I am too old for stealing brides.'

Mung returned from the bath, his body tingling from the hot water, his heart racing at the thought of seeing Saiyo. He nibbled at the food on a low table as the court barber shaved the front part of his head. The long hairs on the side and back were oiled and tied into a queue, then pulled up and forward on to the shaved part. He donned an embroidered kimono, wide silk trousers and black *obi*, into which he slipped his sword with the carved whalebone handle.

Mung looked in the silver mirror. He thought first about his parents and then about the Whittefields. They were his family too, but Lord Nariakira would speak for him at the *mi-ai*.

He stretched his neck forward, crinkled up his bent nose, thumped his chest, and said to the barber, 'Children! I am going to have many children! A man who has no family must make a large family!'

The barber bowed and offered his blessing, 'May your wife bear as many children as there are seeds in a fig.'

The priest who had helped Mung and Ryochi leave Satsuma, guided him to a room where Lord Nariakira sat on a lacquered platform. Mung was directed to a mat on the Lord's right side. Nothing was said. Soon Mung heard a rustling noise outside the *shoji* screen opposite them. The door slid open. Mr Ishikawa had to bend his head to enter. Behind him followed Saiyo, her head tilted

247

slightly forward, her jet black hair tied in a bun held by a pink coral comb. Her eyes were lowered and a touch of powder and colour on her cheeks made her the most beautiful human being Mung had ever seen. In the years of their marriage, Saiyo would occasionally chide him for not remembering what she wore on their wedding day. She would always be secretly pleased at his answer, that her face was so beautiful he saw nothing else.

Father and daughter took their seats on mats in front of Lord Nariakira, Saiyo half a mat to the rear of her father. She turned her head slightly, looked sideways at Mung, then quickly lowered her eyes. He felt a weakness in his stomach; his shoulders, like two weights, threatened to topple him forward. From far away, he heard the voices of Mr Ishikawa and Lord Nariakira involved in the delicate art of negotiating the conditions of the marriage. He wasn't sure just what they were saying and he didn't care, as long as he could marry his lovely Saiyo. Suddenly his body jerked forward as he almost dozed off with his eyes wide open. He had been without sleep for two days. The men turned, giving him harsh looks. Mung straightened his back and realized that Mr Ishikawa had been sitting silently for some minutes. This was a crucial time in the negotiations. Courtesy required Lord Nariakira to ask the tall samurai to reveal what was in his heart.

Finally Lord Nariakira said, 'Sir, please speak freely with me, as with one of your own family, so that this matter may be brought to a happy conclusion.'

The tall scholarly samurai raised his head. 'My gracious Lord, I have sired only daughters.' He paused, then continued, 'Without sons, my family's name will be buried with me.' He turned towards Mung. 'This young man has been given an adopted name and the rank of junior samurai as befits that name.' Mr Ishikawa faced Lord Nariakira. 'There are several precedents in the book of heraldry for a second adoption.'

Lord Nariakira's head pulled back. 'What would you accomplish by that?'

'The continuation of my family name.'

'What about the name already given to Mung? Is that to fade

away? Moryiama Einosuke was a trusted retainer and a man who lived the code of Bushido.'

Mr Ishikawa bent his head and said, 'You asked me to reveal what is in my heart. I hope this has not caused you discomfort, my Lord. I understand the question, but would it be acceptable to you, my Lord, if first we agree that a second adoption is possible before we seek a solution to a problem which may not exist?'

Lord Nariakira nodded, then sent for Sakuma Shozan. The old scholar was excused from prostrating himself and moving about on his arthritic knees. He stood, head bowed, in the rear of the room and listened to the Lord of Satsuma. Mung and Saiyo sat with their eyes fixed on the floor, hanging on every word.

Sakuma Shozan considered the problem for several seconds, then said, 'My Lord, a second adoption and change of name would also entail a problem of rank. The Ishikawa family is one of the oldest and most respected. Mung would have to be raised to the rank of middle samurai.'

'The question of Moryiama Einosuke's name remains,' Lord Nariakira said. 'Is there a solution?'

Mung and Saiyo glanced longingly at each other.

After a short period of polite silence, Mr Ishikawa spoke. 'My Lord, when Moryiama Einosuke still served you, how did you address him?'

'By his first name.'

'As he had no family, my Lord, it is you who would want to hear what was most familiar to you. Would the name Moryiama Ishikawa be acceptable?'

Lord Nariakira looked to Sakuma Shozan in the rear of the room and the old man said, 'It would preserve the memory of a faithful retainer and continue the name of Ishikawa.'

Lord Nariakira slapped his knees, stood up, and said, 'It will be done!' To Sakuma Shozan he added, 'Record that Moryiama Ishikawa is raised to the rank of middle samurai and is adopted into the Kagoshima family of Ishikawa.'

Sakuma Shozan bowed as the feudal lord left the room. He turned and said, 'Ishikawa, I congratulate you on the adoption of a son into your family. The adoption will be registered as taking place after the wedding.' He looked at Mung. 'You leave on the morning of the fourth day for Yedo with Yoshida and Ryochi.'

Mung's head snapped around. He and Saiyo had been gazing into each other's eyes.

The negotiations at the *mi-ai* had taken four hours and Mung had still not rested. Back in his room, Ryochi and Yoshida were helping him dress, laughing and joking about his good fortune.

Mung complained, 'But how can they allow me only three days with Saiyo?'

Ryochi retorted, 'Being with your two good friends is better than being with Saiyo.'

Mung did not agree. Porcelain flasks of sake were brought in. Yoshida and Ryochi insisted Mung join them drink for drink.

There was a tapping at the door and a voice called from outside, 'Are the thieves ready?'

Ryochi offered a last toast, 'Here's to your bride and the children she will bear to serve the Emperor!'

Yoshida shouted out, 'The thief is ready!' They lifted Mung under the arms so his feet were off the ground.

Yoshida said, 'It's time for you to go out in the night and steal yourself a bride.'

Mung's face lit up with a silly grin. He staggered as they put him down. He raised his sake, shouted, 'Onward,' and emptied his cup.

Outside, Mung turned with a bewildered look to his friends. 'What do I do?'

Yoshida took his arm and said, 'Come along. It's all arranged. We sneak over to her room. You go in ...'

'What if her father catches me?'

They all stopped. The two friends shook their heads in exaggerated expressions of sadness. Ryochi said, 'It's the custom to steal the bride and Mr Ishikawa knows all about it.'

'You mean Mr Ishikawa is going to help me steal his own daughter?' Now Mung shook his head. 'You upper-class people have strange customs. I think I would like another drink before I kidnap her.'

'I thought you told me you never drink after that hangover in California,' Ryochi said.

Mung looked at him. 'I'm worried. What if she puts up a fight?'

The two friends took him by the arms to a nearby restaurant where they each finished another flask of sake. Yoshida and Ryochi walked on either side of Mung, for his step had become slightly erratic.

Approaching the Ishikawa house, Mung said, 'You're sure her father won't make trouble?'

'If he does, shoot him with your pistol,' Ryochi said.

'He'll be glad to get rid of that tall, skinny, intellectual daughter,' Yoshida laughed.

They were in front of the house now. Mung spun around, pulled away from Yoshida, and shouted, 'She's beautiful, be-yoo-ti-fulll!'

The two friends hushed him. They each gave him a slap on the back which sent him forward. He stumbled up the porch steps, staggered to the left and, before they could stop him, slid open the wrong door. Mr Ishikawa and Sakuma Shozan were seated in the room facing each other and drinking tea. When Mung realized what he had done, he bowed deeply over and over, excusing himself repeatedly.

Mr Ishikawa looked at Mung with wide-eyed shock, back at the old scholar, and back to Mung. He said in a whisper, 'She's next door.'

Mung bowed twice more, backed up, and slid the door closed. Looking down from the porch, he opened his hands, imploring his friends, 'What should I do?'

Ryochi pointed to the door behind Mung. 'Jump in there and get her, quickly.'

Mung reached out for the door but his hand went through the thin paper. He pulled to slide the door open but it ripped even more. Standing up straight, tugging his kimono, he smoothed the pleats and stepped through the paper screen, tearing a larger opening as he entered the room.

Ryochi turned to Yoshida, eyebrows raised. 'Holy Buddha shit! Did you see that!'

Saiyo knelt in the centre of the room, staring up at Mung with eyes so round, she looked like a westerner. 'I was told you would be expecting me,' he said. Suddenly he noticed the dress she was wearing and, in a shocked whisper, said, 'Why are you wearing white? White is for mourning.' Then his voice rose. 'Who died in this house?'

The *shoji* screen on the left slid open. Mr Ishikawa poked his head in. 'Nobody died yet, but if you don't take her out of here, I will think about killing you!'

Saiyo quickly got to her feet. She took Mung by the arm and directed him through the torn opening in the door. They hurried away with Yoshida and Ryochi.

Behind them, Mr Ishikawa shouted, 'My daughter has been stolen by a crazy man!' and his neighbours rushed out to congratulate him, to wish him well with his new son-in-law.

On the way to their room, Saiyo insisted on stopping at a Shinto temple. Except for the wind chimes tinkling in the soft breeze, there was no other sound. The two kneeled at the altar. They bowed and touched their heads to the ground to pray, each with his own thoughts.

Saiyo became aware of the deep regular breathing of someone sleeping. She looked at her new husband. Still in the kneeling position, head cradled on his arms resting on the floor, with a smile on his face, he slept, for the first time in more than two days. A light sigh escaped the bride's lips. She gently stroked Mung's back, then turned his body so his head rested in her lap. Sitting in this position, thinking of the short time they had together before he would leave for the Shōgun's Court in Yedo, she vowed to make their honeymoon memorable.

At dawn the newlyweds arose and went to their room without a word. For three days their hearts spoke of joy. Thirsting with desire, their bodies drank deeply of each other. Passion consumed them. Pounding blood declared their happiness with each beat. Neither in classical love poems nor pillow books had either read of the pleasures they experienced or the love they felt. Yet, even in the midst of their ecstasy, they spoke of the future, fearful that during their separation they would dream different dreams. So they lay close under the blankets, whispering plans, making love, and swimming in the sea of each other's mind.

On the third day, when the evening mist settled on the mountains and the sun angled into the west, Yoshida and Ryochi called on the lovers. Holding the reins of three horses, they bowed solemnly to Saiyo Ishikawa and promised to protect Mung from harm at the Shōgun's capital. It was a promise more easily given than kept.

CHAPTER
13

30 November 1852

For three months after his wedding, Mung remained in hiding with Yoshida and Ryochi. Time passed slowly waiting for the Americans. Mung felt torn between his service to Lord Nariakira and his love for Saiyo. He had lost more weight and begun to disregard his appearance.

Now, he stood alone on the porch overlooking Yedo Bay. A chilling rain swept the port. The waiting was over. There, below him, near the entrance to the harbour, three American warships swung at anchor. It was five hours since Yoshida and Ryochi had gone to make arrangements for him to act as interpreter for the Shōgun. They were to be given assurances for his safety before he would appear. He pulled his rain cape tighter and stepped closer to the wall as the wind began to gust. He watched hundreds of small Japanese fishing boats heading from the shore, through the downpour, to the large sailing vessels. Behind warehouses, out of sight on the docks, ranks of samurai were forming. In full armour, they stood quietly in the rain.

Mung went into the house. He leafed through half-painted scrolls he had discarded, stopped at a sketch of Saiyo, and his mind began to wander. Hiding from the Shōgun's spies and the separation from his wife was the most depressing event in his life. He hoped it would soon be over. There had been only one message from Saiyo in all this time. She had returned with her father to Kagoshima where he was now the acting governor.

Mung rolled the sketch like a telescope, returned to the porch and held it to his eye, scanning the American ships. Their sails were furled, not one steamer among them. He noted marine sharpshooters in the rigging and sailors at the rails with weapons ready to repel boarders. The cannons were run out and the gun crews in position. On the quarterdecks, officers with telescopes were observing Japan for the first time. The flotilla of sampans and dragon boats were encircling the large foreign ships, hundreds more of the small craft on their way and others preparing to leave shore. Mung was reminded of Gulliver and the Lilliputians. The mass of small boats undulated on the surface of the water like a gigantic bed of seaweed around the Americans.

He brought down the makeshift telescope, unrolled it and looked again at the sketch. He fingered the pouch at his waist. It contained a delicate bamboo pipe finely inlaid with silver, a present from Saiyo who taught him to smoke on their short honeymoon. He chuckled, remembering their time together. Her mother had given her a book entitled *Sexual Pleasures for the Uninitiated*, which she spent many hours studying. Mung was not uninitiated, but found that making love to Saiyo was a spiritual as well as physical sensation such as he'd never known before. He shivered at her memory. During their lovemaking he had thought of the gods he worshipped and the afterlife they promised. He could not imagine it would be any better than the exquisite caresses or ingenious climaxes he experienced with Saiyo.

Rolling up the picture, he went inside and sat near the *hibachi* for warmth, deciding not to light the pipe because he always blew the little fiery pellets of tobacco out by mistake. The burn marks on the floor mats, cushions, and his clothes attested to that.

Yoshida and Ryochi entered the room. Without taking off their shoes or rain gear, they squatted to warm their hands.

Yoshida said, 'It's arranged. Lord Hayoshi assures us of your safety. We are to go now for an immediate audience with the Shōgun.'

'You don't appear pleased,' Mung said.

'No, I'm not. We were made to reconfirm your story from the time you landed on Ryuku. They already knew everything.'

Mung looked from one to the other. 'So what is the problem? You've both said the Shōgun's spies are everywhere. We knew there would be danger and that is why you first received assurances about my safety. Let's get this over with so I can return to Kagoshima.'

Ryochi ignored Mung's comments. 'It makes little difference now. We were followed back here. Put on your rain cape and let's go.'

The three friends left the house and were immediately surrounded by samurai wearing Lord Hayoshi's calligraphic insignia on their winged helmets. No swords were drawn but it was made clear that they were an armed escort to the Shōgun's palace.

The ten-tiered pagoda dominated the centre of Yedo, Japan's most populated city. A stone wall, ten feet high and seven feet thick, surrounded the palace. Samurai, wearing winged helmets and linked chain armour with breast and shoulder plates, stood guard.

Entering the courtyard, Mung heard a scuffle behind him. Ryochi and Yoshida were being led away by samurai guards. He was taken into the palace and was standing in front of the Shōgun's reception hall before he had time to think. The next second the doors slid open and he was knocked to the floor. Lying face down, he was ordered to crawl forward on his belly. He wriggled like a snake down the centre of the hall.

Seated on either side were the councillors of the empire, ahead a raised platform with a canopy supported by four posts. At each of the posts stood a fierce samurai warrior in full armour, over six feet tall. In the centre of the platform, on a raised dais under the canopy, was the Shōgun, the ruler of Japan, Lord Hotta. He sat straight, his right eyebrow cocked, the left lowered. A first impression was of an inquisitive elderly man who pitied the world, but those dark dull eyes held no pity in their depths. Ten feet from the platform, Mung was ordered to stop. He remained arms outstretched, face down, on the mats.

One of the councillors skittered on his knees to Mung's side. He shouted at him in a high-pitched voice, 'Will the Americans use their weapons?'

Mung breathed in deeply, trying to control the weakness in his stomach and the looseness in his bowels. 'I do not believe they will use their weapons unless they are forced to. Americans are generally a peace-loving people, except when angered.'

'Why do they put themselves in danger? What do they want?'

Mung hesitated before answering. If he admitted not telling the officials in Nagasaki everything, it would mean he had withheld information from the Shōgun. He said, 'I do not know.'

The councillor's voice rose to a sarcastic whining pitch. 'Didn't the shipwrecked seamen tell you that American ships were coming to negotiate a mutual trade and aid treaty?'

Mung lay silent, fearing to answer the question.

The councillor shouted, 'Or is it that you only translate correctly for the Lord of Satsuma! And not for the Shōgun who is the Emperor's appointed guardian of the people and lands of Japan!'

Mung pressed his nose harder into the mat, muttering a prayer he had been taught by his adopted brother, John Whittefield. 'Yea though I walk through the valley of the shadow of death ...' Expecting the sound of a sword coming out of its scabbard.

Instead the sarcastic voice continued, 'This scum, who has broken the law by living in a foreign country, expects us to believe he does Japan a service by warning us that three American ships come to topple the empire. He is a fool!' The councillor bowed his head to the floor. Still on his knees, he skittered back to his place.

The Shōgun lifted the little finger of his right hand. Two guards grabbed Mung by his ankles and dragged him out of the hall. As he was pulled into the corridor, a voice in accented English said, 'How are you, my teacher?'

Mung looked up at a group of his students from the Interpreters School, waiting to be admitted to the Shōgun's presence. He arched his back, keeping his head from bouncing on the paving stones. He was dragged through the corridors, then thrown down several flights of stone steps and dumped into a four-by-four-foot hole chiselled out of solid rock. The hole, seven feet deep, was covered by a bamboo grate and guarded by two samurai.

In the reception hall above, the Shōgun dismissed all but his two senior councillors, Lord Hayoshi and Lord Abi. They remained on their knees before the dais.

The Shōgun nodded to the fleshy, intellectual Lord Abi, who then said, 'Each of Admiral Biddel's requests should be dealt with individually. The power of the American weapons should not be discounted. Trade and coaling stations are unacceptable. At first, aid and repatriation of shipwrecked sailors should be denied. Haven in our ports for ships in distress should be refused and then acceded to if pressure warrants. In the case of excessive force, we can accede to one coaling station on some remote island.'

Lord Hayoshi straightened his back. The veins on his clean shaven skull vibrated under the gleaming yellow skin. He looked disdainfully at Lord Abi. 'No concessions! If we give just one, the French, English, Russians, and Dutch will be here with their hands out. If we change one letter of the Exclusion Edict, we will be assaulted on all sides!' He clutched the hilts of his two swords and snarled, 'To the death!'

The Shōgun's right eyebrow rose even further. He looked from one councillor to the other. In a voice just above a whisper, he said, 'Make no concessions. Make no resistance unless the foreigners attempt to come ashore. If Americans regard life as highly as they pretend, we shall let them bombard our boats. After they have killed a few hundred fishermen, we will know if they are serious or not. Lord Hayoshi will be responsible for the military; Lord Abi the negotiations.' His lips parted in a smile, his upper teeth protruding. 'Dress the head of the Butchers Guild in the prefect's clothing. He will receive the American admiral.' As the two councillors bowed, the Shōgun said, 'Don't kill that interpreter Mung. We'll use him for entertainment when this affair is over.'

An admiral in the American Navy can make mistakes only if his directives are not clear. Such a situation existed for Admiral James Biddel in the winter of 1852. His orders from the United States State Department were, 'Set up treaties of trade, assistance to shipwrecked sailors, and coaling stations, with the ruler of Japan. *No force is to be used nor diplomatic incidents to occur.*'

Admiral Biddel had little knowledge of Japan, its government or its people. He was hampered by a lack of ships. The East India Squadron he commanded had, on paper, a complement of twelve fighting ships and seven supply ships. Actually there were only three ships of the line and two supply ships, all of them windjammers.

The Admiral left his supply ships at sea for safety and hove to near the mouth of Yedo Bay on a grey rainy day. Soon after dropping anchor, his ships were surrounded by a fleet of small boats which stood off about one hundred yards.

In the afternoon, a large government barge used by the prefect of Yedo put out from shore. The head of the Butchers Guild, a socially detested group (Japanese rarely ate meat), sat under a canopy clothed as the prefect. Lords Hayoshi and Abi were dressed as messengers. Two samurai from the Interpreters School acted as guards and the third as a Dutch interpreter. The prefect's party was rowed to Admiral Biddel's ship, piped aboard and given full honours.

Back on the prefect's barge after having conferred with the Admiral, the two Lords began to devise a plan to thwart the Americans.

Lord Hayoshi said, 'They have no one who speaks Japanese, can you believe it? They are so sure we can't understand English, they speak freely in front of our interpreters. It is clear these Americans are naïve and confused.'

Lord Abi said, 'Keep in mind that the interpreter Mung was correct about their demands. He could also be correct about the destructive power of their weapons.'

Lord Hayoshi waved his hand as if brushing away a fly. 'I saw the size of those cannon, but the man who commands them is indecisive and that is more important. You can't say this American made demands. They were more like requests.'

Lord Abi said, 'I want him to leave the harbour through negotiation, not a battle.'

'You have two days to negotiate. Then I will enter the picture. The Shōgun wants them out of here.' Lord Hayoshi rose to his feet clutching his sword. 'Two days!'

Lord Abi's first order was for the small boats to close the ring around each American ship, thereby isolating them. When the Americans did not react, he sent a message to the Admiral stating that negotiations were impossible and the foreigners must leave. To his surprise, the Admiral's reply was addressed to the Emperor, a clear indication the Americans had little or no information of Japan's political structure. The Admiral refused to leave the harbour until he had spoken to the Emperor or one of his representatives. Lord Abi issued an order for the fishermen to try to board and harass the Americans.

All that night, American officers and crews stood a one hundred per cent watch. They were hamstrung by orders against using force in trying to prevent the theft of everything not nailed down. In the morning, Lord Abi sent a message inviting Admiral Biddel to come to the prefect's barge to meet with a representative of the Emperor. The Admiral refused, requesting that Japanese civilians be restrained from boarding American ships in order to prevent an incident. Lord Abi's return message consented to the withdrawal of civilians, pointing out that this could be implemented more efficiently if the Admiral would visit the prefect's barge. To relieve the pressure on his men who had been standing at battle stations all night and into the morning, Admiral Biddel agreed.

In the eyes of the Japanese, the Admiral had already lost face when he personally greeted messengers and allowed common fishermen to board his ships. When James Biddel stepped on to the prefect's barge he was purposely bumped by one of the samurai guards and almost fell overboard. That he did not have the samurai killed immediately became an oft-told story in the Shōgun's Court. The samurai was sought after as a guest by Yedo's élite. The yarn that drew more laughs amongst Japan's intellectuals was how the big American tried to sit crosslegged like a Japanese and bargain with a butcher. It was true the Admiral became angered by the refusal of the Emperor's representative to negotiate any point. It was then that Lord Abi, using a clever ruse, reduced the American force by one third. He told the Admiral about the shipwrecked sailors in the port of Nagasaki; and that repatriation would be immediate but time was of the essence since they were being held by a Lord who had been known to implement the death penalty of the Exclusion Edict. The Admiral dispatched the USS *Preble* with instructions to make haste to save the survivors. The fleet of small boats closed around the remaining two ships. Now there was an obvious addition to the fishing boats. War barges carrying archers and sword-wielding samurai with boarding equipment were brought close.

On the morning of the third day, Lord Hayoshi, in full battle armour, strode into Lord Abi's room. He bowed and said, 'Your negotiations have not succeeded. It is time to kill these foreign children and burn their big toys to the waterline.'

Lord Abi answered, 'Allow me one more message.'

Lord Hayoshi slammed his fist into the palm of his hand. 'I'm preparing my warriors! Send your message!' He left the prefect's barge.

Lord Abi's final message warned the Admiral of an impending battle if he did not cease the invasion of Japan's privacy.

James Biddel realistically evaluated his mistakes. He replied that he was prepared to leave but would have to wait for a wind to manoeuvre his vessels. Another indignity was added to the American failure when the Japanese fishing boats took the American fighting ships in tow and hauled them out to the open sea.

A seasoned veteran, Admiral James Biddel had sailed into Yedo Bay with his hands tied. The Japanese Department had not yet been established. It was because of this failure that the Foreign Office of the United States appointed William Whittefield to be its first director.

In the Shōgun's palace, Mung was hauled out of his cell, escorted by guards to a steaming bath and thrown in. He scrubbed himself clean, used oil of jasmine to cover the smell of his imprisonment, and donned the clean white robe he was given. The guards escorted him to an anteroom of the Shōgun's reception hall where several men in similar white robes waited with actors and musicians. The strange clothing worn by the actors seemed somehow familiar to Mung. Because he held the rank of samurai, he was taken away from the others and directly into the Shōgun's reception hall. There he was made to wait against the side wall.

Acrobats performed before the Shōgun and his court, soon followed by the musicians and singers. Then the actors began a pantomime presentation of the American disgrace. Mung now recognized the clothing they wore, as grotesque imitations of American naval uniforms. The exaggerated but deft movements of the actors caused the councillors to double over with laughter. They were brought to tears when the butcher, attired in blood-stained clothing and chewing a piece of raw meat, negotiated with the Admiral. The *pièce de résistance* came when the samurai who had actually bumped the Admiral acted his own part. The councillors tapped their gold inlaid fans and threw them to the actors.

From the opposite side of the hall, four enormous men lumbered in. Except for small aprons, they were naked mountains of muscle and fat. The sumo wrestlers bowed before the Shōgun and faced off into pairs. A fifteen-foot circle was marked on the floor mats by a blue silk rope and the first two wrestlers entered the ring. They faced each other for several minutes, making a series of facial and muscle-flexing movements designed to frighten an opponent. Then they bowed to each other and, with surprising agility for men their size, leapt forward. The smack of flesh and muscle resounded throughout the hall. The giants, locked in combat, pushed and grunted, sweat pouring like rain from their huge bodies. There was a sudden quick movement and one of the wrestlers was pushed over the line. The next two entered the ring, going through the same procedure until two winners stood side by side.

Excitement rippled through the ranks of the councillors when Chikamutsu, Japan's sumo champion, entered the hall. He was taller and larger than all the other wrestlers; each step he took was an entirely separate movement which carried his enormous torso forward. The man mountain bowed to the Shōgun, then to one of

262

the sumo wrestlers who stepped into the ring. The smaller man began the face-making and muscle-flexing exercises. Chikamutsu stood straight, looking at his opponent with a placid bovine countenance. Mung felt the smaller man was defeated even before he leapt forward and was tossed like a bale of rice over the silk rope. The second wrestler fared no better.

From the anteroom came the men Mung had seen dressed in white cotton robes similar to his. They were lined up and the smallest was pushed inside the circle of the blue silk rope, looking fearfully at the sweat slick mass of flesh before him. He sank to his knees, body shaking. Chikamutsu put a huge hand on the little man's shoulder, the other hand on his head and twisted. Mung heard the neck snap from across the room. The man fell dead and was dragged from the ring.

The largest and strongest looking man in the group was pushed into the ring. He moved first to the right, then to the left. Only Chikamutsu's serene round eyes followed the movements. The man leapt forward, fingers outstretched to gouge the champion's eyes. The wrestler took one quick step forward and caught the man in midair. He hugged until the spinal cord snapped, then threw him, like a limp chicken, from the ring.

Mung found himself being led by the arm. The guards stopped him just short of the ring. The councillor who had accused him before he was thrown into the hole, came forward on his knees.

He bowed to the Shōgun and shouted at Mung, 'Your predictions of doom were slightly exaggerated. The threat of American power was a lie. We led the dogs out to sea with their tails between their legs. Show us your American fighting methods against Chikamutsu. Win, and you are free. The Shōgun, Lord Hotta, decrees it.'

Mung's fear of dying had passed in the stone cell. The moment he had given up hope of living, he felt freer than ever in his life. Either he would meet Saiyo in another life, or he would wait for her in the Christian hereafter. He accepted his karma.

The councillor turned but was stopped by Mung's voice. 'If I defeat this gentleman ...' he used the highest form of the word gentleman, 'will my friends also go free?'

The councillor looked to the Shōgun who remained motionless, then slowly closed and opened his dull dark eyes.

The councillor pointed to the rear of the hall. 'Your two friends will bear witness to their fate. It lies in your hands.'

Mung had just a glimpse of Yoshida and Ryochi, flanked by guards, before he was shoved into the ring. He looked across at Chikamutsu who stared down at him like a cow looking at fodder. Mung flexed his knees, hunched forward and brought up his hands in front of him. His mind raced through all the kicks, throws, and death blows he could possibly deliver. None could succeed against this gargantuan. He straightened up, fingering the bridge of his broken nose. Suddenly he remembered his brother's story about the legendary Kappa with the cavity in his head. As his fingers felt the crease in his nose, he thought of the Frenchman in Hawaii. Stepping forward, he bowed low. Chikamutsu looked down with that same placid expression, then slowly bent his huge head forward, returning the bow. Mung planted his feet. As the giant raised his head, Mung drew back his right arm so far the tendons in his neck almost snapped. With all his weight and driving strength, he threw the punch, hitting Chikamutsu squarely between the eyes. The man mountain quivered and rocked on his heels. Mung backed up quickly, ran forward, and leapt into the air. With both feet, he jumpkicked the sumo wrestler in the face. Knocked off balance by the punch, then rocked backward by the double kick, the colossus staggered and tried to regain his balance. He tripped over the silk rope and crashed into the samurai guarding the Shōgun. Both men fell into the corner pole supporting the canopy, snapping it like a twig. The covering slid to the floor. Mung looked at the Shōgun who showed no surprise, no emotion. His dull eyes stared and his mouth opened like a cobra's. Several samurai drew their swords and closed in on Mung.

From the rear of the hall an authoritative voice boomed, 'Halt!' The priest, Mung's guide in Satsuma, wore armour and an insignia of high rank. Mung had been unaware of his guide's status, senior warrior priest in all Japan. The priest strode forward, shaven head gleaming, fists dug into his hips. His voice carried to all corners of the hall, 'The Shōgun has given his word! The code of Bushido demands it be implemented! No harm will come to these three Satsuma men in this Court!'

The only reaction Mung could discern in the Shōgun's face was a slight reddening of his pale cheeks and the lowering of his raised eyebrow. It enhanced the appearance of a snake watching its victim, preparing to strike. Then the fingers of the Shōgun's right hand made a short brushing motion. Mung was pushed from the room.

In the corridor, a samurai stepped forward with sword raised to strike Mung. He died choking on his own blood, a dagger, thrown by the warrior priest, in his throat. The guards closed around Mung and rushed him out into the courtyard, through the compound gate and into the street. Yoshida and Ryochi waited there, bewildered.

'There's no time to speak,' the priest shouted, pointing at the samurai coming out of the gate towards them. He led Mung, Ryochi and Yoshida at a dead run away from the castle, always moving south through the streets of the Shōgun's capital. They ran four miles and only then left the populated area of Yedo.

Completely winded, the three rested while the priest ran into a wood and returned leading four horses. Mounted, they galloped after him, racing onward at top speed. When finally they stopped, the animals stood foam-flecked and spraddlelegged in the road. The men removed bedrolls and saddlebags from the horses and sent the exhausted beasts into a ravine. They sat down to eat.

On foot, they headed for Mount Fuji and beyond. Twenty days and nights, they walked. The warrior priest led them, unseen by searchers, travellers or villagers. They fed on edible roots, herbs and mushrooms in the woods and mountains. Emerging from the forest in tatters, at a small shrine near the shore in the province of Mikawa, they recuperated for a day while the priest arranged for a boat and guide to Satsuma. Then he disappeared, without a word.

They sailed out of the harbour on a moonless night, keeping away from the shore, and made for the far side of Kyushu. They waited until nightfall before coming into the port of Ichiki. From there, the guide led them on a short trek overland to Satsuma.

Seated in a room of the Satsuma castle, Lord Nariakira and Sakuma Shozan faced Yoshida, Mung, and Ryochi. They had been meeting for three days, hours on end, to evaluate the effects of Admiral Biddel's failure in Yedo.

Lord Nariakira spoke, 'The loss of face suffered by the Americans has strengthened the Shōgun. We and other supporters of the Emperor are in a more tenuous position than ever before.' He looked at the senior scholar. 'Sakuma Shozan has advised acceptance of Mung's view that indeed the three American ships had superior fire power, although inferior leadership. Nevertheless, with a straw, the Shōgun has beaten off the American eagle. This show of power will draw those who were undecided to his side.' Lord Nariakira arose and left the room.

Sakuma Shozan's pale, delicate skin hung loose on his cheeks. The lower eyelids showed pink, his dark eyes tired. 'Fifty years ago I joined the Satsuma Court as senior scholar.' He slowly dabbed the dampness from the corners of his lips. 'My life's work has been the restoration of power to the Emperor. I will not see that day.' He looked at Yoshida and Ryochi. 'Henceforth you will both remain at my side. You, Yoshida, will soon succeed me as personal adviser to Lord Nariakira and as senior scholar of Satsuma. Ryochi will begin to study certain military books I have selected, some of which Mung translated in Nagasaki.' He turned to Mung. 'You are herewith appointed first assistant to the governor of Kagoshima, your adopted father.' He smiled. 'Go home to your bride. Spend more time with her. It is not good to leave a young woman alone.'

Mung made his farewells and hurried to Saiyo. As fast as he travelled, Lord Nariakira's messenger still reached Kagoshima first. Mung was met with a fresh horse at the outskirts of the city and taken up the mountain slope above the damage line of the *tsunami*. His guide left him on the path of a cottage overlooking the harbour. On the porch stood Saiyo, her hands clasped in front of her. He moved towards her and saw her smile. A tear ran down one cheek. She bowed.

'Dear husband, it is good to see you. Are you well?'

Mung bowed in return. 'Yes I am well now that I have come home. It has been a long time and I have yearned for the sight of you.'

'And I for you. It has been a hard, dusty road you travelled. There is a bath waiting.'

'Will you join me?'

'I feared you would not ask.'

In the tub-room they disrobed, each using the utmost willpower to restrain from reaching out to touch the other. They entered the steaming tub face to face. As they sank slowly down into the hot water to their necks, their knees touched. Saiyo picked up two bars of perfumed soap and handed one to Mung. She rubbed hers to foaming soap suds and reached over to lather his neck and shoulders, he following her example. Then she stood up, her tiny breasts pointing at him. Her golden skin glowed with the heat of the water, radiating with a burning desire for his caresses. He soaped her body and she his. They stepped outside the tub, embracing, allowing their bodies to slip and slide one against the other until he entered her and she raised her legs to hold him within. With one thrust, he ejaculated. His body quivered but he did not release her. He carried her to their bed still impaled on his erection and they made love slowly. She seemed to anticipate his every pleasure and he pleased her, revelling in her moans and the spasms of her body.

Mung uncovered his wife, gazing at her and drinking in her beauty and grace. His box of paints stood in the corner of the room. Placing her right hand behind her head, he positioned Saiyo on her side, her left hip leaning back to expose the dark V of her pubic hair. He took up his brush and began to work on the silk *shoji* screen door, painting a full portrait. His strokes were bold and quick but each time their eyes met, the strokes slowed. As he worked and gazed upon her, the motion of the brush had an erotic effect on both of them. He saw the rise and fall of her soft belly. The nipples of her breasts stood out. He felt the hardness between his legs. Her lips parted. Her eyes beckoned him. He dropped the brush and went to her.

After breakfast the following morning Saiyo motioned to the symbolic recess set aside for the Emperor in the wall. 'I have waited for your return before preparing the *tokonama*.'

'It's a good thing the mikado didn't arrive while I was away.' They both laughed.

'I'll paint an apricot tree in blossom,' he said.

'And I can arrange a vase of wild flowers.'

Saiyo stayed at Mung's side as he painted their *shoji* screens with apple blossoms, forsythia and other flowering trees according to her wishes.

The only change Mung initiated in the house was to seal his reputation with the townspeople as an eccentric. He built an indoor toilet. Spectators watched him dig the cesspool, line it with stones, then cap it with wood and sod. Many of the old jokes about the whaling ship's toilet were revived to fit this new addition they called a shit storage closet. When the work was finished, Saiyo gave a tea party. Most of the guests queued up to use the indoor privy.

When spring came, the couple walked the beaches and collected shells. They strolled the mountain slopes, gathering flowers and composing poetry to nature and each other. As spring blossomed, so did Saiyo. She was with child.

Thereafter, they stayed close to their cottage amongst the red pines, clover and wildflowers. Saiyo, a fastidious housekeeper, drew pleasure from her husband's comfort. They treasured each moment together.

Mung and Mr Ishikawa's gardener worked together building a rock garden for Saiyo. They diverted water from a nearby stream with bamboo pipes and carefully placed stones according to the gardener's plan. The musical sound of the trickling water gave them pleasure day and night. Where the water formed a pool, Mung planted a weeping willow tree. He was reminded of Lucky and told Saiyo about the kitten. She encouraged him to recount every detail of his adventure in Yedo and the long, arduous journey home. Unknown to him she was keeping a journal of his exploits, a record which eventually entered Japanese folklore.

Often Mr Ishikawa came to visit. He instructed Mung on the political, social and economic structure of Japan. Saiyo listened but never spoke until her father had gone. Then she and Mung would discuss the possibility of applying the American concept of democracy to Japan. They enjoyed playing a game in which all Japanese were equals, Mung always taking the role of the lower class and Saiyo the higher. It never failed to make her laugh.

'Hello there old horse. How are you doing?' says Mung the merchant.

'For your sake I have not heard what you said, detestable slug that you are. Why do you wear such an elegant kimono and *obi*?' says Saiyo the artisan.

'Because I have the rice and can afford them.'

'How did you come by this rice?'

'From oafs like you.'

At this Saiyo hurries away on tiptoe and whispers to an imaginary district prefect, pointing at Mung as she whispers. Then, taking the role of the prefect, she lifts her kimono slightly and strides back to Mung like a samurai. Looking him up and down, she demands, 'Your identity card!'

Mung smiles and produces an imaginary wooden tag. 'I am a merchant.'

Saiyo throws her shoulders back, chin up, and plants her fists on her hips. 'You were a merchant.' She mimics the haughty tone of command. 'I now confiscate all your property!'

'But I am a human being and equal to every other person,' Mung implores.

'You were never a full human being and certainly are not equal to anyone because you are without a head.' She brandishes an invisible sword and falls limp with laughter into Mung's arms.

The one role she could never complete was trying to act a bossy American woman who shook her finger and shouted at her husband. Invariably she would sink to the floor holding her sides in laughter at the absurdity of the idea.

As her pregnancy progressed, Saiyo's face rounded with such beauty that those who saw her remarked upon it. Mung was pleased to have others recognize what he saw every time he looked at her.

Ten thousand miles away, the parting of another young couple would have a significant impact on Mung, Saiyo and the future of Japan.

CHAPTER
14

John Whittefield and Beth Spaulding had walked together under crossed swords in Annapolis. Immediately following their wedding and John's graduation, he was assigned to the staff of Commodore Matthew Calbraith Perry. For two years they led an exciting life in New York City with its concerts, museums, plays and sporting events. They were part of the social whirl of dinner-parties and costume balls. John had long since learned to balance a tea cup. He was always part of the political discussions which surrounded Commodore Perry's staff at these gatherings.

When their son Jeffrey was three months old, John received orders to ship out with the Commodore. Despite his regrets about leaving his wife and son, he could hardly wait to be aboard a ship of the line. He yearned for the sea. It was what he had been trained for.

John and Beth were both from navy families. They often spoke of sea duty. However, Beth had pushed the reality of it from her mind. When the time came, she was devastated. 'How will I sleep without your arms around me?' she asked. 'How will I survive without your kisses and your smile?'

He held her in his arms and kissed away her tears. 'My Beth. Don't cry. Please don't. We knew this time would come. Our parents suffered separations.'

'You'll be gone more than a year,' she sobbed into his chest. 'Jeff will have begun to talk and have taken his first steps before you return.'

John rubbed his chin lovingly on the top of his wife's head. 'Will you tell him about me?'

'Yes my darling.'

'Tell him I love him and teach him to say dad, not father.'

'I will. I will,' she wept.

'Beth, Beth,' he crooned, smoothing her golden hair. 'We both grew up with our fathers away most of the time. My mother and I always appreciated him more than other families whose fathers were taken for granted.'

She chewed the corner of her lip and dried her eyes. 'You're right. You're right. I guess we didn't turn out so bad.'

They laughed together as he hugged her but then she thumped the centre of his chest with her fist and once again her eyes welled with tears.

'Why are you hitting me?' he asked.

From behind a handkerchief, she sobbed. 'I know better than anyone your physical needs. I think sailors call it being horny.'

'Horny!' The word burst from his lips. He snorted.

'Stop laughing,' she said. 'You must admit you are sexually active.'

'In that case,' he said, 'you're a bit horny yourself.'

'John!' She stamped her foot and the words rushed from her lips. 'I've heard about those brown-skinned girls in Hawaii and the beautiful Chinese women.'

John enveloped his wife in his arms, but in the moment before their lips met he had a fleeting glimpse of the enchanting girl in Canton and the Hawaiian girls at Waikiki.

'Dearest Beth. We'll just have to work at getting all the horniness out of me before I leave.'

In contrast to the hazy orders and reduced fleet which had hamstrung Admiral Biddel, Commodore Perry had the full backing of Daniel Webster, the senior senator in the US Congress. He was given his choice of ships, carte blanche to purchase presents, and clear orders from President Millard Fillmore.

'The objects sought by this government are: 1) To effect some permanent arrangement for the protection of American seamen and property wrecked on these islands, or driven into their ports by stress of weather. 2) Permission for American vessels to enter a Japanese port in order to obtain supplies or provisions, water, fuel, and/or in case of disasters to refit so as to enable them to prosecute their voyage. 3) Permission for our vessels to enter one or more of their ports for the purpose of disposing of their cargoes by sale or barter.'

The commodore's personal instructions from the President were, 'Make it clear that the United States is no part of, not even an ally of, the British Empire, or any other European country. Point out that our wealth and population are rapidly increasing, that California lies only twenty days' steaming from Japan, that the Pacific will soon be covered with our vessels, and that even a limited Japanese-American trade would be mutually profitable. Any concessions on these points should be reduced into the form of a treaty for which you will be furnished with the requisite powers to negotiate. But if after exhausting every argument and means of persuasion you are unable to extract any concession from the Japanese, you will then change your tone and inform them that if any acts of cruelty should hereafter be practised upon citizens of this country, whether by the government or by the inhabitants of Japan, they will be severely chastised.'

John Whittefield, as the only Japanese interpreter, was caught up in the whirlwind set in motion by Commodore Perry in his hasty but exacting preparations. All captains and seamen who had any knowledge of Japan were interviewed. Silas Bent and Mercator Cooper both had been imprisoned in Japan and escaped, one from the island of Hokkaido and the other from Honshu. They confirmed that most of the literature about Japan was fantasy and conjecture but could add little about the military, economic or political situation there.

The American ambassador to the Netherlands confidentially obtained a copy of the journal kept by German Doctor Philip von Siebold. Dr Siebold, posing as one of the Dutch delegation from Dishima paying the yearly homage to the Shōgun in 1824, remained in Yedo teaching medicine for six months. His journal was forwarded to Canton to await Commodore Perry and the East India Squadron.

Commodore Perry and his contingent left the United States in

March 1853. Under steam they rounded Cape Horn, missing by several weeks the most up-to-date source of information about Japan. Harold MacDonald had been rescued and was aboard the USS *Preble* which had taken the route around the tip of Africa on its way back to the United States.

In Hawaii the Squadron was joined by three other ships. John had a few days to renew his friendship with Reverend Damon, see the rebuilt church, the beautiful thriving city of Hawaii, and the square named in memory of Dr Judd. He visited Mama's boarding house. She hadn't changed much, a few more grey hairs perhaps but the moneybelt and gun were still at her waist, and the rules of the house were the same. They spoke of Mung who had himself told Mama about Pistchiani and Ben.

John spent most of his time in the Japanese compound improving his understanding and use of their language. Every day he faithfully read a portion of the Bible, continually revising his reading time to coincide with Washington DC where Beth and her parents were reading the same portion. The Bible and its readings made him feel closer to his wife and son, and made their separation more bearable.

The Squadron moved out of Honolulu Harbour on a beeline across the Pacific to Ryuku. The Commodore, aware that the island was a protectorate of the Japanese empire, had an official message of his impending visit to Yedo delivered to the island. He anchored only part of his fleet within sight of land and replenished the supply ships with wood, fresh fruit and vegetables.

He then steamed into the straits of Formosa. For years American whalers and merchantmen had complained of pirates operating from the ports of Tainan and Kaohsiung on the big island off the coast of China. The Commodore applied the same formula to both ports. After his cannon had blown the top off the largest pagoda, he sent in his contingent of marines, led by John Whittefield. John lined up his men on the beach and ordered the town's leader to point out those who practised piracy. When the head man hesitated, John signalled and the guns of the *Susquehanna* fired until another pagoda lost its roof. This procedure led to the imprisonment of the pirates and their eventual turn-over to Chinese authorities on the mainland in Canton.

The Squadron sailed up the Pearl River. Once again, after so many years, John saw the Tiger Gate fort and the bay where the Chinese war-junks, scrambling dragons, and British ships had battled. The boat people were as numerous as before. Two more navy ships waited in the harbour to join the Squadron.

From the upper deck, John's eyes searched the crowd on the quay until he saw the familiar figure of Jake Tillim in his loose three-quarter-length jacket and Panama hat. The unlit cigar was stuck in the corner of his mouth. Ashore, the two reminisced for hours, then John toured the city in a rickshaw, a new, more comfortable innovation of the British which had replaced the palanquin. He bought clothes, lacquerware and trinkets for Beth, their son and families.

The officers and men were warned not to leave Canton. A self-styled Chinese messiah had arisen in Kwan-si Province. Hsui-chuan, messiah, madman or mystic, believed himself to be the younger brother of Jesus Christ. Schooled for two years by Protestant missionaries, he had distorted their teachings and was now leading a popular revolt against the Chinese government. His objective was to establish God's kingdom on earth.

A few days after the fleet arrived, Jake Tillim hurried to the Commodore's stateroom at three in the morning. One of his Chinese agents had staggered in from a six-hour nonstop run with the message that the American steamer, *Mildred R.*, had run aground and was surrounded by religious fanatics. It was believed the American ship was selling opium. Hsui-chuan himself was on his way to direct the final assault.

Commodore Perry ordered John Whittefield and his marines to board the *Vandalia* and take part in the rescue mission. The captain and crew of the *Mildred R.* were to be brought back in irons if there really was opium aboard. Jake Tillim's offer to act as interpreter and guide was gratefully accepted.

The *Vandalia* weighed anchor. Building up to a full head of steam, she coasted by the boat people. Turning west with a bone in her teeth, she ploughed up the centre of the Youngchow River, the dawn's light caressing her wake.

The *Mildred R.*, a low draught English steamer purchased by the firm of Park and Lesser for trading, plied the southern rivers of China. The captain would nuzzle her bow to the river bank of the most populated areas, lower a gangplank, and allow farmers and merchants to file aboard and show their merchandise. Credit slips or cash for completed transactions could then be used to purchase items laid out along the length of the deck. These trading sessions took several hours or sometimes as long as a week.

Now the ship was hung up on a mud flat forty-five miles from Canton. Trading had stopped and the crowd was being incited by leaders from the new religious sect. Under normal conditions, the *Mildred R.* would have reversed her engines and left her troubles behind, but the level of the Youngchow River had dropped three feet in two hours. This was not an unusual occurrence for the river, but with the growing excitement the captain had paid more attention to the commotion around his ship than to the level of the water. When he gave the order to move, the big side-wheeler literally walked away from the river bank over the mud flat on her paddlewheels, but did not quite make it over the mud bar.

The captain sent his shipboard coolies over the side with shovels and mattocks to dig a channel through the mud flat and into the river. But the crowd pelted the coolies with stones, clods of dirt and insults, calling them traitors. Half of them deserted to the crowd, taking their tools worth more than a month's pay with them. The other half scrambled back aboard the steamer. The captain tried reasoning with the crowd, assuring them he carried no opium and offering good pay for those willing to help free the ship, but the instigators would have none of it.

The mob continued to grow. Word spread throughout the countryside. More men came, some armed with wooden spears, slings, knives and muskets. A few scattered shots from the river bank sent the rest of the ship's coolies slipping and sliding over the mud away from the steamer. The captain organized his crew and passengers to defend themselves as best they could with a small number of pistols, rifles, sabres and boat hooks.

The first assaults by the mob across the mud flat were almost good-natured. Like school children, hundreds came running towards the ship, sloshing and slipping knee deep in mud. When the captain laid on the steam whistle, they turned back to shore, frightened by the noise and laughing at their own fear. But people kept pouring into the area and the mob turned mean. A volley of musket fire from the river bank caused the first casualties. A crewman was killed and a passenger wounded. The captain ordered bales of rice and cotton brought up from the hold to form a barricade at the rail. Throughout the remainder of the day, serious assaults were made with the intention of gaining control of the bow of the ship. Every attempt was thwarted but the attackers gained a little more confidence with each effort. It was a matter of time before the defenders weakened and the ship was overrun.

Mob leaders sent word by runners to Hsui-chuan fifty miles away. The new messiah decided a river steamer could add new dimensions to his crusade against the government of China. He made for the river with his soldiers of God. Seventy-five rickshaw men running full speed, six of whom died in the effort, brought Hsui-chuan to the river. He covered the fifty miles in his rickshaw at an average of fourteen miles per hour. Arriving at three in the morning, he immediately ordered an all-out assault.

From the ship, the bank of the river appeared to be covered with giant fireflies. They were torches which were soon thrown at the bow of the steamer by the first group of attackers. The second wave flowed into the battle, engaging the defenders in hand to hand fighting on the burning deck. The captain died trying to hold off the mob. So many wooden spears pierced his body that it propped like a sizzling pig over the fire. With the stench of the smouldering body in their nostrils, the passengers and crew renewed their efforts. They drove the mob from the ship.

The fire soon forced the defenders back to the stern where they barricaded themselves behind rice bales. Before dawn two assaults were made from sampans on the river, but these were easily beaten back with heavy losses to the attackers.

The morning sun revealed dead bodies strewn around the charred, smoking bow of the *Mildred R*. Three red rockets whooshed skyward from the shore and thousands of armed men poured onto the mud flats, shouting and running towards the steamer.

From aboard the *Vandalia*, it appeared they were too late. Coming up river, they had passed several bodies drifting downstream. They saw the rocket trails in the sky before the black smoke pouring from the bow of the river steamer was visible. When she did come into view, her decks were covered with armed Chinese. It was John Whittefield who spotted the defenders, men, women and children, on the lower deck, backed to the stern rail behind a barricade reaching almost to the upper deck. The attackers were firing and throwing spears down behind the bales of rice. The *Vandalia* closed the distance at full speed.

John Whittefield turned to the captain. 'Sir, can you fire your big guns?'

'Yes, but not accurately enough to support those poor souls on the stern.'

'Then fire to encourage them.'

The cannons on the *Vandalia* boomed out, one after another. The attackers on the ship hesitated, not sure if they were under fire. John formed his men on the bow of the steamer as she churned the muddy brown water.

A navy chief sang out the distance between the two ships, 'One thousand yards and closing ... Nine hundred yards and closing ...'

The marines loosened the leather slings on their rifles and pulled their peaked caps down over their right ears so as not to interfere with their sighting. They assumed the kneeling firing position.

'Seven hundred yards and closing ...'

John Whittefield's voice rang out, 'Scouts fire at those on the upper deck!'

Pow! Pow! Pow! The expert riflemen rocked with the recoil of their weapons.

'Six hundred yards and closing ...'

'Company – fire!' The command was not fully out of John's

278

throat before attackers began falling on the upper deck of the steamer. The rifle fire was so deadly accurate and the mob so dense that one bullet often hit two or more attackers. The captain of the *Vandalia* laid on his steam whistle as they closed with the stern of the embattled ship.

John ordered his men, 'Prepare to board!'

The marines straightened their caps, fixed bayonets, pulled leather stocks from the kits at their belts, and buckled them around their necks to prevent sabre cuts; then stood at attention.

John Whittefield spoke in a firm cadenced voice, his eye measuring the narrowing gap between the two ships. 'We go over the rail, up the barricade and clear the top deck! Keep in line! Show them naked steel and use your rifle butts! Don't rush ahead!'

As the *Vandalia* nudged the steamer, John leapt forward from rail to rail, a sabre in one hand and six-shot Colt in the other. He went up over the heads of the defenders on to the rice bales and leapt to the upper deck, shooting two men before he swung his legs over the top rail. With his sabre and pistol, he cleared a place on deck for the leathernecks. The men formed in four ranks of seven each. On his command, they fired in volleys sweeping the deck. The captain of the *Vandalia* cleared the lower decks, port and starboard, with two rounds of grapeshot. Like a huge wounded animal, the mob fled the ship, howling in pain and rage. They lined the river bank, cursing, shaking their spears, and firing ineffectually at the two ships.

Slowly, a silence spread along the bank. A ripple ran through the crowd as a tall, thin man, clothed only in a loin cloth with a garland on his head, appeared at the centre.

Jake Tillim had come aboard the *Mildred R.* and stood next to John Whittefield. 'That's the messiah himself!'

In full view of the two ships and under the guns of the *Vandalia*, the self-styled prophet gave orders for his men to prepare another attack. Bannermen ran with flags to take up positions along the river bank. Signal rockets were being placed. Close to ten thousand armed men lined the shore.

Jake pointed to the guns of the *Vandalia* with their crews at the ready. 'John, if that religious fanatic gives the order, those people are going to be slaughtered. I've come to love them, crazy as they are.'

The new messiah stepped barefoot out on to the mud flat in full view facing the mob, dead bodies strewn around him. Hsui-chuan spread his arms skyward and began a lengthy harangue against those out on the river. John Whittefield took a rifle from his first sergeant, adjusted the sight and brought the weapon to his shoulder. He levelled the barrel and aimed. As the zealot turned to give a signal, John squeezed the trigger. The single shot echoed across the river. Hsui-chuan sprawled backward, spreadeagled in the mud, a hole in his chest. There was hushed silence on the river and the shore.

Jake, the first to recover, pulled John around by the arm. 'You've got to get his body or there's going to be more trouble.'

John looked at the older man, dumbfounded. 'What kind of trouble?'

'There'll be a resurrection.'

'A what?'

'A resurrection. If those people aren't sure he's dead, someone else is going to hide his body and claim to be the soul resurrected.'

'Will they believe that?'

'Look at them.'

Thousands of people stood along the banks of the river staring at their fallen leader. No one moved. No one made a sound. John handed Jake the rifle, then pulled his first sergeant with him. They went over the side on to the mud flat. The crowd watched in stunned silence as the two Americans sloshed across the mud. They picked up the fallen messiah and dragged his body back to the *Mildred R.*

The survivors of the ship were already aboard the *Vandalia*. The fire was put out and the damage to the forward part of the *Mildred R.* hastily repaired so a reverse tow could be effected.

John and the first sergeant stood near the body of Hsui-chuan.

Jake approached them. 'John, you've got to think of some way to show these people that it's absolutely impossible for anyone else to don a loin cloth and say he's the resurrected messiah.'

John looked at Jake for a long hard second, then shook his head and slapped the rail. 'Why didn't you tell me these things before I shot him?'

'I didn't think of it at the time.' Jake pointed towards the shore. 'Look there.' The crowd was following the two ships as they moved slowly downriver. 'They'll follow us to hell and back as long as they think he can rise again.'

John stared over the rail and did not answer. He had avoided a bloodbath and for the moment that would have to do. They passed several sampans and a sand barge moored near the channel. Suddenly John left the rail. He ran to the dead captain's quarters and searched the desk drawers until he found the ship's manifest. Scanning the inventory, he found what he needed, then ran to the quarterdeck and blew the steam whistle to signal the *Vandalia* to stop the tow. He ordered his marines to strip to the waist, board the anchored barge, and dump half the load of sand into the river. The barge was brought alongside, bags of cement were hoisted from the *Mildred R.*'s hold, and mixed with river water and the sand on the barge. In plain sight of the crowd, Hsui-chuan's body was transferred to the barge and buried six feet deep in the cement. The barge was towed to the centre of the river and sunk by cannon fire from the *Vandalia*. For two days, the crowd watched silently, until the last air bubbles rose in the water. Then they quietly slipped away. The *Mildred R.* and the *Vandalia* returned to Canton.

For his bravery, Commodore Perry immediately promoted John Whittefield to the rank of commander. He was presented with a sapphire pendant encrusted in gold by the Chinese prefect of Canton. The United States Navy later awarded him the Congressional Medal of Honor.

It would be ninety years before another naval force the size of the East India Squadron assembled near Canton. Led by the frigates *Susquehanna*, *Mississippi*, *Macedonian* and *Powhattan* steaming down the Pearl River, the sloops of war – *Plymouth*, *Saratoga* and *Vandalia* – followed. The cutters, *Princeton*, *Lexington*, and *Southampton*, brought up the rear. They sailed out into the sea of Japan, then into the Straits of Shimoneski, the war sloops in a protective screen ahead of the Squadron.

While making passage through the Shimoneski Straits at Moji Point where the channel is most narrow, the sloops came under fire from three forts under the command of the Lord of Choshu. The sloops held their fire and turned back out of range, signalling the flagship for instructions. The Commodore ordered them to fall behind the Squadron, and the frigate *Mississippi* to come almost parallel to the *Susquehanna*. Crews of all ships were sent to their battle stations.

Approaching the bluffs overlooking the channel, figures of men standing on the dirt embattlements were seen to be waving swords, banners, and muskets. The *Susquehanna* signalled a request for safe passage in an international waterway. In answer, a cannon boomed from the closest of the three forts and a geyser erupted one hundred yards from the stern of the flagship. Other cannons boomed from the forts. Commodore Perry ordered the *Mississippi* and *Susquehanna* to engage the enemy. Spouts of water shot up around the two ships and several cannonballs bounced off the iron armour plate of the frigates as they cut loose with two successive broadsides, using explosive shells.

The Commodore's log book read, '23 June 1853, 11.00 hours. While making passage through the Straits of Shimoneski in international waters, made signal for safe passage and was fired upon from three different fortifications. Fire was returned by the *Mississippi* and the *Susquehanna*. The forts were levelled and the Squadron passed in safety. Time of actual combat – eight minutes.'

CHAPTER
15

On an evening in early June 1853, Saiyo and Mung sat on their porch watching a small deer push his head forward and delicately lap the cool water under the weeping willow. A bird swooped down to the water from the feeding platform Mung had built. The two creatures stared at each other for a moment before the deer moved to frighten the bird off and then gambolled back into the woods.

'I am like that deer,' Saiyo said. 'Jealous and selfish by nature. But I have read and understand the ways and needs of men.' She lowered her eyes. 'When I am swollen and bloated like a melon with our child and can no longer satisfy your physical needs, you must go to those women who reside in the Willow World to relieve your tensions.'

Mung reached out with both hands and gently lifted his wife's face to him. 'Darling Saiyo. I love you with all my heart and soul and vow my love to you now and forever. I will not lie with another woman for the rest of my days.'

Tears filled her almond eyes. They embraced and she whispered, 'You are a good, dear man. I knew from the first time I met you that it would be good between us because my eyebrows itched.'

Mung took her hand. 'Come let us go between the covers and prove how correct your eyebrows were.'

Shortly after midnight Mung was summoned to the governor's office. Yoshida and Ryochi were there, their appearances telling of a long, hard ride.

Only after Mr Ishikawa left the room did Yoshida speak. He came close to Mung, eyes bright in his tired face. 'They are coming! They are coming again! The Americans have more ships than before! Steamships! Big ones just as you predicted!'

'How do you know?'

'They stopped in Ryuku. The Americans wanted it known. Luckily Ryuku is in the domain of Satsuma. The word came directly to the Court. Since that time every person leaving the island has been intercepted and detained.'

'Where are the ships now?'

'They were sailing to reprovision in Canton, probably to allow time for the message to reach Yedo.'

'What must we do?'

Yoshida said, 'Lord Nariakira orders you to sail the *Shinto Maru* and wait off Point Satasuki at the western end of the Shimoneski Straits to make contact with the commander of the American ships. Ryochi and I will sail north immediately and set up lookouts on the Seven Isles of Izo which are strung across the approach to Yedo, in the event you miss them.'

'What do I tell them when and if we do meet?'

Yoshida took two scrolls from his sleeve. 'One is written in Japanese, the other in Dutch. These are official documents from the Lord of Satsuma as representative of the Emperor of Japan to the Commander of the American fleet, certifying your position as an administrator of Satsuma and appointed spokesman for the interests of the Emperor. No Japanese must ever see these documents. Only I carry a duplicate of each.'

Mung held the two scrolls secured with the Satsuma seal.

Yoshida continued, 'Our task is to inform the new American commander about Admiral Biddel's mistakes and about the true division of power in Japan. Even though it is the Shōgun who will deal with the Americans, they must address all their correspondence to the Emperor. It is the Shōgun who must lose face this time and not the Americans. Advise them to go along with the farce and never to show weakness. Explain to them that the Shōgunate will resist all efforts to open Japan. We, who support the Meiji Emperor, do not wish to give our country away, but desire to stabilize our economy by trade, to benefit from advances in science, and learn of the new freedoms gained by the peoples of the world. Coaling stations and ports of refuge will be agreed upon. Lastly, a meeting must be arranged between Lord Nariakira and the Commander of the American fleet to evaluate the events that will have taken place at Yedo and their effects on the future.'

Once again, Mung packed his seabags. Saiyo accompanied him to the ship. She stood quietly, her thin body leaning back, hands on hips to relieve the strain from the weight of her large stomach. She watched Mung received aboard the whaler with honours amid enthusiastic cheers from the crew. He stood on the quarterdeck looking down at her. As the lines were cast off and the ship drifted away on the tide, he bowed low and long to his beloved wife, and she to him.

The *Shinto Maru* ignored all sightings of whales, paying attention only to ships and the weather with double lookouts aloft day and night. Mung used his free time to read the ship's log, its manifest, and question the captain. It became clear that whaling could become a very profitable industry for Satsuma, and a significant new food source for the people.

On 30 June 1853 at eight in the morning, the lookout in the crow's nest sang out, 'Smoke in the sky! Smoke in the sky!'

Except for Mung, no one else on the whaler had ever seen a steamship. He went up into the rigging with his telescope. Over the horizon came three sloops fanned out in front of four frigates in a diamond formation, followed by three cutters in line. The American flag whipped from the mainmasts. There was a golden eagle figurehead on the bow of each ship. Mung ordered a distress rocket fired and the smoke trail arched high into the sky. Through his telescope, he saw darker and thicker smoke belch from the stack of the closest sloop as she heeled over towards the *Shinto Maru*. He ordered his flag unfurled. From the mainmast the emblem of the Meiji Emperor whipped out on the wind, the rising sun with sixteen golden rays on a field of white. Mung took the signal flags himself.

'Request permission to board,' he signalled.

'Request granted,' came the reply.

Mung was rowed to the *Vandalia*. Speaking Dutch, he asked to see the commander on a most urgent matter.

Although Commodore Perry was anxious to gain as much information as possible before going into Yedo, he knew he must be cautious and retain face in the eyes of the Japanese. Therefore, only after the two scrolls were presented to the captain of the *Vandalia*, then taken to the Commodore aboard the *Susquehanna*, was Mung transferred to the flagship. He climbed smartly up the rope ladder in his robes, two swords stuck in his *obi*. Officers and marines were lined on deck. He bowed to the flag and was saluted in return, then directed to the Commodore's cabin.

The commander of the East India Squadron, six feet two inches tall with sideburns almost to the cleft in his chin, sat straight behind a mahogany desk with his big hands clasped in front of him. Appraising Mung with cool brown eyes, he watched the samurai bow. Neither he, nor John Whittefield, nor the other aides standing behind their commander had ever seen a samurai. He was taller than the stranded Japanese fishermen who inhabited the compound in Hawaii. His head was shaved in front, his hair oiled, tightly bunned, and brought forward in a thick curl on top of his head.

John examined the details of the samurai's costume – white socks with the large toe gloved, grey pantaloons, green brocade robe. John's attention was caught by a familiar brass compass hanging from the man's waistband. Then he studied his face – the firm mouth; calm, sure eyes and a bent nose.

Mung felt himself being scrutinized by the men ranged behind the Commodore. He flashed a glance at them and caught the eye of a tall, blond officer who stared at him with an odd expression. They recognized each other at the same moment.

John Whittefield gasped in Japanese, 'Mung! My God Mung, it's you!'

Both stepped forward but were brought up short by the sharp voice of Commodore Perry. 'What is it, Commander Whittefield?'

Mung quickly regained his composure and answered John in Japanese. 'The fewer who know of our relationship, the better.

286

Does anyone else understand us?'

'No. Not on this ship.'

'Good. There is much danger. I must talk to you and the Commodore alone.'

Commodore Perry did not understand their words but he had seen the recognition flash between the two young men. 'Commander Whittefield! Explain!'

'Sir, it is a most urgent request by our guest that you, he and I be allowed to speak in private.'

'Do you believe the situation warrants it?'

'I do, sir.'

When the room was cleared, John turned to his commander. 'Sir, at my first interview for assignment to your staff, I told you of this gentleman.'

The senior naval officer looked from his aide in dress blues and polished brass buttons to the colourfully apparelled samurai.

With a brilliant smile, John said, 'May I introduce John Mung Whittefield, my brother!'

Mung bowed.

The big squadron commander whose thirty years' service had led him to believe he had seen everything, rocked back in his chair. What a stroke of luck, he thought. Choosing a time-tested method of handling unusual situations, he determined to observe and evaluate. 'John, you have my permission to greet your brother in a proper manner.'

The two young men embraced and the darker Japanese, smaller by four inches, spoke freely in English. 'John, how are our parents? Did you marry Beth? Are you well and happy?'

John laughed. 'Mother and father are well. They'll be so pleased to hear about you. The last letter we received told of your intention to return to Japan. We feared you would be killed.'

'I hope it did not pain your parents too much?'

'They love you and understood. And now I will be able to let them know you were successful.'

'Information about me must be passed on with care.'

John slapped Mung on the shoulders several times in delight, as if to nail him to the floor with both hands.

'Are you married?' Mung asked.

'Yes. Beth and I have a son. He often plays with that carved whale's tooth you gave her.' John reached into his tunic for a photograph of his son.

'He's a handsome boy,' Mung said. He rubbed the tips of his fingers back and forth across the photograph, something he had never seen before.

John, understanding Mung's curiosity, said, 'It's a new technological process which duplicates exactly what is seen. I'll explain it later. But first tell me if you were able to return to your village and see your mother.'

Mung shook his head sadly. 'Not yet.' Then his face broke into a big grin. 'But I'm married too and my wife is pregnant. I told her all about you.'

'Gentlemen,' the Commodore said, 'we have much to speak of. The first subject is how America and Japan can benefit from this act of fate.' He addressed Mung. 'My reasoning tells me you were waiting for us to clear the Shimoneski Straits, Mr Mung.'

'That is correct, sir.'

'Then you have information for me.'

'I do, sir. My authority to speak is contained in the scrolls I presented aboard the *Vandalia*.'

'They have been accepted as valid credentials. We are anxious to hear what you have to tell us.'

'I represent Lord Nariakira of Satsuma who is a supporter of the Emperor. My Lord desires your mission to be successful. He assumes its objectives are the same as those of Admiral Biddel.'

'They are.'

'The failure of the Admiral was a blow to the Emperor and his supporters in his struggle to regain power. Your success in dealing with the Shōgun will be the first major step in weakening the Shōgunate.'

'I've heard and understood every word you have spoken, Mr Mung. But I confess to be somewhat confused.' He tapped the large file folder on his desk. 'Everything we've learned about Japan

288

until now has led us to believe that the people give unquestioned loyalty to the Emperor.'

'That is true, sir.'

'But you've spoken of the Shōgun as the power.'

'That is also true. For two hundred and fifty years the Emperors have remained in their palaces and allowed the Shōguns to rule. Now the Meiji Emperor is desirous of regaining his throne and his power.'

The Commodore looked at both men facing him. 'I had intended to celebrate the fourth of July in Yedo Bay. That schedule will be set aside if Mr Mung will consent to work with me and Commander Whittefield on a plan of action to approach the government of Japan, whomever that may be. We intend to establish coaling stations, ports of haven for shipwrecked seamen, and a treaty of commerce between our two countries.'

'I will fulfil my obligations to my Lord Nariakira by working on the plan. But before we proceed any further, I must explain the necessity for secrecy.' Resting his hands on his sword hilts, Mung said, 'If the Shōgun were to hear about my Lord Nariakira's initiation of contacts with foreigners, the Lord and thousands of his samurai retainers would be obliged to commit suicide. I amongst them. Furthermore, if the Japanese people were ever led to believe that a foreign government was intent on invading our country, they would band together under the banner of the Shōgun and fight to the death of every man, woman and child. There would be no alternative.'

'Your request for secrecy is clear. Only we three will attend these meetings. We will keep no written records and guard this secret with our lives. You have our word as officers and gentlemen.'

Mung bowed and said, 'I will signal my ship that I am staying aboard and we can begin immediately.'

Mung left the cabin and the Commodore spoke to John. 'We've chanced upon good fortune and must make the best of it. Obviously the Japanese Emperor tires of being a figurehead. Mung represents a political faction opposed to the established regime. We must ascertain how powerful that faction is and what benefit our mission can derive from it. I would also like to know where that whaler came from. If the Japanese built it, we can soon prepare for a challenge to our whaling industry and merchant fleet in the North Pacific.'

When Mung returned to the cabin, the Commodore's first question was, 'Who do we negotiate with and what is the best way to proceed?'

In the following days the three men spent every waking hour plotting a course of action which would affect the future of both their countries in ways none could have predicted.

Prior to their final meeting on the fourth day, the two brothers finally had a little time for themselves. 'Let's sit up on the bow,' Mung said. 'I'm not used to the smells aboard an American ship any more.'

They sat on coils of rope facing each other, backs against the rails. 'Tell me,' John said, 'have you found what you wanted in Japan?'

'Yes. I was right to return.'

'You are happy?'

Mung considered the question, then answered, 'Yes, being with Saiyo makes me very happy. I knew from the first look that I had found my wife. And building the whaler was quite a challenge.'

'You built the whaler! I should have guessed. The Commodore would like to know more about your whaler. I'd like to hear how a fisherman became a samurai.'

Mung recounted his adventures with Ryochi and Yoshida, on the island of Dishima and in Kagoshima. Then he asked, 'How do you feel so far from home?'

'I miss Beth and Jeffrey but enjoy doing what I was trained for. The opportunity of being part of the last great exploration into the unknown is more than I could pass up.'

'Japan is unknown to the rest of the world just as the world is unknown to the Japanese. We greatly need application of western technology in our society. For the first time in our history there have been food riots. The worst took place on the Kanto Plains near Yedo itself.'

'What was the result?'

'Everyone was killed by the Shōgun's samurai,' Mung said sadly.

'Everyone?' John was shocked. 'How many?'

'On the Kanto Plains alone they counted eight thousand bodies.'

John shook his head. 'Too many people. Not enough food. Just kill off those who complain. That's a tragic solution to the problem. I'm sure American technology could teach the Japanese how to grow more food.'

'No. Growing food is not the problem. Eight thousand men, women and children died because they wouldn't give up the food they'd grown to the Shōgun for taxes. Had they complied, then they would have starved to death.'

The two brothers sat silently, each with his own thoughts. Then John asked, 'If Lord Nariakira and the Emperor regained power, how would they change things?'

'They are sworn to implement a democratic form of government based on the British system. The Emperor as a monarch, the House of Lords as the domain of the *daimyos* and the House of Commons open first to samurai and then the people.'

'Why not consider the American system of representative government?'

'It wouldn't work. We are a feudal society as England was. Our people still live in the Middle Ages. We have an ancient culture. It won't be easy to break with the past. The leap into the nineteenth century must be done with care. Our first steps in political maturity should be within the framework of our regular social structure. America is establishing its culture now, a culture as varied as the nations of the world which the Americans come from. When I think back on most of the books I've read by American authors, I remember them as excursions into self examination. America is still trying to find out who it is. Japan already has a personality. What it needs is a better form of government.'

John smiled. 'I wish our teachers at Harvard High School could

291

hear you. They would be proud, as I am. But they would ask about religion.'

'Any attempt to missionize in Japan will be met with the same uncompromising force as on the Kanto Plains. Missionary activity in Japan would unite the people under the banner of the Shōgun with the Emperor's blessings. We Japanese may fight each other, but any attempt against the country from outside will draw us together in a common front.'

'I meant your personal religious beliefs.'

'I often think of the teachings of Jesus. The little Frenchman in Hawaii who fought with his feet taught me the truth about turning the other cheek. And the Fairhaven bullies demonstrated the nonsense about love thy neighbour.' Mung saw the disappointment on his brother's face and laughed. 'I was joking. Or half joking. The teachings of Christ are still important to me. You, your parents, and men like Black Ben and Pistchiani make it work. I sometimes pray to Jesus. I also go to Buddhist temples and Shinto shrines.' John's face was still downcast. 'Don't be saddened. I can't believe that a god so great and merciful as the one Deacon Gilhooley taught me about would be angry that I worship my own gods in my own country. I do try to live by Jesus' words, "Whatever ye would that men would do to you, do you even so to them."'

'Yes,' John said, 'the world would be a better place if all men could follow the golden rule.'

Once again there was silence between them. Then John said, 'It isn't religion which troubles me. It's Japan. The solution to every problem is death. Can the Japanese people really be led into accepting a democratic form of government. Can they govern themselves? Do they want to?'

'They will if they're told to do so by their Emperor. At first they'll follow orders. Then they'll go at it with a vengeance. They must live in a democracy sooner or later. The ringing of the Liberty Bell in Philadelphia is still echoing throughout the world. We in Japan are just beginning to hear it.' Mung leaned forward. 'Each people hears the sound differently but the meaning is the same. All men really are created equal.'

292

Now John leaned forward. In a tense voice he said, 'I propose we take an oath between us. We swear to devote our lives to a democratic Japan and lasting relations between our countries.'

'I do swear,' Mung solemnly said.

'I would like it if we could make our pledge before God.'

'Yes,' Mung said. 'That would be fitting.'

The samurai and the naval officer walked to the ship's chapel. They knelt together, praying for guidance to serve their people and the Almighty.

Coming out of the chapel, the two were summoned to the Commodore's quarters where he reiterated the plan they had agreed upon. 'I will take only the *Susquehanna, Mississippi, Vandalia* and *Saratoga* into Yedo Bay. News of our firepower against the ports in the Straits of Shimoneski should have reached the Shōgun by now. He will know from those reports that I have more ships at sea but not how many exactly. We will make our stay in Yedo short to avoid conflict. I will personally present President Fillmore's letter to officials of the Shōgunate. I'll promise them a return visit with a hint of more fighting ships next time. The second visit will be to formalize a treaty.'

Mung nodded his approval. 'I shall inform Lord Nariakira and will effect a rendezvous after your visit.'

A short time later John and Mung parted. But not before they had devised a plan to bring them together again for a longer period of time.

Close to noon on 8 July alarm gongs sounded from lookout points on the approach to Yedo. Men of the Fish Watchers Guild signalled that one or more ships were on fire. In a dead calm, four ships, spewing black smoke from their bellies, were making for the entrance to the harbour. The inhabitants of Yedo were shocked and disoriented by these foreign vessels steaming directly into the bay and forming a battle line in the centre of the harbour.

Messengers arrived constantly at the Shōgun's castle but no one dared wake him with the news. Since Lord Hayoshi was away, the Shōgun's councillors hastily appointed Lord Abi to take charge.

Scrambling dragons, sampans and other small craft were sent to surround the strange fire ships anchored in the harbour. The attempts to attach themselves to the larger ships and climb aboard were met with a no-nonsense attitude from the Americans. Lines were cut and over-confident samurai were butt-stroked head over heels into the water. The small boats stood off. The samurai shouted and waved their swords until the prefect's barge approached. Lord Abi, dressed as a royal messenger, was allowed to board with three interpreters. He was made to stand on deck while the translation from Dutch to English took place with the captain of the *Susquehanna*. The Commodore did not appear. John Whittefield stood aside, close enough to the Japanese delegation to overhear their conversation in Japanese.

To Lord Abi's first question, 'What is it you want here?' the American captain answered, 'Remove the small boats that surround our vessels!'

Lord Abi bowed and said, 'It is for your own protection.'

The captain turned and gave a signal. Two cannons on each of the four ships were loaded with sacks of flour. They fired in unison. When the clouds of smoke and powder cleared, more than half the fleet of small boats and their crews were covered with the white dust. Many Japanese had jumped or fallen overboard in fright and were being hauled out of the water. Lord Abi signalled. All but a few picket boats returned to shore.

'These barbarians are crazy!' John heard Lord Abi say to his interpreters.

Now the captain addressed Lord Abi, 'There is a person of great importance aboard with a letter from the President of the United States of America for the Emperor of Japan.'

Lord Abi's reply was, 'Raise your anchor and leave here immediately!'

The captain said, 'We have come as peacemakers, not to invade Japan. After delivering the letter, we will sail from the harbour.'

The Shōgun was awakened by the sound of the cannon. Informed of what had taken place, he raged and ordered all samurai and soldiers to attack the ships. Then he immediately cancelled that order and sent a message to Lord Abi, 'Use the same story which made Admiral Biddel reduce the number of ships in the harbour.'

When Lord Abi received this message, he judged the Americans and decided against it. John heard him discussing it with his interpreters. Instead, Lord Abi told the captain, 'Withdraw to the harbour entrance before talks can continue!'

The captain ushered Lord Abi, still in the guise of a high-ranking messenger, to the quarterdeck of the *Susquehanna* and barked several orders. Broadsides from the *Susquehanna* and *Vandalia* tore into a barren mountainside to the left of Yedo, a site which had been carefully chosen by naval engineers. The explosive shells tore an area below an overhang, causing a landslide and raising a dust cloud that floated over the entire city.

The captain had Lord Abi escorted from the ship with one last statement, 'Tomorrow the representative of the President of the United States will come ashore with an honour guard. Either Commodore Perry will deliver the letter from President Fillmore to a Japanese cabinet minister on shore, or he and the entire contingent will march to the palace and deliver it there. Should anything happen to the honour guard or Commodore Perry, remember that the entire city of Yedo is under the Squadron's guns.'

While Lord Abi and the population of Yedo were being shown a demonstration of American firepower, word arrived from Choshu about the breakthrough of the barbarian squadron in the Straits of Shimoneski. Upon hearing of the destruction of the three forts, the Shōgun ordered the messenger put to death. Hysterical and incoherent, he retired to a meditation room in the castle. He was not to be disturbed until the crisis was over.

Upon his return to shore, Lord Abi took command. He ordered earthworks built on the road to the Shōgun's castle. The entire male population of Yedo was mobilized. Every feudal lord in attendance at the castle led a contingent of mounted samurai, archers, spearmen, and swordsmen to the harbour area. They formed ranks, each behind his own lord, carrying pennants and flags. The night was pleasantly warm and the skies clear as the warriors gathered. Signal fires burned along the coastline. Temples were crowded with worshippers praying for a storm to blow the foreigners out to sea. At 10.20 P.M. a comet streaked across the sky. Neither Japanese nor Americans knew if it foretold good or evil.

The sea was calm and the midnight watch had taken their posts when a sampan sculled in close to the *Mississippi*. The crew ordered the sampan to stand off but Yoshida and Ryochi used the big stern oar to nudge their boat against the side of the frigate. They had seen the Squadron steaming towards Yedo but with no wind it had been impossible to intercept them. Shouts from the *Mississippi* to get away from the ship were ignored. Speaking in Dutch, then using gestures, Yoshida pleaded to be taken aboard, but he was not understood.

One of the Japanese picket boats moved in towards the sampan. Yoshida barked an order and Ryochi pushed off, around the stern of the frigate. They sculled for their lives across the placid waters of Yedo Bay with the picket boats gaining on them. Quickly Yoshida took the sealed scrolls from his robe, put his short sword through the centre of both and dropped them over the side. He seized the oar and ordered Ryochi, 'Stop rowing and swim for the shore!'

Ryochi let go of the oar. 'I am a samurai! I was born a samurai, bred to fight and die in battle! That is my honour!'

'You do not have the right to die yet!' Yoshida cried. 'Fulfil your obligations to your lord! Bring word to Satsuma that we have failed!'

Ryochi shook his head. 'No! No!'

Yoshida, tiring at the oar, gasped, 'I am neither swimmer nor fighter.'

He leaned down with all his weight on the handle of the long sculling oar and raised it out of the water. Swinging the oar handle, he hit Ryochi full in the chest, knocking him backwards and over the side. With his last reserve of strength, Yoshida sculled as fast as he could, leading the pursuers away from Ryochi in the water.

Seeing the lanterns on the boats closing in on him, Yoshida sculled to the left only to see two pursuers cutting off that escape route. He turned right but another boat shot out in front of him. Gasping for breath, in desperation, he lifted up on the long-handled oar, driving it deep into the water, then pushing it to the side. His lighter craft spun around, facing the attackers. The first was moving so fast it shot past him. The second rammed into his boat, dumping half its crew into the water and knocking Yoshida to the bottom. Their chain link armour and winged helmets dragged them under to their deaths. The remainder of the samurai swarmed aboard. Yoshida staggered to his feet. For the first time in his life, he drew his long sword from its scabbard, his arms so tired he could barely raise the blade. He heard a command barked in the darkness, 'Don't kill him!' and the sword was knocked from his hand. He was kicked and spat upon, bound and taken to the prefect of Yedo.

During questioning his fingernails were ripped off one by one. A rat, placed on his stomach under a hot bowl, gnawed its way into his intestines without his divulging anything about his mission. Still alive, he was thrown into a cage in the middle of a square near the port. A sign, hung on the cage, read, 'Punishment for Traitors'. People threw rubbish and faeces, and urinated on the Satsuma scholar.

The next day Yoshida was dragged from the cage and hacked to pieces in the street by two of the prefect's guards. The parts of his body were thrown onto a dung heap. Among the spectators was a dirty beggar who squatted nearby. No one noticed the tears running down Ryochi's cheeks, nor heard his vow to seek revenge. He set out barefoot from Yedo to Satsuma, a distance of a thousand miles.

On the bay, the American ships weighed anchor and came closer to shore in a battle line. Their guns were run out, crews standing by. Fifteen launches stood ready to take 250 heavily armed marines, sailors, and the Squadron band ashore.

Lord Abi came out to the flagship, imploring the captain to wait until noon before embarking. 'The government will honour your request. A minister will receive the President's letter. Preparations

297

are being made and a pavilion built close to the shore where the ceremony will be held.'

In fact, all Lord Abi said was true. The councillors had decided to avoid a confrontation unless the Americans tried to march on the Shōgun's castle or take up permanent positions in Yedo. Twenty thousand Japanese troops stood in ranks on the shore, banners and pennants waving, in full armour, weapons ready.

At 11.30 A.M. on 9 July 1853, a thirteen gun salute boomed out over Yedo Bay. The launches, in line, headed for shore. Commodore Perry was stepping on to his skiff as John Whittefield became the first American to officially land on Japanese soil. Rank upon rank of samurai, spearmen, archers, swordsmen and mounted horsemen glowered at the marines in their dress blues, white bandoliers crossing their chests and plumed barracks caps. The discipline on both sides was remarkable. The marines performed a series of intricate marching drills to the barked commands of a grizzled first sergeant. They moved forward and to the sides, forming a hollow square which faced outward. Marines stood nose to nose with grim samurai.

Sailors, heavily armed, wearing new white jumpers with blue bell-bottoms, formed ranks on either side of the square. A drum roll started as the Squadron band came ashore. The air was thick with tension. A navy signalman took his place near the water's edge, raising both flags straight over his head. If those flags were lowered, it would be the signal for the warships to open fire.

John Whittefield snapped a salute as Commodore Matthew Perry stepped ashore, preceded by two of the biggest Negro sailors in the fleet. The band struck up 'Hail Columbia' and the first notes of the loud music caused the tense samurai to flinch. The marines clutched their rifles tighter, but the tension on both sides eased as the cornets picked up the melody. The Commodore, with twenty-five selected officers carrying six-shot Colt revolvers loosened in their holsters, marched forward.

The hastily built pavilion was a raised platform with steps leading up the sides, open at the front, the floor covered with silks and the back masked with a canvas wall. There were no seats. Just behind the canvas stood one hundred of the Shōgun's personal guards in full armour, swords unsheathed. Underneath the platform itself, twenty high-ranking samurai crouched, their swords ready with orders to kill the Americans if there was trouble. A portion of the floor of the platform was not fastened so that these twenty men could push up from below to upset anyone standing there.

Commodore Perry, flanked by his two black guards, a Dutch interpreter and John Whittefield, walked up the steps led by Lord Abi who still acted the part of messenger. On the platform, an interpreter and two of the Shōgun's councillors, actually lower in rank than Lord Abi, waited behind a black lacquered table. The Japanese interpreter indicated that the letter from the President of the United States should be placed in the red silk dispatch case. Commodore Perry nodded and the two black sailors came forward with rosewood boxes. One contained the letter from President Fillmore in English, the other in Dutch. They opened the lids and displayed the documents to the councillors who, never having seen black men before, could not take their eyes from them. The two sailors placed the open boxes on top of the red silk case and stepped back.

The Japanese interpreter kneeled, and accepted a scroll from the first councillor. He stood and handed it to one of the black sailors. It was a document officially acknowledging the receipt of President Fillmore's letter.

The two groups faced each other in embarrassed silence.

Finally, the Commodore said, 'We will sail northward off the coast of Japan, then return to Canton. If any Japanese officials desire passage north, they are welcome to travel with the Squadron.'

There was no reply. The two councillors stood with arms folded in front of them, hands tucked into the large sleeves of their kimonos, staring at the Americans.

Commodore Perry then said, 'Thank you for receiving us. I will return in one year to conclude the treaty.' He took a step backwards as if to leave.

The councillors lost their composure at this sudden unexpected turn of events. No inferior had ever been known to end a discussion with a threat. The Japanese interpreter asked a prepared question to give the councillors time to regain their poise. 'We have word of a religious rebellion in China involving Christian fanatics. Do you know of this?'

The Commodore answered, 'Yes,' and now he stared through the two councillors as if they did not exist.

'Do you know its cause?' the interpreter asked.

Perry focused his eyes directly on those of the first councillor. 'Discontent. Discontent of a people with a corrupt and backward government.'

John Whittefield saw the interpreter blanch, suck his breath in through his teeth, then translate the Commodore's answer as, 'They are indeed fanatics and have little support from the population.'

Having regained their equilibrium, the first councillor asked, 'Will Commodore Perry be returning with all ten ships?' This was a clear indication that word of the destruction of the Choshu forts had reached Yedo.

Perry answered, 'It is only fitting when two nations sign a treaty that the ceremony be better attended than the delivery of a letter.' He nodded his head slightly. Before the interpreter could bow, the Commodore turned and left the pavilion.

The councillors looked questioningly at the interpreter who stared after the Americans. They had prepared for a long drawn out series of negotiations. Now they listened as the band played 'Yankee Doodle', and watched the Commodore and his escort board their boats in reverse order and leave Yedo's shore. The official ceremony had taken less than twenty minutes.

John Whittefield wrote to his wife,

Today was the second most important event in my life (marrying you was the first). I had the honour of being the first American to be received officially on Japanese soil. The feudal lords of Japan were decked out in their battle dress.

Behind them stood endless ranks of warriors. They reminded me so much of the stories we read of King Arthur's Court and knights of olden times. I am so pleased the meeting ended peacefully. The conduct of our marines and navies was exemplary. Their precision drills could not but impress those tough-looking samurai. Without submitting to the degrading kow-tow, we landed peacefully and delivered an official document to the government of Japan. The event was unprecedented, its outcome unpredictable. The Commodore believes this to be one of the most important happenings in modern history. Our next meeting will take place a year from now. Only then will we know the true extent of our success. This means a longer period away from you and the baby. Success for me is tinged with sadness. I wish more than anything to be with you.

I have met our friend who gave you the whale's tooth. He landed safely, is married and his wife is expecting a child. He sends his love to all. He has been of great service to us on this voyage. This information is for you and my parents only.

Beth, I miss you and don't know if I am made for the sea. My mind is more often on you and Jeffrey than on what is taking place aboard ship, but I am very proud to be a part of all this. We are about to rendezvous with the remainder of the Squadron. Mail will be taken aboard one of the ships returning to Hawaii. So I close this letter and will again open my Bible, knowing that at the same moment you will be reading the same passage. Sharing our love and knowledge of the Almighty in our prayers together with Him in heaven makes life bearable for me here on earth.

When the *Shinto Maru* had parted from the American fleet, it sailed to the coastal town of Ichiki where Mung left the ship. He needed no guide as he went overland to Satsuma. His memory served him well and he easily found the covering to the tunnel which led under the wall and into the blacksmith's shop. He remained hidden there for twelve hours, until the warrior priest arrived, put a hand on his shoulder and looked at him approvingly. Without a word, the priest led Mung unseen through the dark streets into secret passages in the pagoda castle to a room where Lord Nariakira and Sakuma Shozan sat.

Mung prostrated himself on the floor and was told to be seated. He described all that had taken place aboard the flagship with Commodore Perry and reported the time and place for the next rendezvous at sea. The three laid plans until the hour of meditation before dawn. Then once again the warrior priest led Mung to the tunnel where he slept through the day.

That night, Lord Nariakira, dressed as a middle-rank samurai, followed the warrior priest into the tunnel to meet Mung. Not even the most trusted retainer would be aware the Lord of Satsuma was away from the palace. Sakuma Shozan let it be known that the Lord had entered a period of fasting and private meditation.

Led by the warrior priest, Lord Nariakira and Mung made their way overland by foot. They travelled by night, moving through gullies and river beds, staying out of sight.

Nearing the town of Ichiki in a shallow ravine, the priest suddenly froze. Mung crouched instinctively. Lord Nariakira stood straight, glowering into the night. Mung heard no sound on the warm night air. It struck him that there should be sounds of crickets and other night creatures. At the top of the ravine, on both sides just above them, silhouettes appeared against the star filled sky.

A voice from above shouted, 'Pay and pass!'

The Lord of Satsuma whipped out his long and short swords. 'Come to your death, outlaws!'

Mung crouched lower to the ground, watching the Lord and the warrior priest.

From above the voice answered, 'We are not outlaws. We are trained warriors, *ronin* without a lord to serve. We are starving.'

Mung cocked the new Colt revolver given to him by John Whittefield.

Lord Nariakira pulled a purse of coins from his *obi* and threw it up to the dark figures above. 'Take these coins. If you are scum, eat and drink your fill for you are not long for this world. If you are true samurai who follow the code of Bushido, go to the castle of Satsuma, to Sakuma Shozan. There you and all honourable *ronin* will find a lord to serve and battles to fight.'

Mung heard whispers above, and the clink of coins. The purse came plunking down at Lord Nariakira's feet.

The voice from above said, 'Thank you, sir. It is food we need and we have taken only enough for that. It is our shame that we have done this. We will be on our way to Satsuma.'

When the figures had disappeared from the edge of the ravine, the three travellers continued on to the marsh where Mung had secreted his boat. They rowed out into the open sea. Mung took a lantern from under the transom and in the last hour of darkness made a signal. They rowed the small boat over the ocean swells until the *Shinto Maru* loomed up in front of them. They were taken aboard and Mung ordered the whaler out to sea, to a rendezvous with Commodore Perry.

Aboard the ship, Lord Nariakira and Mung spent hours preparing for the coming negotiations. Yet there was still time for the feudal lord to watch the chase, kill, and trying out of a whale as they waited for the rendezvous. Mung presented figures of whales taken by the *Shinto Maru* and convinced the lord to build another two ships and a whaling station at Kagoshima. The Satsuma Lord made one stipulation – that the *Shinto Maru* and any future whaling vessels be fitted with mounts for cannon.

The log books of the *Shinto Maru* and the *Vandalia* showed simultaneous sightings. The rendezvous was kept on 5 August, 150 miles from the nearest land. Despite all previous descriptions and explanations by Mung, the Satsuma Lord could not conceal his excitement and surprise at the size of the *Susquehanna* and her ability to sail into the wind.

The meeting was held aboard the Commodore's flagship with Mung and John Whittefield interpreting for Lord Nariakira and Commodore Perry.

The Commodore opened the meeting. 'We have no experience with diplomatic procedures in Japan. If offence is given during these talks, it is not intended.'

Lord Nariakira said, 'The words you have used express my thoughts exactly. It is in both our interests to dispense with formalities. Would you be so kind as to describe the events in Yedo.'

The Satsuma Lord listened to the translations impassively. He interrupted only to ask for descriptions of the Japanese officials who were part of the ceremony. Mung tried not to show astonishment at what had taken place. As he translated, John's eyes met his, and both smiled.

After the summary, Lord Nariakira sat silently for some moments, then said, 'The messenger who remained with you during the negotiations was none other than Lord Abi. During the talks with Admiral Biddel he used the same disguise, but then was accompanied by Lord Hayoshi. I cannot identify the two councillors with whom you met, but since the Shōgun's interpreter knelt before them, there is no doubt they were councillors to the Shōgun. Mung has identified the interpreter from your description. His name is Kunaiae, a full-ranked samurai of noble family.' Lord Nariakira bowed his head slightly. 'Your plan was well conceived and brilliantly executed. We Japanese are impressed by pomp and circumstance, and especially by discipline and a balanced show of power. You walked on a sword's sharp edge.'

The Commodore bowed his head, acknowledging the compliment.

Lord Nariakira continued, 'Never doubt for a moment that every one of the samurai you saw would have attacked if given the order, despite your overwhelming firepower. The one who would have given the signal to attack you, Lord Hayoshi, is not in Yedo. On your return, either he will be in command of the Shōgun's army, or I will be leading the Emperor's forces.'

The Commodore said, 'It is my sincere wish that our treaty can be ratified peacefully. To that end, will you accept our hospitality aboard the *Susquehanna* to rest before our next meeting?'

'Your offer is most generous, but Mung informs me it took him some time to accustom his stomach to western food and his body to the bunks or hammocks. I will be more at ease aboard the *Shinto Maru*, although I would like a tour of your ship.'

'You will be our honoured guest.'

During the next two days, there were a series of meetings. Lord Nariakira related the military history of Japan and the Commodore was shocked at the number of troops involved. During the final battles in which the Tokugawa took over the power of the Shōgunate, 250 years before, more men had been in action than the combined French and British armies at Waterloo.

Lord Nariakira said, 'For centuries, battles in Japan have been won either by the larger force or by subterfuge. Now the Shōgun will have interior lines of communication and supply for his armies in the upcoming battle. The feudal lords who support the Emperor are mostly those in the extreme north and south of the empire.'

'How do you know there will be a war?' the Commodore asked.

'There are feudal lords, I among them, who have taken an oath to fight to the death to restore the Emperor to power. We must open our country to the west, but on our terms. We do not want what happened in China to happen here.' The words exploded from his lips, 'This oath is Bushido! There is no turning back! To do so would mean the eternal disgrace of my forefathers and my children's children! I made another decision in a ravine on our way to this meeting. If only Satsuma rises against the Shōgun, then so be it!'

The Commodore studied the Japanese Lord closely. 'There are limitations to the aid we might give you. I must have assurances that we would be received by the Emperor and our requests seriously considered.'

'Your requests are in no way against the policy we hope to implement. You have no understanding of the place of the Emperor in Japanese society. He is descended from the Sun God. Neither you nor any other foreigner will ever see him.' Lord Nariakira looked hard at the Commodore. 'We are, first, Japanese who do not want to become westerners, or have anything to do with your religion.'

'Our intention is not to change your ways, but to implement a series of humanistic and commercial agreements beneficial to both countries,' the Commodore said.

'I believe you, but must put things into perspective. Had you forced your way to the Shōgun's palace, you would have united all Japan against you.' The Lord smiled and bowed his head. 'Your actions in Yedo were well calculated to gain the respect of the councillors and the everlasting hatred of the Shōgun. It was he who lost face. The brevity of your visit, the presentation of your President's letter, your swift withdrawal and promise to return in a year, must have left the Shōgun and his people in an extreme state of confusion.'

'How do you see the future?'

'The moderate Lord Abi may be asked to commit *seppuku*. Lord Hayoshi will be appointed chief councillor and head of the army. He will begin immediate preparations to prevent your landing again in Yedo. He too is bound by the code of Bushido and will support the Shōgunate under all and any conditions.'

Commodore Perry appraised the Lord. 'We Americans have our own Bushido. I have given my word to return to finalize a treaty, and return I will!'

'There is only one possibility for you to avoid a confrontation, and that is the defeat of the Shōgun's forces before you arrive.'

'How can that be accomplished?'

'When I return, messengers will leave Satsuma to call on those feudal lords who have sworn allegiance to the Emperor, telling them to prepare for war against the Shōgun.'

'Isn't there a way for a negotiated settlement?'

'Bushido governs our lives. It is our karma. The Shōgun, Lord Hayoshi and their families have been in power for 250 years while we who supported the Emperor have paid tribute. This Shōgun is a weak personality. For the first time, we have an Emperor who is demanding his divine right as leader of the Japanese people.' Lord Nariakira tapped the table. 'You have hastened the inevitable conflict.'

'What are your chances for success?'

306

'Almost none.'

'Then why attempt it?'

The Satsuma Lord threw his shoulders back. He said one word, 'Bushido!'

During the final hours of the last meeting, as the ships rode easily on the ocean swells far from land and range of seagulls, the Commodore conducted Lord Nariakira on a grand inspection of the *Susquehanna*. The Lord was most impressed with the giant steam engine and the furnace which consumed so much coal. He asked detailed questions, through Mung, about the naval guns and their mounts. When he requested a demonstration of the new exploding shells, the Commodore gladly obliged. It was the Commodore's suggestion that Mung be allowed to study the drawings and schematics of the guns, the explosive shells, and their fuses while the others went to the quarterdeck.

On deck, sails and flags had been rigged to shade the long row of banquet tables. Commodore Perry, Lord Nariakira and John Whittefield took their seats at the head table just in front of the wheelhouse. On one side sat fifty men from the *Shinto Maru*. An equal number of officers and senior mates from the *Susquehanna* sat opposite. Navy chefs served up a whole bullock, two sheep, venison, poultry, vegetables and bottles of various alcoholic beverages. This repast was set before the Japanese. They had brought special savouries to seduce the palates of the Americans – raw sliced fish, boiled seaweed, white gummy rice, shredded radish, sea slugs with ginkgo nuts, and bottles of sake.

The Americans and the Japanese had been warned in a most stern manner by their superiors that the favourable outcome of the negotiations depended on the success of this feast. Both sides began to eat with gusto. However, soon after the gastronomic competition began, John saw a bosun's mate pushing his sea slug around the plate with the tip of his fork. The mate glanced across the table at his Japanese counterpart who was jabbing at a blood red slice of roast beef on his plate with chopsticks. The navy man made motions with his hand. As soon as the Japanese whaler

307

understood, he smiled with relief and passed his plate in exchange. Up and down the length of the banquet table, dishes were handed back and forth.

At the front table Lord Nariakira and the Commodore chose to ignore the exchanges, chewing stoically until their plates were empty. Both politely declined seconds. John, with much enthusiasm, asked for another portion of sea slug and raw fish. The *daimyo* of Satsuma raised his eyebrows but said nothing. He did not know that the relish with which John performed the task of eating was related to the plan he and Mung had worked out with the Commodore.

Matthew Perry raised a cup of sake. 'To Japan and the United States. May we work together for the betterment of our nations and for mankind.'

Every seaman raised his cup. The Japanese watched the Americans toss down the sake which should be sipped. To be polite they did the same, trying to hide the shock they felt as it went down.

Lord Nariakira raised a glass of white Madeira. 'To our countries. May both benefit from the exchange of ideas between a new, infant democracy and an ancient, ordered civilization.'

Once again everyone tossed down their drinks. John toasted with champagne and all joined him. The senior whaling captain countered with whisky. The toasting continued.

One of the Japanese seamen jumped up and leaned across the table. He wrapped his arms around a tough old navy chief. 'We are of one heart, your country and mine,' he shouted.

'What did he say?' The chief looked down at the little Japanese. He broke loose of the embrace and straightened his uniform jacket. 'Old one hundred,' he shouted.

The entire contingent of Americans staggered to their feet and began to sing, 'Before Jehovah's awful throne. Ye nations bow with sacred joy. Know ye that the Lord is God alone. He can create and He can destroy ...'

'Shut up and sit down,' the Commodore bellowed from his seat.

Half the Americans appeared to have been blown over by the

308

roaring command. The other half dropped to the deck.

'Translate that song as an introduction to the afternoon's entertainment,' the Commodore ordered John. Then he roared, 'Bring on the Royal Ethiopians!'

The master of ceremonies stepped forward and announced, 'Part one of our minstrel show is entitled, "A Coloured Gentleman in the North".'

In blackface, carrying banjos and tambourines, members of the crew strutted onto a makeshift stage just below the quarterdeck. They sang and danced to a medley of songs, beginning with 'Virginia Rosebud' and 'Ole Ma Coon'.

Halfway through the act the Japanese guests sufficiently recovered from their initial shock to join in clapping their hands to the music. They laughed at jokes they did not understand, and cheered when the Americans did.

At the completion of the entertainment, when the applause and whistling had died down, Lord Nariakira inadvertently set off another frenzied round of toasts by raising his cup to the Royal Ethiopians. He saw his men gulping the champagne which they preferred to sake. He pointed to the stage and barked the single word, 'Kagura!'

The fifty-man crew of the *Shinto Maru* froze in a sitting position, backs straight, eyes forward. At a command from their captain they all stood and faced right. In single file they marched to the steps leading to the lower deck and the improvised stage. Half tumbled down in a tangle of arms and legs. The remainder trudged over their shipmates wearing silly, drunken smiles. Onto the stage they trod. The captain stood in the centre and waited for his men to form a circle. He glared at each one in turn as they stumbled to their places. 'I see all of you,' he growled, then whipped out a fan from his *obi* and began tapping it. Several men drew small drums from their voluminous sleeves and took up the beat. The others donned colourful masks of animals and mythical beasts and began to dance around the captain, one masked beast chasing another through and around the moving circle.

The Americans kept time by clapping their hands until a banjo player gave melody to the Japanese dance. Some Americans staggered onto the stage and joined the whirling circle. Around and around, faster and faster they went. A dragon mask chased a lion under the arms and through the legs of the flying dancers. Just then Mung appeared on deck. With open mouth he watched the lion get caught between the dancer's legs. The circle of moving men was thrown out of kilter and the drunken dancers of both nations went flying in all directions. Bodies sprawled on the stage, the deck, and against the ship's railings.

'What happened?' Mung asked.

Commodore Perry answered. 'We have just signed an agreement in the most poignant way possible. Both crews have made fools of themselves.'

John translated the comment for Lord Nariakira who bowed and said, 'Only when the topknot is lowered does the truth in one's head show itself and is sincerity of the heart revealed.'

John winked at Mung who nodded, then addressed his *daimyo*, 'Sire, Commander Whittefield has a request.'

The Lord of Satsuma turned to the young blond American. 'Speak!'

'Sir, I respectfully request to be allowed to take my accrued shore leave in Satsuma.'

The *daimyo* looked from one young man to the other, trying to fathom the request.

Commodore Perry, party to the scheme, said, 'Mr Whittefield will gladly work for his room and board.'

Lord Nariakira turned to John. 'What work would you expect to do?'

'I am a military man sir, and know little else.'

Lord Nariakira pursed his lips and grinned. 'It is agreed. There will be much work for a man of your profession in Satsuma.'

He drew the two swords in their ornately silver inlaid scabbards from his *obi* and handed them to the Commodore. Matthew Perry acknowledged the gift with a bow of his head. He took a mahogany case with an American eagle carved on its cover and handed it to the Satsuma Lord.

The case contained two matching Colt revolvers. The gun-metal blue of the barrels, mother-of-pearl handles, and neat row of bullets caught the light and Lord Nariakira's fancy. Bowing his head, he said, 'You would make a good samurai.'

To which the Commodore replied, 'You would make a good American.'

CHAPTER
16

John Whittefield, in full field kit and with a Henry rifle, boarded a longboat with Mung. They were rowed to the *Shinto Maru*, followed by another boat carrying Lord Nariakira and the warrior priest. Once aboard, the *Shinto Maru* caught the wind, heeled to starboard, and headed for Ichiki. The *Susquehanna* and *Vandalia* steamed for a rendezvous with the Squadron, and then to Canton.

On the *Shinto Maru*, John shared Mung's cabin. Because he was so tall and the bunk too short, a straw mattress was put on the floor. The adopted brothers agreed that the most immediate problems were to devise a disguise and improve John's pronunciation of Japanese. They set themselves a daily ten-hour schedule of learning.

Mung was summoned to Lord Nariakira's cabin. Their relationship had changed. Mung was now a trusted adviser, and the bond between them grew stronger. He stepped forward, knelt, and bowed his head to the floor.

Lord Nariakira said, 'Be seated, Mung, and listen to me. I am leading my people to war and yet I feel as if a burden is lifted from my heart.' He made a gesture with his right hand and Mung became aware of the warrior priest sitting in a corner of the room. 'Our high priest believes he can colour the American's skin by using a certain dye distilled from wood. With shaven head and cosmetic touches to the eyes, he will pass as a Buddhist priest of Mongolian ancestry. However, he must learn basic Japanese military commands.'

'His language lessons have already begun,' Mung said. 'I'll teach him. The captain and mates will assist me.'

'Let the others teach him. It was on purpose I enquired about the details of the naval guns and their mountings. The Commodore is a very astute man. He understood my intentions and sent you below to view the drawings and schematics of the weapons. Fortunately, John Whittefield must have told the Commodore about your phenomenal memory.' He looked directly at Mung. 'Your most immediate task is to set down on paper what you remember of those drawings, all about the guns and sighting instruments. On Tanegoshima Island, which was the imperial armoury 250 years ago, there is a family which has retained the knowledge of casting cannon. Even though all weapons have been banned since then, this family passed down the secrets of their craft from father to son. That is where you will go.'

The ship's carpenter built a special table in the hold and attached oil lanterns overhead. Mung spread a scroll of rice-paper the length of the table, pinning it at the edges. Assuming the position of meditation, he cleared his mind of all thoughts, then concentrated until he saw the sheet of rice-paper in his mind's eye. He recalled a particular drawing until it appeared on the mental paper. Trance-like, he began to sketch, his eyes half open. Working from the mental pictures, the brush flicked over the paper. His problem was not in recalling the drawings. In his mind they were sometimes superimposed, interfering with each other. It took extreme concentration. He returned to his cabin exhausted.

The second evening, John, from his mattress on the floor, broke into Mung's thoughts. 'Where do you disappear to all day?'

Mung hesitated for just a moment and felt guilty for doing so. Then he explained.

John listened thoughtfully. Then he said, 'I agree with Lord Nariakira. I did tell the Commodore about your memory, and it's clear that any help I can give you will in no way compromise the United States or our Navy. Meanwhile, learning ten hours of Japanese even for two days so far, is the worst duty I've ever had. I can help you. We can work together at least five hours, speaking only Japanese. It will reduce my problem by half and may solve some of yours.'

They sailed across a rolling sea with a cracking wind under a warm August sun. Ten days lay between them and Ichiki.

The entire crew gathered on deck to watch the warrior priest shave John's eyebrows and straight blond hair. There were cheers and jokes as the razor neatly lifted the hair from his scalp and John traded friendly insults with the crew. The priest meticulously applied the dye to John's face, neck, arms, and hands. Afterwards, John mimicked the bowlegged walk of the whalers, exaggerating their rolling gait. They countered by throwing back their shoulders, chests out, and parading stiff-legged up and down the deck. John put on the wooden clogs the priest gave him and the crew howled with laughter as he clopped around the deck, twisting his ankles or leaving the wooden sandals behind as he tried to stride back and forth. With a great deal of practice, he was able to run backwards, forwards, or to either side with ease before they landed.

It was after sunset when the *Shinto Maru* neared the port of Ichiki. In a saffron robe sewn by a crewman, John went over the side into a longboat with Lord Nariakira, Mung, and the priest. Mung had already given instructions to the captain of the ship. Under no circumstances were any of the crew to be allowed ashore. They were to continue whaling. Every third day the *Shinto Maru* was to lay off the coast from midnight to one hour before dawn. The signal for a rendezvous would be one white and one green lantern.

From their landing at Ichiki, the warrior priest led the party to Satsuma. They moved quickly and silently through the night. Approaching the secret tunnel, the priest stopped and pointed to a strange radiance above the wall on the far side of the Satsuma fortress. Lord Nariakira motioned them to follow him towards the light. The glow lit the night sky as they neared the corner of the fortress. Making the turn, they saw hundreds of fires and thousands of men stretched out asleep on the bare ground. The four passed unnoticed among the sprawled figures. The sound of slow, even breathing and occasional spit and crackle of the fires filled the night.

Walking directly to a man squatting near a fire, Lord Nariakira waved his arms at the sleeping figures and asked, 'What is all this?'

The man stood, revealing two swords in his *obi*. His clothes were patched twice over but he held himself erect. 'Does one samurai ask another a question without first excusing himself?' He threw a hard look at Lord Nariakira. 'Where are your manners?'

Mung and the priest stared at each other in disbelief.

Seeing the look of shock on the Satsuma Lord's face, the samurai laughed and said, 'Come. Sit down.' He motioned to the others. 'Out here formalities are a bit relaxed.'

They sat crosslegged by the fire.

Lord Nariakira regained his composure. 'Please excuse my bad manners.'

The samurai took an old, worn pouch from his *obi* and emptied the last of the tea leaves, mostly dust, into the pot. 'You must have been a real dandy before you became a *ronin*,' he said to the Satsuma Lord.

'How do you know that?'

'Look at you. Good clothes, yet you've sold your swords.'

The Lord of Satsuma clutched at his empty *obi*, then let his hands drop.

'It's not for me to judge a man,' the samurai said. 'Times have been hard. But to sell your swords ...' He shook his head and handed Lord Nariakira a cup of tea.

The Lord accepted the cup, although he was shocked at being spoken to in such a manner.

The samurai waved his arm at the sleeping figures. 'Soon we *ronin* will have a Lord to serve.' He pointed at the castle inside the walls. 'The Lord of Satsuma has been meditating for more than a month. *Ronin* have been gathering ever since, for it is said he will employ all honourable men.' He looked at the cup in Lord Nariakira's hand. 'Drink.'

The Lord smiled. 'Now it is you who have bad manners. It is impolite to tell a guest when to drink.'

'Yes, that is true.' The samurai's face cracked into a big toothy grin and he winked. 'But I have only one cup, and your friends are waiting.'

The Lord put the cup to his lips and drank. Handing it back, he said, 'You are right. I was a dandy. I have had tea at ceremonies performed by experts in the art. Tonight your service surpassed them all.'

The samurai handed John Whittefield the cup, saying, 'I knew he was society. Listen to his compliments.'

The Satsuma Lord stood up and dug his fists into his hips. Turning slowly, he surveyed the sleeping figures stretched out around the fortress. He took the case with the carved eagle from under his kimono, opened it, and removed a bullet. Turning to the samurai, he said, 'What is your name?'

'Showa-kai.'

The Lord of Satsuma bowed deeply from the waist. 'Take this, Showa-kai.' He placed the sleek bullet in the palm of the samurai's hand. 'Bring it to the prefect of Satsuma tomorrow at noon. You have honoured me by your hospitality and gladdened my heart with your news.'

Before the samurai could answer, the Lord of Satsuma strode away. The priest, John Whittefield, and Mung moved quickly to catch up.

Mung and John remained in the tunnel while the warrior priest escorted the Satsuma Lord through the streets and secret passages of the castle to the meditation cell. Once there, Lord Nariakira fell into a deep sleep.

Awakened by the gentle touch of Sakuma Shozan, the Lord looked up into the face of his ageing teacher. Sakuma Shozan's delicate skin hung loose from his cheek bones. There was a touch of grey at the corners of his lips. His voice, however, was still strong. 'How goes it with you, my Lord?'

'It goes well, my teacher. I have taken a path from which there is no turning back.'

'Is it an honourable direction in which we travel?'

'It is the only honourable way. It is Bushido. Please have my two sons brought here at once. Send for the warrior priest and Mung who are in the tunnel with a guest.' The old scholar turned to leave and Lord Nariakira said, 'Have a servant buy the most beautiful tea service in Satsuma. There are to be five cups. Fill each cup with silver and have it given to a *ronin* named Showa-kai. He will come to the prefect's office at noon and present a match to this.'

Lord Nariakira handed a bullet to the old scholar who turned it over in his fingers. 'What is it?'

'It may be the means by which we restore the Emperor to power.'

The old man shook his head. 'I think I have had to wait too long and will not be here to see that day.'

The Lord of Satsuma took the old scholar by the shoulders. 'My teacher, I need you more than ever. The future of Japan will be decided within a year. There can be no long drawn out sieges. We have plans to make.' He turned away. Face flushed, eyes burning, he curled his arm and shook his fist. 'I'm free! I can breathe!' He punched the air and roared, 'No more tribute to the Shōgun! Not a grain of rice! I will fulfil the vows of my father and his fathers before him! The Emperor will rule Japan!'

Before Sakuma Shozan left the room of meditation, the shouts of the Lord of Satsuma were heard. Word raced through the corridors of the castle; out into the streets and fields beyond. The period of meditation was over. People gathered near the entrance to the castle. *Ronin* thronged at the fortress gates.

In the room of meditation, Lord Nariakira carefully instructed his sons, giving them names of feudal lords in the north loyal to the Emperor. He imparted secret words which had been agreed upon for the uprising against the Shōgun, stressing the important points they were to make. 'There should be preparations for war, but avoid battles. All possible pressure should be exerted on feudal lords who may come over to the side of the Emperor. All expert workers of metal and wood should be sent to the island of Tanegoshima with the tools of their trade. The feudal lords are to organize the *ronin* in the countryside to take up arms.'

The two sons bowed their heads to the ground. When they straightened, they pulled a long object wrapped in silk from between them, placed it on the backs of their outstretched hands and presented it to their father. He removed the silk, revealing the fine steel sword which he and his sons had worked in the

317

blacksmith's shop. He hefted it in his hands, testing the balance. He held it high in the air, catching the light and playing with the reflection. Placing it on his lap, he bowed to his sons. In slow even-spaced words, he said, 'There will be no dishonour brought to the house of Satsuma. When the time comes for battle, we three shall stand together!'

The sons bowed and left the room just as Mung, John, and Sakuma Shozan entered.

Lord Nariakira faced Mung and said, 'You and your brother will sail the *Shinto Maru* to Tanegoshima. With your drawings you will supervise the making of artillery.' He turned to John. 'Allow our craftsmen to study your rifle. Have each make one part until he becomes expert at it. Then train men who will return to teach those *ronin* outside the fort how to shoot.' The warrior priest entered and Lord Nariakira addressed them all. 'We have only a few short months to prepare. The battles will begin in the summer. The Shōgun's spies have sent word of the gathering of the *ronin*. We are already in a state of war.'

A senior councillor of the Satsuma Court interrupted with a request for Sakuma Shozan to come on a most urgent matter. The old scholar begged forgiveness and was excused. He hurried to a room not far down the corridor. Entering, he saw a pregnant woman adjusting her body to a more comfortable position against the far wall. It was clear from her dress that she belonged to a family of rank but her hair was dishevelled and her face pale.

'This is the daughter of the governor of Kagoshima and the wife of Moryiama Ishikawa,' the councillor said.

The old scholar stared at her, realizing it was indeed Mung's wife. 'I see you are uncomfortable. What has brought you here at such a time?'

Saiyo attempted a bow but her stomach was too large.

Sakuma Shozan stepped to her side, placing a gentle hand on her shoulder. 'Please, just tell me.'

Saiyo looked at the councillor standing behind the scholar and pressed her lips tightly together.

The old scholar, understanding her reluctance, said, 'You may speak freely. He is a most trusted servant of our lord.'

Saiyo remained silent, staring at the floor until Sakuma Shozan asked the councillor to leave. When she lifted her head, there were tears streaming down her pale cheeks. Her first attempt to speak brought forth only a deep sob. Then she said, 'Ryochi is in Kagoshima. He is half dead. The left side of his body is paralysed and his face is disfigured. How he made the journey from Yedo without food, money, I, I ...' She winced, held her stomach, then continued. 'Three days ago fishermen brought Ryochi to my door. He made me swear to die with the message before telling anyone but you, my husband or Lord Nariakira.'

The old scholar knelt in front of Saiyo. 'I am here. You see me. What is the message?'

'Ryochi said they failed to reach the Americans.'

'But it was not a failure. Your husband did meet with them.'

A heartrending sob broke from her lips. She wagged her head. 'Then Yoshida died in vain. He was cut into pieces, urinated upon and thrown on a dung heap in Yedo.'

Sakuma Shozan rocked back and forth on his knees in front of the weeping woman. His hands came up in front of his face, making fluttering motions in the air, then dropped to his side. Tears bled slowly from his eyes. 'Yoshida was to become my adopted son. To assume the position of Scholar of Satsuma,' he whispered.

A sobbing moan escaped Saiyo's lips. The old man took her head gently to his shoulder and they wept together.

A few minutes later Sakuma Shozan said, 'Please tell me Ryochi's story in detail.'

Saiyo related the events, then glanced down at her stomach. The baby's movement was visible under her kimono.

'Try to bear with me just a little longer,' the Satsuma scholar said.

Saiyo pointed at her belly. 'I will try my lord but I don't know if he will.'

'If you can just tell me what Ryochi saw.'

'He said there was great confusion in Yedo while the Americans were there. People crowded into the temples. Prayer notes from the Shinto priests were selling at exorbitant prices. After the foreign ships departed, the war gong sounded and all the *daimyos* in residence were summoned to appear before the Shōgun.'

She tried not to show it but Sakuma Shozan could see that Saiyo's pains were more frequent. 'Thank you, little mother,' he said. 'I know the trip was long and arduous. You have served your Lord and Emperor well.'

'Was it all in vain? Did Yoshida die and is Ryochi maimed for nothing?'

'No. You have all served the Emperor and Japan. You will be written of in the historical accounts. Plays will be produced in the theatres throughout the empire about your loyalty.' The old man's voice grew bitter. 'I promise you that those who have done this terrible thing to Yoshida and Ryochi will surely die before their time! Now I must leave. There is a matter I must attend to before returning to my Lord. I will send your husband to you.'

Upon Sakuma Shozan's return to the room of meditation, he stood stiffly with fists at his sides. The colour in his cheeks reflected the raging violence in his eyes. He disregarded Lord Nariakira's gesture absolving him from the bow and went down on his knees, touching the floor with his head and the palms of both hands. When he raised his head and looked into the eyes of his lord, he clenched his jaw, drawing back his lips to reveal two rows of blackened teeth.

Lord Nariakira leaned forward, staring into his teacher's eyes. He saw a touch of madness there and shuddered. 'What vow have you made with the blackening of your teeth?'

The damp pink lips accented the blackness in his mouth. 'Death to the Shōgun!' the old scholar shouted. He turned to Mung. 'Go to your wife. She is a brave and courageous woman. I have sent for the midwife.'

The scholar and the feudal lord stared at each other as Mung dashed out of the room. He arrived at the same time as the midwife and her assistant. Saiyo lay propped on pillows in the corner of the room. Her eyes were closed, her face pale and damp with perspiration. She looked like an awkward doll left in a corner by some child, outstretched legs spread by her swollen belly, hands resting at her sides. She stifled a cry as the pain came again. Mung knelt by her side and touched her cheek. Saiyo opened her eyes, wider and wider, engulfing him in her happiness at the sight of him. Another pain came and she grasped him with both hands as she cried out. He felt her pain in his heart.

The midwife donned a robe and began opening Saiyo's kimono. She ordered Mung from the room. He objected and the assistant took him by the arm. Shaking her off, he held Saiyo's face in his hands, looking deep into her eyes. 'I love you more than my life,' he said.

'Go now please,' she whispered. 'The child is coming.' Her body tensed for the next pain.

Mung hadn't the strength to resist the gentle but persistent tugging of the assistant, and was led from the room. He heard Saiyo cry out again. Waiting outside, he sat down in the position of meditation, praying to Jesus, Buddha, and the Shinto gods of wind, water, sun and sky. Thoughts ran wild in his head. I am a samurai. If anything happens to Saiyo, I will cut off the midwife's head. I am a samurai. He felt sick in his stomach. I don't want to kill anyone. I just want to be left alone with Saiyo and the baby, any baby, boy or girl. I am supposed to pray for a boy to serve the Emperor, but all I want is Saiyo. Even if the baby dies. Oh, don't let the baby die!

The assistant massaged Saiyo's back to relieve the pressure on her spine. She checked to be sure the baby was in the correct position and warned the midwife it was moving down. She removed the pillows and laid Saiyo gently back. Raising and spreading her knees, they massaged and pushed on the stomach. The baby's head popped out of the womb, wet and hairy, with squinted eyes and wrinkled face. The midwife cradled the baby's head with one hand and the child pulled its own shoulders through, first the right, then the left. The midwife cleared mucus from the nose, mouth and eyes. Examining him as she worked, she found him sound. She placed him on the floor to signify the earth and he let out his first lusty cry on contact with his new world. The assistant placed her hands on the infant to symbolize humanity. The midwife then held him aloft as far as the umbilical cord would stretch, to indicate heaven and obedience to the Emperor.

Saiyo's head lolled back on the pillow. Through half closed eyes, she watched her son held high. Finally he was placed in her arms. The feeling of his head on her cheek was like warm silk, and his smell was hers. Mung was called. He knelt beside his wife and son, gazing at both of them, unable to speak.

'Did you see what he has?' Saiyo whispered. 'Did you see?'

Mung looked at the baby, frightened.

Saiyo gently pulled the cover from the infant. 'Look,' pointing to the baby's penis, 'he is a man child.'

Mung smiled with tears in his eyes. Ever so gently, he leaned over and embraced them both.

Lord Nariakira and Sakuma Shozan were cheered by the news that Saiyo had given birth to a son. The old scholar cracked a black-toothed smile upon hearing that Mung would name his first-born Yoshida, and said, 'His karma will be good.'

After hours of consultation, Lord Nariakira addressed the warrior priest, 'You understand the importance of a coordinated attack from both the north and south in early summer. We are divided and must force the Shōgun's army to fight on both fronts at once.'

The priest nodded.

'Reach the Emperor and obtain a clear sign that he supports us.'

The priest said, 'Pigeons will leave the temple's loft immediately with messages calling on all fighting priests to gather in support of the Emperor. Furthermore, they will use their influence to sway other feudal lords to join us.' He bowed his head to the floor. 'The fighting priests of Japan will join you here in the south, but, with all due respect my Lord, the new weapons are not for us.'

Lord Nariakira bowed and put his hand on his new sword. 'I understand,' and the priest backed out of the room.

Lord Nariakira looked at Sakuma Shozan who turned to Mung. 'Our fastest means of communication is carrier pigeons. The code we use is simple enough. I will teach it to you. The third day of next week you and John will rendezvous with the *Shinto Maru*. Carrier pigeons have been sent ordering master craftsmen of metal and wood to gather at certain points. As you proceed north to Tanegoshima, you will pick them up.'

'Since we must train men to use the weapons we produce, I would like to begin with the five samurai who guarded me while I received instructions here in Satsuma,' Mung said.

'You will have them. Train them well and train them quickly. We have no more than seven months before the Shōgun's army moves south.'

'How can you be certain they will come south first?'

'Lord Nariakira is the leader for the restoration of the Emperor to his rightful power. We are stronger here in the south than in the north, with just one major weak point. At our backs stands the Lord of Choshu, loyal to the Shōgun. What we will attempt to do by attacking from north and south, Lord Hayoshi will attempt to do to us. It is classic Japanese warfare. In June they will come. It has always been that way.'

On the second day of their second week in Satsuma, Mung, his wife and child, John, five samurai, and twenty porters departed for Ichiki. They made their rendezvous with the *Shinto Maru* in a calm sea on a starry night. Mung wished for a slower passage to spend more time with his family but the whaler ploughed ahead.

In Kagoshima, Mung agreed that John could come ashore. It was a dark night and they had the five samurai as bodyguards. John's disguise as a fighting priest had yet to be questioned. Mung led them to the governor's house. While he met with Mr Ishikawa, John and Saiyo had an opportunity to speak. She questioned him unabashedly about his wife and child, and his parents. She considered them her in-laws and revered them for saving her husband's life. More intensively, she asked about Mung and his life on the *J. Howland*. She wanted to hear how Mung's nose was broken and about his schooling in Fairhaven.

They were still deep in conversation when Mr Ishikawa came out to greet his daughter and grandchild. Then he turned to John. 'Mung is my adopted son. You are his brother, therefore also my son and Saiyo's brother.' He smiled and bowed. 'Once I had no sons. Now I have two, and a grandson. Life is sometimes pleasantly surprising.'

John bowed respectfully. 'It is an honour to have another father and to become a member of the noble Ishikawa family.'

'My father welcomes you to his house as your father welcomed me,' Mung said.

'It is good to have family here. So far from home, I have known terrible loneliness,' John said.

Saiyo and the child entered with her father. John and the samurai guards followed Mung to his house. A servant girl pointed out the room in which Ryochi lay flat on his back, staring at the ceiling. He was pathetically thin, his skin sallow. Slowly, with difficulty, he turned his head towards them. Mung saw his face, one side like melted wax. The eye was pulled down, bottom lip protruding, and the jaw twisted. Ryochi spoke, but neither Mung nor John could understand. Mung bent closer to his friend. Ryochi had to repeat his words before Mung understood and jerked away. He stared down at the broken samurai and watched a tear escape from his good eye. Without a word, he stalked from the room.

John followed Mung outside and asked, 'What did he say?'

'He said, "I have served my Lord. Of what use am I now? I ask your permission and help to perform the ceremony of *seppuku*."' Mung bent his head. 'I,' stressing the word, 'can't do it.'

An incredulous look came over John's face. 'You even consider giving him permission to kill himself?'

'You don't understand. This is Bushido. He is a warrior. It is the most honourable way for him.'

John stood straighter, his lips pressed together in a tight stubborn line, staring at Mung. 'He's a man; a human being; your friend!'

'Because he is my friend, I can't let him rot!'

'Why? Because you can't stand it?'

Mung strode away, then back up to John. The muscles in his jaw twitched, his eyes hardened as he looked up at his brother. 'Yes, I can't stand it! He can't stand it! It is our way of life!'

Now John stepped away, paced back and forth, then pointed a

finger at Mung. Through clenched teeth he said, 'Because you can't bear it, is no excuse. Because he can't, he is too ill to make the decision. That it is his way of life, I understand, but you!' He jabbed his finger at Mung. 'You know another way! There is an alternative to killing him or leaving him here to waste away.'

'What is it?'

'Take him with us.'

'What?'

'If you leave him here, he'll die. If not, you're going to kill him. Take him with us and he just might live.' John moved closer to Mung. 'I've seen men in Fairhaven recover from strokes well enough to work. But they had guts.'

Mung pointed to the house. 'That man in there has more guts than any three of your mythological Greek heroes.'

John lowered his voice, 'Then why help him to kill himself?'

Mung stared up into John's eyes, then stalked away into the house. John could see the silhouette on the *shoji* screen, kneeling next to Ryochi. Then Mung appeared at the door. He gave quick sharp orders to the samurai who went off into the night and returned with a palanquin. Mung ordered them to take Ryochi aboard the *Shinto Maru*. He stood with his fists dug into his hips, reminding John of Lord Nariakira.

'John, you return with them,' Mung ordered. 'I will say goodbye to Saiyo.' Without waiting for an answer, he turned and left.

On the deck of the *Shinto Maru*, carpenters measured out lengths of wood for bunks, washing facilities, and slop pots. The ship's holds were being cleaned by hundreds of workers. Master iron and wood-workers assembled ashore, waiting to be taken aboard. Eighteen hours after reaching Kagoshima, Mung ordered the *Shinto Maru* out to sea. They left the harbour trailing the sounds of hammers, saws, and mallets.

Heading north, Mung brought the whaler close to shore several times to pick up craftsmen from feudal fiefdoms loyal to the Emperor. Mung and John avoided speaking to each other as they explained the drawings of cannons, the mounts, and the Henry rifle to the craftsmen. Mung buried himself in the business of

325

running the ship and working with the drawings of the cannon. John had the craftsmen make six dummy rifles of wood which he used to drill the five samurai. He supervised the craftsmen's duplication of the parts of the rifle, and dedicated himself to curing Ryochi.

The half-paralysed samurai was brought up on deck to observe the rifle drills. For many days he refused to respond. Then one morning John assembled the Henry rifle and propped it up next to Ryochi, aimed at a water bucket. He put Ryochi's good hand on the pistol grip and told him to gently squeeze the trigger.

BAM! The gun bucked in Ryochi's hand and he flinched from the noise. The water bucket shattered.

John saw Ryochi's left arm and leg quivering. He grabbed him by his kimono and shook him, shouting, 'You idiot! You moved your arm and leg!' He shoved his face closer to the disfigured features. 'Try man! Try! I won't let you die until you at least try!'

Ryochi slumped back, looking away from his tormentor.

John ordered a hammock strung in Ryochi's cabin. From an overhead beam, two ropes were tied to his useless limbs. The swaying and rocking of the ship kept those limbs in continuous motion.

John looked down at the helpless samurai. 'You'll remain trussed up like a Ryukun pig until you improve.'

Ryochi tried to twist and curse at John but only spittle dribbled from the corner of his mouth.

John looked down at him. 'Good! Good! Get angry! But live! God gave us life! Fight for yours!'

Day after day, John spoke patiently to Ryochi, encouraging him.

Three weeks out of Kagoshima, Mung invited John to the quarterdeck. Without looking at his brother, Mung said, 'The other samurai are complaining that Ryochi has the right to die. Your torture is taking whatever honour he has away from him.'

'Come and see for yourself,' John said. 'I'll let you decide.'

In Ryochi's cabin, Mung immediately saw that his friend was controlling the sway of the hammock with the ropes tied to his paralysed arm and leg. He realized Ryochi's face was less twisted. His speech was slurred but intelligible and he no longer spoke of death. From then on, Ryochi went on deck with John and slowly took over the drilling of the five samurai. The relationship between Mung and John warmed again with Ryochi's recovery.

'I will yet live to revenge Yoshida!' Ryochi said to Mung and John.

They landed on the island of Tanegoshima in a light rain, the three of them walking down the gangplank, Ryochi with a cane to steady himself. Three hundred and forty craftsmen disembarked, joining five hundred others. More arrived every day. Iron was being smelted. Stacks of seasoned wood, covered with straw against the weather, lined the shore.

Mung, John, and Ryochi met with the head of the family which would cast the cannon. John was impressed with the ability of the craftsmen to grasp new technical problems and offer practical solutions. On one point they were adamant, that each cannon must have its own soul. To accomplish this, each had a name and was cast in the form of a legendary animal. The first was a small dragon whose cast-iron head would spit fire. On the third firing 'Small Dragon' exploded, wounding some of the crew. Then 'Gay Falcon' made its debut, steady and accurate. There followed 'Hawk', 'Fish', 'Eagle', 'Butterfly', and others.

Directed by John Whitefield, metal workers learned to make explosive shells with gunpowder smuggled in from China. The shells and bullet-casings for the rifles proved more of a problem than the weapons. It took a day to make a bullet and three for an artillery shell. More than four thousand of Japan's finest metal and wood workers laboured day after day and into the nights. Smoke from the forges covered the island. Vast amounts of wood were ferried in. Fuel and food shortages were alleviated when the *Shinto Maru* killed three whales and towed them to shore.

Carrier pigeons were continually coming and going. In November, a pigeon came from the north carrying a message from the eldest of Lord Nariakira's sons. It told Mung to beware an attack on the island. Mung had four cannon placed aboard the

Shinto Maru. John and Ryochi, who was making a phenomenal recovery, trained the crews and samurai in the use of artillery. Ryochi had a sixth sense about the cannon, as if he could speak to their souls. His ability to judge distance and time the roll of the ship amazed John, who soon stopped giving advice and allowed Ryochi to work the crews.

On a cold sleety day in December, alarm rockets burst overhead from picket boats posted around the island. In thirty minutes, the *Shinto Maru* was making her way out of the harbour, the gun crews at their stations in the sleet that was turning to snow. Visibility was closing rapidly and the hands of the lookouts froze to the ropes as the whaler picked up speed.

The cry, 'Sail-ho!' came from the crow's nest. Again and again the cry was repeated, 'Sail-ho! Sail-ho!'

John made sure the deck was sprinkled with sand, and buckets were ready to douse fires. Ryochi stood to his guns, and Mung was on the quarterdeck. Half a mile away, out of the blinding storm, a fleet of fifty boats suddenly appeared. Mung gave orders to stand by to fire at targets port and starboard. He was turning to give the order to put the big ship on a ramming course when the long-drawn-out cry came from the crow's nest, 'Sat-suuuu-maaa.'

On the lead ship, the long green banner carrying the Satsuma calligraph fluttered for an instant, then dropped soggy and wet against the mast.

The fleet was led by the two sons of Lord Nariakira. Battered, exhausted samurai filled the boats. Once in the harbour, they told their story. Lord Hayoshi, now the supreme commander of the Shōgun's forces, had rounded up an army which he beat into shape as they moved north in the winter. This was against all known rules of Japanese warfare. Those feudal lords who had wavered when they thought the Shōgun was weak, now stayed at home or actively joined the Shōgun's army. Those loyal to the Emperor, caught unaware, went out to do battle with Hayoshi's army and were beaten one after the other. The two brothers advised the ~ds of Riku, Ugo and Uzen not to fight, but to force a siege. The

being honourable men desirous of serving the Emperor,

disregarded the advice. They met Hayoshi in the time-honoured formation on the fields of Arato, a flat place between two parallel sets of rolling hills. The battle opened in the formal way with champion samurai from each side striding forward to hurl insults. Challenges were accepted and soon there were hundreds of individual duels taking place at once while the soldiers watched. This continued for two days.

On the third day, rockets went up and drums rolled for the charge against Hayoshi. His forces pulled back to the crest of the hill as if in retreat. Archers, spearmen, and horsemen rolled forward towards the enemy of the Emperor. Suddenly, from each flank, came an attack of over one thousand horsemen followed by archers, then spearmen who passed through the archers.

'It was a brilliant manoeuvre,' Lord Nariakira's eldest son said. 'We thought at worst to fight, wound Hayoshi, then force him to hold a siege through the winter. In the end we were routed.' He looked at Mung. 'We did not even have time to send off pigeons.' He chuckled grimly. 'They killed the birds too.'

The messages fluttered off that day to Satsuma. The mood in camp became as sullen as the weather. Three days later a half frozen bird landed in the loft with a message from Satsuma, 'No one is to commit *seppuku* because of the loss of face in the battle with Hayoshi. The output of guns is to be increased. The *Shinto Maru* is to return to Ichiki and Satsuma in February, in time to train the gathering *ronin* to use the new weapons. Hayoshi will move south in the spring and the battle will take place in early summer.'

On 3 January, the *Shinto Maru* left Tanegoshima with twenty cannon, five hundred duplicates of the Henry rifle, ammunition and shells in her holds. Ryochi remained to oversee the continued production of weapons and the training of the men who had accompanied the sons of Lord Nariakira to the island. He travelled around the island in a rickshaw designed by John from the Chinese model he had ridden in Canton.

At Ichiki, the ship was met by two thousand porters who took over the unloading of the weapons. Mung, John, and the sons of Lord Nariakira went by horse to Satsuma. At the castle, they were immediately taken to the chambers of the Lord. He questioned his sons about the battles in the north. Sakuma Shozan pressed for details.

Only after many hours were they satisfied they understood exactly what had taken place. The Lord's sons were excused.

'Now we know what happened, but we don't know why,' Sakuma Shozan said.

'I don't understand,' Mung said.

John spoke, 'From your line of questioning, you can't fathom why Lord Hayoshi went north in the winter. But I see it as a gamble.'

Both Lord Nariakira and the Satsuma scholar bowed their heads slightly in respect. Lord Nariakira said, 'You are perceptive. We are the weakest force because of Choshu at our backs. The move north was brilliantly executed, but it was one of desperation. We can't understand why Lord Hayoshi took the chance.'

Sakuma Shozan spoke. 'Now Hayoshi will move slowly southwards, gathering strength because of his victories in the north. He will rest his men on the Kanto Plains outside Yedo and move south at the first sign of cherry blossoms.' The old scholar stood up and walked to the far wall. He stood there, muttering to himself. Slowly, he turned. 'Choshu.' At first it was a whisper. Then he shouted it, 'Choshu!' Coming to stand in front of Lord Nariakira, his blackened teeth glistening, he said, 'It must be Choshu! For some reason Lord Hayoshi is not sure that the Lord of Choshu will attack us. My Lord,' he bowed, 'allow me to go to Choshu to confirm this. I feel it in my bones. It can be the only reason for Hayoshi's gamble.'

Within two days, Sakuma Shozan was on his way to the fiefdom of Choshu which overlooked the Straits of Shimoneski. Mung and the five samurai began training the *ronin* to use the rifles. John trained crews for the cannon. Every sunrise, rain or shine, whistles blew, gongs sounded and drums beat the men into formation. By February there were more than 25,000 soldiers in the Satsuma ᵥ. The Lord of Osumi sent word he had 10,000 men, Lord of ᵥ 7,000, Hayuga 6,000, Chikuzen 8,000, and Hakusar another

8,000 fighting men. The roads of the Satsuma fiefdom were lined with samurai on horseback and peasants on foot. Porters and carts travelled in both directions, loaded until the axles squealed and backs bent.

In the camps, armed men marched and counter-marched. John worked his unit until he felt they were perfect. Only then did he allow them to fire the precious ammunition. Two of the cannons exploded in practice but the other ornate weapons fired true. Mung and his samurai drilled their riflemen in dry firing at fixed targets until they were proficient. Later, each was allowed to fire twenty rounds of live ammunition, learning to fire in ranks by volley, taking careful aim according to commands.

At the end of February, a column of cavalry burst out of the Satsuma fortress, banners waving, the long green Satsuma pennant whipping in the air. Cheers rolled like the roar of the sea following the column, Lord Nariakira and his sons at its head. Swords, spears, and bows were raised in salute by the troops camped around the fortress. Mung ordered ten riflemen to fire a volley, and John had two cannoneers discharge their guns. Carts, wagons, and people scattered as the column galloped up the main road throwing clods of dirt into the air.

A messenger brought a horse for Mung and told him to join Lord Nariakira. When Mung reached the road, he saw John and other commanders on horseback following the column.

Mung galloped up to John and slapped him on the back. 'No more waiting. We move at last.'

John, with a big grin, shouted, 'Hai!'

They kicked their horses and galloped with more than two hundred commanders following the Lord of Satsuma. Changing mounts three times, they stopped to rest only once after eighteen hours. They slept for three hours and were in the saddle again. The ride was well planned, for when they arrived on the crest of the hills overlooking the Hakusar Valley, tents and food were prepared. The clan banners of Osumi, Bungo, Chikuzen, Hayuga, and Hakusar flew in front of the largest tents. After a meal of rice and pickled vegetables, they slept.

331

Mung and John were summoned to Lord Nariakira's tent before sunrise. The Satsuma Lord was flanked by his two sons. He said, 'Lord Hayoshi has once again shown himself to be a brilliant soldier. He isn't waiting for the cherry blossoms. He is already on the move with 90,000 troops. He will gather more men as he moves towards us. We will meet here. The Valley of Hakusar will be the battleground.'

'Why did you choose this place, and why will Hayoshi accept?' John asked.

'Our fathers chose this site for their battle 250 years ago. This is where the Shōgun gained his power and where I will return it to the Emperor.'

'Can we set no traps or meet him in a place he doesn't expect?'

'It is Bushido that we meet here, and our karma if we win or lose.'

'I am a guest,' John said. 'I accept your traditions and codes of honour, but Hayoshi has taken his karma into his own hands. We cannot sit and wait for him.'

'What do you propose?'

'At least, harass him as he makes his way to the battlegrounds; slow his progress. Force his men to stand extra watches. Reduce the amount of food he can take from the land.'

'Your training in the naval college has stood you in good stead,' Lord Nariakira said. He nodded to his right and left. 'This role of harassment, I have already assigned to my sons.' He looked at Mung and John. 'You two will walk every inch of this battlefield until you know exactly where your weapons will be the most effective.' He pressed his lips together in a tight line. 'I have not heard from Sakuma Shozan. If Choshu comes against us, we will have another 30,000 enemy at our backs. Mung, send pigeons to Ryochi. Order him to return on the *Shinto Maru* with all the weapons and men he has trained.'

Day after day for two weeks, Mung and John walked the grass covered hills on both sides of the valley. They sat at strategy meetings and listened to the Lords and high-ranking samurai discuss who would be given the honour of facing various lords and

332

champions of the Shōgun in single combat.

Then they requested a private audience with Lord Nariakira. Mung said, 'My Lord, you have utilized our knowledge of making modern weapons, yet your senior commanders speak of individual combat with swords.'

John said, 'It is one thing to be outnumbered, but to fight a battle according to rules by which we will certainly lose is ...,' he bowed his head, 'pardon the expression, my Lord, but it is foolish.'

Lord Nariakira looked from one to the other. 'You are both correct. Your guns are my surprise for Lord Hayoshi. We will use your weapons, but you must remember we are an ancient people with deep-rooted traditions. Your country is not old enough to have traditions and so you are more flexible. How would you advise me?'

John thought for a few moments. 'I am trying to take your traditions into consideration, but surely you knew when you sought Dutch Learning you are already breaking tradition.' The Satsuma Lord nodded and motioned John to continue. 'It is an axiom in modern warfare that the number of men on either side is not the determining factor, but the number of men who actually fight is.'

Mung said, 'From my readings of the Latin books about the campaigns of Alexander the Great, the Roman generals, Napoleon, and with John's training, we have drawn up a plan of war utilizing rifles and cannon to the best effect.'

Lord Nariakira nodded. 'I will study this.' And he dismissed them.

Word from Ryochi and Sakuma Shozan was long overdue. Finally, one afternoon, a pigeon rang the loft bell with a message from Ryochi, 'Until the Shinto Maru arrived, I had no word from Satsuma. We are loading and will leave immediately.' At the bottom of the message was scrawled one word, 'Hawkers.'

In fact, both sides used hawks to down and intercept messages. All three birds sent to Ryochi had been hawked in flight.

On a sunny April morning, from the top of the hill, Mung saw clouds of black smoke in the distance. From that day, the clouds never left the sky, always coming closer and closer. The princes of Satsuma were harassing the vanguard of Lord Hayoshi's army. Farms and villages in their path were evacuated and stores carried away or burned. Wounded soldiers and riderless horses became a common sight in the valley.

Mung and John were summoned to the Lord's tent. His sons, still in armour, had the look of lean, hard, seasoned fighting men.

'My sons have performed well,' Lord Nariakira said. 'They have harassed the enemy day and night. We still face an army of more than 120,000. Their commanders and many of their men have been blooded in battles in the south. Their outriders are already in the hills opposite us. The battle should begin in a few days. Be sure to keep the cannon and riflemen out of sight of their scouts.'

Lord Nariakira gestured to his elder son to see what the noise was outside the tent. The son returned, carrying the frail body of Sakuma Shozan. The old man's face was grey, and his breath wheezed through dry blue lips and blackened teeth. The son lay the withered scholar gently on the mat in front of his father.

Sakuma Shozan was barely able to whisper, 'The Choshu Lord has poisoned me. He said it would take seven days to be effective. Choshu people were never a good judge of anything. I shall die sooner.'

Lord Nariakira went forward on his knees to the old man. Before he could utter a word, Sakuma Shozan stopped him with an upraised finger.

A rasping sound came from the old scholar's throat before he cleared it enough to speak. 'The Choshu Lord was so impressed by the cannons of the American ships which levelled his forts in the Straits of Shimoneski that he was not going to join the Shōgun's forces.' The old man breathed heavily, but refused a cup of water. 'The poison constricts my throat. I cannot swallow. They wanted me alive long enough to tell you.' He breathed in slowly and deeply, then continued, 'Until the victories in the north and the defection of some of the supporters of the Emperor to the Shōgun, Choshu was going to remain neutral. A week ago they received a message from Hayoshi that the *Shinto Maru*, carrying the weapons made on the island of Tanegoshima, was captured; the ship and contents burnt.'

They all sat in stunned silence. No word had been received from Ryochi since his last message that he was loading the whaler.

Lord Nariakira said, 'My teacher, it is time for you to rest.'

The old man shook his head. 'Not yet, not yet. You have two more lessons to learn.'

'What are they, my teacher?'

'Treachery and honour. The treachery of the Choshu Lord. He will attack, but not from behind. He will attack your left flank with all his 30,000 troops. This I learned without his knowing from the warrior priest whose people are quietly gathering somewhere here in the south. They number about 5,000.'

'You have told me of the treachery. What is it you want me to know about honour?'

Sakuma Shozan tried to raise himself but could not.

Lord Nariakira cradled his head in the crook of his arm. 'Yes, my teacher?'

The old man's tongue licked his parched, blue lips. 'I have been obedient to you and your father. I have not the strength to die honourably. Will you help me?'

Lord Nariakira smiled into the old eyes. 'Yes, my teacher.'

The Satsuma Lord gave orders for the ritual of *seppuku* to be prepared. He ordered his senior commanders to hear the story of the poisoning and to witness the ritual act.

Clothed in white linen, supported by the sons of his lord, Sakuma Shozan sat on a raised platform in front of the commanders. Lord Nariakira motioned his sons away. He held the old man around the shoulders and picked up the razor-sharp knife. Placing the old scholar's hands on the hilt, he moved the point to his abdomen, and asked, 'Are you ready, my teacher?'

The whispered answer came, 'I am ready, my Lord.'

Lord Nariakira closed his hand over the old man's cold bony fingers and plunged the knife deep, then drew it quickly across the abdomen. Sakuma Shozan sighed once, then slumped forward.

The Lord stood up, tears in his eyes. 'Bury this wise old man who was a father to me. Bury him sitting up, looking over this battlefield to see if we who serve the Emperor have as much courage as he. This is my order.' He planted his fists on his hips and shouted, 'No man will be disgraced on this battlefield!' He pointed to the valley below. 'Here we win or die for the Emperor!'

The commanders' cheering became a roaring chant, affecting Mung and John and spreading to the Satsuma fighting men camped above the valley. The hills reverberated with the voices of 70,000 troops.

Sakuma Shozan's grave was placed on the hill behind Lord Nariakira's tent where Mung and John were now presenting a change in strategy.

Mung said, 'The loss of the *Shinto Maru* and the weapons is a serious blow. Even with five hundred rifles and eighteen cannon, we are 70,000 facing more than 150,000, many with battle experience. Ammunition for our weapons is not plentiful. We must use John's concept of minimizing the number of enemy facing us at any one time.'

Lord Nariakira nodded for Mung to continue, but it was John who said, 'An American general, Andrew Jackson, led a force of untrained men against twice as many veteran British soldiers at New Orleans, and won. He fought from fixed positions behind breastworks, utilizing the lie of the land to make his weapons more effective. We must not order our riflemen to move forward. Allow the enemy to come to them.' He spread a map before the Satsuma Lord and pointed. 'If the army of Choshu attacks our left flank and the Shōgun's forces make a frontal assault, have your commanders prepare for an orderly withdrawal on the left flank. It must be done quickly to pull the Choshu army in front of Lord Hayoshi's troops, effectively screening them. Allow the Choshu to come well within the range of our riflemen and cannon. If you can mass cavalry and bowmen behind the crest of the hill, they can drive into the Choshu flank, push them downhill and into the ranks of the Shōgun's troops.'

Lord Nariakira looked at the map. He traced and retraced his finger over the battlefield, then looked up. 'It is a good plan. You will have two days to build the breastworks. Do it!'

Before returning to work on the defences, Mung took John's arm. 'Brother, we took a solemn vow in the chapel aboard the *Susquehanna*. Now, here in Japan, I would like to renew that vow with you at a nearby Shinto shrine.'

John hesitated. 'I couldn't bow to any idol.'

Mung clapped his brother on the shoulder. 'Nothing like that. You will only humble yourself before the work of the Creator. Come!'

The two mounted their horses and rode a few miles into the hills. The trail led through a glen which narrowed to a footpath. They tethered the horses and John followed Mung under the wide branches of the old pine trees. He heard the sound of rushing water before he saw it. They came out into a clearing fogged by white mist from a cascading waterfall. The two stopped to admire the lush greenery and thirty-foot torrent of ice-cold, mountain water pounding a giant boulder at the bottom.

'This is it,' Mung said.

The only sign of a shrine John saw was a small brass gong and hammer near the boulder.

Mung kicked off his sandals, removed his clothes, and walked into the mist. He picked up the brass hammer and struck the gong six times.

Stepping back, he cried out, 'Purify my six senses that I may use each one of them to defeat the Shōgun and restore the Emperor to his rightful place!'

He struck the gong a seventh time, then leapt onto the boulder and knelt under the torrent. The shock of freezing water beat on his back and shoulders. He saw purple, black and yellow flashes.

Then he heard a gasp. At his side knelt his brother, John. The water beat down on both of them. Their bodies numbed by the pounding and the cold, the brothers, from opposite ends of the earth, grasped each other's hands.

'We are cleansed of all impurities of the body and soul,' Mung said. 'Do you feel it?'

John nodded his head slowly, surprised at how close to Jesus he felt in this faraway land at a Shinto shrine. They both knew they were prepared.

CHAPTER
17

15 April 1854

Shortly after dawn, a breeze rippled the valley grass and brushed the ancient pine trees on the crests of hills surrounding the Hakusar Valley. Smoke from cooking fires wafted up to the pale blue sky. There were no more clouds of black smoke on the horizon. Suddenly a partridge bolted into the tree line behind Sakuma Shozan's grave. A low soft rumble reverberated and grew louder. Small animals ran over the crest before the waves of thunder. Birds took flight. Mule, deer and buck scrambled down the slopes into the valley. The men in the Satsuma camp looked towards the skyline, 900 yards away.

The thunder became a crescendo of distinct deafening drumbeats. The grass and trees quivered to the throb of 10,000 drummers leading the Shōgun's army. Mung felt the vibrations in his feet, and in his teeth. The ground seemed to undulate to the beat. A blue rocket trailed smoke across the far sky. The drums ceased, but the beat continued in Mung's heart.

A single flag bearer came over the skyline carrying the Shōgun's pennant. Lord Hayoshi's banner appeared next. On either side, bannermen came over the crest of the hill, followed by the feudal lords and their retainers. Silhouetted against the skyline, they planted their flags.

Mung heard a Satsuma commander identifying the leaders and their colours to Lord Nariakira, 'Awaju, Bitchu, Wakasa, Yamato, Shimutsu, Iwaki, Hida, Higo, Noto, Echigo, Inaba, Aki, Musashi, Kotsuke, Sanuke, Tajima, Tosa, Tokugawa, Mito, Minimoto.'

The thunderous drum roll started again, and the skyline filled with samurai in burnished chain-linked armour and winged helmets. Once again a rocket exploded in the sky. From the centre of the formation a single samurai trotted his horse down the hill, followed by one hundred men who fanned out on either side of him, each fifty yards apart. As the samurai's horse came closer to Lord Nariakira and his retinue, they heard the clinking of his armour.

He stopped twenty-five yards in front of the Satsuma ranks and shouted, 'Those who hear my voice must pay tribute to the Shōgun!'

The men spread across the field repeated his command.

A senior samurai of Satsuma walked forward. 'Do you pay respect to the Emperor?' He pointed to the ground. 'Bow down before the Emperor!'

'Is it war?' the Shōgun's samurai shouted.

'Hai!' the Satsuma man answered.

A gesture from the Shōgun's samurai sent the men on his right and left running back to their lines. He walked his horse closer and shouted, 'I am Lord Hayoshi's champion. I challenge the champion of Satsuma.' He trotted his horse back and forth, restlessly waiting for the Satsuma Lord's champion to come forward.

John turned to Mung and patted his Colt revolver. 'What would happen if I walked out there and put a hole between his eyes?'

'He would be one very surprised dead man but this must be done according to ritual. Wait and see.'

Lord Nariakira's runner moved forward carrying a silk pillow which held a writing brush. Offering it to the samurai, he said, 'This is the weapon of Sakuma Shozan, the scholar of Satsuma. You mighty warriors of the Shōgun poisoned him. Is that the way of Bushido?'

The samurai kicked the pillow out of the runner's hand and wheeled his horse around, trotting back to his lines. From the Shōgun's camp others came forward to challenge the warriors of the Emperor who eagerly accepted. Soon two hundred individual duels were being fought in the valley, both sides shouting encouragement to their champions. Mung and John watched the combatants fight until one was dead or mortally wounded. No advantage was gained by either side. The day of single combat ended at sunset.

Mung and John were summoned to the last meeting before the battle, half an hour before sunrise. They sat with Lord Nariakira and his commanders in the position of meditation, each one with closed eyes watching his thoughts. Most saw glory on the field of battle. John and Mung would have been surprised to know their images were similar – of their young sons, wives and families.

Barking dogs and the tinkle of bells broke the silence of meditation. The sun spread its warmth over the valley. Out of the woods behind the Satsuma camp came two hundred armed samurai, each holding a ten-foot, two-inch-thick colourful braided leash. Giant dogs with faces like bears strained at the leashes, each dog weighing at least 140 pounds and standing thirty inches at the shoulder. Around their necks they wore collars of thick ruffled material similar to that Mung and John had seen on clowns at the circus in Fairhaven. At sight of the procession, everyone threw themselves to the ground. These were the Emperor's dogs.

Mung and John also prostrated themselves until the dogs and samurai had passed through their ranks headed for the enemy lines. Behind them came five thousand warrior priests with shaven heads, wearing chest armour over their saffron robes. Prayer bells tinkled at their waists. Eight-foot bows and quivers of steel-tipped arrows were slung over their shoulders.

The warrior high priest bowed to Lord Nariakira. 'The Emperor sends his Akita dogs as a sign to the Shōgun that he supports Satsuma.'

All in the Satsuma camp watched the effect on the Shōgun's troops as the dogs approached. Drums rolled, whistles shrilled and gongs sounded, until 120,000 of the Shōgun's men stood to arms, many in the forward ranks prostrating themselves before the royal canines.

The commander of the imperial guard strode up to the banner of Lord Hayoshi and shouted, 'In the name of the living god and embodiment of Japan, the Shōgun's troops must lay down their weapons and return to their homes!'

Lord Hayoshi, seeing several of his feudal lords hesitating, gave a signal. One thousand *ronin* ran forward and fell upon the Emperor's guards with spears. The dogs, trained to kill, were unleashed. Their masters, swords in hand, leapt forward. A wild savage mêlée ensued – ripping, clawing, shouting and barking. Bared fangs and slashing swords. The imperial guards were heavily outnumbered, the battle was fierce but brief. They were wiped out and the dogs butchered.

Then John saw rank on rank of archers move to the front of the Shōgun's line. They took aim at their own *ronin* who had destroyed the Emperor's guards. John looked to Mung in shock as the archers cut down their own men.

'It is Bushido,' Mung said. 'No one is to harm anything of the Emperor's and live.'

'Then how can they fight against the Emperor if he is revered by everybody as a god?'

'It's not logical, I know. The Emperor and his predecessors have been confined to Kyoto for two and a half centuries as a symbol rather than a power able to make change. It's a paradox.' Mung shrugged. 'But that's the way it is.'

From the west came the rolling of drums and firing of signal rockets.

Lord Nariakira said to the warrior priest, 'It is the opening Choshu attack on our left flank. Sakuma Shozan gave us your message. We are prepared. Order your priests to reinforce the riflemen at the centre.'

Across the valley the enemy troops marched into position. The noise from the west grew louder. Mung and John moved, with Lord Nariakira, to a higher position on the hillside. They saw their left flank engage the Choshu army. Choshu commanders had not grasped the advantage of seizing the high ground. Instead they pressed their men forward to roll up the Satsuma flank on the side of the hill.

Lord Nariakira pointed to the Shōgun's line. 'That is why they are not taking the high ground.'

Masses of enemy troops poured down the opposite slopes into the valley. They marched across the valley floor for the uphill assault on the pressured left flank of the Satsuma fighting men.

Lord Nariakira nodded to John. 'Exactly as you predicted.' He signalled and two red rockets whooshed skyward. The withdrawal began in the face of the Choshu army. The Satsuma warriors retreated in a disciplined manner, drawing the Choshu army forward. When the Shōgun's soldiers, coming up the hill, reached the point where the fighting had been, they found themselves on the flank of their allies, the army of Choshu. Effectively screened from the combat, 20,000 warriors milled in confusion.

Lord Nariakira slapped both his sons on the back. They leapt into their saddles and galloped up the hill to their men. He smiled at Mung and John and, with a gesture, ordered them to their positions.

John's eighteen cannon stood gun carriage to gun carriage, facing the flank. Mung's five hundred riflemen, lined in three ranks behind the cannon, protected their flanks. The warrior high priest's five thousand archers, cleverly camouflaged in a ravine which ran up the hill, tied in with Mung's riflemen.

John ordered a double load of grapeshot loaded. The crews jumped to their guns, ramming home the canisters of deadly iron balls. Retreating soldiers ran by the gun crews to regroup behind the riflemen. The last of the Satsuma flags came through the lines. Riderless horses galloped back and forth in front of the oncoming ranks of Choshu. The horses jumped the breastworks or skidded on their haunches, bolting up the hill.

Mung awaited the bannermen of Choshu leading the spearmen, swordsmen, archers, and mounted samurai into his guns. John signalled and Mung ordered half his riflemen to begin

343

firing. The deadly accuracy of their fire on the advancing enemy flanks funnelled them in towards the cannon.

The noise of rifle fire startled the Choshu troops. Lord Nariakira watched them hesitate one hundred yards from where John Whittefield, head shaved, dressed in the battle garb of a Buddhist fighting priest, stood with arm raised, ready to signal. A drum beat began and the Choshu men came forward. Eighty yards ... seventy yards ... John's arm was rigid, his fingers outstretched. Sixty yards ... forty ... Clouds of Choshu arrows whistled into the ranks of the riflemen.

John held his position until the enemy were twenty-five yards from the muzzles. His hand hacked down. Eighteen cannons roared at once, bucking back on their carriages. Smoke and dust enveloped the slope. The cannoneers wrestled their weapons back into position to load a second round of double grapeshot. John's arm came down again and the eighteen cannons fired. When the smoke and dust began to clear, Mung ordered his five hundred riflemen to fire independently. The Henry rifles cracked one after the other, building to a crescendo. A breeze lifted away the cloud. Carnage lay before them – men and horses ripped apart, blood flowing down the slopes into the valley. It ran through the grass in rivulets, forming puddles around the boulders. The attack of the Choshu army was halted.

Lord Nariakira signalled his rocketeer and two royal blue smoke trails streaked skyward. From the upper slope 3,000 cavalry broke from the woods, led by the two Satsuma princes. At the same time the 5,000 archers obeyed a signal from the warrior high priest. They unslung their eight-foot bows and wheeled right, swinging behind the cavalry racing down the hill. Mung ordered his men to fire by volleys into the ranks of the milling Choshu army. The Satsuma horses slammed into the flank of the enemy with downhill momentum. The Buddhist priests strung their bows and let fly the five-foot steel-tipped shafts. The Choshu army staggered and reeled, beginning to move slowly, then more quickly down the hill in disorderly fashion.

Mung saw John stagger away from the guns and ran to him,

thinking he was hit. John was bent double, retching and choking, mucus dripping from his nose and mouth.

Mung grabbed him around the shoulders. 'Where are you hurt?'

John choked, then pointed to the battlefield. 'Look what I've done! Look at it!'

They both stared at the blood-soaked field – at heads, legs, arms, wounded men and staggering horses slipping on the sticky red-stained grass.

Mung held John tighter, grinding his teeth. 'This is only the beginning. Hold on! We need you!'

He left John and took command of the cannons, ordering high explosive shells loaded, the guns trained on the retreating soldiers. The shells burst with devastating effect into the mass of humanity on the hillside.

Lord Nariakira's sons, regrouping the Satsuma cavalry, attacked again. Like a bull goring the flank of a wounded elephant, they drove the Choshu and Shōgun soldiers from the valley floor and up the far slopes.

A single green rocket zoomed skyward from Lord Hayoshi's position. Five thousand armoured cavalry moved forward from the west end of the valley, another 5,000 trotted in from the east. The valley filled with a rumbling which grew to a deafening thunder as 10,000 horses galloped forward. With pennants flying, swords and spears gleaming, they caught the Satsuma cavalry from both sides.

The artillery and rifles were useless in the wild fight below. Mung kept his eye on the Satsuma flag. Satisfied the cavalry was making a stand there, he looked uphill to Lord Nariakira. The Lord watched the action below for another minute, fists dug into hips, then signalled Mung and the warrior high priest forward. Mung marched his *ronin* riflemen in formation down into the valley, setting them in ranks 150 yards from the cavalry battle. On his signal, the first rank knelt and fired. The second rank moved forward through the first, kneeling and firing. The third moved forward as the others reloaded. The priestly archers moved behind the riflemen and a corridor was blasted through to the entrapped Satsuma cavalry. Led by the two princes, some were able to extricate themselves and gallop to safety, leaving more than 1,500 dead.

Mung, beginning a withdrawal of his riflemen, suddenly caught sight of a mass troop movement on his right. Thousands of warriors, led by Lord Hayoshi's spearmen, charged towards him. He reformed the ranks – front line in the prone position, second line kneeling, third line standing. The spearmen advanced to within a hundred yards. Mung's hand was raised. He was directing his men. 'Steady ... steady ... steady.' Suddenly, by some prearranged signal, the front ranks of charging spearmen dropped to the ground. Mung's riflemen were looking into the barrels of hundreds of muskets which had been screened by the charging spearmen. Both sides fired simultaneously. At that range the muskets were as effective as the rifles, but the riflemen's ability to reload was three times faster. Mung ran up and down the line encouraging them to pick their targets and aim true.

He was losing men, and their weapons were beginning to overheat. The ranks of the Shōgun's spearmen leapt to their feet and charged into the blazing muzzles. The riflemen would have been overrun but for a rain of arrows which poured onto the spearmen. The fighting priests were supporting Mung's men but they too began falling to enemy arrows. They were all in danger of being outflanked and surrounded as Lord Hayoshi sent more troops into the battle.

Three arrows were deflected by Mung's chest armour but a fourth skewered his left wrist. With extreme concentration he knelt, placed the long shaft over his knee, and broke it off. Fighting dizziness and pain, teeth clenched, he pulled the arrow through.

The enemy cavalry had reformed. Led by a sword-wielding samurai, they made a daring charge at Mung's position. He blew the big samurai out of the saddle with one shot from the Colt revolver and emptied the rest of the bullets into the oncoming horsemen. Then the ground erupted under the enemy's forces. High-explosive shells smashed into their ranks. John's guns were in action again. His men were loading and firing like the demons of hell. Under the covering artillery fire and umbrella of arrows from

346

the warrior priests, Mung disengaged and took the remainder of his men back to the breastworks.

The court surgeon tended Mung's wound. Now he sat with his arm in a sling, next to John, listening to the army commanders' battle reports to Lord Nariakira. Major battles had taken place on the right flank. Although the line held, casualties were high. The Choshu army was badly mauled and the Shōgun's soldiers had been routed but they still outnumbered the imperial army by more than two to one. Mung reported he had lost more than one third of his men. Those remaining had only eight bullets per rifle. John had eleven shells per gun.

Lord Nariakira nodded to the warrior priest who said, 'I have learned from a captured senior commander of the Mito clan that the *Shinto Maru* was never taken. This commander led a force of 150 boats to invade Tanegoshima. Bad weather capsized many of the craft and scattered the rest. None ever reached the island. He said it is doubtful that those on the island even knew they were to be attacked. The message sent to Choshu was a lie and a trick.'

'A trick that worked,' Lord Nariakira said. 'Choshu entered on the side of the Shōgun.'

The warrior priest spoke again, 'The muskets that were used against us today were purchased from the Dutch. They knew of our rifles and cannon through their spies but were doubtful the weapons would affect the outcome of the battle.'

Lord Nariakira said, 'Had we more of these rifles and cannon, it would have.' Calmly, he gave his commanders their final orders to draw the line in closer and reinforce the flanks, then dismissed all but Mung, John, and the warrior priest. He turned to John. 'I commend you for your invaluable assistance to us. You are a good samurai.'

John bowed, acknowledging the compliment. Lord Nariakira picked up one long and one short sword with the Satsuma seal on their scabbards. Placing them on the back of his hands, he offered them to John. Mung and the others bowed.

Lord Nariakira said, 'Take these as a token of my gratitude and as the sign of your rank of Satsuma samurai.'

347

John held the weapons at arm's length and looked from one to the other until his eyes met those of Lord Nariakira. 'My Lord, you speak as if I am leaving.'

Mung and John listened carefully as the Satsuma Lord said, 'The new weapons saved us today. Tomorrow, Lord Hayoshi will throw all his men into the battle. Your ammunition would be used up in minutes. The outcome is certain.'

'You will need me more than ever,' John said.

Lord Nariakira cut off further comment by a wave of his hand. He turned to Mung. 'You will both instruct your men, then, without being seen, take the shortest route to the sea. There you will put John on a ship with orders to sail to Canton. When you have done this, your obligations to me are fulfilled.' He took a scroll from his sleeve and handed it to Mung. 'You are hereby appointed the Satsuma scholar. It may be an empty title after tomorrow, but in our family it has always been an honourable one.' With a gesture, he dismissed them both.

John drew himself up and saluted the Lord, then smartly turned and followed Mung. They walked dejectedly to their positions.

Mung said, 'I feel like the night we watched Honolulu burn. It was terrible and there was nothing we could do.'

John nodded. He began to speak, then threw up his hands in a futile gesture.

Mung selected a samurai familiar with the area to lead them. They slipped away, moving in single file through the forest until they came to the end of the tree line where the Hakusar Valley narrows. The light of the half moon played tricks with shadows as they made their way. An hour's walking time into the narrow valley, they heard noises ahead. Mung signalled to move up the slope. They crawled as fast and as far as they could. The three crouched in the dark and watched shadowy figures approaching below. Mung made out a formation of foot soldiers screening for a larger body of troops. He heard the clink of armour as they passed and behind them a low deep throated rhythmic chant. The light of the moon lit the top of the hill and moved slowly into the valley. As the chanting drew closer, the silvery moonlight revealed a dragon-headed cannon held shoulder high by more than a hundred men under eighty-foot bearing poles. They shuffled forward to the rhythm of the slow chant.

John grabbed Mung's arm, whispering, 'Holy Jesus Christ! God forgive me for swearing, but . . .' He pointed to a rickshaw moving with the column.

Mung stood up, cupping his hands around his mouth. 'Town-hooooooo! Town-hooooo! Ryochiiiii! Ryochiiii!'

They slipped, slid and tumbled down the hill and were immediately surrounded by guards until Ryochi came bouncing up in his rickshaw. Mung and John stared at their friend as he got out of the carriage. His face was straightened and he barely limped. Hugging Mung and then John, it was the old Ryochi.

'How did you know where the battle would be?' John asked.

Ryochi shook his head. 'You should learn more about the history of Japan. For 250 years everyone knew where it would be.'

'What have you brought?' Mung asked.

'Forty-three cannons with trained crews, 130 shells per gun. I trained the men who came to Tanegoshima with Lord Nariakira's sons as gunners and riflemen. There are 600 riflemen with 200 rounds per man. The craftsmen found a quicker way to make the bullets.' He motioned to the column. 'We have barrels full.'

Mung looked up and down the line of porters and at the heavy guns being borne on the shoulders of farmers and peasants. 'Where did you find all these men to carry the guns and ammunition?'

'I commandeered every carrying pole and man of every village and temple from the coast to here. They had a simple choice. Carry or die.'

Mung laughed and slapped Ryochi's shoulder. He was convinced they could influence the outcome of the final battle. 'I'll take 400 of your riflemen. Each man will carry an extra hundred rounds of ammunition and one artillery shell. We'll move forward as quickly as possible to be in position before dawn. These weapons must be a surprise for Lord Hayoshi.' Now he addressed John. 'You have the right to continue on with the guide.'

A thin smile creased John's lips and he shoved Mung as he had when they were boys. 'You may be the Satsuma scholar but,' patting his two swords, 'I'm also a Satsuma samurai.'

Mung rubbed his bent nose. 'We're going to succeed, John! Position your guns to support us on the right flank. Use the remaining 200 riflemen to protect your guns.'

John said, 'Tell Lord Nariakira we need as much time to place these cannon as he can give us. Explain to him that the closer he can bring the enemy to the guns, the more effective they will be.'

Ryochi grasped Mung's forearm in a grip of steel. 'I am alive because John would not let me die. But more than that, he made me remember my oath to avenge Yoshida. I want to command the guns.'

Mung looked questioningly at John who stepped forward and slapped his hand down hard on top of Ryochi's, saying, 'I will obey according to Bushido.'

CHAPTER
18

Lord Nariakira made no reply to Mung's news. He sat like one of the graven images Mung had visualized when Deacon Gilhooley was teaching him the Bible. Slowly, the colour in the face of the Satsuma Lord changed. His eyes took on the light of the rising sun flooding the Hakusar Valley, and his cheeks flushed. Reaching out on either side, he grasped his sons' arms. They stood shoulder to shoulder. 'Summon the warrior priest and my commanders,' he said.

Across the valley, drums and whistles sent the enemy horses and troops into formations. The flags of the Tokugawa, Minimoto, Hojo, and Mito clans flapped in front of Lord Hayoshi's tent. To the right and left, other clan flags stood out against the skyline. The Shōgun's army stood to arms.

From the tree line above Lord Nariakira's tent, more than 4,000 fighting monks followed the warrior high priest down the hill. They carried bows and quivers over their shoulders, the silver bells tied at their waists making tinkling music. The leading monk carried the Emperor's flag with its bright red sun and sixteen rays on a field of white. The flag caused a ripple of uneasiness to wash over the ranks of the Shōgun's army. The priests passed through the Satsuma lines and formed ranks on the floor of the valley. Lord Hayoshi watched his men carefully, then barked orders to send the Tokugawa cavalry forward. The Minimoto and Mito horses followed, charging down the hill, gaining speed as their hooves trembled the earth.

The priests calmly strung their long bows and fitted their arrows. The warrior high priest fired a smoke arrow into the air. As it reached its apex, 4,000 bow strings snapped, a twang like that of a harp filled the valley. Before the arrows reached their marks, another cloud of deadly missiles was on the way. The first wave of cavalry was decimated, the horses suffering more than the men, who wore armour. The second wave of mounted warriors buffeted through or jumped their horses over the first, only to be cut down by another flight of the long, slender shafts. Kicking, screaming animals thrashed about, lashing out with their hooves, crashing into men and beasts.

The disciplined cavalrymen of the Shōgun, on foot, drew their swords and charged the priests. Mung watched the savage battle. The Shōgun's men hacked at the unprotected heads of the priests with two-handed swords. Then the third wave of Mito cavalry rode full force into the ranks of the warrior priests.

Lord Nariakira stared down at the uneven battle. He neither moved nor showed any emotion. Even as the last priest was slaughtered, he was silent. The flag of the Emperor remained planted in the field near the bloody body of the dead warrior high priest.

Lord Nariakira stood on the side of the hill and addressed his commanders. 'The priests have given us time. We do not prepare to die. We prepare to fight and win. On our right flank, somewhere in the hills, more artillery is being brought up. All my orders are designed to manipulate the enemy into moving east, within the range of the guns. An order to retreat or disengage is not meant to dishonour. It is to trap Lord Hayoshi.'

The samurai raised their fists in the air and cheered, 'Hai! Hai! Hai!'

Lord Nariakira stayed them by holding up his clenched fist. 'When you see the Satsuma riflemen, make way for them. They have priority over all marching orders.'

'Hai! Hai!'

'Prepare to do battle!' Lord Nariakira shouted.

'Hai! Hai!' the commanders roared, brandishing their swords.

'Prepare to win for the Emperor!'

'Hai! Hai! Hai!'

The chant was taken up by the troops. It rolled across the valley. 'Hai! Hai! Hai!'

Just after mid-day, the commander of the army, Lord Hayoshi, mounted on a Mongol pony, raised both his arms. He held them up for a moment, then brought them down. Rockets blasted upward, etching green, blue, and yellow trails over the valley. A gust of wind dented the smoke trails and pulled silk battle-flags over the ranks upon ranks of spearmen, swordsmen, archers, and cavalry. To the beat of war drums, 135,000 men of the Shōgun's army moved forward.

Mung, along with his men in the original breastworks, could taste the sound of drums on his tongue. He looked to the remaining twelve cannons. Ryochi's 400 riflemen were hidden behind the guns.

The enemy formations executed a series of marching manoeuvres to skirt the dead bodies where the priests had made their stand. The troops moved eastward, the first step towards Ryochi's guns hidden somewhere in the hills.

The riflemen, faces taut, weapons at the ready, watched the enemy coming over the lush green grass on the valley floor. Mung gestured and a white rocket roared into the air. His cannon opened fire, lobbing shells into the oncoming troops. The shells blew holes in the formations but they were quickly filled by other winged helmets.

Lord Nariakira raised his sword and signalled. His sons raised their swords, saluted him, then led the last of the Satsuma cavalry forward down the hill. The two brothers rode stirrup to stirrup, followed by 1,500 mounted men. The horses gained speed as they stretched out, foam flicking from their mouths, clods of dirt thrown high, the ground trembling under the weight. The stunning impact of their daring charge directly into the ranks of the enemy halted the Shōgun's army. The battle-line moved backwards at the centre, pulling the attacking force further east. Having absorbed the initial impact of the charge, the Shōgun's forces moved relentlessly forward over men and horses, killing everyone and trampling their bodies into the earth.

Lord Nariakira watched his sons die, and he was proud. They had served the Emperor, faced the enemy and fulfilled their karma.

He was distracted by the sound of rifle fire as Mung ordered his men into action, mowing down rank after rank of the attacking swordsmen and spearmen. The Shōgun's archers manoeuvred into position, sending their deadly arrows into the ranks of the Satsuma riflemen.

In the western part of the valley, the left flank collapsed and Mung's riflemen were screened from firing at the enemy by their own retreating soldiers. Their position was in danger of being overrun. Mung ordered them back two hundred yards but they were hardly in place when they came under fire from Lord Hayoshi's muskets and more archers. Rather than accept the challenge, he moved them another two hundred yards further east. The left flank was gone and they were beset by muskets and archers on the front. Shōgun samurai wielding two-handed swords hacked their way through retreating Satsuma soldiers trying to reach Mung's position.

A runner from Lord Nariakira reached Mung with a message. He tore the seal with his teeth, his wounded arm throbbing. 'Withdraw immediately and defend the cannons. The Lords of Hayuga and Chikuzen have betrayed us and withdrawn from the battle, leaving the right flank exposed. We are surrounded on three sides.'

Mung tucked the message in his kimono and for the third time gave the order to withdraw. On his signal, the riflemen ran three hundred yards to the artillery position. They barely reached the position before they were under attack again. The front was in danger of collapse. By sheer weight of numbers, the Shōgun's army overwhelmed all opposition. The regiment of enemy muskets came marching up the slope towards the cannon. Mung signalled the four hundred riflemen hidden behind the guns. They straightened their ranks, and coordinated their fire on the muskets with the remaining two hundred of Mung's riflemen. Their accuracy was exceptional. In three minutes, the Shōgun's muskets were eliminated. Mung now wheeled his men to face the left flank. Their withering fire halted the enemy advance. Lord Nariakira held the right flank with all the archers in the Emperor's army. The rifle fire drove the Shōgun's troops back, dead and wounded piling on top of each other, but the constant use of the weapons was causing them to overheat. Mung saw his men urinating on the smoking barrels to cool them down.

Only eight cannons were still operating. Convinced they had not brought the enemy within range of Ryochi's guns, Mung ordered his artillery men to prepare grapeshot to forestall the final attack. Just then he saw a shell explode in the valley a little short of Lord Hayoshi's headquarters. Another shell burst just beyond. Mung looked to his guns. They had not fired. He looked eastward and across the valley. There, on the rim of the hill, fluttered the Emperor's flag. Forty-three cannons in line were silhouetted against the clear blue sky, the sunshine reflecting off their ornate barrels.

Mung shouted to Lord Nariakira, 'Ryochi! Ryochi! He's bracketed them! He's got the range!'

It was impossible for the Satsuma Lord to hear Mung but he followed the line of his outstretched arm in time to see the muzzle blast and hear the roar of the barrage. Mung knew exactly where to look. The earth across the valley erupted. Men and horses were blown to smithereens. The battle on both sides halted as the ear splitting noise pierced the air. All eyes looked to Lord Hayoshi's headquarters. Another barrage, and another ripped the ground. Smoke, dust, dirt, parts of human bodies and animals flew in the air. Slowly the wind cleared the valley. Not a man nor animal was alive where the Shōgun's general and feudal lords had been.

Mung rubbed his nose and slammed his fist into his hand. He turned to see Lord Nariakira signal to his rocketeers. Red, blue, green, and yellow star rockets zoomed skyward. The Lord whirled his two-handed sword around his head and leapt forward, leading the counterattack. The entire imperial army moved after him, roaring their war cries. Mung's riflemen faced front. In two ranks, shoulder to shoulder, advancing, halting every five steps and firing on command, one rank passed through the other. The cannons, blasting at point blank range, blew holes in the ranks of the Shōgun's soldiers. From further away, Ryochi and John brought their guns to bear on the centre of the Shōgun's lines.

With Lord Hayoshi dead and their feudal lords killed before their eyes, the soldiers of the Shōgun hesitated. The roaring cannons, exploding shells, and the oncoming deadly fire of the Satsuma riflemen caused fear to spread. Slowly, the centre of the Shōgun's army began to move backward like a large beast avoiding a forest fire. Some *ronin* turned and fled. The effect was contagious. The centre broke, then the right flank melted away. The Satsuma riflemen wheeled to sweep the left flank. The enemy wavered, then retreated. The retreat became a rout. Ryochi and John directed barrages of high-explosive shells on the fleeing enemy.

The battle-flags of the Shōgun, Lord Hayoshi, the clans of Tokugawa, Minimoto, and Mito fell and were trampled with others of the Shōgun's supporters. Lord Nariakira wielded his sword with abandon, singing an ancient war chant. The Satsuma samurai picked up the chant, fighting side by side with their Lord. The war song, sung by their forefathers 250 years before, spread through the ranks of the attacking soldiers of the Emperor. They cut, hacked, slashed, and stabbed at the retreating enemy. Their arms wearied from the bloody work and the war chant became a hymn of death filling the Hakusar Valley.

Mung and his riflemen joined the pursuit of the Shōgun's army. On the third day, having neglected to change the bandage on his arm, he ran a high fever. By the time he was brought to the court surgeon, he was delirious. Lord Nariakira's physician treated the discoloured, swollen hand with poultices and herbs but gangrene had set in. Mung was close to death when he was given opium. Lord Nariakira, John, and Ryochi held him during the amputation of his left hand at the wrist.

In the following weeks, it was Ryochi and John who nursed Mung and gave him the will to live. When he was well enough to travel, Lord Nariakira summoned the three to his tent.

The Lord looked at Mung and John, so opposite in appearance. 'Your weapons and courage made the difference. Forty thousand Japanese died in the battle of the Hakusar Valley.' He looked at all three, his head back, chin up. 'Our nation will be stronger for this loss. The Meiji Emperor will lead us to take our rightful place amongst the nations of the world. There we will participate in trade and exchange of modern knowledge in order to stabilize our economy and raise the standard of living of our people.' He addressed John Whittefield, 'You deserve more than the honours I can bestow upon you. I have written a letter to Commodore Perry. I will leave it in his hands to see you rewarded; your deeds noted and credited by your government.' He smiled. 'It is time for you to leave, John. Your yellow hair and white skin are showing through the dye.'

John bowed respectfully.

The Satsuma Lord turned to Mung and said, 'Go home to your wife and child and recuperate. My sons made jokes about her thinness, relating it to her courage. They said if she became more courageous, we would not be able to see her. I have commissioned a poem to be written in her honour. When you are well enough, return to your fishing village and pay your respects to your departed parents.' He pulled a scroll from his sleeve and handed it to Mung. 'This is a commission for the erection of a shrine over your parents' graves. They birthed a son who has changed the course of Japanese history. When you have completed your filial obligations, go home to Kagoshima. We will await Commodore Perry.' Lord Nariakira turned to Ryochi and handed him a scroll and two swords. 'You are now a senior samurai in the service of the Emperor. The long sword belonged to my eldest son. The short one to my youngest. Wear them well.'

Ryochi bowed deeply.

'Accompany Mung and John to Kagoshima,' Lord Nariakira said. 'See John aboard the *Shinto Maru* with orders for the captain to take him to Canton. When you have done this, you are to return and take full command of the imperial rifles and artillery.'

The three warriors bowed in unison to the Lord of Satsuma. He stepped towards John with an outstretched hand. 'A custom I learned from the Commodore.'

The two men's hands met in a firm grasp.

In easy stages Mung, John and Ryochi made the journey to Kagoshima. At Mung's reunion with his family, John felt pangs of loneliness and longing for his wife Beth and son Jeffrey. Each time he held little Yoshida, his thoughts were of home. He was anxious to be on his way.

Within two weeks he bade farewell to Saiyo, her father, Ryochi and Mung, boarding the *Shinto Maru* laden with presents. Before the two brothers parted, they renewed their vow dedicating their lives to the principles of democracy and good relations between their countries. It was a promise both would keep as long as they lived.

Mung's period of recuperation was shortened by his desire to honour his parents. He, Saiyo and Yoshida arrived at Nakanohama by boat. The villagers prostrated themselves before the Satsuma scholar with the two swords of a senior samurai. Mung revealed nothing. He led Saiyo and their son directly to the village cemetery. He was surprised to see the graves of his parents immaculately kept. When he questioned the village headman, an old fisherman was summoned.

The old man shuffled forward and bowed before the Satsuma samurai with the bent nose. 'Yes, I attend these graves. I have done so for fourteen years since the sons of these worthy people were drowned on the fishing boat of which I was master.'

Mung took a step forward. With his good right arm he held the old man's shoulder and looked into his eyes. 'Have you ever heard how to catch a Kappa? It is a strange beast with magic fluid in the cavity of its head.'

The old fisherman looked up, his eyes searching the strangely familiar face of the one-handed samurai.

'Fudenojo,' Mung said, 'only one son died. The other stands before you ready to sing the sea bass song.'

For two days there was a feasting in Nakanohama. Mung learned from Fudenojo how he had used the sealskin bags thrown to him by Deacon Gilhooley to make a tub-like vessel from the water barrel and flotsam. The wind and then a current had taken him closer to

358

Japan where he was picked up by fishermen.

On the last day of festivities, Mung presented the scroll allocating funds for the building of a shrine at the site of his parents' burial place. The headman accepted it with deep bows. The project would bring prosperity to the village for years to come.

Mung, Saiyo, and Yoshida boarded the ship. Their course was set for Kagoshima and the meeting with Commodore Perry.

BIBLIOGRAPHY

Albrecht-Carrie, Rene, *Europe after 1915*. 4th edn, New Jersey: Littlefield, Adams, 1964.

Billington, Ray Allen, Loewenberg, Bert James, and Brockunier (eds), *The Making of American Democracy*. New York: Rinehart, 1950.

Boyd, Maurice and Worcester, Donald, *American Civilization*. Boston: Allyn & Bacon, 1964.

Bragdon, Henry W. and McCutchen, Samuel P., *History of a Free People*. New York: Macmillan, 1958.

Bronfenbrenner, Martin, *Academic Encounter*. New York: The Free Press of Glencoe, Crowell-Collier Publishing Co., 1961.

Callahan, J. M., *American Relations in the Pacific and Far East, 1784–1900*. 1901.

Chamberlain, Basil Hall, *Japanese Things*. Rutland, Vermont & Tokyo, Japan: Charles E. Tuttle, revised 1905.

Cole, Y. S. (ed.), *Yankee Surveyors in the Shogun's Seas*. Princeton: Princeton University Press, 1947.

Crawford, David & Leona, *Missionary Adventures in the South Pacific*. Tokyo: Charles Tuttle, 1967.

Daily Life in China.

Downs, Ray F. (ed.), *Japan Yesterday and Today*. New York: Praeger, 1970.

Dulles, Foster Rhea, *Forty Years of American–Japanese Relations*. New York: 1937.

Fairbank, John K., Reischauer, Edwin O., and Craig, Albert M., *East Asia: The Modern Transformation*. Boston: Houghton Mifflin, vol. 2, 1965.

Faulkner, Harold Underwood, *American Political and Social History*. 6th edn, New York: Appleton-Century-Crofts, 1952.

Ferrell, Robert H., *American Diplomacy*. New York: W. W. Norton, 1969.

Finnemore, John, *Peeps at Many Lands – Japan*. London: Adam & Charles Black, 1907.

Flenley, R. and Weech, W. N., *World History*. London: Dent, 1936.

Fullard, Harold (ed.), *China in Maps*. London: George Philip, 1968.

George, M. B., *Basic Sailing*. New York: Hearst Corp., 1971.

Graebner, Norman A., *Empire on the Pacific*. New York: 1955.

Griswold, A. W., *The Far Eastern Policy of the United States*. New York: 1938.

Hale, William Harlan, 'When Perry Unlocked the "Gate of the Sun".'

Hammond Historical Atlas. New Jersey: Hammond, 1968.

aHammond World Atlas & Gazetteer. New Jersey: Hammond, 1976.

Historical Statistics of the United States, Colonial Times to 1957. Washington: US Dept of Commerce, 1960.

Hoffmann, Yoel, *The Sound of One Hand*. New York: Bantam, 1975.

Hofstadter, Richard, Miller, William, and Aaron, Daniel, *The United States*. 2nd edn, New Jersey: Prentice-Hall, 1957.

Ihara, Saikaku. *The Life of an Amorous Woman*.

Jacobson, Helen, *The First Book of Mythical Beasts*. New York: Franklin Watts, 1960.

Japanese National Commission for Unesco, *The Role of Education in the Social and Economic Development of Japan*. Japan: Ministry of Education, 1966.

Japan in Transition. Japan: Ministry of Foreign Affairs, 1972.

Jones, Evan, 'The State', *Americana*, vol. 5, Number 4 (September/October 1977).

Kaneko, Hisakaya, *Manjiro: The Man Who Discovered America*. Boston: Houghton Mifflin, 1956.

Lane, Richard, *Masters of the Japanese Print*. New York: Doubleday, 1962.

Latourette, Kenneth Scott, *A Short History of the Far East*. 4th edn, Toronto: Macmillan, 1969.

Lederer, Ivo J. (ed.), *Russian Foreign Policy Essays in Historical Perspective*. New Haven: Yale University Press, 1962.

Mark, Fredrick, *Manifest Destiny & Mission In American History*. New York: 1963.

Ministry of Education 1964 White Paper. *Higher Education in Postwar Japan*. Tokyo: Sophia University Press, 1965.

Morison, Samuel Eliot, *'Old Bruin': Commodore Matthew Calbraith Perry*. Boston: Little Brown, 1967.

Morrow, James, *The Journal of Dr James Morrow* (ed. Allan B. Cole). Chapel Hill: University of North Carolina Press, 1947.

Murasaki, Lady, *The Tale of Genji*. New York: Doubleday, 1925.

National Geographic magazines, 1947 to 1982.

Rand McNally New Cosmopolitan World Atlas. Chicago-New York-San Francisco: Rand McNally, 1965.

Reischauer, Edwin O. and Fairbank, John K., *East Asia: The Great Tradition*. Boston: Houghton Mifflin, vol. I, 1960.

Roehn, A. Wesley, *et al.*, *The Record of Mankind*. 3rd edn, Boston: D. C. Heath, 1965.

Rubinstein, Alvin Z. (ed.), *The Foreign Policy of the Soviet Union*. New York: Random House, 1960.

Scalapino, Robert A., *Democracy and the Party Movement in Pre-war Japan*. Berkeley & Los Angeles: University of California Press, 1962.

'Tsunami', in *Scientific American*.

Scoresby, William. Log books. Capetown: Capetown University Library.

Shoals of Time.

Shulman, Frank J. *Japan and Korea: An Annotated Bibliography of Doctoral Dissertations in Western Languages, 1877–1969*. Compiled and edited by Frank J. Shulman. London: Frank Cass, 1970.

Statler, Oliver, *Japanese Inn*. New York: Pyramid Books, 1961.

Statler, Oliver, *Shimoda Story*. New York–Toronto: Random House, 1969.

Stevens, Sylvester K., *American Expansion in Hawaii, 1842–1898*. Harrisburg: 1945.

Storry, Richard, *The Double Patriots*. Boston: Houghton Mifflin, 1957.

Swisher, Earl, *China's Management of the American Barbarians: A Study* of *Sino–American Relations, 1841–1861*. New Haven, 1953.

Tazawa, Yutaka *et al. Japan's Cultural History.* Tokyo: Sophia University Press, 1972.

Te-Jen, Yu, *The Japanese Struggle for World Empire.* New York: Vantage Press, 1967.

Toynbee, Arnold J., *A Study of History.* London: Oxford University Press, 1947.

Treat, Payson J., *Diplomatic Relations Between the United States and Japan, 1853–1895.* Stanford: vol. I. Stanford University Press, 1932.

Treat, Payson J., *The United States and Japan, 1853–1921.* Boston, 1921.

Underhill, R. L., *From Cowhides to Golden Fleece: A Narrative of California.* Stanford, Stanford University Press, 1939.

Walworth, Arthur Clarence, *Black Ships Off Japan.* New York: Knopf, 1945.

Warinner, Emily V., *Voyage to Destiny.* Indianapolis: Bobbs-Merrill, 1956.

Weinberg, Albert K., *Manifest Destiny.* Baltimore, 1935.

Wells, H. G., *The Outline of History.* New York: Macmillan, 1921.

Wildes, H. E., *Aliens in the East.* 1937.

Yanaga, Chitoshi, *Japan since Perry.* New York: McGraw-Hill, 1949.

ACKNOWLEDGEMENTS

Any author, looking back on the road he and his manuscript have travelled, must think of those who helped him along the way. My parents, Charles and Grace, gave me life. When I was thirty-three, Mr Jules Rubinstein, then aged ninety, gave me the world of intellect. My wife, Janet, has given me the world of love. Her moral support, editorial expertise and common sense, during the decade and a half it took to research and write this book, made everything possible. 'A woman of valour who can find? For her price is far above rubies.'[1] I have found her and we are one.

Fifteen years ago, in a lecture on Far Eastern history, Professor Robert Lee of Stony Brook University, New York, told a brief aside about a shipwrecked Japanese fisherboy, named Mangiro, who became the bridge for western knowledge into feudal Japan. Thus began my research into the subject with the idea of writing this historical novel. Professor David Trask, then Chairman of Stony Brook's History Department, and members of the university's faculty, especially Dr Mark Goldberg, helped me lay the foundation.

I was assisted with materials and advice by Professor of Far Eastern Philosophy, Yoel Hoffmann, of the University of Haifa, and Dr Frank Joseph Shulman, Curator of the East Asian-language library collection at the University of Maryland. For reading the chapters and making suggestions, I wish to thank David and Elsa Epstein, Dr Mervyn Abrahamson, Lillian Cohen, Edyth H. Geiger, Bernard and Bea Greenbaum and Edith Lowell.

Special mention goes to my daughter, Barbara Shefer, who has taught her father a thing or two, and to my mother-in-law, Malka

[1] Proverbs 31:10.

Rabinowitz, who every morning pokes her head into the cistern where I write and says, 'Today you'll do better than yesterday!'

For support and encouragement along the way, my gratitude goes to Marilyn Beck, Sylvia and Mel Springer, Shane and Jack Birns and many others.

I also thank my agent, Bill Hamilton, for his expert criticism. His sharp comments and imaginative suggestions led to the rewriting that benefits the reader as well as the author. Many thanks to the editors of Grafton Books, Patricia Parkin and Penelope Isaac, for their help in seeing this book through to publication.